Bordeaux

Books by Janet Hubbard

The Vengeance in the Vineyard Mysteries
Champagne: The Farewell
Bordeaux: The Bitter Finish

Bordeaux: The Bitter Finish

A Vengeance in the Vineyard Mystery

Janet Hubbard

Poisoned Pen Press

First Edition 2014

10 9 8 7 6 5 4 3 2 1

Library of Congress Catalog Card Number: 2012920265

ISBN: 9781464201523 Hardcover
9781464201547 Trade Paperback

Poisoned Pen Press
6962 E. First Ave., Ste. 103
Scottsdale, AZ 85251
www.poisonedpenpress.com
info@poisonedpenpress.com

Printed in the United States of America

For
My mother, Lily Whitten Hubbard

Acknowledgments

I raise a glass to the following people who helped to take this novel to another level:

Poisoned Pen Press editor Barbara Peters, and the rest of the team: Jessica Tribble, Suzan Baroni, Nan Beams, Pete Zroika, and Beth Deveny

Editors extraordinaire Kate Vieh Redden and Valerie Andrews

Agent and magic-maker Kimberly Cameron

Inspirationist Astrid Latapie (who, as always, provided the French essence)

Readers and proofreaders Dana Barrows, Colette Buret, Mary Moffroid, Sammye (Frances) Vieh, Lisa Doherty, Richard Gaillard, Dana Jinkins, and Kelly Johnson

Wine critic and blogger Barbara Ensrud

My personal hero—and role model for Max—NYPD Detective Jennifer O'Connell

Wine consultant and food writer Dawn Land, who contributed to the chapter set at Veritas Restaurant, New York City

Chef Sam Hazen of Veritas Restaurant, New York City, whose tasting menu transports

Jiu-Jitsu expert Regina Darmoni

My son, Luke Brown, and daughter (and role model two for Max), Ramsey Brown

Wine gives great pleasure; and every pleasure is of itself a good. It is a good, unless counterbalanced by evil.

Samuel Johnson, *Boswell's Life of Johnson*

New York City
March 2012

Chapter One

March 31

Max Maguire watched as her boss, NYPD Captain Walt O'Shaughnessy, rolled his ungainly frame out of an old-fashioned oak office chair. He gouged out a Rolaid from the packet on the desk and slipped it into his mouth, then walked across the floor in the cramped and overheated West 82nd Street Precinct and leaned against the doorjamb. Max was in the hot seat and it burned. She'd gotten herself into a jam. One so bad Walt had called her father, about to retire from the elite Homicide North uptown, for a consult.

"Let me see the last part of that video again," Hank Maguire muttered in his gravelly voice.

Max felt frustration rising in her. "Oh, come on," she said, first looking at Hank, who maintained a stoic, intractable expression, then shifting her gaze to Walt, who she could tell had slipped back into his usual role of mediator between father and daughter. "We've looked at it twice already."

A YouTube video uploaded by a tourist showed Max in top form, using the Jiu-Jitsu moves she'd been practicing for a decade. At thirty, she had won too many tournaments to count. Walt clicked "Play" and the three of them watched as she approached a short, dark man dodging in and out of baby strollers and bicycles on a crowded street. Max gained on him, and he spun around to face her, apparently deciding he could take a woman cop. He seemed a little excited by the prospect. In fact, women were his main targets. Max gained speed and crashed headlong into him and both fell to the ground. That was a horrible couple of seconds, she recalled.

When he scrambled to rise, she jabbed her left hand across his Adam's apple, cutting off his wind. Max quickly moved behind him and punched at his right ear, and, dropping her left hand into the crook of her right elbow, squeezed his neck in her forearms, until he went completely limp. As he fell to the pavement, his head bounced. With the perp nearly unconscious, she rolled him over, cuffed him, and then simply walked away. Max felt a surge of pride that she had brought the guy down with a perfectly executed guillotine choke.

"Where the hell was your partner while you were using excessive force?" Hank asked, his eyes hard as steel. "The press was right: you *did* use excessive force. And you had no back-up." Hank put up his hand and Walt paused the video, freeze-framing Max in her instant of triumph.

"How would *I* know?" Max knew she sounded on the defensive, and quickly switched to explanatory mode. "I was too busy chasing this guy. Look, we found the woman bruised and totally hysterical. Joe took one path at the 72nd Street Entrance off Central Park West and I took the other. I got to the guy first…"

Walt said softly, "Joe made a statement, Hank. He told us he got to the scene too late to help with the arrest."

Hank's voice was tight. "I disagree. See that shadow in the background? He's watching. Like a voyeur." Max felt her stomach go queasy. He turned the full force of his gaze on his daughter. "I thought you and Joe ended things before you went to France last year."

"We did."

Hank turned to Walt, "They need to be officially separated."

Max leapt up. "Hel-LO. I'd like to have a say in this."

Walt's voice was kind, but firm. "Joe will be reassigned." He looked at Max. "And I'm going to put you on temporary suspension." Max cringed. She'd hoped it wouldn't come to this. "Just until the YouTube thing dies down. Meanwhile, you've got a bit of freelance work."

"What's your agenda?" she shot back.

"It's the wine critic, Ellen Jordan," Walt said. "She received a threat and wants protection." This had to be a ruse—something her father and her mentor had cooked up. Ellen Jordan was her mother's friend. They saw each other regularly when Ellen was in town but Max had not kept up with her. She hadn't even seen her when she was in France last year, involved in one of the biggest murder cases in the country. Now Max felt like a child who was being sent to time-out. She was pissed.

"So what am I supposed to do? Hang out in a bar and watch her drink?"

"Better than that," Hank said. "You follow her to Bordeaux, and get to use that French that made your mom so proud."

"Yeah," Walt said. "You can order QUA-SONTS every morning." He said to Hank, "She won't touch our donuts, you know."

Ouch. Max's years abroad, before she made the leap to follow in her dad's footsteps, was the source of much teasing from her fellow cops who tried to knock her down a peg. Hank's fame as the NYPD version of Clint Eastwood didn't help. Max had to prove herself over and over, to everyone. Once she had hooked up with Joe, she thought she'd no longer feel like an outsider. Now all this was about to change.

Before she left for France last spring, and ended up solving a murder, Max learned that Joe had slept with another female officer. Feeling a little reckless after the breakup, she had had a brief fling with Olivier Chaumont, the examining magistrate on the case. When she returned to New York, she refused to go back to Joe when he tried to reignite their relationship. It had been awkward being partners after that, but neither wanted to complain for fear of being reassigned. There was no way she could explain all this now.

Hank sat blinking like an old turtle. "Your plane leaves at ten."

"Tomorrow morning?"

He stood up, an intimidating presence at six four.

"Tonight. You'll fly with Ellen Jordan to Bordeaux. Someone will pick you up and take you to the village of Saint-Émilion, a half-hour away."

Recalling the days in Champagne without technology, Max said, "I want a phone that works this time."

"You got it," Walt said.

"And bodyguards carry guns, right?"

"You're covered," Walt said. "I'll talk with our contacts at Interpol, but I don't think you'll need them." She knew what he meant. She was really going as a babysitter, not a bodyguard. Max hopped up and grabbed her short leather jacket off the back of the chair.

"By the way," Hank said, as she headed to the door, "your Jiu-Jitsu moves were impressive. It's that 'Kill Bill' attitude at the end that got you into trouble with the public."

She stared hard at her father. "He raped that woman, Dad. What was I supposed to do? Congratulate him?"

"Max..."

She walked out. When she got to the subway station, her cell phone rang. It was Hank.

"What?"

"Your mom and I will drive you to the airport."

"I have a ride, thanks."

She hung up before he could call her on that lie. Hank had been discreet as he watched her climb from rookie to second level detective, but now it appeared he was going to start micromanaging again. She jogged down the stairs of the subway station, and hopped on the express train to Times Square. She didn't know who to be more furious with, her father or Joe. Until fifteen minutes ago, she had believed Joe's excuse that he had shown up too late to help. Now she had a mountain of doubt. On top of that, Hank had seen the couple of seconds she was out of control. She also knew that he was terrified for her.

She hit Joe's name on her speed dial.

"Hi, babe."

"Can you drive me to JFK in an hour? We need to talk."

"Guess so. Where're you going?"

"Bordeaux. A short assignment."

Joe was silent for two beats before he said, "You'll catch hell from the rest of the team for this plush job...."

Wait until you hear you're being transferred, she thought. "I wouldn't be going anywhere if you had covered my back!"

"You had just accused me of always taking over. I decided to give you free rein."

"You didn't jump in because you were teaching me a lesson? I'll find another ride!" She hit end.

Within moments, she received a text from Joe: *u pms?* Ignoring it, she rushed for the shuttle to Grand Central that would take her to the East Side, and an express train to the East Village. When she emerged from the station, she had new texts but ignored them. Instead, she tried to absorb the information that she was on her way to France again. And what's so wrong with that? she asked herself. If I stop acting like I'm being punished, it could be an interesting gig. She and Ellen Jordan would be staying at a hotel in Saint-Émilion, far from Bordeaux, where he had been transferred.

Entering her rent-controlled apartment building, she took the steps two at a time to the third floor. Selecting a Grace Potter tune on her iPod, she began gathering up her clothes and stuffing them into a suitcase. Her phone rang again. "Ma?"

"*Chérie*, Hank just called to tell me that you are being given a great opportunity to go to Bordeaux with my friend Ellen."

"I'm trying to get out of the doghouse."

Juliette de Laval Maguire sighed and switched to French. "I hardly believe that traveling with a famous wine writer to Bordeaux is such an awful thing, chérie."

Max began explaining in French to her mother that she was on the verge of blowing the career that she had committed to a year ago. Using excessive force during an arrest was a strike against her—regardless of the fact that she collared a rapist. Max was about to hang up when her mother said, "And Olivier? He's now in Bordeaux, isn't he?"

"Let's not go there."

"Oh, Max. This is difficult for you, *n'est-ce pas*? I'm sure there's a good reason why he hasn't been in touch."

"Maman. It was a fling, *une amourette*. Nothing more. Gotta go. Love you."

"Je t'aime, sweetie. *Au revoir*."

Max began to sing along with Potter to her song, "If I was a judge I'd break the law. Oooh. Oooh…" as she tossed her sneakers into the suitcase and zipped it closed. Having given up on Joe—this time, for good—she called her friend Juanita for a ride to the airport and was told to be waiting at the curb in twenty minutes. Standing there with her suitcase, Max read her messages from Joe: *didn't mean it; call me; fuckin CALL me*. She typed in a simple response: *I'm already gone*.

◇◇◇

Ellen Jordan had an abundance of charisma. Passengers flocked around her in the first-class Air France lounge where she and Max waited to board their flight. Instantly recognizable from her TV appearances, Ellen joked with them and offered wine advice freely. Every half-hour Ellen would mouth the words to Max, *the case?* And Max would lift up the impact-resistant metal carry-all for her to see. Max had had no problem securing permission to carry the wine onboard, which had impressed Ellen.

Ellen had been firm when she handed it over, "Forget me, this is what you have to guard." Max had been surprised by the weight of it when she lifted it, but when she asked what was in it, Ellen had said simply, "wine."

Max sipped bottled water and kept her eye on Ellen as the passengers began lining up to board the aircraft. She was deep in conversation with a man who was also going to Bordeaux for the *en primeur*, a significant wine event in the region. Brokers, retailers, distributors, importers, and exporters from all over the world descended for barrel tastings of wines from the previous year.

Max knew Ellen's history from her mother. The two women had met in Paris in 1984. Juliette hailed from a long line of French aristocrats. The daughter of a car manufacturer, Ellen had been raised in Grosse Point, Michigan, and ventured to Yale for college. When she was twenty, she toured the wine districts of France with a classmate and discovered she had an impeccable nose, able to distinguish without any coaching the nuances in taste required for professional tasting. Through a friend she met Juliette, who was soon on her way to New York to visit Ellen. Juliette happened to meet Hank Maguire, who proposed the day she was to return to France.

Ellen had gone on after graduation to create a newsletter that initially had only a handful of subscribers. Half a million readers later, she was considered, next to Robert Parker, the most influential critic in the world. "It wasn't easy," Juliette had told Max, "the wine world wasn't open to women during those years." Neither was police work, Max had reminded her.

Once settled in their seats, Ellen, ordered a glass of red wine for each of them and said, "I'm glad I'm going to have the chance to get to know you. Are you aware that I was your brother's godmother?"

Max shook her head. Ellen turned back to the flight attendant to answer a question, and Max's thoughts turned to her brother, Frédéric, who, had he lived, would be twenty-four. She looked out her window, replaying that dreadful moment in her mind. The phone call announcing that her twelve-year-old brother was DOA after being hit by a car on his way home from school. Hank going into a stupor for weeks, and her mother erupting daily into paroxysms of grief.

Max realized much later that she carried enough guilt to keep the Catholic Church in business for the next fifty years. No one had addressed her self-blame: Had she picked her brother up and walked home with him instead of hanging out with her friends, the accident never would have happened.

Ellen interrupted her thoughts. "How about a quick course in wine? I don't know how much your mother taught you, but as with painting, there are layers upon layers of color and complexity. The more you understand of this, the more you can enjoy."

Max wondered if Ellen had any idea how strained her parents' finances were. If her mother hadn't married an Irish cop, causing her parents to disown her, Juliette would have inherited a small fortune when her father died.

"I've never tasted a rare wine," Max said. "But, sure. Let's begin my education."

After a brief tutorial, Ellen announced that she needed to sleep, reaching for her mask and moving her seat into the horizontal position. Max pulled the latest Cara Black mystery novel out of her backpack. Tucked in its pages was the last email that she had received from Olivier. Dated February 12, it read: *I'm sorry I went incommunicado back in November. I was struggling with lots of things, and I'm afraid I was a lousy friend and correspondent. I trust that life is going well. I hope to hear from you. Fondest, Olivier.* Max folded the piece of paper and stuck it in her jeans pocket. She had been hurt when he suddenly stopped emailing and, when he started again, she didn't respond. She wished now that she had.

Being with Joe on a daily basis hadn't helped. They had to remain partners and live with their broken relationship each day, or one of them would be sent to a new precinct. In Max's mind it was a little like staying in a bad marriage because neither spouse wanted to move out. Joe was cajoling one day, sarcastic the next, yet as work partners they still clicked, and were known for their boldness.

Max pulled out her little notebook that she used as a journal and wrote: Note #1 for therapist: Why is my trust level around men at an all-time low? Note #2: Why do I carry a printout of an email from Olivier around with me like a lovesick teenager? Note #3: Once I get to France, will I have the courage to call the grandmother I've never met?

She put her seat back and glanced over at Ellen, who was snoring lightly, her precious cargo on the floor between them. Max sighed and closed her eyes.

Bordeaux, France
April 2012

Chapter Two

April 1

Olivier Chaumont scanned the headlines in *Sud Ouest,* Bordeaux's daily paper, while waiting for his assistant to show up. It was the start of the *en primeur*, when retailers and importers from places like the U.S., Hong Kong, Singapore, and Russia arrived to purchase "futures" after the first wine-tasting, then waited three years for the vintage to arrive in bottles. After the tasting, a courtier, or broker, connected with a *négociant,* or trader, who then sold it to an importer in another country. A distributor finally sold the wine to a retail store and other outlets.

Spring 2011 had been extremely hot, with drought conditions. Summer had been like autumn, then autumn like summer again. Olivier knew what that meant. The wines would not be as round and voluptuous as they were in 2009 and 2010. Already critics were up in arms because the *négociants* were quoting the same prices for the inferior 2011 wine. It smacked of greed, which came as no surprise when Olivier considered the vast sums of money involved in the fine wine trade.

Bordeaux had over centuries produced the most sought-after wines in the world, and in the global community the more established vineyards were selling at higher prices than ever before. Olivier had read about the rich Chinese who arrived with fistfuls of cash with the intention of purchasing the most precious vintages, which they were rumored to mix with soft drinks. Some had gone on to purchase *châteaux*. Before the Chinese arrived, the Americans exhibited their lust for the best vintages, driving prices up, and making the wines unaffordable for all but the most elite collectors.

To add to these concerns, a new ratings system on the Right Bank demoted some winegrowers in the area while promoting others. The slightest changes in ratings could either raise profits significantly or bring a vineyard to ruin. A couple of vintners had sued over their loss of status, the most vocal being François Laussac. At the same time as Laussac's vineyard was ranked lower by the appellation committee, Ellen Jordan had lowered his 2010 tasting score, and he had taken to publicly blaming her for all his woes. Olivier found him insufferable, but he had a lot of clout in Bordeaux.

A light knock on the kitchen door, and Commissaire Abdel Zeroual entered, wearing the traditional blue *Police Nationale* uniform. Now thirty, Abdel had been involved in a bad crowd back in Paris as a teen. Olivier had taken him under his wing, shaped him up and gotten him a job out of the city. They had been together in Champagne, where Abdel's grandmother, Zohra, housemaid to the Chaumont family, lived. Both had decided to move to Bordeaux when Olivier was assigned there.

"*Bonjour*, Abdel, I was just reading about the *en primeur* event starting this evening. I predict there might be an arrest or two due to excessive drinking."

"To a teetotaler it sounds like a lot of fuss over nothing. Something smells delicious, by the way."

"It's a joint effort of your grandmother's and mine, using a recipe from an old friend named Bruno, the local police chief over in Saint-Denis."

Abdel sniffed the air. "*Gigot*?"

"*Oui*. Lamb shanks cooked for hours in a bed of red onions and red wine. I have guests coming for dinner." Olivier handed Abdel the newspaper. Page three contained an article on the American wine critic, Ellen Jordan. "She called me to say she had something to discuss that couldn't wait. Of course the Laussac dinner is this evening, but she declined his invitation, a blasphemous act. I invited her here for dinner instead, an even more blasphemous act."

Abdel glanced up from the paper. "I saw on the news that her nose, like the critic Robert Parker's, is insured for a million. She also said publicly that Monsieur Laussac's wine was not much better than…piss."

Olivier winced. "No wonder she wasn't interested in his posh gathering this evening. I'm curious what's so urgent." He got up and headed to the oven to check the lamb.

Abdel stuck his head into the dining room. "She must be pretty special for you to go to all this trouble."

Olivier smiled at the sight of the table, covered with an ancient white linen tablecloth, fine Sevres porcelain, silver, and crystal. The *centre de table*, the yellow tulips that he had bought to display in the silver *jardinière,* an eighteenth-century relic he had found in a secondhand market, was perfect. He took a moment to admire the tapestried raspberry-colored walls that created intimacy, blending beautifully with the room-size Persian rug. He held up the bottle of wine he planned to serve at his dinner, and examined the label. A 1982 *Cos Estournel.* "I was wise to have purchased a case of this fifteen years ago," he said.

"At twenty-two you were buying cases of wine?" Abdel chuckled.

"Wine is a living organism. When you taste, you are inhaling *terroir,* where you get a sense of the land that grew the grape, the rain that fed the roots, the wind that rustled the leaves, the sun that warmed the ripening fruit. It ends up on your tongue and finds a permanent place in your mind…"

Abdel interjected, "Sorry for interrupting, *Monsieur*, but you wanted to talk about a plan of action for this evening?"

"Oh...right. I want you to keep an eye on things in Saint-Émilion. Check for drunk drivers. Stop in at the Hôtellerie Renaissance and make sure the Laussac evening is going smoothly. At 7:30, escort Madame Jordan and her assistant out the back door of the hotel and bring them here."

"Why such secrecy?"

"The press knows Ellen Jordan is in town. I'd prefer that they, and Laussac, not know her dinner plans, especially since my other guests are Pascal and Sylvie Boulin."

Abdel said, "It's a rumor that Madame Jordan and Monsieur Boulin are in bed together with the promotion of his wine."

"She is the reason for his success, after all."

"And in bed together, literally. I read it on a local blog that pretends to be about the wine industry."

"That's absurd," Olivier said. "From what I understand about this style of writing, and it is very little, anyone can write whatever they want, true or not."

Abdel, accustomed to Olivier's prejudice against bloggers, and the Internet in general, steered the conversation back to the dinner. "And the assistant Madame Jordan is bringing with her? A calm presence among all the renegades?"

"You're putting *me* in the renegade category?"

"Compared to your peers, yes. I'll bet you five francs the assistant's a woman."

Olivier laughed. They had been making wagers since Abdel was a teenager, ever since Olivier had taught him to play poker. It wasn't in Olivier's nature to be silly, but somehow he felt at ease enough to be so with Abdel. "I don't see her as the type to travel with a doughy little secretary. A young man who has just awakened to his senses would be perfect for Madame Jordan."

Abdel gave a toothy grin. "So you think she's a *cougar,* eh? I have to go. But don't expect me to fit in with the people at the Laussac dinner."

"Meaning you'll be the only sober one?"

"The only Arab is more like it. I might get sent to the kitchen to wash dishes."

"I hope that's a joke."

"I wish I could say it is. Don't worry, I'm used to it."

"That makes it worse." Olivier walked outside with Abdel.

"This weekend is the perfect opportunity for us to launch Opération Merlot. Is everything in place?"

Abdel came to attention. "Our agents have infiltrated all the export offices and are marking any suspicious cases with the letters *OM* on the bottom of the crate. A global alert has gone out to customs offices and importers where the wine is shipped."

"Not that any of them will read it, but let's see if we get a bite," Olivier said. "Our biggest deterrent is our revered, and I'm being sarcastic, Minister of Justice Philippe Douvier, along with Minister of the Interior Katia Alban. Both claim that my request to pursue an international counterfeit wine ring smacks of self-aggrandizement and will cost the government too much. Of course, they are trying to make my job obsolete."

Olivier liked being a *juge d'instruction*, or investigative magistrate. He had dealt with a lot of political corruption, but only occasionally took on major murder cases like the Champagne murders of the previous year. Appointed by a *procureur* to those cases, he was one of the few judges who relished solving a crime. One of Philippe Douvier's jobs was to oversee the major cases, and Madame Alban was in charge of the police and gendarmes.

"The people believe in the judges," Abdel said. "Without them, who would keep an eye on the elected officials?"

"But it's our president who will determine the next three years for me. No worries if Hollande wins the election, but I'm not in Sarkozy's good graces, as you know. I have to walk gingerly these next few weeks." Recently Olivier had gone after Douvier for protecting a German suspect during the Champagne murder investigation. The German had brought such a large sum of cash into France that Olivier was sure he was intent on buying land on the periphery of Champagne that would quadruple in value once it was officially designated as a part of that region. It was a difficult accusation to prove, but Olivier fervently believed that people like this needed to be brought to justice.

Abdel pointed to a small headline in the paper, "How about this article on the scam invented by that investment company, Bordeaux Advisory? Perhaps we should send it to the ministers."

"Are you referring to the company that bought wine for 4.75 euros a bottle and sold it to unsuspecting buyers for 1,100 a case?"

Olivier felt this had paved the way for an even bolder move: a counterfeit operation in Bordeaux. Counterfeit wine was now a global scam costing up to thirty million dollars. The wine world had become more sensitive about counterfeiting since the arrest in California on mail and wire-fraud charges of an Indonesian named Rudy Kurniawan. There was more to it than met the eye. Back in 2008 Kurniawan allegedly consigned for auction eighty-four bottles of counterfeit wine, which he expected to sell for $600,000; since then, many had issued complaints that they had been ripped off by him. Olivier put some of the blame on the collectors, who wanted bragging rights for owning the most expensive bottles which they then hid away in their cellars, behaving more like hoarders than true oenophiles.

Since moving to Bordeaux, Olivier had compiled a list of *châteaux* that had been robbed. The thieves no doubt thought that a simple way to make money would be to steal cases of the rare wine and sell it on the black market or through private sources. Or better yet, drink it, and fill it with cheaper wine and sell it for a fortune. What was also frustrating was that vineyard owners didn't want the negative publicity surrounding an investigation, which thwarted authorities' efforts to find and punish the culprits.

Olivier's thoughts were interrupted by an Etta James tune on the radio, reminding him of the last night he and Max McGuire spent together in Champagne. They were at the home of mutual friends when Etta James singing, "I Want to Make Love to You," began playing. Olivier had spontaneously taken Max in his arms and led her out to the balcony to dance. He had been completely smitten with the American detective, who was his opposite in every way. All they shared, aside from their strong attraction to each other, was a mutual passion for solving crimes.

Abdel said, "That song sounds familiar. I know. It was the night we closed the de Saint-Pern case..."

"You have a good memory," Olivier said, walking across the room to turn the radio off.

"You never hear from Detective Maguire?"

"Oh, you know, New York is a great…distance." Olivier wondered if he looked a bit chagrined. When Max hadn't responded to the email he had sent in February, he assumed she had moved on with her life.

"I'm surprised," Abdel said. "I received two postcards from her. She invited me to visit New York. She knows that's my dream."

"Did you write back?"

"Sure. I sent her a postcard of Bordeaux." Olivier realized he must have been scowling, because Abdel said, "I won't write to her anymore if you think it unprofessional."

"I don't know why we're discussing postcards. I'll see you at eight."

Abdel waved, and left the house. Olivier picked up his cat, Mouchette, and absently stroked her head while watching Abdel climb into his car and drive away.

Chapter Three

April 2

Sitting in a Louise XVI fauteuil chair in an elegant hotel suite, Max nervously jiggled her long legs as Ellen began tasting wine. Soon after they'd arrived at the Hôtellerie Renaissance, bottles began to arrive. If Ellen gave a first-growth a score of 95 or higher, a bottle might be priced as high as $1,000 or more. If she dropped the score below 90, the winemaker would begin losing profits. Ellen had adopted the scoring system started by her fellow American critic Robert Parker. Ninety-five to 100 was the equivalent of an A, and B was between 90 and 95; after that, no one paid much attention.

The wine gurgled in Ellen's throat before she spit it into a small bucket. "It's interesting to note the *caudalie*."

"Never heard of it."

"There isn't a word in English that matches it. It's the number of seconds we use to measure the aftertaste of a vintage. How long it lasts on the palate. The finish, as it were."

"Wine is a numbers game, right? The scores. The vintages. The number of minutes it's supposed to breathe before you can drink it. The seconds of aftertaste. The ten years before you're supposed to drink it."

Ellen chuckled. "You've just put a new slant on wine. I'll quote you in my next newsletter."

She crossed the room and picked up the shiny aluminum case Max had toted onto the plane and set it down in front of Max. "Here's a number for you. This magnum of *1945 Chateau Mouton-Rothschild* could be worth over $30,000." Max whistled through her teeth. "It was sold as part of a four-magnum lot to a friend of mine at a New York auction. A collector named Bill Casey with an ego the size of the Empire State Building, but I adore him all the same."

Max sat at full attention, listening.

Ellen's face grew troubled. "I tasted the first bottle in the lot, and declared it counterfeit. Casey called a mutual friend of ours, Paula Goodwin, who is an auctioneer, to taste it, and she's adamant that it was authentic."

"Don't you need somebody objective to taste all four magnums?"

"That's the ideal solution, of course, but Bill won't agree to it. I could go to the Major Theft Squad at the FBI, and they could confiscate the bottles, but Casey would never speak to me again."

"Imagine if none of the rest turned out to be counterfeit. Ninety-thousand down the tube, right?"

"Exactly. I doubt that that's the case, though." Max turned her attention back to the specially contained magnum in front of her. "I made a deal with Bill," Ellen continued. "The man who is hosting a small dinner this evening in my behalf not only has an incredible knowledge about wine, but he knows of a company in Bordeaux that has developed a high-tech method for testing wine for authenticity. I've decided to defer to him."

"What's the deal you and Casey made?"

"If this bottle is declared authentic, I won't pursue it any further."

"Meaning you will be conceding that Paula Goodwin was right."

"I wouldn't go that far. What's going on, Max, is that I'm convinced, as are others, that there's a counterfeit ring operating under our noses. This is the third time this year I've been handed fake wine to taste."

"My dad could have put you in touch with the right people."

"I don't want to create another Rudy Kurniawan scandal. I thought you and I could be on the *qui vive* while we're here."

"Us? What are we on the alert for?"

"Counterfeiters!" Ellen said in an impatient voice. "I have some ideas."

"Don't tell me you're thinking of unearthing a counterfeit scheme on your own?"

"What do you think I brought you along for? You solved that big murder case in Champagne last year."

"I assisted the French in solving it…"

"I'm not going to do anything rash."

"Who do you suspect?"

"If you agree to help me, I'll tell you."

"I'll agree to nothing until I know the whole story. I was sent here to protect you. Somebody sent you a threatening note. Why?"

"It isn't the first one, trust me."

"Somebody was telling you to stop. Stop what?"

"Okay. I'm having an affair with…someone who shall go unnamed…there's no sense in burdening you with that information…and I think his wife, whom I happen to know, was in New York at about the time the note arrived. I think she sent it."

Max realized she was being offered up a different version of the Ellen Jordan than the one her mother talked about. The woman her mother described wasn't a femme fatale, and certainly not an aspiring investigator. When Ellen opened her closet door and peered in, Max took the opportunity to study her. Of medium height, Ellen had, as Hank would say, curves in all the right places. Her dark, chin-length hair curled slightly, and soft, brown eyes and a long, aquiline nose made her striking, if not beautiful. Divorced five years ago, Max didn't find it surprising that Ellen was involved with someone, but again, why the secrecy? No doubt someone else famous, Max thought.

The little excursion to her mother's homeland had suddenly turned into a mad tangle. "Let's deal with the bottle first," Max said. "Can we put it in the hotel safe?"

"Good idea."

"And pardon my nosiness, but is your lover American or French?"

"French. And due here in forty-five minutes." Exhibiting no modesty, she stepped out of sweatpants. "And no, I won't cancel."

"Let me guess, the wife's in Paris?"

Ellen had the decency to blush. "They live here." She slipped into leggings and a blue tunic. Turning back to Max, she said, "I'll tell you what. I promise not to leave this suite. I will wait for you. We will be picked up for dinner at seven-thirty." Max hesitated. "Listen," Ellen said, "I wouldn't have hired you if I hadn't felt anxiety about my safety. I won't do anything stupid."

Max nodded. "I've been thinking. How many people know you have this magnum of wine with you?" Ellen shrugged. "My point being that if there is a counterfeiter, or a gang of counterfeiters, they won't be happy with your interference. Would Bill Casey spout off about sending this bottle to France with you?"

"Not to anyone involved in criminal activity."

"Criminals come from all classes."

Ellen looked skeptical. "I'll email Bill to stay mum."

Max thought it was already too late. "And what am I to do while you're…entertaining?"

"Let's go down together and put the magnum in the hotel safe, then you can take off and see the sights. Practice your French. Check in when you return to the hotel."

Ellen stopped for a moment to run a brush through her hair. "You look great," Max said.

"Thanks. Tonight I'll reveal everything. The name of my suspect, the name of my lover, and by then you will already be acquainted with our host. Be sure to wear your signature fragrance."

Max's eyes narrowed. "You're not fixing me up, are you?"

Ellen was already out the door. Max picked up the case containing the magnum of wine and bounded down the short flight of stairs in her jeans and cowboy boots. She spoke in French to the concierge, whose eyes kept darting over to Max, who hovered around her employer, and back to Ellen. Max made note of his name displayed on a name tag. Edouard Cazaneuve.

"Madame, may I help you?" he asked, his face showing disapproval.

Ellen said quickly, "Oh, she's with me."

Max gave him a broad smile, which seemed to irritate him further. He was tall and broad-shouldered, with blondish-gray, coiffed hair. A maid appeared from the room behind and said meekly, "Monsieur?"

"*Pas maintenant!*" he barked at her. The maid quickly disappeared. Turning back to Ellen, he said, "Come this way, Madame. May I ask what is in the container?"

"Is that really necessary?" Max asked in French.

He shot her a nasty look. "No, of course not." Ellen glanced over at Max as if to ask what the big deal was, but Max ignored her.

"Someone is always here to open the safe for you," Edouard said.

"I want to make sure that my assistant can also ask for it," Ellen said. "Her name is Max Maguire."

"Of course, Madame." He made a note on a form.

Ellen glanced at her watch, "Okay, Max, I'll see you at the end of the day."

"Ellen!"

Both women whirled around, coming face-to-face with a woman of Max's height, with a body that yelled a minimum of an hour and a half a day in the gym, and a face that hid intense alertness behind a strained smile. Ellen smiled, and gave a perfunctory hug to the tall woman wearing a designer suit, and then introduced Max as her assistant.

"You're coming up in the world." Paula Goodwin shook hands with Max. "What does an assistant do?" she asked, her gaze fixed on Max.

"Answer emails. Make travel plans. Taste wine whenever I can."

Unamused, Paula said, "You have a great coach. Except for one particular wine, Ellen and I are usually on the same page with our tasting notes."

Ellen frowned. "Of all wines for me to select to drink on my birthday, why did I choose the *45 Mouton*? With the size of Bill's collection, it could have stayed there for decades, untouched."

"He told me he gave you a second bottle in that lot to take to another expert?" Exactly as I predicted, Max thought. "Why don't we taste it together back in New York, and see if we can agree?"

"I'm going to give it to someone completely objective," Ellen said.

"Okay, here's a different solution, one that Bill Casey is considering. I have a client who will pay top dollar for the three bottles left."

Max watched Ellen's lips compress. "I don't think it's fair to the person wanting to purchase," she said. "These bottles need to be tested."

Paula ran her hand through her long mane of hair. "You're really going to pursue this counterfeit thing?" Max was ready to side with Paula.

"The bottle that was entrusted to me will be out of my hands as of tonight," Ellen said. "I'll step away then."

Paula smiled. "Fine."

Ellen deftly changed the topic. "I thought you were sick and couldn't make it to the Laussac dinner."

"I had a two-day virus. I'm still not well enough to put up with Laussac for an evening."

Ellen laughed in sympathy. "Same here. I'm playing hooky."

"I came for some special wines for a client. I'm taking a train to Paris in an hour," Paula said. She reached in her handbag and handed Ellen her card, and Ellen stuck it in her wallet. "By the way, I have a friend I want you to meet while you're here. I'll call you from the train and explain."

Ellen nodded. When Paula was out of hearing distance, Max said, "I wish Bill Casey had been a little more discreet. You don't want people to think you're running around with such valuable property."

"Paula is his new go-to wine expert. He won't admit it, but he's a little miffed that I pronounced his prize bottle a counterfeit."

"Nobody asked me, but it seems to me Bill Casey is playing you against each other by telling Paula to sell the lot and handing you a bottle to be authenticated."

Ellen led the way back to her suite. "I think Paula was seeing if she could get a reaction out of me when she said she wanted to sell the rest of the lot." She laughed. "She'll go crazy figuring out who I gave the bottle to. She's one of those people who likes to be in the know."

Once in her room, Ellen opened her laptop and scanned emails, while Max stood waiting. She read out loud, "*Ellen, bring the bottle back and we'll discuss further. I don't want it opened.*" She glanced up at Max, a stubborn expression on her face. "I never saw this email. I'm hitting delete." She waved her hand in the air. "Now go. Check in around 5:30."

"The bottle leaves our hands tonight, though, right?" Max asked.

"That's the plan." Ellen disappeared into the *salle de bain*.

Max returned to her room and called her mother, who listened as Max described all that had transpired with Ellen. "I thought that affair was over," Juliette said, tut-tutting. "I've told Ellen it's not a good thing for her, but she won't listen."

"Who is he?"

"Pascal Boulin. Famous in the wine world."

"I figured it would be somebody like that. Would his wife send her a note that says 'stop' in French and English?"

"That isn't French. If anything, she would confront her in person."

So who sent the damn note, Max thought. "And this stupid bottle of wine?"

Juliette laughed. "Once Ellen has a plan, she is not flexible. Tonight it will be gone, so don't worry."

"Do you know who we're dining with tonight by any chance?"

The pause was long enough for Max to wonder if her mother was lying when she said no. She exited the hotel and stopped to peer at the gates, spires, and old stone houses. The sky was grayish-blue, the air brisk. Bright red geraniums in window boxes provided a perfect accent to the monochrome color of the stone buildings. A large, monolithic church dominated the village. She entered a gate that was ajar and stepped into a garden where a guide spoke in a reverent tone to a small group of tourists about the thousands of men and hundreds of years it took to carve the stones for the church building. The guide pointed in Max's direction, describing a stone bench where women came to sit when they found themselves infertile. "Feel free to try it, if you like," she said with a wink to Max, who shook her head vigorously, making the tourists laugh.

Max walked out of the church and stopped to look around. Just beyond the rim of the village undulating rows of vines climbed to the horizon. Gnarly stumps, with small, bright green shoots, protruded two feet out of the ground. At harvest time, they would be covered with lush, green leaves, and heavy with deep crimson grapes. She continued walking the narrow roads leading to the outskirts of town. In a couple of days she would accompany Ellen to some of the most famous *châteaux* in the Médoc and Pauillac regions—names like Margaux and Saint-Julien.

The week will fly by, she thought, and if all goes well, I'll make a stop in Paris to see my grandmother. She still felt unsure about meeting the woman who had caused her mother so much pain—but there had been a reconciliation of sorts, when Juliette rushed to her mother's bedside after she had had a stroke two years ago. Max knew for certain that she wanted to avoid her uncle, the Minister of Justice Philippe Douvier, who was married to her mother's sister. Their brief meeting last year around the Champagne case had confirmed her mother's opinion that he was an ass.

By the time Max arrived back in the village, she felt overcome by hunger. At L'Envers du Décor, a bistro across the street from the hotel, Max ordered a glass of *Château Milon* and a plate of cheese to tide her over until dinner. The waiter recommended *Tome de Bordeaux,* an herb-encrusted goat cheese made in the Loire Valley. When it arrived Max could distinguish the taste of thyme, savory, fennel, and something else she couldn't quite identify. It occurred to her that she was happy, not a pinch-me kind of happiness, but the kind of unexpected contentment that comes from suddenly feeling at home in a foreign land.

A man at the next table sat reading a book and sipping an *express*. An attractive couple on Max's other side began to bicker.

"What's happened to you, Pascal?" a petit woman asked. You can do nothing without that woman telling you how to do it!"

The man she had called Pascal slowly cut his eye over at Max, then shifted his attention back to his companion. The woman was almost perfect, Max thought, with her shoulder-length fair hair casually swept back from her face and petite, well-proportioned figure. Although he had lowered his voice, Pascal, his dark hair pulled back in a ponytail and wearing jeans and a sweatshirt, appeared to be pleading with the woman as he gestured with his massive hands.

Max thought she could be watching a silent film. What would the hero do? "*Désolé,*" she heard him say, wondering why he was sorry. He started toward the door, then came back to kiss her hard on the lips and marched out. The woman watched him disappear, then gave Max a wan smile as she gathered her purse and left the restaurant.

A man at the next table said, "Pascal is in trouble as always. Poor Sylvie."

"*La Papesse* is in town," the waiter said. "I hear she's going to be tough with the wine scores this year." Clearly he meant Ellen Jordan. Max took another sip of her wine, listening intently as the waiter refilled his patron's glass. "*Oui. Elle a déjà cassé les couilles de Pascal.*" Max suddenly couldn't wait to tell Ellen: the critic had been accused of cutting Pascal's balls off.

"That's what Pascal gets for having an affair with her," the patron said. "Hoping to get high scores on his wine." Both men laughed.

"*La Papesse* had better watch herself," a man standing at the bar said. "She's pushed people too far. Monsieur Laussac was here two days ago ranting about what he'd like to do to her."

"He's a lot of hot air," his companion added in a dismissive tone. "Who knows what Sylvie would do if she learned of her husband's philandering? Especially with the Female Pope of Wine!" This was now quite a public discussion, Max thought, of a very private matter.

A few minutes later, Max paid her bill and crossed the lane to her hotel. Waiters were buzzing around setting tables. She ran up the stairs to Ellen's room and knocked. "I'm busy!" Ellen called out. "Come back at 7:30."

Max wanted to insist that she open the door, but she also didn't want to interrupt a romantic moment, if that was what was going on. "Okay!" Max went to her room and set her alarm for 6:30, stretched out on her bed, and fell into a deep sleep. When the clock buzzed, she felt refreshed and hungry, and full of energy. She took a quick shower, then slipped into boots, black jeans, and a cropped leather jacket. The little Boy Scout knife that her brother had cherished, and that her father had given to her several months ago, was a comforting weight in her pocket.

She rapped lightly on Ellen's door. "Second call," she said. Inside Ellen's room the phone was ringing off the hook. Max knocked again, this time harder. *What the hell*, Max thought. Ellen had promised not to leave her room. She called her name. No response. "Shit and *merde alors*," she said out loud. Ellen had given her a key to her room but Max had forgotten to take it. She rushed down to the concierge and explained that she needed to get into Madame Jordan's room.

"I will come with you," he said in a bored tone.

"May I just have the key, Monsieur Cazaneuve? Someone is coming for us in ten minutes."

"I can't give you the key," he insisted. They went up the stairs together. He knocked loudly several times and when there was no answer, he unlocked the door and pushed it open. Max strode into the bedroom and was shocked by the stench. Ellen was passed out on the bed, covered in vomit.

"Madame? " the concierge called, stepping into the room. "Is everything okay?"

Time for damage control. Max rushed over to Cazaneuve and spoke to him in fluent French to ensure no confusion on his part. "*Monsieur, Madame Jordan est indisposée. Elle est à moitié nue. S'il vous plait.*" Telling him that Ellen was naked might make him leave. Cazaneuve refused to budge. Desperate to return to

Ellen, she told him that she had things under control, and to please leave. When she tried to close the door, he wedged his foot in. She kicked him hard on the ankle with the sharp point of her cowboy boot. He yelped and hopped back, and she shut the door and locked it.

She raced back to Ellen, shrugging off her jacket and leaving it on the floor. "Ellen! It's me, Max. Wake up!" She tapped Ellen's cheek, which was clammy but warm, then hustled to the bathroom and ran a washcloth under cold water. Rushing back to the bed, she placed it on Ellen's forehead. When Ellen didn't stir, Max flicked on the bedside lamp. Ellen's face was so white it looked bleached, her eyes were closed, and the sour smell overpowering. Max felt for her pulse. Nothing. Reaching for the hotel phone, she dialed 112 for the ambulance and explained in French that the tenant in room six had asphyxiated and was in acute distress. Then she jumped up on the bed and started performing CPR. Three minutes passed. No response. Max continued, pressing rhythmically on Ellen's chest.

For a moment, she felt a sense of utter despair. Just focus on the facts, she thought. The woman she had been hired to protect was dead. The strong possibility was that she had drunk too much and thrown up, asphyxiating on the vomit. On the other hand, there was a threatening note somewhere in Ellen's possessions. Someone known to Ellen but not to Max was due to pick them up at 7:30. Ellen had planned to take a magnum of wine that she suspected of being a counterfeit to her host. Just when Max thought she couldn't continue the CPR, she heard footsteps in the hall and ran to open the door. The EMTs made a beeline to the patient.

Max stood back, the horrible truth starting to sink in. Glancing at the bedside table, she noticed a sizeable remnant of blue cheese, which, mixed with the odor of the vomit, almost made her gag. Where had that come from? Suddenly, Hank's words came back to her, words she had never read in a police manual—always cover your own ass first, for if you don't, how will the problem get solved?

Chapter Four

April 2

Olivier was preparing to leave his office in the Tribunal de Grande Instance, which, with its great glass wall beneath an undulating copper roof, made him think he was in some futuristic film, especially when he looked out his window and saw the medieval cathedral next door. He didn't share the opinion of a certain architectural critic who wrote that the expensive, contemporary building improved the people's perception of the French legal system.

He had driven to his office to meet with a representative from the minister's office, only to learn that his superior was giving him three months instead of the six he had requested to prove the existence of a counterfeit wine operation. Olivier hated the bureaucratic nonsense, but knew he had no other option than to listen to the cynics blather on about how counterfeiting had gone on for decades and no one seemed the worse for it.

Glancing at his watch, he realized that this small detour meant he would be rushed to have everything ready by the time his guests arrived. His cell rang as he started the drive home. "*Allo*, Sylvie."

"Have you spoken with Pascal?"

"*Non.* Is everything okay?"

"He's nowhere to be found, as usual. He told me he was

bringing our *Terre Brûlée* wine for dinner. Now that it's been elevated by the INAO, he'll give our entire profit away."

Olivier knew she was referring to the organization responsible for regulating French agricultural products.

"*Ça ne fait rien,*" Olivier said. "I prefer to serve from my own collection anyway." Though he respected Pascal's and Sylvie's newer methods of making wine, he preferred the traditional, blended wines that had first made the region famous. In a tiny shed in Saint-Émilion, Pascal had created a bolder, fruitier wine that could be consumed right away. His method, inspired by the established and elite vineyard, *Le Pin,* involved cutting away excess bunches of grapes, then tending to the grapes largely by hand right up to the bottling. Pascal's wine received glowing reviews from critics, especially from Ellen Jordan.

"You and Pascal decide what to open," Sylvie said. "Who else is coming?"

"Ellen Jordan and her assistant."

Olivier found the silence that followed unsettling. He vaguely recalled Abdel quoting a blogger who hinted of an affair between the famous wine critic and some winemaker she had put on the map.

"I need to speak to you later, Olivier," Sylvie said, "as a friend."

"We'll find a moment. Come at 8:30." He continued driving up the winding road to the house he was renting in Bouliac, one that offered splendid views of the city below. His cat, Mouchette, dashed across the driveway and onto the porch as he pulled in, always there to greet him at the end of the day. As he paused on the porch to check his mail, she brushed up against his pant leg, letting him know that it was past her dinnertime. He reached down and picked her up to carry her into the house. Aromas drifted out from the kitchen, where Zohra was busy with last-minute preparations.

"Monsieur,"she said, smiling brightly. "The *haricots verts* are ready to cook and the gooseberries already poached for the compote with *Muscat syllabub*."

"I'll decant the wine. You are welcome to stay in your room here for the night," he said.

She smiled at him, "Are you asking me to serve dinner, Monsieur?"

"I am saying I can't do it without you, which is what I've been saying for years."

"You're still a sentimental boy," she said, but she was smiling.

Olivier went upstairs to shower, and had dressed and was decanting the wine when the house phone rang. It was Abdel. "I'm at the Hôtellerie Renaissance and the concierge, Monsieur Cazaneuve, says that he thinks something suspicious is going on. Ellen Jordan's assistant frantically demanded a key to her boss' room, but when he let her in, she shut the door in his face."

The word *she* jumped out at Olivier, as he realized he had lost their bet. "Go on?"

Abdel was sounding uncharacteristically animated. "The room reeked of vomit and from what he could tell, Madame Jordan was passed out."

"*Putain*! I'm on my way. Call the ambulance just in case and tell them to pull around to the back. I should be there by the time they arrive. It's probably nothing."

"The assistant has called the ambulance. They just drove in."

Olivier couldn't guage the seriousness of what was going on. Madame Jordan's secretary had probably panicked. "Get her room key from the concierge. No drama."

Olivier told Zohra to put the dinner on hold until he called to confirm, and dashed out to his car. Once on the road, his thoughts raced at the speed of his Audi R7. Glancing at the clock on the dashboard, he made note of the time. 7:40. When his mobile rang he slowed down slightly and answered in a peremptory voice, "*Quoi*!"

"Monsieur… "

"I'm entering the village limits. I'm going to lose you."

"The news is bad."

Abdel's voice faded out. Olivier came to a screeching halt just in time to avoid hitting a man who had darted out in front of him. He pulled in behind Abdel's Renault parked at the rear entrance to the hotel. The haunting notes of a saxophone punctuated the air. The Laussac dinner event was in full swing.

A dim light illuminated four *ambulanciers d'urgence* loading a gurney into the back of the vehicle. As he approached, he saw the profile of a woman with bobbed, blond hair which struck him as familiar. She spoke English in an agitated voice. "This ambulance is not leaving without me!" He watched her turn to the gendarme who was moving toward her, her body in attack mode. "If you touch me, you'll be sorry."

Olivier thought he must be hallucinating as he studied the woman's full, luscious mouth, now locked in a pout; defiant azure eyes; and impossibly long legs sheathed in tight jeans.

Abdel broke the spell. "You may ride with the patient, Max. No problem."

She turned then, and seeing Olivier, froze. All five feet nine inches of her, five ten in cowboy boots. "Olivier."

"Drive to the hospital in Libourne," he ordered the driver. "Hurry. Max, get in."

"But where are you…?"

"Never mind about me. I'll see you there." He watched as Max folded her tall frame into the back of the ambulance, and the attendant closed the door. Abdel hopped into the passenger seat of Olivier's car and they took off after the ambulance. "Did you know she was here, Abdel?"

"*Non*! She was trying to revive Madame Jordan when I arrived in the room."

"Is Madame Jordan going to make it?"

"She's dead. Max insisted on taking her to the hospital anyway."

Ellen Jordan dead! Olivier's brain was having a hard time computing. "Do you know why Max is here?"

"No idea. The local *gendarmes* told me they attempted to arrest her after she kicked the concierge on the ankle when he tried to remove her from Madame Jordan's room. She gave me a wild embrace when she saw me, and the *gendarmes* wanted to arrest her again for further demonstration of insanity."

Olivier pulled up behind the ambulance and watched Max hop out, then stand back as the stretcher was unloaded and rushed inside. Max followed, taking long strides and keeping her head down. When Olivier and Abdel entered the waiting room after speaking to the ambulance attendants, she was at the desk, looking stricken. "Max," he said, "you know the victim?"

Max nodded. The doctor on duty approached them and announced in a quiet voice that Ellen was DOA.

Olivier said, "I'm sorry."

"I already knew. I couldn't get her pulse."

"We're going in to see the body. You can wait for us here," Olivier said kindly.

Her eyes met his, and he was taken aback for a second by the familiarity. She said, "You know I can handle the sight of a corpse, Olivier. Just so you know, I came here as her bodyguard."

Olivier tried not to look shocked. "I don't understand why I wasn't informed."

"It was last-minute. And you and I weren't exactly in close touch."

He wanted to retort that it was she who hadn't responded to his last email, but the time and place were inappropriate.

The doctor suggested they go to a small waiting room and he would join them there. "Did you spend the day with her?" Olivier asked.

"Ellen was fine when I left at one or so, and looking forward to a dinner at someone's home. Some straitlaced guy who loves to cook."

"I don't know this term straitlaced."

"Stuffy. Old-fashioned. Conservative."

Olivier tried to ignore the insult. The local medical examiner joined them. "I've seen Madame Jordan," he said. "I can do further testing, but I'm quite sure the cause of death is asphyxiation due to inebriation."

Olivier translated for Max. She said in English, "He's wrong. We should get the body to our old friend in the Paris suburbs for some good forensic work."

"But there's no crime," Olivier said, recognizing the fragrance she had left on his pillow in Champagne ten months ago, chagrined that his senses could be charged at a time like this.

"I think there is," she whispered.

"I can do a simple autopsy," the local doctor said.

"Give us a minute alone," Olivier said. When the doctor closed the door behind him, he turned to Max. "Are you saying you suspect foul play?"

"She was murdered. I would bet my brother's knife on it." He knew she'd never make a bet on her sacred talisman if she wasn't completely sure. Still…

"There has to be some proof of foul play before I can order a forensic autopsy."

"Order it and we'll find the proof."

Olivier looked over at Abdel, who shrugged slightly, then fixed his gaze on Max, trying to guess what was going on beneath her façade of professionalism.

The words tumbled over each other. "My boss, Captain O'Shaughnessy, assigned me to Ellen when she received a threatening note and went to my father. She is…or was… a good friend of my mother's, and so of course it seemed natural to send me." Olivier thought he might as well get used to the shock waves that he knew would continue throughout the evening. "By the way, my Uncle Philippe gave permission for a bodyguard to accompany Ellen to France, but he has no idea it's me. We're not on the best of terms, as you know, so can we keep it that way?"

"*D'accord.*" He knew that Douvier would want to send Max back to the States immediately so Olivier would keep her secret for now. "Okay, I'll ask for a forensics team to come later this evening after the Laussac dinner has ended. If we find any proof of foul play, I'll order a forensics autopsy."

"That's better than nothing."

They left the room and Olivier ordered the medical examiner not to leak Ellen's death to the press. He joined Max and Abdel at his car, and they returned to the hotel, taking the back flight upstairs to Max's room where two *gendarmes* stood in the doorway. "What the hell!" Max said. "Do they have a search warrant?"

Olivier realized someone had tipped off the *capitaine de gendarmerie,* who had in turn put in a call to the local prosecutor. "I don't know quite what's going on," Olivier said, "but I'll find out."

"Who turned down the bed?" Max asked once they were in her room.

"The maid must have come in," Olivier said. Turning to Abdel, he asked, "Didn't you tell the proprietor not to allow anyone in?"

"I hope she didn't go to Ellen's room," Max said. "I'm worried about evidence being destroyed."

Abdel offered to check and left the room.

Max recalled the events of the day, including the part about Ellen telling her she was going to have an assignation with someone. "When I stopped by at 5:30 and knocked, she called through the door to come back later. I assumed her lover was still there, so I went to take a nap."

"Did she slur her words? The emergency room doctor said he could smell alcohol on her."

"No. She sounded sober as a judge when she called out to me. Excuse the pun."

"Monsieur Cazaneuve told the police that your behavior was aggressive."

"How so?"

"You kicked him hard enough to require a trip to the doctor. I bring this up because he may decide to press charges."

"He's a nosy bully. If Ellen had passed out from drinking too much booze, I wanted to protect her."

"But she sounded sober as a judge?"

"It's a manner of speaking." Max stood up in frustration.

A light tap on the door and Abdel re-entered. "The concierge said he put out the word to the staff not to enter, but the maid went in anyhow."

"In other words, Madame Jordan's bed was turned down for the night?"

Abdel nodded.

"Assign an undercover officer to the hotel," Olivier said.

"Why don't we go in there now?" Max asked. "I worry about a small-town forensics team screwing up."

"Abdel and I will be overseeing it. I need to ask you some questions, Max, before I turn the investigation over to you."

"I know I'm being a pain in the ass."

She's the same Max, Olivier thought, a bit overwrought, acting on pure instinct, needing to be in charge, and one of the finest detectives I've ever observed. He said in a patient voice, "I'm trying to wait until most of the guests have left before bringing in a team of guys in space suits. How about if I have dinner sent up, and we can talk?" Olivier included Abdel with a look in his direction, but Abdel declined. "I'm sorry this happened," he said to Max. "You're a bodyguard now?"

Olivier recalled how Abdel and Max had become fast friends while working on the Champagne murders the year before.

"I'm on suspension from the NYPD for using excessive force on a rapist that I chased through Central Park. Some tourist caught me on film and put the whole fiasco up on YouTube. My boss thought sending me here was a good, temporary solution."

Olivier thought the force she used on her victim must have been extraordinary to create such a public outcry. "Did you bring a gun?" he asked her and she pulled the 19 mm Glock from her bag and handed it to Abdel. "I'm going to ask you to stay in your room tonight," Olivier said. "The news is already out, I'm sure, that Ellen Jordan was taken to the hospital. If you go downstairs, reporters will descend on you like vultures."

Max nodded. Olivier followed Abdel down the stairs, shaking his head. "I forgot to call your grandmother to tell her that my dinner is off."

"I let her know and she called the Boulins."

"Excellent. What's your gut feeling about Ellen Jordan's death?"

"Max knows something we don't."

"That's why I want to have this opportunity to get to the

truth. But first I'm going to circulate around the dining room to see if I can pick up any information."

"The proprietor found a space for us, which wasn't easy, as the hotel is full. I'm going to view the YouTube video of Max's fight with the rapist."

"She seems more confident than last year," Olivier said.

"Less ambivalent."

"Madame Jordan was planning to bring her to my home for dinner tonight. What a surprise that would have been."

"A better reunion for sure than the way it ended up happening."

"Napoleon said, 'There is no such thing as accident. It is fate misnamed.'"

"There is a similar Arab saying."

"Then it must be true."

Chapter Five

April 2

The evening had a surreal quality to it. Tragedy in slow motion was the way Max referred to it in her journal—the delicious afternoon of exploring the village, the return to the hotel and falling into a deep sleep, then awaking to Ellen dead. The surprise, and okay, she could admit it in her journal, the unexpected joy of seeing Olivier. She forbade herself that distraction, and instead tried to write rationally her reasons for thinking Ellen was murdered, when she had nothing to base her certainty on but an innocuous note and a bottle of wine—and a big dose of intuition.

She needed to remove the wine from the safe, but would wait and have Olivier accompany her. Thinking of dinner made her wonder what had happened to the mystery man who was to be their host. Did he arrive to collect them while she was at the hospital? It was time to run events by her dad and Walt. She didn't call the main number at the NYPD. Instead she dialed Walt's cell phone number known to very few, and when he answered, she spilled the whole story. The silence that followed lasted so long she thought they had been disconnected. "Have you called your father yet?" he asked.

"I thought I'd call you first."

"Are you okay? This wasn't what we had in mind when we sent you there."

"I guess so. The wine that I was supposed to be guarding with my life, which may not be authentic, is in the safe downstairs. It may provide the motive."

"We weren't told about any counterfeit wine." He paused. "Nothing that you've said is any proof of murder. What was the weapon?"

The answer felt clear to Max. "Poison."

"Hard as hell to prove."

"Olivier and Abdel are here, and I'm having a hard time convincing them that there's been foul play."

"If my memory serves me right, they're pretty rational guys. They know you speak French yet?"

"No, but the pretense is getting old."

"Keep it that way for now. It worked in your favor the last time. I'll call Hank."

"Okay." She bit her lip to keep the tears at bay. "I half-suspected until now that you and my folks concocted the bodyguard thing just to get me out of town until things settled down."

"We're not that generous. And don't get any big notions about trying to solve this thing on your own. The French won't take kindly to it."

"If we learn Ellen was murdered, I want to stay and solve it."

"We've got the FBI there. I'll bring you back here."

Max picked up the pillow on her bed and threw it against the wall. "I'm not going home," she said out loud.

Ten minutes later her phone rang. "Dad."

"I just talked to Walt."

"I turned out to be quite the bodyguard, huh? My client killed while I'm napping?" Max hated the way her voice started going shaky on her at the sound of her father's voice.

"Stop sounding like a sick toddler." Before she could object, he said, "Give me the one-minute rundown."

Max obliged.

Hank said, "The police will know soon enough that they're dealing with a homicide. You hear me agreeing with you, right?

You have to go through the whole rigmarole like the last time, with everybody on hold until the judge is appointed?"

Max was impressed that he remembered. "Olivier steps in, only if he's appointed to the case, after twenty-four hours. There's no official investigation as of this moment, but Olivier is sneaking forensics in to do a quick tour of Ellen's room, though the maid has already been in there. He hasn't decided on the forensic autopsy yet."

Hank's voice softened. "This is a tough one. I sure as hell hope you don't plan on putting your tail between your legs and running back here."

"Walt said the FBI here can take over."

"If I had listened to my bosses, I wouldn't have accomplished anything. You know my motto."

She said it by rote. "Detective work is solo business."

"The first step is to get in Ellen's room and see if you can figure out what happened."

"Do you know how much trouble I'll be in if I get caught? It's easy for you to say…"

"Ellen's room will tell the story, but once it's filled with the forensics guys, forget it."

"Okay, okay. I'll do it. How's Mom taking it?"

"Hard. She'll feel much better if you figure out what happened."

He was gone. A light tapping at the door startled her. She glanced at her watch: 9:30. It had to be Olivier, returning at last. She'd have to forget searching Ellen's room. A handsome man with an insouciant air about him stood in the doorway looking at her. "Oh!" Max said, surprised. This had to be the mystery man they were to dine with, but there was nothing old-fashioned about this guy.

"*Bonsoir*," he said. "I'm Vincent Barthes."

"Max Maguire," she said, shaking hands with him. "Ellen was taken ill and is in the hospital. I didn't know who we were to dine with, and so couldn't leave a message."

"I'm a little slow with my English, forgive me," he said. "And I'm a little drunk. Yes. I have been downstairs saying hello to old friends. Is she okay?"

Max looked at him. "I'd wager a bet those friends sent you up to find out what happened." He didn't deny it. "She's quite ill. Probably food poisoning."

"Are you Madame Jordan's daughter, by any chance?"

"Assistant. Sommelier-in-training." Max recalled Ellen's cheshire grin when they spoke about the dinner and realized that she had been matchmaking. The man standing before her was a pretty perfect bundle of good looks and charm.

Abdel, appearing out of nowhere, suddenly loomed over Vincent, a look of disapproval clouding his face. He was followed by a short, stocky man in casual street clothes Max sensed he was undercover. Vincent stood at mock attention. "I didn't do anything, your honor," he said.

"Just why are you here, Monsieur?"

"Max will explain." Vincent turned to gaze at her. "You'll be hearing from me. *Au revoir*."

She waggled her fingers. "You know him?" Abdel asked.

"No, but I realized when I opened the door that he must be Ellen's friend who was picking us up for dinner."

Abdel stared at her.

"What's wrong?"

"Did he acknowledge that he was your dinner host?"

"I think so. On second thought, he didn't seem to know Ellen was bringing an assistant."

"My hunch is he saw you and was determined to meet you. Women, to a man like that, are prey." Max had learned about Abdel's strong morals last year, and understood where he was coming from. "Where did you tell him Madame Jordan was?"

"In the hospital with a sudden onset illness."

"Maybe he was being *fouine*. Nosey. I'm sure that half the village was trying to guess your identity as you walked around this afternoon. That's how small towns operate." He smiled at her, "Monsieur Chaumont has ordered dinner, and should be along within half an hour or so. He's scoping out the formal affair hosted by Monsieur Laussac."

"I think Olivier likes detective work, don't you?"

Abdel smiled in agreement. "The policeman who was with me will be keeping an eye on things here tonight. If Madame Jordan was murdered, as you insist, then someone could also be targeting you."

It hadn't occurred to Max to be concerned about her own safety.

Chapter Six

April 2

Olivier instructed the hospital authorities to send Ellen's body to a suburb of Paris for a forensic autopsy, issuing a warning about secrecy at the same time. He had met with the *procureur*, or prosecutor, briefly, who had reluctantly given his approval. Though he had learned to trust Max's intuition the year before, he was going out on a limb tonight with the autopsy and forensic team. Max surely had some information to back up her conviction, he assured himself. He stepped outside for a moment to breathe in the night air. The ancient village was bathed in moonlight, the monolithic church a symbol of faith and struggle.

Max is back, he thought, looking strong, full of vigor. He, on the other hand, was still recovering from the depression that had descended upon him after his friends in Champagne were murdered. He had never felt so unmoored. Night after night, he had been unable to sleep, haunted by the murders. For months after arriving in Bordeaux, he got up and went to work like an automaton, barely aware of others. Other than Pascal and Sylvie Boulin, he hadn't made friends with the locals.

Zohra made all of his favorite dishes, which he picked at, and then one night in February, instead of going home, she sat with him while he drank until three in the morning. He had sobbed uncontrollably, and she held him as she had when he was a boy.

The next day the despair started to lift, but he still lived with the anxiety that the depression could return and bring him to his knees again. He had longed to contact Max, but somehow she was associated with the cause for all this endless mourning. He hoped over dinner he could explain some of this to her.

A high-profile case involving Ellen Jordan could easily land him in a political quagmire, so he needed to stay as detached as possible with all his senses on alert. He re-entered the hotel and went to the room behind the proprietor's office where Abdel had quietly set up an operations center. Abdel told him that the *capitaine* from the *gendarmerie* had been a little prickly when asked to bring the forensics team in the back door, but in the end he had agreed that discretion was called for. Olivier scurried to the kitchen and shook hands with the chef, ordered a dinner to be sent to Max's room, along with a bottle of *Château la Vieille Cure 2007*, then braced himself as he wove among the crowd in the dining room.

The pale yellow dining room could seat 150 diners, yet had a quiet elegance rare for such a vast space. Damask draperies covered a wall of windows on the far side of the room. Olivier paused to admire the round tables, each covered in rich linen tablecloths and yellow china, with the three requisite glasses—for water, white wine, and red wine—arranged to the right of the plates. The waiters moved in and out among the tables, balancing trays of glasses.

Vincent Barthes had a reputation as a playboy, and was often seen on the news with women who served as arm candy. Of medium height, and with fair hair and blue eyes, he was a standout as far as looks went. Watching him glide around the room, Olivier observed that he treated each woman he spoke with as though she were the only person in the room.

Olivier didn't think he had any particular interest in Max, just in seeing how quickly he could net another fish. Vincent's father, Yves Barthes, and his father before him had been successful *négociants*, selling wines from the best vineyards. Since dropping out of his family firm and starting a company that produced cheap commercial wine, it was rumored that Vincent had lost a fortune, and then regained his footing—a last-minute save most people attributed to his father's largesse.

Olivier was interested in the cultural mix he saw before him as he continued to scan the room. A large number of Asians mingled with Russians and Americans, with English the dominant language. Chantal Laussac made her way over to him. She had been born into this glamorous world, and her correct posture and subtle manners, the elegant chignon, the Chanel suit, and Hermès scarf were symbolic of that upbringing. *"Vous êtes resplendissante,"* Olivier said as she approached.

She didn't pause for the requisite kiss on each cheek before saying, "Olivier, a rumor has spread that Ellen Jordan declined our dinner invitation because she was planning to have dinner with a mystery man. Do you have any idea who she was cavorting with, other than Pascal Boulin?"

"The key word is rumor," Olivier said. "And as she isn't well, and dined with no one, it doesn't matter, does it?" Olivier reminded himself that the only people who knew of his planned dinner with Ellen and her assistant were Abdel and Zohra, and Sylvie and Pascal. He wished he knew what had been urgent enough for Ellen to insist on seeing him her first day in the village.

"François is upset," Chantal went on. "She re-tasted his 2010 wine, but won't tell him if she has changed the score. That woman shouldn't have such power over us."

Olivier was hardly in the mood for placating the various egos in the room. "You have to admit Ellen Jordan has sold a lot of French wine."

François Laussac approached. "You decided to come after all. Welcome, Monsieur."

Olivier shook hands with him, and explained that he couldn't stay for dinner. "You understand the politics of my position, I'm sure."

"Then you're here on business?"

Olivier judged Laussac to be astute, a bit grandiloquent, but also polished, and certainly a great advocate for the Bordeaux region, though he usually went too far. "Nothing official," he said. Olivier removed a glass from the tray as the waiter passed by. He sniffed the 2000 wine, gently rolled it around in the glass, and sipped. It had been a good year for Laussac, and he had good reason to be proud of it. His wine in the past had been compared to the exquisite *Château Ausone* that was held up as a benchmark for others, but the more recent vintages were causing him trouble.

"*Pas mal*," Olivier said, and François smiled. "I might make an appearance tomorrow at Chantal's family estate in the Médoc for their wine tasting, if that's all right with you. It isn't the time now to discuss it, but I understand that you had some wine stolen from your cellar."

"They took some bottles dating back to the fifties from my wife's family cellar which is under lock and key. She didn't want to report it."

"I'm investigating a series of break-ins and will encourage her to file a report."

"Bordeaux can't afford the bad publicity. There's been quite enough around the newly announced Saint-Émilion ranking." François had a way of speaking for the entire Bordeaux wine world, which Olivier found irritating.

"But it's against the law to steal," Olivier said, his tone sarcastic. "And it is a policeman's job to find and punish the thieves."

"It will no doubt turn up at some auction house. I suspect some of the Moroccans who've been working in our vineyards."

"Why?"

"I've heard there are some trained thieves among them."

Olivier felt disgusted at the racist remark. To change the subject, Chantal told her husband that Ellen Jordan had gone to the hospital with food poisoning.

Olivier was about to ask her who told her that when they were interrupted by a man who took Olivier's hand and pumped it. "Hello. I'm Larry Wexler," he said, glancing from one to the other. "Wexler's Wine Importers and Distributors in New York? I don't know how you guys sleep after eating so late. It gives me heartburn."

Olivier prided himself on his English, but could barely make out what this man was saying because of his strong accent. He spoke in a sing-song manner, and elongated his vowels. Muscles bulged beneath his suit jacket. Of medium height, with dark curly hair, he reminded Olivier of a boxer. He had read about New Yorkers' obsession with gyms, and thought this man had gone to an extreme.

Chantal repeated what she had just learned about Ellen Jordan.

"I've been waiting for Madame to arrive before telling my guests to take their seats," François said. Olivier was tempted to call him on his lie, but refrained. "You know, Monsieur Chaumont, Mr. Wrestler sells more of Chantal's and my wine than any other distributor in New York."

"It's *Wexler*," the man said. "And to tell you the truth, selling wine is no different in my opinion than selling toilet fixtures. You're either a salesman or you're not. I happen to be damn good at it."

François uttered a humorless laugh.

"To what do you attribute your success?" Olivier asked with genuine interest.

"Chutzpah," Larry said. "And somehow I developed a decent wine palate. I have people back home clamoring for everything I'm purchasing here over the next three days."

"Your commerce system is almost as complicated as ours," Chantal said.

"It's a racket is what it is. I'll give you an example of when I started out. I was a small company. I wanted Chantal's family's famous wine, which always sells out early. I talked to your *courtier* and *négociant* and the next thing I knew I'd agreed to buy a lot of inferior wine in order to have the fine wine. It made me mad as hell. They can't do that to me now that I've gotten so big."

Olivier noticed that Chantal was bristling, but he also knew there was some truth to what the American was saying. "Who do you sell to?" Olivier asked in an attempt to sidetrack the conversation.

"Retailers, private buyers, restaurants…"

"Auction houses?"

"Not allowed."

"There's a woman at an auction house who has developed a reputation for finding extraordinary wines and quadrupling the price," Laussac said.

"Paula Goodwin. She's fantastic."

Chantal excused herself, leaving the three men to carry on.

"Not as big a star as Ellen Jordan, though, right?" François said.

"Paula holds a Masters of Wine certificate, held by maybe six women in the U.S."

Olivier knew that anyone with the initials "MW," or Master of Wine, after their name had reached a unique status. It took years and many thousands of dollars to complete the training in London.

"Ellen Jordan is not popular in this area," François said, obviously pleased to have someone whose disdain for her was as great as his. "She practically admitted this morning to making a mistake with my 2010 wine. Do you know what that mistake has cost me?"

"I can guess," Wexler said, then excused himself. He strode off, wobbling.

"He smells like gin," Olivier said to François, who shrugged.

Over his shoulder Olivier noticed Abdel standing in the door, wide-eyed, trying to catch his eye. Nodding to another couple he knew slightly, Olivier thanked his host for the wine and made his way to his assistant. "What is it?"

"Monsieur Barthes knocked on Max's door. She assumed he was the man who was to be Ellen Jordan's and her host for the evening. Here's the thing: he didn't disavow her of that idea after she brought it up."

"I just learned from Madame Laussac that Vincent met Max, and wondered how."

"Predatory instinct," Abdel sniffed. "He followed in his father's footsteps and took a suite to entertain customers. He probably saw Max pass by." Abdel paused before asking, "You're going to tell Max that she was going to your house for dinner, aren't you?"

"I'll have to now," Olivier said. "Make sure to get a list of all the guests at the Laussac dinner, and names and addresses of people staying at the hotel."

Olivier's mobile rang, and while still talking into the phone, he jumped up and hurried up the stairs with Abdel at his heels. "The policeman heard a loud crash in Madame Jordan's room and Max has gone missing," he said to his assistant.

Chapter Seven

April 2

Max thought of Hank's words—*the story of what happened is in Ellen's room.* There was only one thing to do—get into Ellen's room and look around. She would try Ellen's balcony door, and if it was locked, she'd let it go. Olivier must have forgotten about dinner, she decided. She ransacked her suitcase for a small flashlight and a pair of latex gloves, items that went with her everywhere as a matter of habit. Her watch read 10:30. From her balcony she heaved her body over the wrought-iron railing to Ellen's balcony next door and tried the door. To her surprise it opened. A narrow swath of light came in under the door from the hallway.

It took her a second to get her bearings. Clicking on the mini-flashlight, she did a quick survey of the room, making note of the wine bottles looking like sentinels standing at attention in the shadows. A half-empty bottle of a wine labeled *Château d'Yquem* 1995 stood separate from the others. Various cheeses wrapped in white butcher paper were in the mini-fridge. She didn't know if someone had brought them, or if Ellen had ordered them up, but they weren't there when she'd left to walk around the village. Tasting was verboten, but she was sorely tempted.

In the salon she looked around for the cheese that had assailed her senses when she was doing CPR on Ellen. The plate was there, but the remnant was gone. Forensics hadn't arrived yet, so where was it?

She directed the narrow beam of light to a couple of tailored suits in the closet that hung like ghosts, then scanned the bed and night table, noticing a pair of reading glasses on the table and beside them the leather notebook that Ellen used to record wine scores. She walked over and picked it up. There were ten entries, the Laussac wine and Pascal Boulin's among them. Boulin's score had dipped down to 88, a baleful score for a wine that had, in the past, reached 98. Laussac's 2010 score had climbed a couple of points, enough to redeem his reputation.

She next thumbed through Ellen's address book which was also lying on the bedside table, and a slip of paper fell out. Bingo! The threatening note. Max jammed it into her jeans pocket. A business card was tucked inside. She removed it and shone the light on it. It was Olivier's, with his home, mobile, and private office number scratched on the back. How curious, she thought. Why would he have given her his personal contact information? She slid it into her pocket and put the tasting book back on the table. Enough rummaging. She picked up Ellen's laptop and put it next to the balcony door.

Typical party noise wafted into the room. A quick look in the *salle de bain* and she'd be back in her own room. She closed the door behind her. A blue silk robe hung from a hook behind the door, and Ellen's cosmetic pouch hung from a towel holder. Max's eyes followed the course of the light into the wastebasket. She picked up tweezers from the shelf and saw beneath the condom wrapper the spent condom. A DNA dream, Max thought. In the world she operated in, lovers and husbands were first persons-of-interest. All she had to go on so far was her mother's statement about Pascal Boulin, but that could have changed. For a fleeting second she speculated about Olivier.

She left the bathroom, carefully rotating the skinny beam of light around the room, and froze. A hulking figure wearing a ski mask stood facing her. As he lunged, she stepped back and threw the flashlight at him. A soft thud told her she had hit her mark, but she didn't wait to see where. Her instinct made her turn sideways into his attack. She rammed the side of her head into his belly, while grabbing and lifting his leg. He fell backwards. Hard. Max planted her foot on his exposed throat and reached down for the small flashlight, focusing the beam on his face.

She spoke in French in a low voice, "I'm going to remove your mask. Do not struggle or I will crush your neck. You'll take your last breath ever." He lay still, panting. As she started to lean over to yank off his mask, she heard a sound at the door. Startled, she lifted her foot from the intruder's throat, who took advantage of the distraction, grabbing her ankle with both his hands, and giving it a twist. Max went sailing into the table holding the wine bottles, creating a tremendous din as they crashed to the floor.

A loud baritone voice yelled from the hallway, "*Ouvrez! La police!*" Max reached down and grabbed the laptop, looped the strap around one shoulder and hurried onto Ellen's balcony, where she saw the back of a man rushing down the cobblestoned path. She made a split-second decision to jump from the balcony in pursuit. Grasping the railing with both hands, she swung her body over it, and landed right side up on her feet, the laptop still attached. She went past the church as fast as she could on the cobblestone path and paused to listen. Accompanied by jazz music emanating from the hotel, she backtracked to the front of the hotel, then raced to the street that ran past it. A couple had stopped to kiss under a streetlight. She ran up and asked them if they had seen a lone man running and they shook their heads.

What if he was clever enough to blend in with the hotel staff, she wondered. She walked into the kitchen from the back entrance and looked around. How would she know if he was there? She saw the stairs and rushed up to the ground level floor, noticing a small bar. A perfect place to get her bearings.

The dimly lit room was divided into four areas; the far section occupied by two men having a drink and engrossed in conversation. A soaring arrangement of lilies in the center of the room emitted a sweet, pungent aroma. In the corner, next to the bar, was a table with three stools placed around it. Winded, and trying to appear normal, Max sat on the far stool and looked out at the lobby. Her back hurt like hell from crashing into the table in Ellen's room, but it helped to think the masked intruder was probably in worse shape than she was. She set the laptop case down beside her. It was no good to her if she didn't have Ellen's user name and password. She glanced at her watch. As much as she hated asking Joe for anything, he was the precinct's computer guru, and would know exactly what to do.

She cast a surreptitious glance over at the two men in the corner who were arguing in stage whispers. One of them got up and listed across the room, stopping in the middle to regain his balance. She continued watching him out of the corner of her eye as he lurched past the reception desk and entered the hotel restaurant, his muscles bulging under a tight gray suit jacket. One of those guys who lives in a gym, Max mused to herself. The other was none other than Vincent, who made a beeline over to her, carrying a small plate of food which he placed in front of her, as though he had been expecting her. "You changed your mind," he said. He smiled down at her, and despite herself, she smiled back. He picked up a morsel of squab and chickpeas and slid it into her mouth, a sensuous act that would have given anyone watching the impression that they had known each other a long time. "I'll order a proper dinner for you," he said. "You're jet-lagged and can't sleep?"

"Don't order dinner," she said. "I'm only here for a minute."

"A glass of wine won't hurt," he said. "Here, take a sip of this *Graves*," Vincent said. "It's a *Smith Haut-Lafitte*, to be exact, a wonderful château you should visit while you're here." Max obliged, and then took another taste of the squab, grateful to have something in her stomach. Though the wine was delicious, it wasn't helping in the least to allay her anxiety. Her status was rapidly deteriorating from intruder-chaser to fugitive. It was time to run upstairs and confess everything to Abdel, who was surely on the prowl for her. She hoped that Olivier had forgotten all about dinner and gone home.

Vincent's mobile rang, and while he was talking, it occurred to her that he might let her make a quick call. When he hung up, she asked if he had international minutes, and he handed her the phone. "Call China if you want," he said, and wandered off to greet a man who had just entered the bar. She had only been there fifteen minutes at most, but that was an eternity if they were searching for her upstairs. It wouldn't take Joe long to figure out the codes. It was 5:30 in the morning in New York.

"Detective Laino."

"Joe, it's me, Max."

"Yeah?" His voice softened. "You back?"

"I need you to refresh my memory about hacking into a computer."

"You're not in enough trouble? Whose?"

"Ellen Jordan's. The wine critic."

The silence that followed told her he was paying attention. "Give me a good reason why."

"She's dead."

"Shit, Babe. She was offed?"

"I'm trying to find out."

"This isn't free, you know." He was enjoying his few seconds of power over her.

"Hurry," she whispered.

"Okay, here's what you do." He started giving clear instructions.

"Got it. Call you later."

She walked toward the table where Vincent was sitting to hand the phone back, but Abdel stopped her in her tracks, wrapping his hand around her upper arm. "People are looking for you," he said. He took the phone from her hand and handed it to Vincent.

Vincent looked up at Abdel, "I hate watching men manhandle women."

Abdel released Max's arm as though he had been burned, never taking his eyes off her. She stepped over to the little bar and picked up Ellen's laptop, and trailed out behind him as he continued texting as they climbed the stairs. She was sure that

Olivier was the recipient. Abdel turned back to look at her, "We thought something had happened to you. Someone broke into Ellen Jordan's room, and you were nowhere to be found."

"I'll explain."

They entered her room where Olivier sat in a chair facing the door. A tray with a bottle of wine and two dinners sat on the table. Looking from Abdel to Olivier, she couldn't believe the hostility on their faces.

Chapter Eight

April 2

"I found her in the bar with Monsieur Barthes," Abdel said in French, obviously put out with her.

"It never occurred to me that you might be enjoying yourself," Olivier said to Max, "I apologize for disturbing you."

"No need for sarcasm, Olivier. You've got it all wrong. I stopped at the bar to collect my thoughts after losing the guy who attacked me in Ellen's room."

Just as he had suspected, she caused the ruckus in the room next door. Remembering her penchant for starting her stories in the middle, he said, "Start at the beginning. You wanted to beat forensics to the evidence. At least admit it."

"Okay, I confess. It feels like a stupid move now, but my gut feeling that Ellen was murdered needed some back-up. I wanted a couple of items before forensics got in there."

Olivier wasn't appeased. "Was the intruder waiting for you?"

"He came in while I was in the bathroom. Ellen's balcony door was unlocked, which I thought odd. I slipped on my gloves, and quietly went about the business of finding clues. I was ready to leave, but decided to give the *salle de bain* a quick look. When I exited the bathroom, a stocky guy wearing a mask came at me and we fought. It ended with him throwing me against the table and the wine bottles went crashing to the floor."

"And here you are. No bruises, no scratches."

"My back hurts, but he might have a hard time swallowing. I was this close to smashing in his windpipe."

"You followed him to the hotel bar?"

"When I rushed to the balcony I saw a man rushing down the street past the church and jumped down and gave chase. He vanished, so I thought he might have re-entered the hotel and hidden in a broom closet or in the kitchen. No luck. I happened to pass the bar on the way back to my room and decided to catch my breath. Vincent was there, and I wanted to tell him that Ellen was bringing him a magnum of wine that she suspected was counterfeit."

So that was what Ellen Jordan was bringing me, Olivier thought. "Do you have the bottle?"

"It's in the safe downstairs. I decided to wait for you before I reclaimed it. Ellen put my name on a form that allows me access."

Olivier stood up. "Let's go, then." They moved quietly down the stairs in order not to attact any attention. Olivier spoke to Cazaneuve, holding up his identity card. "*Bonjour, Monsieur.* I want the aluminum case from the safe belonging to Ellen Jordan."

"May I ask what size and shape, Monsieur?"

Max stepped forward and spoke in English. "Ms. Jordan and I went with you to put it in the safe. I saw you personally write my name on the form. It's a vertical case, aluminum, and heavy."

He gave an exaggerated shrug. "Many guests put items in the safe. I'll go look."

"We'll come, too," Olivier said.

"His sudden amnesia is maddening," Max said, as they waited for him to wait on another guest.

Olivier said, lowering his voice, "Do you recall the label?"

"*1945 Château Mouton-Rothschild.*"

"What? That's a famous vintage!"

"Worth $32,000 if authentic, and nothing if counterfeit." She gave him the short version of the bottle's journey.

Cazaneuve told them to follow him as he stepped out of the office and down a narrow hallway to a locked door. He opened it and led them to a larger-than-average safe, and began turning the dial. Madame Cassin entered. "Is everything okay?" she asked. The safe door opened, and Cazaneuve peered in. "What are you looking for, Edouard?" Madame Cassin asked.

He explained in a terse voice.

He stooped down and moved a few items around, then beckoned Max over to see for herself. The aluminum box was gone. "Edouard, return to the desk," Madame Cassin ordered her employee, ignoring his hostile look. "We'll call you if we need you." She apologized to Olivier, explaining that it was their busiest day of the season.

"We will have to bring the police in this evening," Olivier said. "How many people have access to the code?"

"Monsieur Cazaneuve and I."

"Do you keep a copy of the code somewhere?"

"Yes." She walked to a mahogany desk, and reaching under the drawer extracted a key and unlocked the drawer. She nervously rifled through it until she found a small sheet of embossed stationary from an envelope, which had the code written on it.

"How long has Monsieur Cazaneuve worked here?"

"Eight years. I trained him."

"You've never had a problem with theft before now?"

"We have smaller safes in the rooms. Only a few people have complained over the past five years."

"Any problems with Monsieur Cazaneuve?"

"I have to remind him from time to time who's in charge."

"Has he had any accusations by guests or others?"

She stopped to think. "My senior maid, Martine, and he don't get along, but that's to be expected in this business. Nothing serious that I know of."

Olivier and Max went back up the stairs, their shoulders slumped. "We definitely have a case," Olivier said. "I'm not sure about murder, but we have a major theft."

◇◇◇

Back in Max's room, he lifted the silver dome covers off the plates, and poured the wine. "Our dinner is getting cold. Duck breast is a specialty of Bordeaux. "And I think you'll like the wine."

"You're going to relax enough to dine?"

"Chaos reigns. Reflect. Repent and reboot. Order shall return. It's similar to a Japanese haiku." He handed her a glass.

"I thought it was advice from your life coach."

"We don't have those. What do they do?"

"Tell clients to repent and reboot. I'm teasing you, you know." She ate with relish. "Thanks for not being mad at me for going into Ellen's room."

He was content to be in her presence again, surprised at how comfortable it was. "Why did you do it, Max? You knew I'd be upset."

"My dad."

"He told you to ransack her room?"

"He told me the whole story was there, and better to beat everybody else to it. He's old school." She looked into his eyes. "I shouldn't blame him, though. I wanted to find something that might offer up a clue. Something concrete that would confirm what I'm thinking." Olivier thought he would have felt the same way, but probably wouldn't have acted on it. "I thought I could get over to Ellen's room and be out in fifteen minutes, with no one the wiser."

"So what story did you find in the room?"

"I have to admit I was shocked to see your card with all your phone numbers on it."

"H-mm."

"I thought for one fleeting second that you were her mystery paramour this afternoon, except it's likely that whoever was with her killed her, and you're not in that league."

He had come to full attention. "How kind you are to let me off the hook. It's the most absurd accusation ever directed at me, by the way." He remembered that she took every piece of evidence to its extreme in her imagination, sometimes finding uncanny solutions. "Why was she so intent on bringing the wine to me?"

"I think once she succeeded in convincing Bill Casey to let her have a bottle, she decided to take it to someone she trusted. She told me that you got her off a DUI charge, and she liked you."

"We got along well."

"You're a magistrate, which to her meant you could decide what to do with it, either take it to a new company she had heard about in France, or maybe taste it with her."

"I wouldn't trust myself far enough to determine the authenticity of a wine, though I do have a good nose, which is the key to tasting."

"Ellen was secretive this afternoon, but did say before I left that this evening she would reveal the name of the person she suspected might be involved in a counterfeit operation, and the name of her lover. I called my mother who told me his name: Pascal Boulin."

Olivier set his glass down, too shocked to say anything. "I don't believe it."

"If anyone would know, it's my mother," Max said.

A light knock on the door interrupted them. Abdel stuck his head in to announce that forensics had arrived, and Olivier told him to take charge and that he'd join him in a minute.

"Continue," Olivier said to Max.

She sipped her wine. "I was thinking about Vincent," she said. "The odd thing is he doesn't match the strait-laced description Ellen gave me of our host."

"I have a confession to make," Olivier said. "I am the chef and the host that you keep making disparaging remarks about."

Max's head jerked up. "*You*?"

"You and Ellen were due at my house at eight for dinner. Abdel was planning to pick you up, which is why he was near the hotel."

"I'll be damned." It was the first time he had seen her speechless. "The only explanation is that my mom and Ellen were matchmaking."

"I did think it strange when Madame Jordan called to ask if she could bring her assistant."

"I would have died of embarrassment."

"It would have been amusing."

"Better that than what ended up happening," she said. "It still hasn't sunk in that Ellen is gone."

"It will come in increments," Olivier said.

"We say in the department that there is a murder that will haunt you, and I think this is mine."

Olivier needed to go across the hall. He stood up. "Why was Vincent at your door, Max?"

"I don't know. I thought he was our host and prattled on about it. He was flirtatious to the point that I thought Ellen was fixing me up with him."

"Abdel thinks he saw you out during the afternoon and decided to introduce himself. He took a room on this floor to entertain clients and was probably a little drunk."

"He was sweet to me in the bar."

Olivier laughed in spite of himself. "His credentials are fine. Who can blame him, really, for taking an interest in you?"

He was amused to see her look self-conscious.

Abdel returned, "Monsieur, we found a condom in the bathroom wastebasket."

"*Un préservatif?*"

Abdel nodded, and coughed to hide his embarrassment. Olivier said, "Have them bag it."

Abdel made a quick exit.

Max said, "I made note of a smelly cheese that was on a small plate when I was giving Ellen CPR, but when I went in an hour ago it was gone. Do you think the gendarmes collected it?"

They put their dinner plates on the tray. "Let's go see what forensics has uncovered," Olivier said. "What else do you have?"

"I have Ellen's laptop."

"Abdel will take it and figure out the codes." Max handed it to him.

"I found the threatening note that got me here. It's pretty innocuous. It says stop in English and French." She pulled a small plastic bag from her pocket, and gave it to him.

"Did you leave anything for the forensics team?"

"The condom."

Olivier laughed. His mobile rang, and he saw that it was Philippe Douvier returning his call. Douvier's loud baritone voice echoed throughout the room. "What the hell's going on?"

"Ellen Jordan is dead," Chaumont said.

"Morte? But she brought a bodyguard."

"I wasn't told about her, by the way."

"*Her?"* Douvier bellowed. Olivier glanced over at Max, then remembered she couldn't understand French.

"*Eh oui.*"

"Cause of death?"

"To be determined."

A long silence followed. "You're not thinking murder, are you?"

"I'm not ruling it out."

"What did the medical examiner say?"

"Asphyxiation due to alcohol inhalation."

"Then why are you pursuing this as a murder? It will create a huge scandal."

"The bodyguard gave me sufficient reason, which I will explain later. I've called for a forensic autopsy."

"Without my permission, I might add. Where are you?"

"At the Hôtellerie Rennaissance."

It was clear that Philippe Douvier had no idea that his niece was back in the country. Olivier would keep her secret.

"I want to be kept informed," Philippe said.

"Of course."

"Send the bodyguard home."

"I need her for a couple of days to answer questions. I want this case, Philippe."

"You better be damn sure you know what you're doing. I'll speak to the *procureur.*"

After they hung up, Olivier spoke in French to Abdel, "The bastard *did* know Madame Jordan was bringing a bodyguard." He glanced over at Max again, who was casually flipping through a magazine, and continued his conversation.

Abdel said, "Will you let her"—he tipped his head in Max's direction—"in on Opération Merlot?"

Olivier answered quickly. "The language barrier is a problem."

"It wasn't last year," Abdel said.

"The wine business, and the potential fraud that is going on, is beyond her realm of expertise."

"I don't know about this wine either." Max had a strong ally, Olivier realized. "Except perhaps there's a correlation between the two," Abdel added.

Olivier stopped and looked at him. "What do you mean?"

"What if the counterfeiters knew somehow that Madame Jordan was in possession of a magnum of fine wine that she announced was fake? It makes sense that they would want it back. On the other hand, what if someone came to Madame Jordan and demanded the wine, thinking it authentic, and she refused to remove it from the safe?"

Olivier thought Abdel was becoming an abstract thinker like Max. "You have a point, Abdel. As for the detective in question, let's first see if there is a murder."

Ellen Jordan's suite was filled with uniformed people working under the harsh glare of work lights. Olivier instructed Abdel to locate the sheets that were taken off Ellen Jordan's bed, and he took off.

Max came up, "Unless it's been bagged, Ellen's wine tasting book is gone. I'm glad I took what I did."

Olivier turned to a policeman walking by. "What about a small plate that had a blue cheese on it?" The policeman retrieved a plate from a small pile. Olivier sniffed. "It was a *bleu d'Auvergne.* You're sure you saw a remnant on the plate, Max?"

"Absolutely. A little more than a remnant, actually. A small slice."

"Maybe the intruder ate it."

"I hope so. Then we'd know if it was poisoned or not."

"We have nothing but the condom and the note so far?" Olivier said.

"And the computer."

Olivier was known for being thorough, a perfectionist in fact, which had garnered him quite a lot of praise over the years. But at this moment, with the cheese, tasting book, and magnum of wine that might be counterfeit gone missing, along with the tale of a masked intruder, he felt inept.

Abdel returned. "I'll stay here until they're done," he said. "The sheets were in the laundry room, already washed."

"*Merde,*" Olivier said.

"I'll get busy with her computer," Abdel said.

"Let's meet tomorrow morning at 7:00," Olivier said. Abdel took off. He turned to Max. "We might as well give it up for the night. You must be exhausted."

"I'm okay," she said. "I slept when I returned from the bistro."

He walked with her back to her room. "Max, now isn't the time to discuss what happened after you left Champagne. I went through…some things…after my friends were murdered."

"Depression."

"Yes. It took months…"

"I understand. My peers and I see so many gruesome things we'd like to blot out. It helps that we have each other. You don't have that."

"I felt quite alone, it's true. You wouldn't have known the person I turned into."

"You don't stop being you because you're depressed, Olivier. I'm sorry it's been such a rough time. I thought that could be the case, but then I assumed when you stopped writing that you had moved on with your life."

"I thought the same of you when you didn't respond to my last email."

"I printed it out and keep it in my journal. How ridiculous is that?"

He wanted nothing more than to take her in his arms. She was suddenly before him, soft, receptive. All it would take would be one small step forward.

A tap on the door, and the moment was gone. Abdel stood holding a small French dictionary. "Pardon," he said, looking from one to the other, "This had fallen to the floor, and I thumbed through. The word poison is circled."

"Let me see," Max said, and Abdel held the page up.

Olivier looked over her shoulder. "I wish Madame Jordan had left the name of the murderer," he said.

"She probably only had a couple of seconds of awareness."

"On that somber note, we'll say good-night."

"'Night," Max said, as she gently closed the door behind them.

Chapter Nine

April 3

At midnight Max dialed her most reliable source, her mom. The answering machine came on, "*Bonjour. Hello. You have reached...*"*Oui*, hello?"

"*Maman.*"

Chérie. It's heartbreaking news. Hank told me everything. I'm in pieces."

"I'm so sorry, *Maman.*"

"Ellen could be very headstrong, her only *défaut*. This time I think she went too far." Max knew from the silence that her mother was wiping away tears. "It isn't real to me yet, *Maxine.*" Maxine. A sure sign her mother was distraught.

"Can you let her close family members know?"

"Of course. Hank said Olivier is there."

"Did you know we were to have dinner with Olivier our first night here?" Max blurted.

"She wanted to take the dubious wine to Olivier, and we thought it would be fun to take you to Olivier's as a surprise."

"The dinner was to be a matchmaking effort?"

"It's water over the bridge, or however you say it...." Juliette started to weep softly, and Max decided not to unload her indignation onto her grieving mother. "How did she die?"

Max explained, then waited for her mother's response.

"She was happy to go to France, happy to be taking you, and happy to see Pascal. She wasn't drinking as much as when she first divorced."

Max wondered if Ellen had drunk more than usual the day she died, perhaps in the doldrums after Pascal made his announcement. "She gave her *amour* a terrible score after he dumped her."

After a five-beat silence, Juliette said. "She could be a little vindictive. Who isn't when being dumped?"

Max silently agreed. "Speaking of which, Olivier and I had dinner, then he left."

"He wants to be sure."

"Sure about what? You got your Tarot cards out on the table?" Juliette laughed. She had kept a deck in her secret drawer for years. "What I want more than anything right now is to work this case."

"Oh, Max. Be careful. Ellen should have exercised more caution."

"I have to go," Max said, knowing that a lecture was coming. "Love you." She picked up the remote and turned on the television. Olivier was making an announcement that Madame Jordan had been taken to the hospital with an illness, assuring reporters that he would issue another bulletin the following morning.

Max couldn't deny how attractive he was with his longish and slightly unruly brown hair, almost black eyes, and sculpted eyebrows. When he spoke, his elegant hands conveyed the gravity of his words. He listened intently to a question from a reporter, and just once, he smiled slightly. For the first time, Max noticed something about his manner, the combination of diffidence and politeness, that reminded her of Juliette when she was in a social setting. It had to be a French thing. He had behaved similarly all evening with her, until the moment at the door when he looked as if he could devour her. The investigation, if he allowed her in, was going to be tricky, with the old push/pull between them as she raced ahead and he moved cautiously, not to mention the flare-up of emotions around their reunion.

She picked up her phone and texted a message to him. Her phone rang. Joe. She picked up. "What's up?"

"I gotta move to a Bronx precinct because of you."

"I had nothing to do with it, Joe. I'm thousands of miles away."

"Like hell you didn't."

"Okay, Hank watched the video ten times. He saw that you didn't have my back. You stood by and watched."

"You lost control for a full minute there. I wonder if your Pop made note of that."

She hated it that Joe had picked up on it. When she didn't respond, he said, "Around here you're coming across as a hero for stopping that guy. It's my ass that's getting burned."

"I've been put on leave and right now I'm under house arrest." Max thought it best not to mention that she was drinking a lovely wine and sleeping on 600-thread count sheets.

"The issue is blowing over. Maybe we can work something out and still be partners."

"We'll talk about it when I get back."

She wondered why he was trying to worm his way back into her good graces. He had complained often that there wasn't enough action in the 20th Precinct, which covered an area that was inhabited by the rich who presumably didn't go around killing each other. Now he was about to be moved to a more violent area of the city. Wasn't that what he wanted? More tough-guy action-movie stuff?

After they hung up, Max went to her iPad and Googled "wine thefts in Bordeaux." Olivier's mention of Opération Merlot had made her curious. A short article in the Bordeaux City newspaper, *Sud Ouest*, quoted the head of the Direction Générale de la Concurrence, de la Consommation et de la Répression des Fraudes regarding his concerns around wine counterfeiting. A very rare *Cheval Blanc*, a 1921, bought in Bordeaux, was deemed a fake in London. Next she clicked on a case in Colorado of a man who had made eleven million dollars selling older bottled wines and futures that he didn't own. He was never charged.

Max climbed under the covers, and mused about her mother's friendship with Ellen. Solving this crime, she realized, was something she owed her mother. Juliette had never blamed her for her brother Frédéric's death, for not being there to save him from that fatal accident, but this time, she had every reason to blame Max for not preventing her friend's death.

Chapter Ten

April 3

Dinner with Max had revived Olivier's warm memories of last June, when they had been inseparable, albeit for a short period of time. Enough to create a vivid portrait of a woman he kept returning to in his dreams. Now here they were, reuniting over another murder. He knew Max would feel compelled to solve this crime, just as he had done when his friends were murdered in Champagne.

Television crews swarmed around him as he exited the hotel, and he agreed to give a quick update on Ellen Jordan. Under the boom lights, he spoke for a few minutes about a sudden illness that had sent her to the hospital. He walked to his car, stoppping to glance up at Max's window. The light was still on, as though she were expecting him. He went back into the hotel, walked past the desk and up the stairs, and when stopped by the undercover policeman, explained after showing his identity card that he had an appointment with Mademoiselle Maguire, choosing to ignore the smirk on the young man's face.

He tapped lightly at Max's door and when she opened it, he pulled her to him, and kissed her. She responded with a passion that he found almost startling.

"Olivier…"

Pressing his lips against hers as he walked her gently backwards to her bed, never taking his eyes off her face that seemed radiant to him, he lowered her slowly to the bed and gently peeled off her clothes, remembering the curves of her body. He felt the heat of her skin against his, his heart racing as she wrapped her long legs around his, whispering his name. All boundaries vanished in an instant and nothing else mattered at this moment as they became reacquainted with each other's bodies.

◇◇◇

Olivier slipped Hélène Grimaud playing a Brahms concerto for piano into the CD slot in his car, and slowly drove out of Saint-Émilion. At a stop sign, he observed the few lights that were still on in windows of the village from his rearview mirror. It was a restored medieval village, the perfect setting for a fairy-tale marriage, except in most fairy tales he knew, there was hell to pay for falling in love. Last year he had tried to draw an imaginary line in the sand to keep the personal and the professional separate, which had been a moderate success, but tonight he felt that with the surprise death of Ellen Jordan, Max showing up, and his overhwhelming desire to be with her, that the only solution was to give up control and see where it took him. He was surprised by how liberating it was to act in the moment, and not fret about results. Max, he thought, already knew how to live this way.

Vineyards spread out on both sides of the road. It seemed a pity that the commercial aspects of the region had started to outweigh the agricultural. He had heard others blame the Americans for their insatiable thirst, but the impulse to go global had to have been pulsating in the minds of the Bordelaise. Commerce was the backbone of the city, and had been for centuries. It was the American influence on taste that bothered Olivier. Some estate owners refused to price their wines until they knew how they would be rated in the press. As a result, the *vignerons* were now trying to appeal to the American palate with ripe, rich, over-the-top wines that emphasized fruit rather than *terroir*. These were so fruit-forward on release that they peaked early, unlike those made in the traditional style that took ten to twenty years to release their character and fragrance. And so, slowly, an entire way of life—of tasting and experiencing the bounty of the land—was about to be lost.

Olivier slowed down due to the fog that had descended. Passing through the tiny village of Bouliac that was perched high above the city of Bordeaux, he looked down at the lights of the city reflected in the Garonne River, and admired the great bridges that were on a par with those in Paris. If Paris was equated with New York, then Bordeaux was most often compared to Boston, a city that he wanted to visit for its history.

The cherry tree in the center of his yard was in bloom, and he inhaled its fragrance. Mouchette met him at the door as usual. The kitchen was still fragrant from the lamb that had cooked for hours. The 1982 *Cos d'Estournel* that Zohra had decanted was on the counter, and he poured a glass. It's scent of cedar wood and mocha titillated his senses. He turned on the jazz radio station that he always listened to, and Charlie Parker's saxophone filled the room.

Olivier sat with his eyes closed, and swirled the ruby-colored wine in his glass, noting the scent of smoked cherries. He would devote a few moments to recalling the nuances of his reunion with Max. Her lingering fragrance on his shirt, her quick shedding of the protective stance, replacing it with a softness that he thought few had seen, her arms gathering him in as she whispered his name. A man should not be without this, he thought, and yet for years he had inhabited an emotional desert.

As much as he tried to avoid thinking of murder, it was as though someone snapped his fingers, and he, Max, and Abdel were back together, crime-solving. It was going to be an onerous task to determine just what crimes had been committed, and finding those responsible. Sylvie's remark that she wanted to talk to him about something personal flitted through his mind, and he tried to will it away, but it clotted. Max's mother had revealed that Ellen's lover was his friend Pascal. French men had a reputation for maintaining affairs outside their marriages, and he had wondered at times if their wives really condoned such behavior, or if they felt they had no choice. He couldn't imagine

Sylvie being tolerant of Pascal straying. Not for a minute. Now the consequences of Pascal's infidelity were huge. Max, it was obvious, had already pegged him as Ellen's alleged murdered.

He took another sip of wine and decided it was excellent. Ellen Jordan would have clapped her hands over this one. Sadness descended over him as he thought of her bright eyes and deep dimples. She had helped to put Bordeaux on the map, at least for Americans, and he hoped that this would be noted in the many articles that would appear about her. He would go the extra mile to find what had happened on that fateful night.

He got up, reluctantly, and passed through the dining room where he could hear his mobile making strange and insistent sounds. Text messages, he imagined. Horrors. Normally he would wait until morning to see who wanted what, but it could be Max. He picked up his phone, and saw that his former girlfriend, Véronique Michaud, had a modeling shoot in two days and was invited to a dinner at Château Cheval Blanc. Would Olivier escort her? About to decline, Olivier thought perhaps this would provide an opportunity to probe more deeply into the counterfeit operation. He considered posing as a collector, as few in the area knew him.

His ex added, *Apologies for my nasty behavior last year. I've gone through another round of rehab and it's time for the usual amends.*

He texted back his acceptance, then opened an email from Max:

Your friend Destiny has brought us together again, for which I am glad. I hope you can remain objective and allow me to work this case with you and Abdel. I owe it to Ellen to see this one through. Sweet dreams.

Olivier smiled. He typed: *It was bliss having you back in my arms, Max. I would like nothing more than to have you work Madame Jordan's case with Abdel and me. IF the powers-that-be agree with me that we have a case. Bonne nuit.*

Chapter Eleven

April 3

Max was running as fast as she could, but couldn't escape her pursuer's damp, hot breath on her neck. She awoke with a jolt and lay still, slowly opening her eyes and allowing them to adjust to the morning sunlight spilling into the room. As a way of centering her thoughts, she studied the details of the voluptuous, damask draperies that hung in the French windows. An image of Olivier appeared in her imagination, and she smiled. Forgive me, Ellen and God, she whispered, but I have to take a moment here to revel in last night's lovemaking. This was a different Olivier from the one she was with last year who exercised extreme caution at every turn.

The alarm on her phone played, and she reached over to check messages. Olivier had texted her back at 2:10 a.m. "Bliss," she said out loud. "Bliss! God! What was he drinking?" She jumped up and went to the balcony, taking her notebook with her. Abdel was walking toward the hotel, holding his mobile phone up to his ear. He glanced up, and waved. When he came closer, she waved and said, "I need coffee."

"That's why I'm here," he said, replacing his mobile in his pocket, and grinning up at her. "Are you ready to go with me to a café?"

"Give me two minutes." She changed into sweats and a long-sleeved tee shirt. The face and hair would have to wait.

The concierge glanced up as she sauntered past the main desk, a frown creasing his forehead the moment he saw her. He spoke to her in French, "*Madame, est-ce que je pourrais vous aider?*"

"I don't understand French," she replied in English. What was that goon doing at work so early?

"You spoke perfect French to me when I was at the door of the hotel room," he argued. "By the way, I was told to call an officer if I saw you attempting to leave the hotel."

"So call. I have Olivier Chaumont's home phone and mobile number if that helps," she added, removing his card from her pocket and placing it on the desk.

Flustered, he glanced at it and said, "I have a different number."

"Try yours, then. I need a cup of coffee." She leaned her elbows on the desk to further annoy him. He punched in the numbers. Abdel entered the lobby, holding his ringing phone.

Abdel's eyes met Max's briefly, then he quickly switched his attention to Cazaneuve. "Why are you calling me?"

"Is this some kind of a joke?" Cazaneuve demanded, slamming down the hotel phone. He pulled his shoulders back and spoke in French, "I want to know who will be responsible for *la note*?"

Abdel interjected, "You don't have to concern yourself with such trifles. Maître Chaumont will tell you what to do when he arrives."

Max followed Abdel outside. "He's still mad because I kicked him. Once I'm officially in on the investigation, I'm going after him."

"You're part of our team?"

"Olivier said yes to me joining you two, *if* there is an investigation. You and I both know there will be."

"Great. I need help with Madame Jordan's password." Abdel led the way to a café. "I'll have a double *espress*," Max said to the server. "And a *pain au chocolat*."

Abdel ordered a tea, then handed her Ellen's laptop, and she went to work, clicking on letters. "I knew her email address, but had to call my old partner Joe for the password."

"When did you do that?"

"From the bar. Vincent let me use his mobile."

"What is it?"

"*Bonvin.*"

"Cool." He scrolled down. "There are hundreds of emails."

"Check out any from Bill Casey."

"Paula Goodwin wrote a few days before the *en primeur* that she was sick and couldn't make it to France," Abdel said.

"She ended up coming. I met her with Ellen. She wanted the magnum back and Ellen wouldn't budge."

"Why?"

"It sounded legit. Bill Casey wanted it back to sell to someone who was interested."

Abdel said, "I'll print out all of the emails from her. A more recent one is from a man named B. Casey who writes, 'I want the bottle back. I have a different plan.' And here's one on the evening she died, from P. Boulin, that says *je ne regrette rien.*"

Max got up and ordered another coffee, and sat back down. "He slept with her, then dumped her by the end of the day. He's going to end up with some regret, I'll bet on that."

"How much?"

She laughed. "You and Olivier are still making those wagers?"

"You bet." They burst out laughing at his cleverness. "Shall we head back to the hotel?" asked Abdel. They paused at a stone wall surrounding a large terrace overlooking the village and the vineyards that crawled to the horizon. "Being in the country makes me homesick for Algeria," Abdel said. "Though my memory of my visits there have grown vague."

"Why did your family leave?"

"After the Algerian War with France ended in 1962, citizens of my country, who had been colonized by the French for thirty-two years, were given the opportunity to live in France. My grandfather came here to make a better life for his family. He died two years later, leaving four children, my father among them."

"Where did you grow up?"

"I was born in 1982 and grew up in Clichy-sous-Bois outside Paris. It was developed in the 1960s. Today it is referred to as the *banlieue*."

"Where the car-burnings take place? The ones we see on television?"

Abdel nodded, "It's the area where politicians like to do walkabouts and make promises to the cameras that they will rid the streets of what they refer to as the *racaille* who live there."

"What's that?"

"Scum."

"And here you are a commissaire with the national police."

"I'm the rare success story. I thought this the best way to fight the injustices I have witnessed, but I would never have pursued this career without Monsieur Chaumont's assistance." He sipped his tea, and picked up instantly when his mobile rang. "I have to go," he said. "Monsieur Chaumont is at the hotel early."

He stopped to purchase *Le Figaro* from a *tabac* shop, the front page headlines announcing Ellen Jordan's death. Her photograph was spread across the page.

"Imagine, people don't have a clue about what really happened," Max said.

"It might have continued like that had you not been here," Abdel said.

"It's humbling to do the work we do." She hesitated, "Thank you for believing me."

"After you were so sure about Monsieur Antoine in Champagne being a victim of foul play when he drowned, I'd believe your allegations."

"That's going too far."

"Time to part ways," he said. "Have a good run," Abdel shouted after her.

Max took off at a lope. She already knew the lay of the land from her walk yesterday. The air was crisp, perfect for running. Once her rhythm was set, she felt like she was on cruise control. She rounded a curve and slowed down as the sun was in her eyes. The sound of a motor coming up too close made her turn, and just in time she leapt out of the way. The motorcycle didn't stop or turn around. It whizzed by, at a furious pace. She wondered if the driver was blinded by the sun, or if he was trying to scare her. Maybe Olivier had been right to assign a *gendarme* to the hotel, she thought.

◇◇◇

"We're officially opening up an investigation," Olivier said when Max and Abdel joined him at the makeshift office in the hotel. He had greeted her warmly, but was in strict professional mode, which she understood. "I've been put in charge. We need a liaison in New York. I spoke with your boss, Captain O'Shaughnessy, Max, and he thinks you'll have your shield back in another day or two."

Max felt deflated, and tried not to show it. "You're sending me home? I thought your text meant I could work the murder case."

"I haven't explained the counterfeit operation we have inaugurated. Abdel mentioned last night that he could see the two crimes overlapping, and the more I think about it, the more I think he has a point. You will be here for a couple of days at least."

"With the emphasis on the missing magnum of wine, right?"

"We're grasping at straws, I know. It could be a simple theft. We haven't heard from the medical examiner in Paris yet." He turned to Max, "It's Docteur LeGrand, the same man who helped us with the Champagne case."

"He's good."

Abdel's phone rang and he left the room.

"Are you okay, Max?" Olivier asked.

"Personally, great. Professionally, not so sure. I'm getting a sense of how you must have felt last year. It's much harder knowing the victim."

"It takes great fortitude to move beyond it, I know that. Finding justice helps."

"My father said the same thing."

"I think this case is going to be much more convoluted than last year's," Olivier said. "Please be patient with me." He gave her an imploring look. "Know I want you here with me, personally and professionally."

He had read her mind. He leaned forward. "By the way, Abdel and I saw the YouTube video. My take on it was that you were afraid of him."

"The guy freaked me out with his vile language. He was also starting to overpower me and I thought I was alone."

"I thought you were, too, but Abdel saw a figure in the shadows."

"My soon to be ex-partner."

"How cowardly of him to stand back."

"He was mad over something I said, and wanted to teach me a lesson. I had to continue working with him when I went back after Champagne, but no more."

"And what about the personal?"

Max knew what he was driving at. "It was over when I returned from France last year."

Their intimacy was broken by Abdel entering the room. Olivier asked him to interview the hotel owner again about the wine. "Max, can you start by working with the U.S. consul to get the proper papers for shipping Madame Jordan's body back?"

Oh crap, Max thought. First I'm in charge of a bottle and now a body. "Of course," she said, hoping that her face wasn't a dead giveaway to how she really felt about that task. The waiting and grunge work were the downside of investigations, and this one was feeling extra slow because they were waiting to hear from the medical examiner, and they didn't know where to start. She also knew it would pick up, and somebody somewhere someday would make a mistake, and they would be off and running.

"Why don't you both come with me to the *fromagerie* to find out who has been purchasing blue cheese recently?" Olivier asked.

Abdel and Max stepped outside. Max shouted, "Shotgun!" to him, and jumped into the passenger front seat. Abdel laughed. "Whoever calls 'shotgun' first gets the front passenger seat," he explained to Olivier.

"Americans are crazy," Olivier said, smiling at their antics.

"And you're old-fashioned," Max teased.

When they were in front of the *fromagerie,* Olivier said in French to Abdel, "She has a big appetite. Let's make a bet on how many cheeses she samples. I'll place five euros she tastes at least four."

Max couldn't believe it. They were going to have fun at *her* expense? She had almost forgotten that they still thought she didn't understand French. She would confess, but not until the cheese tasting was over.

Abdel said, "She ate her croissant and half of mine, and drank a double espress this morning. I say two. Five euros is too much for my low salary."

"We'll make it three."

"Don't forget I won the last time," Abdel said. "Ellen Jordan brought a woman assistant, not a man, so you still owe me for that."

"If I win this one, we're even."

Abdel chortled.

I'll make losers out of both of you, Max almost said out loud in French.

Chapter Twelve

April 3

Matthieu Delorme was a fourth-generation *affineur*, responsible for aging the cheeses put in his care at the right humidity and temperature. His was a labor-intensive occupation that few understood. Half the flavors in the cheese aged in his shop could be attributed to his talent. Olivier found Delorme's shop soon after moving to Bordeaux, and returned often. A large case at the front of the small store contained a variety of cheeses, and beyond the shop area, Olivier could see rounds as large as bicycle wheels. Delorme's wife, Christiane, hurried over and shook hands with each of them, then excused herself to tend to customers waiting in line to purchase. Monsieur Delorme suggested a tour of the cheese caves—a cool, damp area of the cellar.

Olivier was pleased to see that Max seemed intrigued. They descended a flight of stairs to a cavernous room with several passageways. Delorme explained that Bordeaux was not known as a cheese-producing area. "That doesn't mean that the Bordelaise don't consider cheese to rest among the Holy Trinity, along with bread and wine," he said with a laugh. "I bring in the best from all over France."

He cut off a piece of a favorite of Olivier's, a chalky, herb-scented *brin d'amour* from Corsica, and offered a sample to each of them. Max closed her eyes and inhaled the fragrance, "Hmm. It smells lovely, but no thank you."

They ascended back to street level and wandered around the store until they arrived at a block of a mild blue cheese called *Fourme d'Ambert.* Max watched as Olivier and Abdel accepted a sample and she remarked that it was *pas mal.*

"You don't like blue?" Monsieur Delorme asked her.

"Not today."

"Oh, here's something you'll like," the proprietor persisted. "It's irresistible." He chuckled. "It's from the Marayn de Bartassac dairy in Landiras near Sauternes, and is shaped by hand."

Max shook her head gently, and said, "I have to watch my figure."

"Oooh, your figure, it is *magnifique*," the proprietor said in English with a strong French accent. "Don't you agree, Monsieur Chaumont?"

Olivier felt annoyed when Max flashed him a smile. When had she turned down the opportunity to sample such delicious fare? The little betting game he and Abdel had concocted seemed absurd under the circumstances, and he attempted to convey that to Abdel by holding up his hand as if to say enough, but Abdel was too busy trying to entice Max with yet another sample of cheese. He suddenly didn't like their playfulness.

Olivier then focused his attention on the proprietor. "Do you keep a record of the specific cheeses you sell each day, Monsieur?"

The cheese maker nodded his head vigorously. "My great-grandfather started the practice and I kept it up," he said. "Sometimes the girl over there makes mistakes, but for the most part, yes. Why?"

"This is extremely confidential. I need to know who has been in here purchasing cheeses over the past week, and the amount of various cheeses that have been sold."

Monsieur Delorme's cheerful countenance instantly switched to one of concern. "Monsieur Chaumont! Has someone become ill from my cheeses? If so, I need to know."

Olivier hesitated, "Unfortunately, someone did become ill. You're not to blame, however."

"What are you suggesting? The fact that it's you standing before me, asking me questions, suggests that someone committed a crime with my cheese. That's *sacrilège!*"

"I agree. May I have the list no later than tomorrow?"

"I will do my best, but as you can see, every housewife in the vicinity comes in here several times a week. And these days it's not just housewives. We have many male customers as well, along with tourists."

"Try to recall anyone coming in who wasn't a regular customer."

Monsieur Delorme's wife beckoned to him and he stood up. "Who's the poor victim?" he asked before walking away. "Anyone we know?"

"It will be announced soon. I'm especially interested in anyone who purchased blue cheeses."

"Do you know which one?"

"It was *bleu d'Auvergne.*"

Monsieur Delorme's mouth turned down. "I feel sorry for the *producteur de fromages,* and for myself," he said. "People will be afraid to buy the cheese once the news is out."

Olivier nodded his head in commiseration. Local producers had dropped to around three-thousand, compared to the many thousands who were producing unpasteurized cheese in the 1970s. Instead of cheese-making being a natural occurrence, it was now artisanal, a word Olivier had grown to dislike for its snobbishness. "Commissaire Zeroual will check in with you tomorrow."

The proprietor watched Max and Abdel for a moment. "What woman doesn't like cheese?" Shaking his head, he strolled over to his wife, equally distressed that an attractive woman was steadfastly refusing his fare.

Olivier joined his assistants. "These used to be the rooms of a medieval convent," he said in an attempt to be civil.

"I'd like to see more," said Max.

"There's no point if you don't eat cheese." Just like that, he was back in the game, unable to control his competitive spirit, and annoyed with himself because of it. He ambled over to a small table. "Here's a *chèvre*. A goat cheese."

"I know what goat cheese is."

"But you've never tasted anything quite like this. French women don't put on weight eating cheese by the way." He cut a thin slice, "Here, this is the best on the market."

Max shook her head slightly and started toward the door. "Later."

Abdel wore a smug expression. He was winning again, and Olivier wondered if he had confided their game to Max. Olivier watched as Max turned and smiled at the proprietor, explaining that she would be back to taste, but that today she wasn't feeling well. Olivier shook hands with the Delormes, and quickened his pace in order to catch up.

As the three colleagues climbed the hill, Olivier spoke to Abdel in French, "We both lost. What got into her?"

"She wasn't hungry," Abdel said,

"I think she understands French. It's subtle, so subtle that I almost missed it. And why not, with a French mother, and a semester abroad when she was in college? Everyone in Champagne was amazed by her intuition, when maybe it was simply that she understood everything she heard."

Abdel stared at him as though he were crazy.

"Come," Olivier said. "I'm going to test her."

Max was slightly ahead of them. The two men caught up and Olivier spoke in French to Abdel, loud enough for Max to hear. "Véronique Michaud is coming to do a photo shoot at Château Cheval Blanc and invited me to a dinner tomorrow evening. I may have to ask you to meet her at the airport."

Max stopped to gaze in a window, seemingly in her own world. "I saw Véronique on the arm of a famous rock singer," Abdel said. "She continues to be a sensation wherever she goes."

"The public is obsessed with celebrities," Olivier sniffed.

"What will Max do while you're at the party?" Abdel asked.

Max turned and spoke in French, her voice steely. "I don't need either of you arranging my evening fun. I'm sure that I can find something to entertain me."

Olivier looked at Abdel as if to say, 'I told you so.' Obviously sensing a spat, Abdel excused himself to go and make phone calls.

Max turned and locked eyes with Olivier. Hers were narrowed, and he knew she was angry. "I played the game in the cheese shop because I wanted you to know," Max said. "I thought I was being funny. I don't see any humor in Véronique coming to town, however."

Olivier suddenly realized that he and Max could be on a slippery slope. He had swept her back into his life last night, and while he didn't regret it, he couldn't believe how suddenly he was on the defensive. "I hardly find it amusing that you lied about your language ability the entire time you were in Champagne. Even at the end, you didn't feel like revealing the truth?"

"I did, but the moment didn't come up."

They walked along in silence, both feeling betrayed.

When they entered the hotel lobby they were interrupted by someone calling out "*Madame*! *Madame*!" Madame Madeleine Cassin, the hotel owner, handed Max a bouquet of flowers, then extended her hand to Olivier for a handshake.

"For me?" Max asked. She took the flowers, then opened the card and read out loud in English, *Please join me for a wine tasting at the Château Laussac tomorrow at four, followed by dinner at my favorite restaurant. I don't take no for an answer. I look forward to seeing your smile again, Vincent*

"You have an admirer," Olivier said.

"The answer to our problem of what to do with me tomorrow night just dropped out of the sky," Max said, smiling. She paused to ask Madame Cassin for a vase of water, and the woman took the flowers and said she'd have the maid deliver them to her room within the hour.

Olivier regretted using his invitation from his ex as a means of exposing Max's subterfuge, but at the same time there was nothing to apologize for. "About our respective invitations…"

"As far as I'm concerned, Olivier, this is not about us, but about an opportunity to acquire information. It makes sense for me to go with Vincent." Olivier nodded in agreement, but didn't feel happy about the way things were turning out. They entered the office, where Abdel hovered over the desk, making notes. He glanced up, appearing slightly nervous, but relaxed when Max was all business.

"I need to add a few things to our growing list of evidence," she said. She sat, and Olivier did, too. "Before Ellen's tasting book was stolen, I looked through it. She had only graded around ten wines, and Pascal's was among them. She lowered the score of his *Terre Brûlée* to an 88."

Olivier said, "You must be mistaken. He's never come in that low."

"I'm not mistaken, but of course we can't prove it because the tasting book was stolen. I could imagine Pascal being desperate to get his hands on it, though some of the other scores were also lowered."

"Are you implying that Pascal was the intruder in your room?"

"If he's big and stocky, I'd look into it."

"He would have to know that she lowered it," Olivier explained. "And no matter what, I don't see him breaking and entering."

"Monsieur Laussc's 2010 wine went up two points," Max said. "He might also want that book to use as proof in his suit against the appellation committee."

Olivier thought it far-fetched that either man would risk his reputation to acquire the scores, and said so. "What do you have so far?" Olivier asked Abdel, who was busy typing their discussion into his computer.

Abdel was ready. "I spoke with Monsieur Bill Casey. He verified that Ellen Jordan left his apartment with a magnum of *1945 Mouton-Rothschild* that she was taking to Bordeaux."

He needed to verify the obvious? thought Max stifling her annoyance. Abdel continued reading from his notes. "Monsieur Casey said that Ellen Jordan's birthday dinner went sour once she declared the wine fake. He's now sorry he gave her the second magnum to bring to France, and wants it back."

"Sounds like he wants to give up learning the truth in order to make more money," Max said. "Wait until he hears it's been stolen."

"He's offering another tasting from the same lot," Abdel said. "He knew that Madame Jordan was taking the wine to you, Monsieur, and called your office to extend an invitation. He was no doubt assuming that you would be attending Madame Jordan's funeral."

"You're flying over for the memorial service?" Max asked.

"We can discuss this later," Olivier said. "Find out the name of the maid who cleaned Madame Jordan's room, Abdel, and put her at the top of the list to be interviewed. She may have seen something. Continue with your notes."

"Monsieur Barthes told me he took a room here and was entertaining a few clients between the hours of 5:30 and 8:00, a few doors down from Madame Jordan. I checked with Madame Cassin and it's true. The room was charged to his company. This is how he had such ready access to the private floor."

"That makes sense. Anything else?"

"The wine auctioneer, Paula Goodwin, is to attend the dinner at Cheval Blanc." Not waiting for Olivier to ask, he listed a few facts. "She's a big success story. Started out working in a retail store, and went on to acquire a Master of Wine certificate. She has been at Blakely's Auction House for a decade. I have an entire report here." He placed it on the desk in front of Olivier.

"She sent regrets to Ellen that she couldn't make the *en primeur* because of illness," Max recalled aloud, "then showed up at the hotel the day Ellen became ill. She was on her way to Paris."

"Make sure that's what she did," Olivier told Abdel.

"She flew over on Bill Casey's private plane," Max said. "She had a client who wanted to buy the three remaining magnums of Mouton-Rothschild, which Ellen wasn't happy about for obvious reasons. They seemed friendly enough."

"I wonder if they were allies in the rarified world they inhabited," Olivier said.

"I think they tried to present a united front as the two most powerful women in the wine world, but I wonder, too." Max paused. "A friend of Paula's wanted to meet Ellen, and she told her as she was racing off that she would call her from Casey's plane back to New York and tell her who. I just remembered that."

Another leaf blowing by, Olivier thought, that probably needs to be picked up and examined. Every hand wave or smile took on significance after someone was murdered, he realized. "Abdel, see if there is a phone record of Madame Goodwin calling the hotel late afternoon," Olivier said.

It was time to map out the day. "Abdel will check on the maid's status, and continue collecting information about guests at the hotel," he said. "I have to make a quick trip to Paris later today for a meeting with Douvier, and tomorrow morning I will meet with Monsieur LeGrand and see what the forensic autopsy revealed."

Just as he thought, Max's eyes were wild with hope. He had already decided that this small, investigative excursion would give them a chance to spend time together. "Any chance I can go?" she asked. Imagine, Olivier thought, Max is becoming predictable. Or maybe, he thought, he was just getting better at anticipating her responses.

"I don't see why not. The train leaves at 3:00. We'll be in the city by 6:15 or so."

"It might be the only chance for me to meet my grandmother. I'll call to see if I can stay with her."

Olivier felt flattened by her pronouncement. How could he object, though, without sounding as though he had an ulterior motive?

Chapter Thirteen

April 4

It was more challenging than Max had imagined maintaining a professional boundary with Olivier, especially now that they had rushed into bed together. There were still a lot of questions left unanswered, and no opportunity to air out feelings. Olivier, she knew, had hoped for a night in Paris—she could still read him pretty well—but she had jumped in with the grandmother visit, which she knew was more a reaction to the threat she was feeling around Véronique's arrival than to any sense of urgency about meeting her grandmother.

She dialed the number of the consulate and was told that the mortuary certificate, the foreign death certificate, and transit permit could be picked up tomorrow in Paris. She next telephoned her grandmother. *"C'est ta petite-fille, Max Maryse,"* she said in French to the woman who answered. "I'm going to be in Paris this evening and would like to meet you."

"C'est trop spontanée! Mais je n'ai pas le temps de préparer quelque chose!" Isabelle de Laval replied. Max apologized in her best French for being too spontaneous and said that a simple meal would be fine. Isabelle hesitated, then said, *"Alors, Maxine, viens a diner à sept heures. Au Revoir."*

I am no longer Max, nor am I to speak English, and I am due for dinner at seven, Max repeated after hanging up. She tossed a few items into her tote bag, and sat down to scribble notes in her journal. She listed the missing magnum, wine-tasting book, and blue cheese as evidence, then made a second list of what she had seen that provided clues—the condom, the threatening note, the emails from Pascal Boulin, Bill Casey, and Paula Goodwin. She made an additional note: word had gone out quickly about Ellen Jordan's pronouncement that a famous vintage wine was fake. Mistake # 1: Ellen opened the door to someone she trusted. Mistake #2: Ellen didn't open door when I knocked, but cheerfully sent me on my way. Mistake #3: I didn't insist on her opening the door.

She decided to go to Pascal Boulin's wine shop to find a special bottle for her grandmother. She ran down the carpeted stairs, but stopped when she heard a woman's voice exclaim, "*Morte! Ce n'est pas possible*!" Max stepped back out of sight, straining to hear the conversation. "Two deaths in twenty-four hours in my hotel!" the proprietress said, "Madame Jordan, and now my head maid." Max peered around the wall and saw that Madame Cassin was in conversation with the concierge, Edouard Cazaneuve.

Cazaneuve said, "I forgot to tell Martine that staff was not to enter Madame Jordan's room. She changed the sheets after Madame Jordan was taken to the hospital. I went up to tell her, but it was done and she was in the assistant's room, turning the bed down."

"Why are you telling me this?" Madame Cassin asked.

"I'm saying that she may have caught the virus from Madame Jordan. Or eaten something that Madame Jordan ate…"

"Such as?"

"Something from the kitchen? Or cheeses that were in Madame Jordan's mini-fridge. There was a nice variety."

"How do you know?"

"I saw them." His voice had taken on an arrogant tone. "I've caught Martine stealing a few items in the past and told her if it happened again I'd report her. She looked guilty when I looked in on her in Madame Jordan's room and caught her standing in front of the refrigerator."

"You should have come to me immediately."

"I saw no point. It's my job to oversee the maids." He stopped to answer the telephone and when he hung up said, "That same night Martine was responsible for Monsieur Barthes' suite. She told me as she was leaving that she thought she had enough in tips to buy her and her husband a mini-vacation."

"What sums of money are you talking about? I don't like this."

"No idea."

Exasperated, Madame Cassin said, "With Olivier Chaumont personally involved, there is more going on than we know. With only you and me having the code to the safe, well…the heavy package was quite valuable, evidently."

"What are you saying, Madame?"

"I certainly didn't remove the package. Did you by any chance leave the door to the office unlocked?"

"No. Maybe Madame Jordan's assistant took it. I've been keeping my eye on her. She sneaks around like a lizard."

Max stood rooted to the spot, too horrified over the maid's death to be insulted by Cazaneuve's remark, though she wouldn't forget it. They were dealing with a double homicide, she realized, even though one was unintentional.

◇◇

Abdel was making a chart of names when Max entered the office. "I'm making a list of the people staying here at the hotel," he said, "and a list of the guests who attended the Laussac dinner. Pure drudgery."

"I have news…"

Before Max could utter the news of Martine, the door flew open and Madame Cassin entered and said in French, "I've just learned that our senior maid Martine has died! Her husband called."

Abdel asked Max to go find Monsieur Chaumont adding, "He's at Monsieur Boulin's wine shop at the bottom of the hill."

She took off. The wine shop was tucked between two limestone buildings, but stood out because of its red gabled roof and red door. It was difficult for Max to negotiate her way around the shop that was no bigger than the average living room, with boxes piled up everywhere. She paused to look around, then stepped into a dimly lit hallway, and was about to shout hello when she heard Olivier's familiar voice. She stepped behind a high stack of wine boxes to listen.

Olivier said, "Pascal, you were, as far as I know, the last person to see her alive. A maid saw you knock at her door at 2:30 in the afternoon."

Max recognized Pascal's voice from the bistro. "I never checked the time, but I went to her around that time and stayed a couple of hours, then met Sylvie at the bistro across the street. I know it was 4:20 then because I was supposed to meet Sylvie at 4:30 and I arrived a few minutes early."

"What time did you leave the bistro?"

"I had to check on something at the winery before driving to your house for dinner. Perhaps 5:15 or so. I sent Ellen an email from my office." Max recalled that it came in at 6:45. "Ellen never responded. Why all these questions?"

"Ellen, we are almost certain, was murdered."A stunned silence followed. "Forensics took a used *préservatif* from Ellen's room. We're conducting a DNA test."

"*Merde!* I'm being accused! I don't want my name bandied about. Sylvie… "

Max thought the popping sound she kept hearing was Pascal cracking his knuckles.

"Does Sylvie know about the affair?" Olivier asked.

"Of course not."

"Did you go back to Ellen's hotel room after you left the bistro?"

"No. I told Ellen before I left her room that I had to end the affair."

"How did she take it?"

"She was upset, naturally. I tried to tease her by saying, 'Ellen, let's try not to have a bitter finish.' Max knew the term 'finish' defined the after-taste of a wine, but she thought the play-on-words in that situation was unkind. Pascal continued, "She said to me, 'You are the one who will end up with the bitter finish, Pascal.'"

"Do you know what she meant?"

"No. But I knew she could be vindictive."

"Someone broke into her hotel room and stole her tasting book. Abdel will have to take your fingerprints."

"I'm not a thief!"

Max considered Pascal a strong suspect. He was a farmer, familiar with plants, and he had a chemical lab for testing wine. The motive was there.

"When did the affair start?" Olivier asked.

"A year ago. We met in Paris for dinner, and later I went to New York. I explained to her from the very beginning that I would never leave Sylvie." Olivier was quiet, and Max could imagine him studying Pascal with his penetrating gaze. She wondered if Pascal knew about the magnum of wine Ellen had with her. If so, could he have somehow gotten access to the hotel safe?

"Did she mention a special bottle of wine she brought with her?" Olivier asked.

"No."

"She was going to confront someone about counterfeiting."

"She said nothing to me about that." Pascal said, sighing, "I won't be a scapegoat. If I have to, I will find the murderer."

"Ellen had many enemies. Let me do my job," Olivier said.

"You know, Ellen was waiting for someone. She told me that she was expecting someone after I left. She also demanded that I cancel the evening with you."

"And?"

"I left a message at your house with Zohra, and told Sylvie that I was too busy to go."

"Ellen didn't mention the name of who was coming to visit?"

"No."

Max heard them stand and prepare to leave. She took a step back further into the shadows, not daring to breathe. Hearing their voices in the retail shop, she quickly moved out into a narrow corridor, and nearly colliding with a woman a foot shorter. It was the hummingbird from the bistro. What is it about these tiny-boned women that makes me feel like I drank too much milk as a child? Max thought.

"Customers are not allowed to come back here," the woman said in English.

"I'm sorry. I was looking for someone to help me." Max followed behind Sylvie and saw from the window that Abdel and Olivier were huddled in conversation. Their heads turned simultaneously as they looked toward the shop. Abdel was probably telling Olivier that he had sent her to the shop. Just then someone bellowed from the rear of the store, causing Max and Sylvie to freeze. Pascal stomped into the room, swearing. Max pretended to be studying the bottles of wine on the shelves.

"Where are our vintage cases of wine that were waiting to be loaded on the delivery truck?" Pascal demanded of Sylvia.

"They are where they were this morning. In the shipping room."

"Call Olivier on his cell. They're gone." Sylvie said *pardon* to Max, and ran to the door to call to Olivier, but he and Abdel had reached the top of the hill. She pulled out her mobile and in a moment was speaking rapidly to someone about the theft.

Pascal noticed Max for the first time, and walked over to her. "I'm guessing you are…were…Madame Jordan's assistant?" He spoke with a strong accent.

"Yes. I'm Max Maguire." She wondered if Ellen had told him anything about her.

"Were you with her when she died?" he asked in French.

"*Je ne comprends…*"

"*Putain,*" he said under his breath.

The front door bell jingled. Abdel entered and shook hands with Pascal and Sylvie, and gave a brief nod to Max. "Monsieur Chaumont is waiting for you to accompany him to the maid's house," he said.

While waiting for change from her wine purchase, Max overheard Pascal demanding to know why Olivier couldn't return. Abdel replied, "He's a judge, not a detective. I can either inspect your storage room now, or you can deal with the local gendarmes who usually take care of these kinds of break-ins. What's missing?"

"Fifty cases of our famous 2010 *Terre Brûlée.*"

"You don't have a professional security system?" Abdel was asking Pascal as Max slipped out the front door and quickly climbed the hill to Olivier's car.

Olivier looked grumpy. Before she had buckled her seatbelt, he said in French, "I know you were behind the boxes eavesdropping on my conversation with Pascal. You forget that my olfactory sense is highly developed, as attuned to your scent as a dog is to his master's."

Dear God, she thought, as the image of a bloodhound came to mind.

Olivier was taking the curves too fast. She said, "You know from last year that I'm not beyond eavesdropping, sneaking around, acting, whatever it takes when I'm on a case."

"This investigation requires a lot of subtlety. You have to understand the mindset of the Bordelaise and the role that wine plays in their lives."

Max hoped she didn't look askance. "If you try to carry on this way in New York, you will find there is a plethora of mindsets. Wine will be perceived by the guys in my precinct as the thing that makes people steal and kill. It's all glorified here, but when taken down to the lowest common denominator, we're looking for a bunch of crooks, and maybe a murderer."

"*Bon,*" Olivier said. "Now that you admit to eavesdropping on my interview with Pascal, what is your impression?"

"Strong motive. And if he has financial problems, even stronger. It's easy for him to make counterfeit wines with his set-up and to create a poison. It also occurred to me that he could have gotten access to the hotel safe."

Olivier couldn't find a counterargument to any of her points, except the last. "I don't know how anyone would have succeeded there."

"All it would take is someone who is willing to be bribed. Like Cazaneuve. He mentioned that the maid was thrilled with the tips she made." She repeated the conversation between the hotel owner and the concierge. "Cazaneuve nosed around and saw the cheeses in Ellen's room."

"You and Abdel seem positive that the cheese is the murder weapon," Olivier said. "I agree that the cheese is the more logical answer, but the killer was stupid to leave it behind. It doesn't make sense."

"He—or she—could have left the room in a hurry once Ellen started throwing up and he knew it was over. Or become alarmed when I knocked on the door at 5:30. I don't know why Ellen's million-dollar taste buds didn't save her. Wouldn't you think she could taste a poison?"

"It may have only taken one bite or sip. And some poisons are tasteless," Olivier said. "If I had it to do over, I wouldn't have held off the forensics team for so long. If I had called them immediately, the maid would never have had access to the cheese. And your assailant wouldn't have entered. If I start blaming myself for these failures, though, I'll have to change careers!"

"I've carried blame for so long I don't know what it would be like to feel free of it."

"From your brother's death, you mean?"

My brother and fourteen other things that now include Ellen, she thought. She nodded, and he reached over and put his hand over hers. She found herself hoping the maid lived a long way outside of Saint-Émilion.

Chapter Fourteen

April 4

The village they entered was typical of little towns scattered about the French countryside that housed field workers. It had a square in the center, a small grocery store and bar adjacent, and a decrepit hotel across the park. An ancient stone church dominated the square. Olivier turned into a dirt road leading to a small dwelling, where two window boxes filled with geraniums were the only hint of color. The late morning breeze had a bite to it, and he thought it would rain soon. An aura of gloom hung over the little house as they approached.

A man built like a bulldozer stared hard at them from the front stoop as they got out of the car. Olivier introduced himself, and could see the suspicion in Alain Seurat's eyes. "I'm sorry about your wife," Olivier said, shaking his hand. "May we come in? I'm interested in the circumstances of Madame Seurat's death."

"Who is this woman?" Monsieur Seurat asked, his attention now on Max.

"My assistant, Maxine Maguire."

"*Entrez.*"

They were led into a small dark parlor that smelled of wood smoke and artificial pine. An old, lopsided photograph of Charles de Gaulle hung on the wall, along with a couple of faded posters of generic vineyards. Olivier said, "I'm concerned about food poisoning because your wife and a guest at the Hôtellerie Renaissance died within hours of each other of similar symptoms. Please try to recall if she mentioned eating anything at the hotel."

"The help isn't allowed to eat at the hotel," Alain said. They followed him into a small kitchen with a sloping floor and shelves nailed to the wall. The room was plain but immaculate. He reached into a cupboard and brought out a large opaque bottle that had no label, and three glasses. "But there was a big dinner," he continued, "and the hotel owner used extra staff to make it all work. Martine told me she helped in the kitchen, and after, she went to the guests' rooms to turn down their beds for the evening."

The room they were in was hot and stuffy, the ceiling low. Alain lit a *Gauloise*, and smoke swirled in front of their faces. He poured the dark liquid into the glasses "To my wife," Alain said, and downed the contents of his glass. Max sipped and thought she had tasted worse.

"*Pas mal, eh*?" Alain asked, already pouring another glass for himself, and holding the bottle of homemade wine out for their refills. Olivier shook his head, but Max held out her glass for him to top it off.

"Continue, please," Olivier said. Alain described how he had picked his wife up at the hotel and how weary she had been. He turned on the television when they got home and she put some cheese and bread on a plate and joined him.

"You didn't want to join her?" Olivier asked.

"I know it's not French, but I don't like blue. In no time she told me her feet were feeling numb," he said. "She went upstairs and started throwing up. Soon she was pleading with me to take her to the hospital. A few hours later she was gone."

"Do you happen to know where the cheese came from?" Olivier asked. "Is it still around somewhere?" Alain shrugged and walked over to the refrigerator. He opened the door and pulled out a plate which held several slices of bread and a lump of cheese. Olivier reached for it and instantly recognized the aroma of the *bleu d'Auvergne.*

"It's supposed to smell like this?" Max asked.

"The aroma will be much stronger after it has come to room temperature." Olivier pulled plastic gloves from his pocket and carefully picked up the lump of cheese. He figured there was half an ounce left. Turning to Alain, he said, "I'll need to take this with me."

"What's this about?" Alain asked.

"We're checking every possibility to see if there's a connection between Madame Jordan's death and Martine's. Your wife was working in the kitchen. I don't know yet if Madame Jordan ate anything the hotel prepared, but it's a possible link."

"Martine was always bringing tidbits home. Like the cheese. We didn't think of it as stealing, as it was just going in the trash anyway."

"Was your wife by any chance carrying a heavy object, like a small metal suitcase, when you picked her up?"

"No. She had her *grand sac*, and that was all."

"May I see the *grand sac*?"

Alain hesitated, then said, "Follow me. It's upstairs somewhere." Olivier and Max followed him up the narrow, steep stairs. Alain ducked his head as they filed into the bedroom. "Now, where is it?" he asked, looking around the room that had peeling wallpaper, and one small window. The bed was unmade, and a sick odor hung in the room. He walked over to a chair and picked up a large, black faux leather tote bag, which he turned upside down on the bed. Out fell an ancient tube of lipstick, a wallet, some balled-up Kleenex, a romance novel, a pamphlet on knitting, and an envelope containing a one-hundred-euro bill.

"Hey! What's this about?" Alain demanded, picking up the money.

"I need to take the contents of this bag, but I'll make sure it's all returned to you," Olivier said. He asked Alain for a plastic bag, and the man lumbered back down the stairs.

"What do you make of the one-hundred euros in the envelope?" Max asked.

"A tip? Bribe? Grocery money?" Olivier picked up a framed photograph of a woman he assumed to be Martine from the dilapidated dresser in the corner. She had grey, wavy hair and wore glasses, and was smiling broadly.

Alain returned with the plastic bag and handed it to Olivier. "Martine was at our son's thirtieth birthday party last May," he said, looking over Olivier's shoulder at the photograph. His eyes suddenly began to fill with tears. Feeling at a loss over what to say, Olivier put his hand on the man's shoulder. Max stood at the window looking out at the gloomy day while trying to breathe something other than smelly cheese, which didn't mingle well with the cheap wine.

Olivier asked Alain if he knew where the money came from. Alain shrugged. "Madame Jordan always left her a big tip, but not this much. That's all I can think of." He thought for a moment and said, "So the little piece of cheese makes my wife a thief?" His words were slurred.

"It's possible she took it from Madame Jordan's room," Olivier said. "At great cost to herself. I need your permission to conduct an autopsy."

"*Pourquoi une autopsie*?"

"We're looking for the cause of death," Olivier said calmly.

"You said food poisoning."

"Someone may have intentionally poisoned the cheese."

Alain suddenly bellowed. "You think my wife was *murdered*? I will make somebody pay!" On the way to the front door he poured himself another glass of wine.

Back in the car, Olivier said, "We have two men threatening revenge of one kind or another. This investigation could quickly get out of hand if I don't make some progress. I'll advise the minister of justice to announce immediately that a murder investigation is underway. It might shake up the murderer who no doubt thinks he's gotten away with it."

Max was leaning back, her eyes closed. "Good idea."

"The countryside here is beautiful," he said. "I wish we had time to drive through the Dordogne region nearby." She cocked one eye open. "Are you okay?" he asked.

"I tried to pretend I was taking communion while drinking that rotgut," said Max.

"Drinking wine like that so early in the day can take its toll, but you seemed to be enjoying it. You took a second glass."

"It was my way of commiserating with the poor man."

"In another hour he'll be completely drunk, and then wake up and have to face his wife's death all over again."

"That's how some people cope with death," Max said. "It's how my father reacted to Frédéric's death. I, on the other hand, rebelled. Jiu-Jitsu finally straightened me out."

Olivier cast aside the memory of his own depression after his friend Léa's death last year, and asked, "And your mother?"

"I'm not sure. I think she went to mass a lot."

"I wish I had that much faith."

◇◇◇

Abdel was waiting for them in the temporary office when they returned to the hotel. Olivier said that they could still make the 3:00 train to Paris. Abdel agreed to drive them to the station, and Max ran for her tote bag. Olivier turned over the cheese and the contents of Martine's bag to his assistant. "Abdel, you're in charge until I return."

Max strode into the room, and was glad after seeing her colleagues' admiring glances that she had changed into the vintage Chanel jacket she had thrown in at the last moment, and black pants. On the way to the Gare de Bordeaux Saint-Jean, Olivier gave Abdel the details of their visit with Alain Seurat. Abdel jumped in to share his research on poisoning. "The person who poisons is uncomfortable with confrontation. A man who poisons tends to be shy and perhaps emotionally submissive. The one who targets a particular person is often a woman."

"That's interesting, Abdel," Olivier said. "But we have no female suspects at the moment." Olivier was relieved that Sylvie's name didn't come up.

"The report is probably based on women poisoning their husbands," Max said. "It's a cowardly act that's hard to prove."

Olivier reminded Abdel that they would be back early afternoon tomorrow as he and Max boarded the train. Max announced she was hungry and they made their way to the food bar and ordered a cheese sandwich and a beer. "Are you going to tell my uncle that I've been assisting with this case?" Max asked, taking a seat at a tiny table.

"Yes, it's time to give a full report to Monsieur Douvier."

Olivier asked about her conversation with her grandmother. Max laughed. "It was short. I asked her if I could come to dinner and she said my request was too spontaneous, but yes, come. She sounded younger than I imagined, and she issues commands like a general."

"Did she invite you to stay over?"

"To my surprise, she didn't."

"The French are not as quick as Americans to invite people into their homes."

"But I'm her granddaughter."

"A stranger, though. You are welcome to stay with me. My place is convenient…"

"If I stay with you, Olivier, it won't be for reasons of convenience."

"I wasn't thinking about convenience."

"Then I accept."

Olivier felt caught off-guard again, but pleased. "You're sure?"

"You've picked up my habit. The answer is yes."

He leaned into her, and kissed her on the lips. "You know," she said, "I've always wanted to be a woman kissed on a bridge or beneath a bridge or in the pouring rain in Paris." Olivier laughed. "Or on a train or in a medieval doorway or at the top of the Eiffel Tower." He kissed her again. As they entered the outskirts of Paris, she asked, "Do you think I'm dressed appropriately to meet my grandmother?"

"Just right."

"I have mixed feelings about this meeting. I've never understood how parents can disown a child, for anything. It's so heartless."

"But your mother and grandmother have reconciled?"

"My mother flew to see her two years ago after my grandmother had a minor stroke, but my mom said it didn't heal the emptiness she had felt for so long. They exchange little notes back and forth on crisp, white paper, but I think their relationship is far from warm."

"It's up to them, and I would even dare to say that nothing you try to do will help. You'll show off your French, of course?"

"I have no choice."

"But you studied in Paris."

"For a semester, and I was drunk most of the time. It was after my brother died, and I didn't give a rat's ass about school."

"A rat's ass?"

"A figure of speech."

"I've never felt rebellious," Olivier said. "I don't know what it would be like. What were you rebelling against?"

"Maybe the conflicted expectations. My mother wanted an intellectual and my father wanted a cop, and they both wanted their son back. I didn't really care about any of it."

The conductor announced that they would be at Gare d'Austerlitz in half an hour. "I wanted to explain how Véronique and the dinner tomorrow night came about," he said. He told her about the text arriving out of the blue.

"The way I see it," Max said, "is I arrived in the nick of time." Olivier had forgotten how open she was, and how it delighted him. They jumped into a waiting taxi once outside the station and Max gave the address.

"Welcome to the world of the bourgeoisie," Olivier teased. "Where rebellion is a foreign term."

"If this visit with my grandmother turns out to be anything like my introduction to Philippe Douvier last year, I'm outta' there in about ten minutes."

"You have my number."

"Stop worrying. I'll call."

Olivier thought it wasn't worry but delicious anticipation that might kill him. The taxi stopped and Max issued a low whistle at the sight of her grandmother's apartment building.

Chapter Fifteen

April 4

The elegant *Belle Époque* building constructed from the classic *pierre de taille,* or limestone used all over Paris, was on rue des Sablons, in the Chaillot quarter of the sixteenth arrondissement. Max's mother had compared the area to New York's Upper East Side, though only certain pockets in that section of New York were like this quiet oasis, where civility ruled.

Olivier accompanied Max to the door. "I'm certain this building was designed by Georges Haussmann," he said, "who is also responsible for all the wide avenues in Paris. The Trocadéro is behind us, which, as you know, offers a fabulous view of la Tour Eiffel."

Max scanned the street, making note of the similarly majestic buildings that lined it. She walked over to Olivier, who stood appraising the building. "Tonight the height of elegance," she said. "Tomorrow the morgue." He smiled, and asked if she wanted him to accompany her.

"I have to do this alone," she said. "*Merci.*" He pulled her close and kissed her again. This time she didn't feel she was in a fairy tale haze, but that her life was somehow unfolding exactly as it was meant to.

She quickly grabbed the tote bag that she had set down, and walked up to the massive door that led into the courtyard, not looking back. A concierge bounded out of his loge to welcome her. "*Laissez-moi vous aider,*" he said, taking her tote. He told her that she was expected and led her to an ornate, wrought iron elevator and touched the number three. As she stepped into the hall, a massive door with a gold latch slowly opened and a tall, formidable looking woman appeared. Max shifted her gaze from silver hair swept back, to arched eyebrows, to high cheekbones, and rested on eyes the color of the Mediterranean. No one had ever told her that she was a clone of her grandmother.

"*Bonjour,*" her grandmother said as Max approached, leaning toward her granddaughter for the obligatory kisses from a family member, which Max dutifully applied.

"*Bonjour,*" Max said softly. She followed the stately woman into an entrance hall with parquet floors and a high ceiling. Max imagined her mother running in and out of this place as a teenager.

"*Viens,*" her grandmother said, "We can have an *apéritif* in the drawing room. It's good that you're here early, as I don't dine as late as I used to." A clock chimed seven times. Max looked around, and thought the furniture and old portraits appropriate for Versailles.

"Sit," Isabelle said in her imperative voice. "And let me look at you." Max stared into her blue eyes. "You resemble my side of the family," Isabelle said finally. "We're from Burgundy. Your grandfather was from Paris." She picked up a bottle of chilled *Lillet Blanc* from an ice bucket and poured the golden liquid into two glasses. "Why are you in France?"

Max's carefully rehearsed answer escaped her. "I came to Bordeaux with the American wine critic, Ellen Jordan, whose death was announced this morning."

"I saw it on television. Was she murdered, or will the authorities continue to try to convince the public that she died from food poisoning?" Max remained quiet. "Your aunt Hélène, don't forget, is married to an important official, and she can't keep her mouth shut."

Max said, "The announcement that she was poisoned will be made tonight."

"I was acquainted with Madame Jordan, you know. She brought out your mother's delicious humor." Isabelle Limousin de Laval sipped her drink. "How is your mother dealing with this awful tragedy?"

"She's devastated."

"You have no choice but to solve this, Maxine." She's echoing Hank? Max thought. She was tempted to tell her, but thought better of it. "I heard all about your involvement in the Champagne murders last year. Hélène told me that you met with Philippe, but weren't interested in meeting the rest of us."

"That's not true! *He* didn't want me to meet anyone."

"Wasn't his mistress involved in that horrid murder scandal?"

Max nodded. "She was more evil than most murderers I've locked up. She was drawn to his power, but I don't know what he saw in her."

Isabelle sniffed. "Power on the outside. Weak inside." She sighed, "Philippe seems to have tremendous influence over my daughter. She had every right to leave him after learning he had a mistress, but like so many French women, she was loath to let go of 'family.'"

"And status?"

"Perhaps."

"Olivier Chaumont is with him right now telling him that I'm back in France working another high-profile case."

"I know Olivier's parents. I saw his photograph in the newspaper with the famous model whose name I forget. Too bad he's not available."

"He and the model aren't together now," Max was quick to say.

Isabelle waved her hand in the air. "Who knows who's together these days? I keep up with Olivier's attempts to bring our corrupt politicians under control. Unfortunately, our judges are at risk of becoming extinct." She smiled at Max, "But not NYPD detectives, right?"

"If New York becomes much safer, we might be."

"I suppose you like being in the business of solving crimes?"

"It's in my blood. And yes, most days I love it."

"You know that detectives aren't held in high esteem here. But we don't have so many murder cases that require such expertise."

"I'm not so sure that we're held in high regard in America, either. Our television shows abound with cops and detectives, which create a lot of myths about us, as well as a mystique."

"What do you think you would have chosen to do had your father not taken you under his wing?"

Max didn't like the phrasing of the question. "Perhaps become a psychologist or a social worker."

Isabelle couldn't hide her disdain. "You need to help people? Is that it?"

"The two people I admire most in the world help others. My parents. What about you? What would you have done with your life if you had had the freedom to choose?"

"I chose marriage with my own free will," Isabelle said. "I suppose if I had a secret longing it was to become an actress, but my parents considered that equal to being a prostitute."

"You couldn't rebel?"

"Oh, no! Look at your mother who rebelled. Look at the mess this family is in as a result."

"It's her fault?"

"Blame it on your late grandfather and your mother. I begged your mother and Frédéric to reconcile. He refused, and wouldn't hear of me going to visit her. Nor would he allow her to come here, and when he was dying, and finally asked to see her, she refused. You know the story…"

"No, I don't. My mother never talks about it."

Isabelle sniffed. "Just as well. What good does talk do?"

"My mother suffered a lot." Max regretted the statement when she saw her grandmother's eyes fill with tears.

"It's a tragedy," Isabelle said, "when families split apart. I want to repair the damage that was done before I die, if your mother will allow it."

"What was it like two years ago when my mother came to visit?"

"It was a miracle to see her enter my hospital room. But of

course, the healing doesn't happen overnight. She won't accept money from me, which means she can't come often."

"I can't believe my mother grew up in such a rarefied atmosphere," Max said. "I'm not sure I could feel at home here. Nothing against you personally."

"You'd be surprised at how easily you would adapt," Isabelle said with no sarcasm. "A lifestyle like this imposes great responsibility." Max felt chastened. "Come," Isabelle said. She led the way to a vast dining room to a table that sat twelve, and they took their seats at the same end.

The maid brought in soup, and Max watched as her grandmother dipped her spoon into the bowl. "*C'est potage velouté aux champignons*," Isabelle said. Max recognized the mushroom soup as one her mother made often. Isabelle said, "Your mother will never get over your brother's death, and it sharpens her pain that he never knew his French family. She named him for her father."

"You don't like my father, do you?"

"I believe that had he really loved your mother he would have sent her back to France, and not married her."

"But she was pregnant with me. My father's love is what got her through everything, and still does. He's a good simple Irishman…"

"There's nothing simple about Hank Maguire, my dear. He would never admit it, but he didn't want Juliette to be connected to her family and this lifestyle. He knew he couldn't provide for her in the same manner."

"My father is a legend…"

"On the New York police force. And legends are human, don't forget." Max thought there might be a grain of truth about her father's resentment of the de Laval family.

"How did my grandfather acquire all his money?"

Isabelle smiled, "To the French that question is considered vulgar, but I don't mind. Those who have it go out of their way to pretend they don't, except for the *nouveau riche* who do just the opposite. I'm the one who inherited vast wealth. Your grandfather's family, the de Lavals, were aristocrats centuries back, and the name still carries weight, but over time they squandered their wealth. When I met Frédéric he was a local functionary, his fortune spent."

"I'm curious about his looks."

Isabelle suddenly put her spoon down. "I don't think I've ever left the table mid-meal, but maybe it's time to break a rule or two. Let's go back to the drawing room and I'll pull out the photo albums."

The maid entered to remove the soup bowls and Isabelle, sounding almost girlish, told her they'd be back in a few minutes. The maid and Max exchanged a smile. Max sat beside her grandmother on a love seat, the album on their laps. Juliette resembled her father, who was dark-haired with a roman nose and an impish smile. "Were you madly in love with my grandfather?"

Isabelle said, "You're a romantic like your mother!" Max had never been called a romantic, and thought the notion absurd. "I fell in love the way all young girls are in love with someone who pays attention to them. I had been extremely protected, and Frédéric was older and ready to marry. My parents wanted their potentially independent daughter to settle down. He had the correct pedigree."

"Buy why, then, would Frédéric disown his daughter?"

Isabelle sighed. "He hated poverty. His father lost everything. And he was certain that your father wanted our money. We fought bitterly over this for years, and one day I accused *him* of marrying me for my money." The image of the Laussacs came into Max's mind. "He barely spoke to me for a month, and I found myself having to make a choice. I didn't want my marriage to end. I don't think I've ever told that to anyone. Maybe you would have made a fine psychologist."

"Detective work is similar," Max said. "We dig around, finding motives, and it usually leads back to childhood upsets and broken dreams."

"How was your childhood, Maxine?"

"It was great." Seeing the look of skepticism on Isabelle's face, she said, "No, really. The city has its challenges, and we didn't have any extra cash floating around, but my parents loved each other and they loved my brother and me."

The maid re-appeared. "Oh, our main course has arrived," Isabelle said. They returned to a *boeuf Bourguignon*. The maid poured wine into delicate, cut crystal wine glasses, then put the decanter on the table and quietly slipped out. Isabelle, relaxed and smiling regaled Max with stories of her one trip to America, when Juliette was twelve. "She was crazy about New York. Perhaps it was that, more than meeting Hank, that determined her destiny."

Salad was served. Isabelle whispered to her maid, "Are there fresh sheets on the bed in the room next to mine?" Just then the telephone rang, and the maid scurried away.

"I'm staying with Olivier tonight," Max said. "I meant to tell you when I arrived."

"This is a little more serious than I thought," Isabelle said. "If that's the case, I want to meet him."

The maid entered and discreetly whispered something to Isabelle, who excused herself and left the room. The telephone conversation quickly grew argumentative, and Max heard the sound of the phone being returned to its cradle with a bang. When Isabelle rejoined Max, she said, "It was Hélène. Philippe called to tell her you are here and they are racing to rescue me."

"What should I do?"

"Stay and say hello. Philippe and Hélène will insist that you are making me tired. You're sure you can stay with Olivier? This won't happen again."

"That's no problem, Madame."

"Call me anything but madame. I'm your grandmother, for god's sake."

"Mamie, then?"

Isabelle laughed. "*Très bien.* If you want to return, and I hope you do, we won't tell Hélène. And if you need an informant on this case, I'm all yours." Max was suddenly intrigued by the thought of using her grandmother as a secret information source. It could replace her language deception.

Chapter Sixteen

April 4

The taxi ride to Place Vendôme had given Olivier a few minutes to bring his focus back to the meeting with Douvier. When Max's name came up, he would emphasize to Douvier that Max was an asset in the investigation. One of his agents called him in the taxi to cast a slight cloud of suspicion around Vincent's business activities. He had invested his father's money in the production of lower quality wines, and the wines hadn't taken off, yet it was obvious there was no dearth of cash. It could be nothing more than faulty bookkeeping, Olivier thought, but still, he would let Max know about it. It was perfect the way tomorrow was unfolding. Max could get an inside perspective on Vincent Barthes as she mingled with people at the tasting and spent time alone with him.

The evening with Véronique was trickier, for he had to enlist her help in posing as a collector. If she revealed that he was a judge, the evening would be a bust. Collectors liked to brag about their latest trophies to other collectors, and he knew that all kinds of deals would be made at the dinner that would never happen in front of a judge. He hadn't heard from Véronique since he cast her out of his house last year, and then had Abdel arrest her for her own safety and keep her under lock and key in a hotel until she sobered up. There was some residue of guilt left over from that episode. He learned later that she had gone back to rehab, which is where she had met her current fiancé.

He walked into the splendidly appointed office of the minister of justice, and took a seat. Twenty minutes later Philippe Douvier entered, in hyper-frenetic mode as usual. "I don't have long," he said.

"I don't need much of your time," Olivier said. "I wanted you to know that your niece is in the country temporarily working on the Ellen Jordan case."

Douvier picked up a decanter and poured a small amount of wine into two glasses and brought them back to the desk, placing one glass in front of Olivier. "Don't tell me she's the woman who arrived here as Jordan's bodyguard?"

"The same. I knew nothing about anyone coming, as I mentioned on the phone."

"And I apologized for the oversight, didn't I?"

"Did you?" Olivier sniffed the 2009 *Yquem* that Philippe had poured, and was almost overcome by the mind-altering bouquet of pear and apricot that enveloped him, for a moment making any conversation seem mundane. It flashed through his mind that Ellen Jordan was sipping *Yquem* the hour she died, which jolted him back to reality, and to the fidgety man pacing around the room.

"Max's father set up the bodyguard thing," Philippe said. "He had to have a reason." Olivier explained about the threatening note, the magnum of wine Ellen Jordan had declared counterfeit, and how she had brought a second bottle with her that was now missing.

Douvier slapped his forehead. "So how'd she die?"

"What I'm about to say sounds sadly like a movie script. I'm almost certain Ellen Jordan was poisoned. Max and I are meeting with Doctor Legrand tomorrow for details."

"This is madness! I hope like hell the motive is personal and has nothing to do with a disgruntled Bordelaise citizen." His pacing made Olivier nervous. "Ellen Jordan's death could be accidental, right? Mixing alcohol with a medication, for example? I thought the local coroner was going with alcohol poisoning."

"A maid also died after eating a blue cheese that we suspect she took from Ellen Jordan's room. We found the remnant at her house."

"*Merde!* Is the killer French or American?"

"I assume that's an editorial question..."

"The presidential election is around the corner," Douvier said. "This case needs to be solved by then." He stopped pacing, "What does my niece say? She obviously wasn't an effective bodyguard."

"She was sent away for the afternoon, and Madame Jordan promised not to leave her room."

"So Jordan opened the door to her killer."

Olivier shrugged. "They ate a blue, accompanied by a Sauternes, an *Yquem*. The same as what we're drinking, I believe, but a different year."

"This is an eighty-eight," Douvier said in the tone of one who knows he has something unusually precious.

"The cheese was a *bleu d'Auvergne*..." said Olivier.

"So strong that it affects all the senses," Douvier said. "Better that the murder weapon be a cheese than a wine. Bordeaux doesn't have its own cheese so the association won't be as strong in peoples' minds." He was obviously ready to wrap up the meeting. "The minister of the interior and I will announce on the 10:30 news that investigators suspect foul play in the case of Ellen Jordan."

"I hope it doesn't send the murderer into hiding."

"Better that than have the public screaming about political malfeasance. Hiding the truth and all that.Where'd the missing bottle come from?"

"An American collector named Bill Casey. I want to go to New York for one to three days." Olivier realized he was holding his breath.

Douvier stared at him before asking why.

"I want to trace the bottle back to the person who sold it to Casey. My agents have marked a number of cases of wine as suspicious and some are turning up in New York.

"You're still on that tangent? Thinking somebody is shipping out counterfeit wine from Bordeaux?"

Olivier wished that everything out of Douvier's mouth didn't sound like either a question or an exclamation. "I also want to attend Madame Jordan's funeral."

The stillness that followed was unsettling. "You mean you want to represent France? I guess I can see that, but we have our French ambassador there."

"I knew Ellen Jordan slightly."

"Oh."

Olivier thought he'd gone this far, he might as well mention Casey's tasting. "I know it sounds strange, but I'm invited to another tasting of the *'45 Mouton-Rothschild* at the collector's house. I see it as an opportunity to step into that exclusive world."

"I hate American boldness. No collector here would phone a perfect stranger and invite him to a gathering. It makes me suspicious."

Olivier thought he quite liked that aspect of Americans.

"It all sounds vague, Olivier, but I guess I owe you one for not telling you Madame Jordan was bringing a bodyguard with her. Who will be in charge while you're gone?"

"My assistant, Abdel Zeroual. He's quite capable."

"I'll keep an eye on him while you're gone, just in case." He paused, "Where's he from again?"

"Algeria. Born here."

"I might be curious to meet him. We need to honor successful immigrants."

Olivier reminded himself to warn Abdel. "Max is picking up the papers tomorrow that will secure the release of the body."

"She'll accompany Madame Jordan's body to New York?"

"She's on Air France, and they can't fly cargo to New York. Madame Jordan will be on an American Airlines flight." Douvier nodded, and Olivier breathed a sigh of relief that the meeting was coming to an end.

"Where's my niece now?"

"With her grandmother. I dropped her off."

Douvier scowled. “That’s a terrible idea. Madame de Laval has had a stroke, and this will cause too much excitement.” Douvier picked up his cell and tapped. “Hélène, your niece, Maxine, is with her grandmother tonight. Surely you know…” He stopped speaking and turned to Olivier. “What time did you drop her off?”

“Half an hour before coming here. Around 7:00.”

Douvier relayed the information to his wife and hung up. “Madame de Laval should have called us first.” His cell rang and he picked up immediately. “*Quoi*?” He listened, then said, “I’ll be there in twenty minutes.”

Turning to Olivier, he said, “My wife called her mother who told her to mind her own business. Now Hélène is upset and she’s going straight away to check on her. I think you know what to do, Olivier. About the case, I mean. Monsieur Laussac is an adequate spokesperson for the Bordeaux area when it comes time to making announcements there.”

“He’s a suspect.”

“François Laussac? What the hell did he do?”

“He and Madame Jordan were in a public feud over his wine score being lowered, and her tasting book has gone missing.”

“He surely has an alibi…”

“He was in the hotel preparing for his dinner. So far Abdel hasn’t found anyone who can vouch for his exact whereabouts between the hours of five and seven, not even his wife who was supervising the table settings in the dining room. Vincent Barthes says that he stopped by his suite and mingled with retailers.”

“Those two are not a great combination.”

Olivier accompanied Douvier out to the street, and watched him jump into a black SUV, then roll his window down and gesture for Olivier to get in. “Maxine is partly your responsibility,” he said. “You can help me get her out of there. Hélène won’t allow her to stay, I know that.”

Olivier hesitated. Max’s family was none of his business, but he was full of curiosity. Just then his mobile rang and when he picked up Max said, "We'll be late for our party if you don't come right away."

He recognized her code talk as *get me the hell out of here*. "On my way, Maxine."

He thought he heard her say, "You'll pay for that."

They were there in fifteen minutes. Hélène was waiting in front of the apartment building, an impatient expression on her face. "I thought you'd never get here," she said to her husband. *"Bonjour, Monsieur Chaumont, comment ça va?"*

"*Bien*," he said, shaking hands with the high-strung woman who wore bright red lipstick and her hair pulled back in a tight chignon. They entered the vast courtyard that exuded old-school luxury.

"The thing is," Hélène explained in a tart voice, "my mother can't take too much excitement. She grieves over Juliette and having Max show up will only add to her sadness."

"It could have the opposite effect," Olivier said.

"I know my mother," Hélène said firmly, as they boarded the elevator.

They arrived at the first floor and Philippe and Hélène marched to the door. It opened, and Isabelle and Max stood side by side. "What grim faces," Isabelle said as her daughter and son-in-law entered. Olivier was stunned by how much Max resembled her grandmother.

"Maxine?" her aunt said, making a beeline to Max and shaking hands. "I'm your aunt. And you've met your Uncle Philippe." She moved past Max to her mother, "*Mon Dieu, Maman,* are you okay? Why didn't you call me?"

Isabelle, unruffled, replied in French, "There was nothing to call about, dear."

"I could have arranged a dinner. How did you communicate?"

"Hélène, stop," Isabelle said. "You're making a fool out of yourself. Of course my granddaughter speaks French."

Philippe interjected, "Hélène, I told you she wouldn't be staying. We should all repair to the living room..."

Olivier stepped forward, and Max strode purposefully over to him. Linking her arm through his, she said, "We can't stay. Olivier and I are due at a party. Right, Olivier?" She led him to Isabelle, "Mamie, Olivier Chaumont."

Olivier was impressed at how Max skillfully took control of the situation. He shook hands with Isabelle, and they entered into the *de rigueur* brief conversation about their family connections.

Isabelle said with a twinkle in her eye, "Go to your party. I will try to set my daughter straight about my health." Max said a quick good-bye to her aunt and uncle, who seemed disappointed that the drama was ending, and steered Olivier toward the door. Once they were on the elevator, she said, "I feel like celebrating."

"*D'accord*. But what are we celebrating exactly?" Olivier hailed a taxi and directed the driver to take them to the Hemingway Bar at the Ritz Carlton.

"Meeting my grandmother. I love her. She said I was a romantic like my mother. Do you agree?"

Olivier laughed. "I can't answer that out of context."

The driver stopped in front of the hotel at Place de la Concorde. The Hemingway Bar seated only thirty-four people and was tucked into the back of the hotel like a well-kept secret. It was reminiscent of a masculine lair from the days when Hemingway frequented one of the secluded tables on a regular basis. His rifle still hung on the wall above the original bar. The dark wood and dim lighting provided an atmosphere of intimacy that encouraged bent heads and hushed voices.

Olivier and Max took a seat in one of the small nooks, and were greeted warmly by a waiter. Olivier ordered a raspberry martini for Max and a "Serendipity" for himself, both original creations of Colin Field, the hotel's world-renowned bartender.

"They'll be closing down for two years at the end of this month for renovation," Olivier said. "I'm glad you could experience it." He held up his glass and Max followed with hers. "To romantics everywhere," Olivier said.

"And here's to finding Ellen's killer."

"That's the least romantic toast I've ever heard," Olivier said.

Max tossed her head back and laughed. Olivier glanced at his watch. "It's a little after 10 o'clock. Douvier was going to announce on the 10:30 news that Ellen Jordan was murdered. Let's go."

They left their drinks, explaining to the waiter that they would return in a few minutes. The concierge in the lobby directed them to a small room with a television. Douvier and Madame Alban stood before reporters holding up microphones. Douvier stepped up and began to speak. *It is with regret that I announce that foul play is suspected in the death of the celebrated American wine critic, Ellen Jordan. The cause of death will be announced when we have more information, possibly tomorrow.*

Olivier and Max didn't stay to hear reporters' questions, but returned to their drinks instead. "The announcement will trigger a firestorm," Olivier said.

Max raised her glass, "To Ellen." Their glasses clinked in mid-air. "Let's talk about something other than death, Olivier. Tell me about Australia. When were you there last?" Olivier told about his brother who had moved to Australia several years ago to start a vineyard, describing the landscape and the culture in detail. They sipped, and kissed, and held hands, deliberately blocking any mention of the turmoil their world was in.

"Are you sure you want to go home with me?" Olivier asked, enjoying their little joke.

"That's a no-brainer."

"What's *that*?"

"The answer doesn't require any thought." The evening air was cool, and Max tucked her hand in his arm as they waited for a taxi. Once in his apartment, she said, looking around, "Nothing has changed since last year."

"Including my feelings for you."

She whirled around, "Olivier…"

"I don't know about you, but…"

She was in his arms before he could finish the sentence.

Chapter Seventeen

April 5

Max awoke early and made coffee, surprised by how soundly Olivier slept. At 7:30 she couldn't delay any longer. She poured two cups of coffee and went to wake him. "I think you like one-shot espresso, right?"

He looked alarmed for a second. "Did I sleep too late?"

"No. I woke up early."

She walked over and placed the coffee next to his bed. "I'm going to dress and go for a run. Back in half an hour..."

"Max."

She put the cups down, and climbed back into bed.

In an hour a car pulled up outside Olivier's apartment, compliments of Douvier. They were driven to the U.S. Consulate, where Max picked up papers needed to transport Ellen's body. Soon they were pulling into the familiar driveway of the Hôpital Raymond Poincaré in Garches, a suburb of Paris. Docteur Legrand, who had helped them solve the Champagne murders, greeted his two visitors warmly. "I followed the Champagne case last year to the end," he said. "If you hadn't come to me, I think the drowning death of Antoine Marceau would have been forever listed as an accident. I'm glad to have the opportunity to tell you that."

"The credit goes to Max," Olivier said, and Legrand nodded in agreement. Max silently passed the praise to her father, who not only taught her to trust her hunches, but also to persevere.

"I think we have another tough one on our hands," Olivier said, "Poisoning is difficult to prove."

"I sent the contents of Madame Jordan's stomach to a private lab because the government tests are quick, inexpensive…and often unreliable. May I ask what made you suspect poisoning when an initial examination would suggest alcohol poisoning, or perhaps food poisoning?"

Max told him about accompanying Ellen as her bodyguard, and mentioned the threatening note. "The lab has come up with aconite poisoning," he said. "There are four kinds of aconitum alkaloids, and one of them, jesaconitine, was detected in the vomitus, stomach contents, plasma, and urine. Hemorrhagic pulmonary edema was revealed during the macroscopic autopsy and I found diffuse contraction-band necrosis in the myocardium."

Olivier said, "It would help if you spoke in layman's terms."

"Sorry. Let me start with aconite. It's easily available, and easy to administer, but not so easy for us to isolate the poison from viscera. In this case, a gas-chromatography/mass-spectrometry screening was used. My ruling is that the cause of death was aconite-induced centrogenic arrhythmia. I won't go into too many details of the symptoms of poisoning, but it starts with numbness in the feet and fingers and progresses quickly to vomiting, diarrhea, and often leads to death."

A horrible death at that, Max thought.

"I'm quite certain you'll find the same results with the body of the maid," Olivier said.

"The poison was in a blue cheese."

"I know.

The driver rushed them to Paris, where they caught the train back to Bordeaux, feeling quietly vindicated by their obsession that Ellen was murdered. "I'm grateful to you, Olivier, for going out on a limb for me."

"I had the same hunch. We've barely started the investigation and I'm already feeling overwhelmed."

"We'll start with today."

Olivier teased, "We're clear that we'll both be on assignment this evening?"

"Watching you run off with arguably the most beautiful woman in France is a challenge, but the answer is yes."

He took her hand. They were both more vulnerable now. "I'm sending you off with our most notorious *bon vivant*, who obviously has a crush on you."

"I disagree. He wants something from me, but I don't know what it is."

"It's only fair to tell you that he is one of several traders who have been targeted by my agents. That can mean anything from his books being off to hiding money to something more serious."

"Abdel told me that he's rumored to use drugs to get women to go home with him. He and his peers think Vincent is protected because nothing has happened to him."

Olivier said, "Abdel didn't tell me. Maybe because it's rumor. You're still okay with tonight's plan?"

"I can handle him. I've seen what happens with date-rape drugs and, trust me, I won't become a victim."

"Okay. Let's do a quick rundown of what we have ahead of us," Olivier said. "Thirty of around four hundred exporters in the Bordeaux area have been tagged by my agents for infractions of various rules. Signs of tampering, shipments leaving from unassigned ports, or financial books that aren't in order are some of the criteria for the agents. Vincent's company is among the places where we have an agent planted. A call came in that he has certain shipments taken to a more distant harbor than is normal, and so that's being checked."

"What's the port that aroused suspicion?" Max asked.

"Le Havre. He has a driver taking a truckload of wine there two nights a week, which I don't find particularly alarming. His father's firm ships wines all over the world, but all these cases are going to two different importers in New York City."

"A good starting place for me when I return."

Olivier said, "I'll be going to Bill Casey's special tasting the evening I arrive."

"Won't I be confiscating the rest of the magnums in that lot when I return?"

"I want to use them as lures. Someone went to great lengths to get their hands on the one Ellen Jordan brought here. My preference, when possible, is to allow things to disintegrate of their own accord."

"Sounds kind of passive."

"I'm far from being passive. At least we can agree about that." Max laughed. "It's more about being a cat than a dog," Olivier continued. "To be aware and wait to pounce requires far more discipline than just barking and jumping."

"I don't think you'd survive at the NYPD," Max teased. "We're all dogs. Dobermans and the like."

"Ellen was also tenacious as a dog. Taking the bone and running with it. She was foolish to ignore the warning note. On the other hand, no one has ever died at the hands of a counterfeiter."

"She took it seriously enough to hire me, although my parents pretty much thrust me onto her. Hank thought it the perfect job to get me out of town, and my mother and Ellen thought it an opportune time for me to reconnect with you. Awful, huh?"

"She succeeded in reuniting us, but under the most dreadful circumstances. You know, I resisted accepting your help last year, but I don't know what we would have done without you. I'm not a seasoned investigator in the same way you are."

"You have some talent."

He smiled. "You're different from last year. I think you've been flourishing in the Big Apple."

"In Champagne, I was on my own. No dad, no Walt, no Joe. I learned I could function without them."

"What waits when you go home?"

"I'll continue as a second-grade detective, but I'm going to ask to be transferred to a different precinct."

"Because of your ex-boyfriend? Maybe he's the one who should be transferred."

"He already has been. I just want a change."

"What about France?"

The question felt loaded. "That would be a big change."

"We'll be entering the station soon. Véronique has a hotel room in the village, and I will be driving home to Bouliac. Can you come there after your dinner?"

"Sure."

The conductor announced their destination as Olivier answered his ringing mobile. "Our little respite is over," he said to Max. "Abdel informed me that cases of wine just arrived at customs in New Jersey with our Opération Merlot marker on them. They'll call back with all the data."

"Things are picking up."

He pulled a sheet of paper from his briefcase and handed it to her. "Names of people at the hotel the night Madame Jordan died. Introduce yourself as the assistant, and no French."

"With my Amazonian build, platinum hair, and ignorance of French, I'll be labeled the American bimbo. People are more prone to reveal secrets when they feel superior, and among the Bordelaise, I've noticed, there is no lack of arrogance."

"I admire your acting skills," Olivier said. "I could use a lesson in portraying a wine collector tonight."

"Just be your usual erudite self. Pontificate."

"Is that how you see me?"

"It's actually a compliment."

"You have your cell. Call me if you need to."

Olivier pulled up in front of the hotel. Max reached over and gave his hand a quick squeeze and was gone. She doubted that either of them would uncover anything significant, but what was wrong with an afternoon and evening of fine wine and entertaining company?

◇◇◇

Max sat in the passenger seat of Vincent's Ferrari as he drove along the famous Route des Châteaux in Médoc, pointing out some of the great houses built on properties that had made the region famous. The landscape was flatter and plainer than Saint-Émilion with its rolling hills and valleys, yet boasted an endless expanse of perfectly tended vineyards. The surrounding waters of the Gironde Estuary and the Atlantic Ocean added a maritime quality.

Vincent explained that Bordeaux was divided physically and culturally by the Garonne River—the old wine aristocracy inhabited the Left Bank and the newer, more innovative winemakers were on the Right, with few exceptions. The wines in this area were made predominantly from the cabernet sauvignon grape, Vincent explained, responsible for those fabulous wines that aged well. Merlot was another important grape to the region.

"What about Pascal's wines?"

"He was one of the first to bring attention to the Right Bank. Like him, his wines are mercurial, undeveloped, and lacking subtlety. There is no *terroir*. Simply stated, no roots or pedigree. But he's in the mainstream now, and the division is much less pronounced than it was even twenty years ago."

"No one can argue with his success."

"You could almost say that the American craving for strongly flavored wines with more alcohol created the new trend. Your critics raved about wines that remind me more of California wines."

"What about the wine you're producing?"

"You mean my $10-dollar-a-bottle wine?" He sounded bitter. "You know, Pascal will be exposed as an opportunist when it's leaked to the press that he and Ellen Jordan were having an affair. I need someone to promote my wine the way Ellen did his." He reached over and put his hand on her thigh. "You interested?"

She shifted her position. "This sounds like sour grapes, Vincent. Sorry, I couldn't resist the pun."

Missing her play on words, he said, "Actually, I have someone as powerful as Madame Jordan who has promised to help me."

"Oh? Who's that?"

"A woman in New York named Paula Goodwin. I have created a fine wine from the two hectares of land my father gave me."

Max feigned ignorance about Paula Goodwin. "Never heard of her."

He rolled his eyes. "She will be bigger than Ellen Jordan, mark my words." Has he no sensitivity? she wondered, suddenly finding a great deal wrong with his character. "She will be attending the Cheval Blanc event tonight."

Max suddenly didn't want to spend the evening with Vincent. She didn't like the hand on the thigh, the bitterness, the insensitivity. "Don't you want to go?" she asked hopefully.

"Because Paula Goodwin's going to be there? I can see her later." He smiled at Max. "Besides, I want to be with you. The *Cheverny* wine that we'll taste today promises an extraordinary blend that will hold for decades, if not centuries. It has amazing depth." He gestured at the building ahead. "There awaits our castle. I shall be your Prince Charming for the night." That's pushing it, Max thought, determined to pull herself out of the bad mood that had overtaken her.

The long, winding driveway lined with trees led to a Gothic revival *château* that stood majestically in the middle of seventy hectares of grapes. Neatly planted rows of vineyards stretched to the horizon. It was one of the few estates that had not been either bought outright in recent years by the nouveaux riches or foreigners, or taken over by international companies that were determined to purchase prestigious property.

"These fields will be transformed into a sea of lush green vines laden with grapes by July," Vincent said. Max had read that Bordeaux's skies were vast ocean mirrors, an apt description of the shimmering light surrounding them. The *château* was even more impressive up close than from a distance. Vincent took her hand as they started up the steps. Max's black, silky pants, shirt, and vintage Givenchy jacket felt just right. She paused a second to get into character. The Lone Rangeress is on the prowl, she thought, smiling at her own humor.

Chapter Eighteen

April 5

Everything about the Barthes *château* in Paulliac was understated. The buildings, the landscape, including the pond below the house, had a pure and natural elegance. Olivier much preferred this type of estate to those on the tourist route. Glancing around the entry hall as he entered, he was certain that some of the paintings had been hanging there for centuries. An attractive woman whom Olivier figured to be around his age, and who was pregnant, opened the door, and shook hands. "I'm Gabrielle. Please excuse the chaos. We're in the midst of preparing for an extended trip to Australia."

He recognized her Australian accent, and thought of his brother who had moved there. "What area of Australia are you from?"

"Melbourne."

"I have a brother there attempting to grow grapes. Jean-Louis Chaumont."

"I've actually heard of him. Please wait here in the library. I'll get Yves." She disappeared through a door, and Olivier walked across the room to admire some Renaissance prints.

"Monsieur Chaumont." Olivier turned and shook hands with the silver-maned man with a courtly manner who Olivier assumed to be in his sixties. "Come with me." They entered Yves' office, which made Olivier feel as if he had stepped back into another century. Yves Barthes was the quintessential Bordelaise *négociant*. Olivier knew that of all the traders in the area, he was the one who would be most informed when it came to who had bought what over the past decade. "Please, sit down," Yves said.

"I won't take up too much of your time," Olivier said. "I'm looking for any clues to a counterfeiter who could be operating under my nose."

"That's getting right to the point. I know of a few bottles that have turned up in recent months with a questionable pedigree. Mostly in Hong Kong. Again, an auction capital. It's awfully difficult to catch counterfeiters, as you know, and when they are caught, they get off with a slap on the wrist. I was glad to see Rudy Kurniawan arrested at last."

Olivier knew he was referring to the arrest in Los Angeles only a month ago of the Indonesian national who had allegedly swindled wine buyers out of a million or more dollars. "Which reminds me," Olivier said, "I'm interested in a bottle that was stolen from Ellen Jordan. A *1945 Mouton-Rothschild* that she had tasted and deemed a fake."

"Stolen?"

"From the office safe at the Hôtellerie Renaissance."

Yves shrugged. "Do you know its provenance?"

"No, but I intend to find out. A collector named Bill Casey bought a four-magnum lot."

"From?"

"Again, I don't know. He bought so much wine five years ago that he can't remember."

"Someone must know. I'd venture a guess and say Blakely's."

"Really?"

"Paula Goodwin is a magician. She has come up with some astounding wines to sell, while at the same time turning these auctions of hers into free-for-alls. She's adored by many, especially young investors. Maybe I'm being a curmudgeon."

"You know her?" Olivier asked.

"We've met a few times."

"Has she purchased from you?"

"Oh, sure. I've been a little suspicious of some of her sources. I can tell you where every bottle of wine I sell comes from, but I'm from the old school. *Vieux jeu*."

Olivier smiled at him calling himself old-fashioned. "Are you implying counterfeiting?" Olivier asked.

"No, no. Not at all. It's illegal in the states for an auction house to purchase wine from a distributor, for obvious reasons. I think she has a secret source, and what better than a distributor, illegal or not?"

"The reason it's illegal is the wine loses its rarity?"

"Exactly. People would just purchase it at a retail store. Or what if Parker scored a '95 *Lafite* very high? The auction house could simply buy it all up, and start the auction at any price it chose. I saw on the news last night that foul play was suspected in Ellen Jordan's death?"

Olivier nodded.

Yves grew pensive. "There's more at stake than a bottle of wine, don't you think?"

"Yes, but what?"

"Millions of dollars? Someone who can't bear to have his name sullied? Reputations count for everything in this business. Look at Monsieur Laussac, who is making a fool of himself by suing the appellation committee of Saint-Émilion for demoting his wine. He's an investor in that vineyard, nothing more, but my god, you'd think he was from a long line of wine growers."

"I noticed you weren't at his dinner?"

"I can't stand the man. I sent my son instead."

"I saw him."

Yves hesitated. "Your look tells me he wasn't behaving." It was clear that Yves treated Vincent as though he were a ten-year-old. "I'm trying to get Vincent on the right track. One minute he's helping with the operation of my company, and the next he has blown-up ideas about this cheap wine he's making that will take the world by storm. He was in Australia a couple of years ago and decided he could make something as equally affordable as Yellow Tail."

"What a stroke of luck for the Australian producers, having the Americans go wild over their wine."

"I told Vincent that it was pure luck, but luck doesn't strike that often. I may have to swallow my words if he has indeed created a fine wine. Suddenly Vincent is not failing at all, but making enough money to start paying me back."

"It's rumored that you have to keep the business afloat."

"On the contrary, I hate his entire concept of cheap wine. I wanted it to fail. He won't let my accountant touch his books. He says he has a much more modern system."

Olivier felt a flutter of excitement, mixed with dismay. "Some unusual shipments have left his business for New York. Do you have a list of his accounts there?"

Yves looked worried. "I hope you're not suspecting *him* of doing anything illegal?"

"At the moment many producers are under suspicion."

"What a mess. I'm glad to be getting away for a while. With all the competition here, everyone selling each other out for another euro, and prices jumping all over the place, I need a break."

"Vincent seems to be on a roll. He entertained clients in the hours leading up to the Laussac dinner. I heard he sold a lot of wine."

"That is our tradition." Yves was no longer leaning back in his office chair, but sitting upright. "I know that Ellen Jordan met up with a murderer that night at the hotel. You've jumped from counterfeiting to murder in a few minutes."

"Did I mention murder?"

"Not specifically."

Olivier realized that he was pussyfooting around Yves, and said, "The two might be related, it's true, but our information is quite scant. I'm focusing today on the counterfeiting."

"I think you want to talk to Vincent. Shall I call him?"

Olivier thought about the evening and didn't want any of his plans disturbed. "I can talk to him tomorrow."

Olivier thought Yves might know why Vincent pursued Max with such enthusiasm. "A final question. Yves called on Madame Jordan's assistant that evening...."

"I know where you're going with this." Yves visibly relaxed. "He told me all about the wildly sexy American who arrived with Madame Jordan. He's taking her out to dinner tonight. With your investigation underway, you must have spent a little time with her. What's she like?"

Olivier, surprisingly, felt at a loss for words. "Like?" None of the words that came to mind—full of chutzpa, enigmatic, exciting, coquettish, stubborn, impulsive, sometimes infuriating—seemed the appropriate thing to say. "She's…interesting."

The older man cried. "That's *all?* Not delicious, beautiful, quirky, funny, as my son claims?"

Olivier relented. "She's beautiful, I agree. She'll be returning to New York in a couple of days."

"Perhaps she'll take my son with her," Yves said. "Vincent is known for his *conquêtes*," he added, eyes twinkling. "But since his marriage ended, he doesn't hold onto anyone." Yves stood, "I must continue packing if you don't have anything further to discuss."

Olivier felt compelled to say something to alert Yves. "I dissembled when you asked me if I suspect Vincent of doing something illegal. I'm concerned, and that's why I'm here."

"Are you referring to the shoddy accounting I mentioned?"

"That's part of it."

"Surely I would know if something was going on." Yves' eyes grew hard. "You're on the wrong trail, Olivier."

Olivier knew that it was almost impossible for a parent to blame a child. "I hope so. When do you leave?"

"In two days."

"*Bon.*" Olivier stood up. "It's just you and your girlfriend going?"

"Yes."

The two men shook hands in parting, and Olivier offered to let himself out. He glanced at his watch, then called Abdel to say that he could meet Véronique. He rushed into the airport terminal. All heads turned as the supermodel sailed across the floor and planted a passionate kiss on his lips. He heard a camera click, and groaned inside. She gave him her trademark smile and he picked up her small suitcase and put it in the trunk of his car.

"When is your shoot?" he asked.

"Tomorrow morning. I'm not sure how I was invited to this evening's event. My new fiancé just spent a couple hundred thousand euros on wine, so I'm thinking that's what it's about." She buckled her seatbelt, and gave him a coy look. "Did I mention that I'm engaged?"

Olivier pretended not to know. "Who is he?"

"A British singer in a fabulous rock band. No one you know. And you? Any luck with the American blond detective you threw me over for?"

Olivier knew how vindictive she could be, and decided to be vague. "We see each other when we can."

"I still hate her, you know. She's the only competition I ever had. She made me drink again."

Neither Vincent nor Véronique had ever learned to accept personal responsibility, Olivier thought. Vincent's father took care of any trouble Vincent got into, and Véronique was on her own at fifteen, and a drug addict by eighteen, yet both had narcissistic personalities. "You're well now?"

"I'm off drugs, if that's what you mean."

"A rock musician doesn't seem the best solution."

"I wasn't looking for a solution. Now that he's into wine, maybe I'll finally learn something about it." She lit a cigarette and blew smoke in his direction.

"I need your help tonight," Olivier said. "I'm on the Ellen Jordan case, and need to pose as a wine collector."

Her eyes narrowed. "I wondered why you agreed to go with me. What do I get if I don't reveal your true identity?"

"I hadn't thought of an exchange. What do you want?"

"To sleep with you."

Olivier couldn't believe that Max had been right from the start. "You have a beautiful room in Saint-Émilion. It's close to the *château*."

"Half the reason I accepted this gig was to see you, Olivier. I miss you."

"I'm sorry," Olivier said.

She pouted. "You should have told me."

"I didn't think it mattered."

"Maybe not to you."

"I can leave you at the hotel while I go to a tasting at the Laussac Château. I should be there no more than an hour."

"I'll go with you. I don't have to change."

He acquiesced, figuring that this would put them on reasonably good terms. There was no question that her earlier hold on him was gone. But that didn't prevent him from admiring the golden hair falling around her shoulders, and the face that women all over the world tried to imitate.

Chapter Nineteen

April 5

Max and Vincent entered the fabulous entrance hall where dozens of people had gathered for the tasting. Original abstract paintings by Braque and Léger hung on the walls. Chantal Laussac wove in and out among her guests, impeccably dressed in a beige suit, white silk blouse, Hermès scarf, and pearl necklace. Max had to admit that she was impressed at the grace of the woman who had lived her life as a BCBG, or *bon chic-bon genre.*

She came up and briskly shook hands with each of them, then led them to a large table covered with glasses and uncorked bottles of their more recent vintages. A bevy of young people manned the tables, chatting up the elegant clientele. Guests stood in clusters swirling the wine in the glass, then sipping, rolling it around in their mouths, and spitting into special porcelain basins located along the walls.

A slender, wiry man approached them, and shook hands. "What a scandal we have with Ellen Jordan," he said to Vincent in French. "We almost canceled today's tasting, but thought about all these people from afar who would be disappointed."

Vincent introduced Max to Monsieur Laussac. "This has been a busy week for you," Max said. "The dinner, and now a tasting..."

"Two separate properties," he said. "It's an important time for us." He gave her a skeptical look. "Madame Jordan has never come with an assistant before. Do you speak French?"

"*Un petit peu…*"

"A little. That usually means not at all. If you don't speak French, what was your job?"

"Actually, I'm in training to become a sommelier. Mrs. Jordan agreed to accept me as an intern."

"I hope you aren't going to tell me you fall into the group of young tasters in the U.S. who are shunning Bordeaux wines for Burgundy."

Max didn't know that was the case. "I don't follow trends."

"What did you taste with Ellen Jordan?" he asked, looking up at her. His bald pate was so shiny she could see her reflection in it.

Max decided to lie to see if she got a reaction. "Pascal Boulin's *Terre Brulée.*"

He made a face. "What did you think?"

She wracked her brain for something to say. "It was young, but it had a kick to it. More a Miles Davis riff than say, a melody by Franz Schubert, which is what this staid wine I'm sipping is like. His is sexy." He stared at her as though she had lost her mind, and she suppressed a laugh.

Vincent had reappeared at Max's side, and now guffawed. "We're switching to musical metaphors now?" He took Max's arm and asked Laussac if he could show her around. "Of course," François replied. As they walked away, she overheard Laussac say in French to a guest who had joined him, "American women. So full of themselves." Feeling their eyes on her, Max fluttered her fingers behind her, praying she wouldn't trip in her new pumps. She was surprised to find that she was having fun with the bimbo role.

Vincent led the way down a flight of stairs into a room where six stainless steel thousand-liter vats stood, and continued down another flight of ancient steps that brought them to a vaulted underground chamber lined with barrels that Vincent spoke of reverently as made of French oak. The glow from soft ceiling lights bounced off the wood. Max had the sensation of being in a cathedral.

Vincent explained that the juice from the grapes fermented in these for a few weeks, then once the sugar converted into alcohol, the new wine would be transferred to oak barrels for aging. Max felt Vincent close behind her and when she turned to say something to him, he pulled her toward him and kissed her on the lips. Max stepped back, flustered. The awkward moment was broken by Chantal speaking from the doorway. "Oh, *pardon*. I am taking my friend Éloise to see our private collection."

Vincent handled the interruption with aplomb by asking if they could join them. "We were admiring the barrels," he said, and the two women twittered. Max was speechless with embarrassment. Chantal motioned for them to follow her as she passed through the *chai* to a door marked *privé*, which she unlocked with a key. The walls were covered with mold. They stepped gingerly over cobblestones until they approached a massive iron gate.

Chantal reached over and switched on a light that illuminated hundreds of cases of wine carefully arranged in rows. "*Voilà*. We save at least ten cases from each vintage," she explained. "And we have wines from other *châteaux* that my family has collected over a long period, some of them dating back to the 1700s."

"How do you protect it?" Max asked, thinking of how easy it had been for someone to break into Pascal Boulin's storeroom.

"We haven't had to until recently. We were broken into a few months ago, and some of our finest vintage wine was taken, including a magnum of a *Château Haut-Brion* 1945, impossible to get today, and a *Chateau d'Yquem* 1900." Max thought about the *Mouton-Rothschild* that had gone missing.

"Why wouldn't they take it all instead of a few primo bottles?" Éloise asked.

"A bottle or two is rarely noticed, or noticed when it's too late. François only discovered these missing because he came down for a bottle to celebrate my aunt's birthday."

Éloise interjected, "They also took cases of more recent vintages, didn't they?"

"Yes. Several cases of our '92 that we were preparing to lock in the private collection."

"And the value?" Max asked. She realized from the change of expression on Chantal's face that she considered the question gauche.

"The two bottles were priceless. I don't know about the others."

"What will the thieves do with it?" Max persisted, having instinctively switched into detective mode.

"Sell to collectors, many in Asia, who have recently been insatiable in their thirst. The old vintages add to the owner's social status. I've heard recently, though, that there were so many scams in Asia last year that collectors are exercising more caution this year. Many of the brokers who sold to them lacked integrity. Obviously, I'm not referring to someone like Vincent, whose father and grandfather before him have sold our wines, but there are many newcomers out there."

"I hope you won't be like Cheval Blanc and start selling from your *château*," Vincent said. He explained to Max that some producers wanted to eliminate the *en primeur* weekend, and sell their own wines, breaking a long tradition. "If that happens," he said, "we middlemen could be eliminated one day."

"François continues to support the current way of doing things," Chantal said. "With my encouragement."

"What's an example of a pricy wine?" Max asked.

"The 2009 Bordeaux was a great recent vintage," Vincent said. "And prices reflect that. For their wine that was still in the barrel, *Château Cheval Blanc's* 2011 *en primeur* release price was $622 a bottle, and the 2010 vintage was $1,200 a bottle."

That's around $300 a glass, Max calculated. More than I earn in two days. And it's not even bottled yet.

"I really must get back to my other guests," Chantal said. A grating sound caught their attention and they grew quiet.

"*Ohe*?" Chantal called down the dim corridor, and hearing no response, she marched down the alleyway, calling out.

A voice came from the shadows. "*Madame*." A swarthy man, stocky and of medium height, wearing a baseball hat and a brown jacket, stepped out into the light. His dark eyes shifted to Vincent, and lingered on his face, but Max couldn't read his expression. She noticed that his shirt collar was buttoned at the neck.

"What are you doing here, Monsieur Martin?" Chantal asked. "Monsieur Laussac gave you strict orders to ask before you entered the cellar again. I heard him."

The man's expression was defiant. "I left my jacket here last week, and I came to fetch it."

"I see." Chantal stood looking uncertain as to what to do next. "*Bien*. I'll wait. We've just had a new lock put on our family cellar gate."

"I don't see what for," he said. "If somebody wants something they'll get it, no matter what you do."

He lit a cigarette and blew the smoke in front of him, causing Chantal to wave it away from her face. "I need to return to my party."

She stood with a stoic expression on her face until he said, "I can get my jacket later. But I need to see Monsieur Barthes for a minute before I go."

"Monsieur Barthes? Now?" She looked from one to the other.

"This isn't a good time, Yannick," Vincent said.

"It's a shipping problem." Vincent hesitated, then told Max she should continue back to the tasting room with Chantal. He politely excused himself and joined the man.

"I'll send my husband down to lock up," Chantal said.

Vincent stopped, and looked back. "I can lock up for you if you like."

"Okay," Chantal said simply, handing him the key and moving quickly toward the stairs.

When Max glanced back, she saw that the two men were making a rapid retreat down the alley, their voices raised in argument. She caught up with Chantal and Éloise. "Sometimes it feels like Yannick Martin is taking over," Chantal said. "He seems to have some control over François, which I know sounds ridiculous." Max was alongside them now. "Oh, Mademoiselle, I'm sorry, we will speak English."

"Thanks. The man back there. Who is he?"

"He's our foreman."

"I notice he limps," Max said.

"Limp?" she asked. "I don't know that word."

Max demonstrated, and Chantal shrugged, "His work is physical," she said, uninterested. The women went back to speaking French, and Max heard Éloise say, "You think she has her eye on the foreman as well?" This was followed by a giggle.

"Oh, Éloise," Chantal said. "How unkind. I was thinking, though, of warning her about our local ladies' man."

Max suddenly felt disenchanted with the role-playing, especially being associated with Vincent. He caught up with them, and possessively put his hand on Max's arm. She wanted to shake it off. "I'm sorry," he said. "Yannick occasionally drives a truck for me and needed directions."

"Yannick Martin drives for you?" Chantal asked. "With that wife of his always complaining about her circumstances, I suppose he has to do some moonlighting. It's strange, though, to have our foreman taking on other jobs. My husband knows about this?"

"I assume so."

"Everything's changing," Chantal said to Éloise and Vincent. "The old loyalties are gone." They arrived back in the chai. Chantal and Éloise went up the stairs to the tasting room. Max started to follow, but Vincent held her back, telling the two women that he and Max would join them in a minute. "Take your time," they said, and closed the door, leaving them on the dimly lighted stairs.

"Ignore those old conservatives," Vincent said. "Chantal probably hasn't been kissed in a decade and it's been longer than that for the giggling idiot."

"You need to know something, Vincent," Max said in a firm voice. "I'm unavailable. Don't think for one minute this is going anywhere."

"*Pardon*, Max," he said. "A kiss is harmless enough, *d'accord*?" He opened the door and, gripping her elbow a tad too tightly, led her into the crowded tasting room, where they came face-to-face with Olivier, his eyes so dark and unfathomable that they seemed to be burning a hole in her. "*Bonsoir,* Monsieur Chaumont," Vincent said, "I think you two know each other?" Olivier shook hands with Vincent, and nodded to Max. Noticing Véronique at his side, Vincent continued, "That was quite a photo of you two kissing at the airport. A friend sent it to my phone."

Max's heart thumped uncontrollably. The model looked fabulous in a silk blouse, short skirt, and tall boots. "Oh, may I see?" Véronique asked in a whispery voice as she tossed her wild mane of hair back dramatically. Max was struck by how her hair, skin, eyes, and even her teeth sparkled." Vincent was too happy to oblige, whipping out his phone and finding the photo in record time. "It's sweet," the model said. Max couldn't believe how jealousy could so quickly swamp the few social graces learned from her mother. Véronique, flashing a brilliant smile at Vincent, said, "Oh, are you going to be at Cheval Blanc?"

Vincent, keeping his hand on Max's arm, said, "We're going to the Le Saint-James for dinner."

"You can't beat the view," Olivier said, as he and Max exchanged glances, "and the food is *pas mal.*"

"Maybe we should switch to the Cheval Blanc event instead," Vincent said to Max. He squeezed her elbow, and she considered the awkwardness that might ensue, but preferred that to being alone with him. She couldn't think straight enough under the circumstances to say why she had taken such a sudden dislike to Vincent, other than to say he was smarmy, a term that Olivier wouldn't be able to grasp.

"The Saint-James is a better choice," Olivier said, not giving her a chance to respond.

Why do I want to kick Olivier in the balls and leave him on the ground? Max thought. All resolve to treat the evening with a degree of objectivity had dissipated. The superficial charm of the people surrounding her was starting to get to her. She longed for her father's blunt verbal kicks in the ass, Walt's avuncular, somewhat grumpy, reassurances, or Joe's asshole-ness. She stood at full height, once again eye-to-eye with Olivier, reminding herself that two nights of lovemaking did not instill loyalty.

Someone beckoned to Vincent, and he excused himself. Véronique removed her hand from Olivier's arm and sashayed over to say hello to Chantal. Max followed her with her eyes, noting how warmly Chantal received the model.

Olivier said, "I'll drop her off at her hotel when my event is over. The Saint-James is only a kilometer from where I live."

"You're repeating yourself."

"Are you upset?"

"You could have encouraged Vincent to go to Cheval Blanc."

"We agreed that this was a work night, didn't we?" He lowered his voice. "I'm worried about Véronique going volatile if she's in the room with you all evening. And besides, Vincent knows my identity."

"Véronique was obviously shocked to see me. Why'd you bring her here? So Vincent could parade his photograph of the two of you in a kiss at the airport around?"

"The kiss was nothing, and she insisted on coming. It's okay, Max."

"Do you know how stupid you sound? And it's not okay. I had bad feelings about this evening from the start."

All of Max's defenses sagged as the model came to claim Olivier. "Come on," Véronique said, taking his hand. "I have someone I want you to meet. You have the dinner tickets?"

Olivier shot Max a guilty look. Max had had it. What was going on was primal, but she couldn't control it. When Véronique turned to pose for a photographer, Max took the opportunity to say what was on her mind to Olivier. "You had a problem with my language subterfuge? I have a problem with the way you're manipulating two women. You know what I think the problem is? There's nobody in your life to call you on your shit. Your parents think you're a god, Abdel also worships you. You have no wife, and when you did, she walked off with someone else, which is a nasty-ass statement of saying you didn't add up. Who says to you: 'Are you kidding me? Are you really treating her this way?' My father does that. And so do my fellow detectives. I don't get away with anything." Olivier looked stricken. "You go your way and I'll go mine tonight," Max said. "And we'll see where we are later."

"Max."

"Don't 'Max' me. Please. Go."

Max thought the man she was in love with and his ex-girlfriend the quintessence of a gorgeous, wealthy French couple as she watched them walk away. She took a deep breath and joined Vincent, and they strolled out into the waning evening light. He stopped to look across the vineyard, where tiny buds were forming on the stalks. The light was pristine, the air moist. He said in a wistful voice, "The wine will always be here, but it extracts higher and higher prices from us all."

"That's a gloomy thought," she said. "What does it mean?"

He gave a vague smile. "It's about regret, but it's a long story." He looked into her eyes. "An even gloomier thought is that you are more attracted to Olivier Chaumont than to me. Or did I read it wrong?"

Max blushed at being caught out. "I find him interesting."

"You have some stiff competition, that's all I can say." What effrontery, she thought.

François, who had been seeing a guest off, strutted over to them. Placing his hand on Vincent's shoulder and, ignoring Max, he spoke rapidly in French. "Chantal told me you bumped into Yannick Martin in our private collection?"

"Yes, Monsieur, he was in the alley, looking for a coat he had left."

François frowned, "I don't like his opportunism. He would sell his mother for money. And his wife is no different."

"I know a landowner in Italy who's hiring," Vincent said.

So, Max thought, the precocious foreman had overstepped boundaries, and the solution might be to send him away.

François said, "Let me know." He paused, "What's the story with Madame Jordan's assistant? Is she really in training to be a sommelier?"

Vincent laughed. "From my travels I find that Americans are always studying something, and it's usually temporary."

François was in good humor. "She strikes me as a *fille facile*. American women have that reputation."

Vincent joined in. "She plays hard-to-get."

"I'm glad to see you have a challenge for a change." Max stalked off to Vincent's car, not caring in the least what they thought.

Vincent quickly caught up and opened the passenger door for her. "I'll take you by the hotel and pick you up again at eight," he said. "I have to see my father briefly." He was eager and chatty once they were on the road. "Many of us are flummoxed that Ellen Jordan was traveling with an assistant. Did she tell you why?"

"She was good friends with my mother." Vincent's eyes widened in surprise. "I'm between jobs, as it were, and Ellen was trying to get me interested in wine."

"You mom must be really upset. Is she okay?"

"No, she isn't. Would you be okay if someone murdered your close friend, Vincent? I wouldn't be. People never seem to realize that when someone is murdered, or dies tragically, it has a ripple effect, touching the lives of many."

Vincent interrupted. "What about you?"

"You mean how do I feel? I'm sad, but I'm also angry as hell. I'd like to come face-to-face with the murderer."

"Most people would want to run from a murderer." The conversation had taken a bizarre turn. "If it helps," he said, "I'm sorry she died." Max nodded, and quickly exited the car.

Sailing past the flowers at the reception desk, she continued up the stairs to her room, wondering if she should cancel the evening, and decided by the time she reached her room that a detective didn't cancel because she was feeling a touch of heartache.

Olivier had mentioned that his agents had Vincent's business under watch. She might challenge herself and see if she could extract some information from him that would help the investigation. Soon, a quick glimpse in the full-length mirror told her that the black *décolleté* V-neck, short silk dress she had changed into was perfect. She pulled up black netted stockings and stepped back into the pumps. She added mascara to her eyelashes, and put on a more subdued lipstick. Vincent called from his mobile and she picked up her little evening bag and ran down the stairs.

He entered the lobby, dashing in a black Armani suit. "*Fantastique*!" he whispered, rushing up and bestowing kisses on each of her cheeks. Flattered, she felt her mood lift.

Chapter Twenty

April 5

Feeling verbally pummeled, and deserving of some of it, Olivier retreated into his thoughts on the drive to dinner. Véronique didn't seem to notice as she prattled on about herself. There was no need to say yes to her when she invited him to the dinner, but some remnant of guilt hung on from their break-up the year before, and he had thought this would make up for previous bad behavior. He had seen the look of surprise on Abdel's face when he told him, and chosen to ignore it. Max was right. He had orchestrated the entire evening, assuring himself that it was all for professional reasons when, in reality, he had ignored Max's look of quiet desperation around Vincent, which was out of character for her. He could have said, you and Vincent come to dinner, and we'll survive together, or some such.

The driveway to Château Cheval Blanc curved up through pine, cedar, and redwood trees. Bought in 1998 by Bernard Arnault, chief executive of LVMH Moet Hennessy Louis Vuitton, and one of the two wealthiest men in France, the vineyard was in the top six first-growth wines in Bordeaux. The 90,000 bottles produced each year were consistently ranked among the best wines in the region. The two-story, ivy-clad limestone *château* built in the nineteenth century was graceful, but unassuming. It was the new winery behind the house that was considered an architectural masterpiece, with descriptions attached to it like "made of air," and "having the appearance of floating over vines."

Véronique moved like a ballet dancer around the tasting room filled with guests from the Bordeaux elite, and journalists from all over the world, some of them photographing her instead of the architecture. She had changed at the hotel into a magnificent black strapless dress that only heightened her allure. Olivier knew she would not be content until every eye was on her. He tried to call Max, but didn't get through.

His host, collector Thomas Chevalier, had been made aware that Olivier was undercover. He greeted him warmly, proffering a *coupe de champagne.* Olivier was relieved to see that there were no familiar faces at the dinner, otherwise he would have to give up his Pierre Guyot identity. The real challenge, he knew, was to keep Véronique from blowing his cover.

He steered the conversation with Chevalier toward collectors and their prizes, bringing up such notables as the 1870 *Lafite*, 1961 *Latour*, and 1947 *Lafleur* that Chevalier had offered at a recent dinner. Their conversation veered to the six-liter bottle of 1947 *Cheval Blanc* that had sold at auction to a private collector for over $304,000 the year before. "My trophy is an imperial of *Cheval Blanc* of that same vintage that I paid approximately 100,000 euros for in 1999," said Chevalier. "It completed the Bordeaux section of my collection."

Olivier couldn't imagine such a strong obsession. "What do you know about the collector, Bill Casey?" he asked.

"I've spent many wonderful evenings drinking wine with him," Chevalier said. "The rumor is that he purchased a large number of Burgundy wines from an alleged counterfeiter, who has since been arrested. Casey felt doubly stung when Ellen Jordan declared the *Mouton-Rothschild* fake."

Olivier pressed on. "Casey didn't take action against the seller who sold him the dubious *Mouton-Rothschild*?"

"*Au contraire.* He's convinced that Ellen Jordan was wrong."

"And now he has Paula Goodwin backing him up, so he has switched his allegiance."

"How do you know that?" Chevalier asked.

"Logic. Casey invited me to an authentication tasting in a few days."

"I know about it. If the one he opens is declared fake, then the assumption will be that all four are counterfeit. And of course, vice versa."

"Do you know if Madame Jordan found something amiss with the label or cork, or was the taste off?"

"It was about the taste. She claimed it was a recent vintage, lacking the depth and profundity of a rare wine."

"Taste is personal," Olivier said. "If Casey has a professional declare the wine authentic, I think everyone will be satisfied that Jordan made a mistake."

"Especially now that she can't protest. I can't imagine what led to her murder. Surely it doesn't have anything to do with that bottle?"

"I don't know. She brought a second magnum here and it's gone missing. I'm seeking clues, but being discreet about it." Olivier thought he should mingle with others, though the conversation with Chevalier was exactly what he had in mind when he accepted the dinner invitation. He hoped Max was having equal success gathering information. "I don't know how Monsieur Kurniawan got away with selling counterfeit wine for so long," he said.

"He was selling mostly to Americans who weren't all that familiar with old French wines. Kurniawan made wine that mimicked the taste, color, and character of certain rare wines," Chevalier explained. "His method was to purchase a hundred-dollar California wine and doctor it to make it resemble a Pomerol or Graves dating back to the twenty-year span from the 1940s through the 1960s."

"You think he was a lone wolf?"

"Some are convinced that there were others involved. Who knows?"

Chevalier waved to a striking woman who wore a chic, black cocktail dress and pearls. She smiled back at him. "That's

Paula Goodwin, who flew in today and will return to New York tomorrow," he said.

"I want to meet her," Olivier said. "She might know who sold the *Mouton-Rothschild* to Casey."

"At which time we might be able to discover the wine's provenance. Come, I'll introduce you."

Paula was as tall as Max, and also had an athletic body, but whereas Max had curves, Paula was built like a man. Olivier guessed her to be in her mid-forties, though Max was convinced from her photo that she had had a facelift. "Paula has turned the auction world on its ear," Chevalier said admiringly as they made their way over to her. "She's been driving up prices at her auction house, though, and I'm not happy about that. I guess we can't have it both ways."

Olivier cut his eye over at Véronique who had attached herself to a journalist from *Le Figaro.* She was tossing her hair back and her laugh had a slight edge of hysteria that made him think she was using again and flying high. She waved lightly, and he smiled at her as he followed behind Chevalier.

The tent was lit by crystal chandeliers. Waiters stood at attention in black tails and white gloves. A string quartet played Vivaldi's Concerto in D. Looking around, Olivier thought that evenings such as this had been occurring for centuries, though in the distant past such feasts were prepared for royalty, not for a mob of cosmopolitan people from all over the globe.

Paula Goodwin had a firm handshake and a raucous voice. He found her energy galvanizing as she turned from one admirer to the next. She put her focus on him when she understood him to be a collector, handing him her card, and responding warmly when he complimented her on her wine blog "Paula's Post." Guests were invited to sit. Olivier looked around for Véronique, but she had disappeared. Paula Goodwin sat in her reserved chair and he noted that he and Véronique had been placed across from her.

The first course, beetroots in a chocolate and honey glaze arrived, accompanied by a 1990 *Haut Bages Libéral,* which he judged a perfect marriage. He listened to Paula discuss golf scores with Chevalier. Turning to the woman on her left, who happened to be from California, she compared notes on running. "I run six miles a day," he overheard Paula say. He had read an article that compared her to an attack dog, but he saw no signs of aggression. "And you," she said, switching her attention to Olivier, "are you like most French who don't believe in exercise?"

"We aren't fitness fans, that's true," he said. "Though most would agree that we believe in exercising our brains to full capacity."

"Are you saying the French are smarter?"

Olivier chuckled. "I won't be caught in that trap."

A noise distracted them, and Olivier turned in time to see Véronique trip in her stilettos, and fall in slow motion. He jumped up and rushed to her. She was grasping her leg and cursing under her breath. "This is your fault," she said, her eyes glassy and hostile. "Get me out of here." Thomas Chevalier came up and assisted by helping Olivier half-carry her out of the tent. She started to cry. "Olivier, I can't possibly stay alone tonight."

"You have a room in a fine hotel, and I'll make sure you're well looked after."

Véronique looked at him, dry-eyed, a smug expression on her face. "I heard your detective was making out with Vincent Barthes in the Laussac cellar. Ask Chantal Laussac."

Olivier, embarrassed, exchanged glances with Chevalier, who said quickly to Véronique, "You must go to my house nearby," he said, "where there are people who can care for you. But first, we need to get you to the emergency room."

She began to swear again. "I don't need an emergency room."

"The ambulance is on the way," a stranger said.

Chevalier turned to Olivier, "I can take it from here," he said. "My assistant, a woman named Béatrice, is here, along with my wife, and it's no problem."

"If you're sure."

"Of course. Go back to your table."

"Go back to being Pierre Guyot," Véronique said, "the wine collector extraordinaire. I told Paula Goodwin what you were up to."

Chevalier called his assistant over. Olivier thanked her, and told Chevalier that he would check in tomorrow. He returned to his seat, feeling unnerved by Véronique's confession. Paula focused her attention on him. "Is everything all right, Mr. Guyot? You know the woman who fell?"

He had to think of a way to test Paula to see if she knew his identity. "I used to be her boyfriend. She saw you and me talking and mentioned that she found her conversation with you earlier this evening interesting."

"Really? I didn't meet her. It wasn't even possible to get near her with so many men gathered around."

Relieved, he turned to the subject he was most interested in. "Your auction house has a reputation of attracting young investors," Olivier said. "How did you manage to do that?"

"It's a new crowd of young people who're sick of the stodgy old-fashioned auctions. You've probably heard of a group of young investors who call themselves the DDD. Dozen Dirty Dudes." She laughed, and he tried to look amused, though he wasn't in the least. "They taste with abandon, and set trophy bottles against each other."

"How do they know the difference?"

"You have to taste two great wines side by side in order to know the difference, and I make that happen."

"You open the wine there?" He noticed that the diners at their table were listening, fascinated.

Paula laughed. "Of course. It's quite rowdy! What about you? You haven't told me what wine you're on the prowl for."

"I have a humble collection. Price is a consideration, but not if that perfect bottle is there before me."

"I'm glad you added the 'perfect bottle' part," she said. "If someone mentioned price to me in the states, I'd suggest they find another hobby."

The main course arrived. Olivier was pleased to see that accompanying the roasted veal was a *Château Cheval Blanc* 1975. Paula sniffed and swirled the wine around in the glass, then sniffed again. "It's perfect," she whispered. She sipped, and rolled the wine around in her mouth. "There it is," she said to Olivier. "I detect the aroma of leather, and the famous tobacco and spices that you don't find in more recent vintages. The finish is long, as expected."

Thomas Chevalier returned and sat beside Olivier. "All is well," he whispered. Without missing a beat, he said to Paula, "I've only recently been made aware of how many of the wines from this region are going to auction houses. It's a fairly new phenomenon, isn't it?"

"Auction houses have been allowed to sell rare wines since the nineties," Goodwin explained. "The demand for our services is huge. Though Bordeaux wine is a luxury item, and always will be, the restaurants don't stock half as much of it as they once did."

"Why?"

"There are so many more outrageous wines from other countries competing," she said matter-of-factly. "And the young investors have different preferences."

"I'm planning to be there for Monsieur Casey's authentication tasting," Olivier said. "If those wines are deemed authentic, and he wants to get rid of a magnum or two, I could be interested."

"I'm to be one of his tasters," she said.

"It would help to know who sold them to him. And I'm interested in their provenance. Any collector would want to know."

"It was five years ago, and Blakely's sold it to him. Ellen Jordan's proclamation that the wine was fake tarnished my company's reputation, but I'll have it restored in no time."

"It sounds like you took it personally."

Her voice became a throaty whisper. "I take everything personally, which is how I've managed to succeed in a world where people judge your every move. Ellen could have come to me instead of starting a rumor."

"I heard it was Bill Casey who started the rumor, which makes sense as he was protecting his purchase."

"You're taking Ellen's side?" Paula demanded to know.

Olivier was taken aback. Undercover work was more effective, and more difficult, than he had realized. Before he could respond, she had turned her back and was chatting up the person next to her. Olivier's mobile beeped, and he excused himself and went into the library so that he could hear what Abdel had to say. "*Oui?*"

"I decided to check out a couple of things before going home. I hate to disturb you, but the marked case of wine that was shipped from Anvers originated at Barthes Négociants. I drove over here to see if anyone was around and I just saw a truck enter and drive around to the back. The driver looked like the Laussac foreman."

Olivier glanced at his watch. It was 10:30. He wondered if Max was still at dinner with Vincent. "I have to drive to the city from Saint-Émilion. Zohra is staying over tonight, so she will be there in case Max comes." He knew Abdel's pause was a question, but he wasn't going to go there.

"What about the truck?" Abdel asked.

"It will take him a while to load the goods on. Delay him until I'm there. It won't be long."

"*D'accord.*" Olivier was glad to have an excuse for leaving early. Véronique had managed to cast a shadow over the event, and the earlier altercation with Max hadn't helped either. He returned to the tent to bid good-night to Chevalier. "Véronique has a slight sprain," the host said. "She'll be out tomorrow."

It was as Olivier thought; she had feigned her injury as a way of getting him to relent. As for Paula Goodwin, he decided that she had been cleverly evasive when answering his questions, even though her admission that Blakely's sold the wine cast a new light on the situation. The question remained: Where did Blakely's get it?

Max hadn't been off his mind for a second, nor had the image of her kissing Vincent in the cellar. Could he have misread her? Were she and Véronique both actors, Véronique hiding her feelings in a public persona that was worshipped by the masses, and Max changing roles the way some people changed lovers? As often happened when thoughts were allowed to dominate the brain, he began to feel self-righteous, wondering what gave

Max the right to be so moralistic. He inserted Schubert's Trout Quintet into the CD player of his car. A musical meditation on the fate of a fish about to be ensnared.

◇◇◇

Olivier entered the Quartier des Chartrons, the section of the city close to the river where wine merchants had conducted business out of stately old buildings for centuries. Most of the area had been turned into galleries and antique shops, but the Barthes business had remained, an anachronism. The company logo, Barthes Négociants, loomed over an impressively tall and decorative wrought-iron gate that was open. Olivier drove through and parked next to Abdel's unmarked car. A uniformed caretaker stood at the entrance, smoking a cigarette. Olivier displayed his carte d'identité. "Monsieur Barthes told me not to let anybody in here without his approval," the man said.

"I have authority over your employer," Olivier said impatiently. "Commissaire Zeroual is already here?" The man scowled, and led the way down a long corridor and out a door to a huge structure. "He's in the shipping area."

The guard walked at a painstaking pace to a vast room where thousands of cases of wine rested on racks that stretched to the ceiling. The place was empty except for Abdel, walking toward him at a brisk pace. A loud grating sound caught Olivier's attention. A gate went up and a truck started rolling toward it. The solidly built driver climbed down from the cab. Olivier noticed his slight limp. His shirt was buttoned at the collar.

Olivier asked him what he was doing. "What does it look like? I've picked up a shipment of wine and I am about to drive it to the loading area. Commissaire Zeroual has already asked me all these questions." Olivier glanced at Abdel, who nodded in agreement.

"In the Bordeaux area?"

"I think so. I haven't looked at the bill of lading."

"Let's look at it together, shall we?"

The driver's eyes darted from Olivier to Abdel. "This is a rush order," he said.

"So, let's hurry," Olivier replied. The driver thrust the paper at Olivier, who scanned it, making note of the name of the shipping company, Axel Van Den Kerkke. "Antwerp. You're going there tonight?"

The driver lit a cigarette. "Yuh."

"Your name?"

"Yannick Martin."

"You're the foreman for Monsieur Laussac, correct?"

Yannick's eyes widened. "Yuh."

"How did you hurt your leg?"

"It ain't my leg. It's my back. Fell off a tractor."

"Did you see a doctor?" Yannick shook his head.

"Unbutton your collar."

"*Quoi*?"

Olivier remained stoic and Yannick did as ordered. "I ain't done nothing," he muttered. Olivier detected the slightest trace of redness, but not enough to question him about it.

"I hate to put you to the trouble," Olivier said. "But I want these cases unloaded."

"But Monsieur Barthes..."

"We're conducting a search for some specific wines," Olivier explained. "We'll assist you."

Abdel, who had stood by listening, hoisted himself up to the back of the truck to help unload. Yannick begrudgingly followed, swearing with every box he lifted. Neither of them liked what was going on.

When Abdel lifted the last case down, Yannick strutted over to Olivier. "This is an abuse of power. You think because you waltz in flashing an I.D. that you can do what you want. Let's see what Monsieur Barthes has to say about this." He got into his truck and roared out.

"Do you agree with the foreman," Olivier asked Abdel, "that I abused my power?"

"His papers seemed in order. I wish we had found stacks of fake labels, or a cache of old bottles. Some concrete proof."

"We have time." Olivier's mobile rang and he pulled it from his pocket. When he hung up he said to Abdel, "Max is taking Vincent home. He's passed out in the car, and she's going to have a look around when she drops him at this house. We will pick her up after we finish up here. Let's see if we can find those labels. It's our only opportunity."

"I could have the police come in tomorrow and do it properly," Abdel said. "You think we should have had Yannick followed?"

"To Antwerp?"

"Something feels off."

"Okay, okay. We could wager a bet as to whether or not Yannick is driving to…"

"I'll bet a week's salary that he's racing to Monsieur Barthes' house, and Max is not expecting company.

Olivier swore as he got into his car. Max had on her professional voice when she checked in—cold, impersonal. What he didn't tell Abdel was that when he asked if she would come to his house tonight, she had said no. Just when he was ready to apologize.

Chapter Twenty-one

April 5

Le Restaurant Saint-James, known for Chef Michel Portos' cuisine and the contemporary design that had been described as a metallic Zen temple, sat majestically on a hilltop in Bouliac overlooking the River Garonne and the city. It was surrounded by a park and a garden that boasted citrus trees and ancient roses.

The chef rushed over and shook hands with Vincent, then had a waiter seat them in the dining room at a table where they could see the twinkling lights of the city below. Vincent instructed the server to bring a bottle of *Château de Fieuzal 1995*. "It's a sauvignon blanc from the Graves area," he said to Max. "The bouquet reminds me of a garden in full bloom, and goes perfectly with the appetizer."

Max had forced herself back into detective mode on the ride over. She was to try to pry information out of Vincent while simultaneously keeping at bay his seduction attempts, which might include a date-rape drug. Great, she thought. Despite her resistance, she found herself succumbing to the charm of her surroundings. The entrée, or first course, Morroccan *foie gras*, arrived; a hint of curry and coriander wafted up. For the main course, Vincent ordered the chef's trademark dish for her, the *filet mignon de Saint-Pierre à la planche*, grilled John Dory served with pepperoni and candied kumquats, and a *pigeonneau à la rhubarb* with green vegetables for himself.

Satisfied, he turned to her. "I learned through my father that the ministers are suggesting that Madame Jordan's death might not have been due to food poisoning. What are the mysterious circumstances under which Madame Jordan died? As her assistant, you must know."

"And as the area's informant, this is why you brought me to dinner, right?"

His look of annoyance was quickly replaced by the charming smile. "You can't accept that you are an attractive woman who turns me on?"

Max felt her face flush. She supposed she should try to appear coy, but instead she gave a blunt answer. "To answer your question, the authorities have asked me questions, but they don't tell me anything."

"I'm surprised Monsieur Chaumont kept you here after her death."

"He didn't force me to stay, Vincent. I was hoping to find a few answers about her shocking death, but I don't think it will happen. Her death will remain a mystery." She thought about what Olivier had said about the suspicious cases leaving Vincent's business. With his impeccable background, assumed wealth, and charm, Vincent had been placed at the bottom of the list as someone involved in a criminal operation. She sipped the white wine after watching the waiter remove the cork and pour. The silence that had arisen between them was awkward. From the expression on his face he had now taken a dislike to her, which would mean no information if she didn't turn it around.

She asked him in a gentle tone what it was like to grow up in Bordeaux, and he launched into the story of his life. He was an only child, adored by his mother, and when she died when he was ten he had been devastated. His father, who hadn't been around much, gave him whatever he wanted. He married at twenty-five, but he didn't know what he was doing, and the marriage ended after two years. She listened with wide eyes, nodding in sympathy.

A mere glance from Vincent activated the waiter, who would glide over and ceremoniously pour more wine, though she had only taken a sip from her second glass. Vincent ordered a *Château Margaux,* 1983, to accompany their main course, and Max was glad she had waited.

Vincent leaned back. "You're not drinking."

"I'm waiting for the red."

He nodded. "Smart girl. One who knows how to wait. That's rare these days." First time I've ever heard that, Max thought. "You're still an enigma to me," he said. "Usually wine is a passion that drives one to become an apprentice, not a sudden whim."

Uh-oh, she thought, we might be plunging into some murky water. "Who says a whim can't become a passion?" she asked. Max found the verbal ping-ponging stressful. The server appeared with the decanted wine, and poured a small amount into Vincent's glass for his approval. "Excellent," Vincent said, waiting for Max to be served. She sipped, and thought for the first time she understood how people could lose their minds over the stuff. Vincent leaned forward. "I see a little rash on your cheek. Do you think you're allergic to something?"

"Really? I'll go check." Max looked in the mirror in the ladies' room, and didn't see anything. The oldest trick in the book, she thought. Send the girl to the restroom and spike her drink. Then she called Olivier. When he answered, she said in her most professional tone, "I'm at a dead end here. I'm so bored I'm about to fall asleep."

They would work it out. "Okay. I have another hour here."

She returned to the table, and told Vincent the rash must have been the play of light on her face. The server arrived with their plates, and when Vincent looked up at him to ask a question Max hastily switched their glasses, just in case. The filet mignon looked perfect. She was hungry. They clinked glasses and drank. Max said the Margaux was like liquid velvet, making Vincent laugh. "I have to remember that one," he said, reaching under the table and putting his hand on her knee. She gave him a hard look, but he ignored it. She sipped from the glass of wine meant for him, and closed her eyes, feeling a moment of what she could only describe as inner awakening.

"I'm obsessed with you," he said, jolting her back into reality. "You can ask my father. I told him that a goddess had arrived in our area. I have a big crush on you." He was slurring his words. She noticed that he had consumed his glass of wine, and was now showing the side effects of a club drug. She shifted into hyper-alert mode, realizing that the evening might end up offering up a clue or two after all.

Most date-rape drugs caused amnesia, and she decided to take a risk. She asked, "Vincent, a magnum of *'45 Mouton-Rothschild* has gone missing. You know everybody. Do you have any ideas?"

"It's the talk of Bordeaux. Some people I know think you stole it."

Max was nonplussed. "Blame-the-American syndrome," she said.

"But you had access to it."

Cazaneuve, she thought. He was the only one who knew that her name was on the form. He was spreading his own gossip. They needed to find out if Vincent hadn't greased Cazaneuve's palms in order to get his hands on the magnum. That begged the question if it turned out to be true: Why did he want it so badly?

He reached for her hand, but she withdrew it. He tried to stand, but couldn't. It had thrown her slightly to learn that she was associated with the missing bottle of wine. Olivier was right. It could put her at risk, especially if the missing magnum was the motive for killing Ellen.

"Are you okay?" she asked.

"A little dizzy. I need to go home."

"Shall I drive you?"

He grinned at her. "Only if you sleep with me." Inhibition gone bye-bye, she thought. "Relax, Max." He laughed. "I'm harmless."

Harmless as any other sociopath, she thought. She wanted to check out his house. "We'll go after you pay up." The server arrived as if on cue and took Vincent's credit card, and they waited while he signed. Max helped him out to the car, and guided him into the passenger seat, where he collapsed. Making her way around the car to the driver's side, she called Olivier and quickly filled him in. He said he and Abdel had a little more work to do and would join her at Vincent's.

"Okay if I take a quick tour of his house?"

"What will you do with Vincent?" Olivier asked.

"Leave him in the car. He had some nausea, but is calm and dreamy now. He's about to drift off to sleep. It'll last a while."

"Lock the car doors. We'll be there to help get him into the house." He paused, then said, "Then we can go to my house."

"No." She hit End on her phone.

On the winding road down to the city, she had to pull over for Vincent to throw up; when she pulled him back in, his head fell back and he gazed at her. She pulled up in front of his townhouse, and he tried to get up, but fell back against the seat. Max said, "*Connard!* You got a dose of your own medicine. We'll see what the courts have to say."

"It's my anxiety medication," he said. "Completely legitimate here in France." The drug is GBH, Max thought, no longer allowed in the U.S. She turned to him, "Vincent, did you kill Ellen Jordan?"

"I wouldn't kill an insect," he said, smiling, still in euphoric mode.

"Do you know who did?"

He smiled, and his head lopped over.

You're disgusting, she thought, as she parked in front of his house. She checked his breathing, and knew he wasn't close to OD'ing, lowered the windows slightly and got out and locked the doors behind her. His house key was attached to the key ring. She stopped to look around, checking out the house next door, one of which still had lights on upstairs. Beautiful street, she thought, admiring the antique lampposts. She walked quickly to the front door and entered. She found the light switch and flicked it on. A portrait of a woman in evening attire, her golden hair swept up, greeted her. Vincent had his mother's aquiline nose, high cheekbones, and hair.

Max stepped into the salon, flicked the light switch, and looked around. It was a formal room with high ceilings and wainscoting. Seeing nothing unusual she turned the light off and returned to the wide foyer, then walked toward the back of the house looking for the kitchen. She felt around and found the switch. The kitchen was bathed in soft lighting. She opened the refrigerator and took a swig of water from a large bottle and replaced it, then looked around, admiring the tiled wall. Beams criss-crossed across the ceiling and as she observed them, she noticed a camera in the ceiling. She went back to the salon and, turning on the light, saw a camera in the upper right part of the ceiling. She ran lightly up the stairs, and entered an open door, which she figured was Vincent's bedroom. It was filled with heavy, antique furniture, and after turning on a lamp, she saw there was another camera. A large mirror was attached to the ceiling over the bed. Max shuddered.

The answering machine light was blinking. Max pushed play and listened. The message was in English, spoken in a deep baritone voice, *Vincent, if the assistant gives you a problem, you know what to do. Stop all shipping. Call me.* Max listened again. The caller had a New York accent, but the call came in as private. For the first time, she felt the chill of fear. Vincent's come-on had been a set-up. He had let it slip that they thought she had the missing magnum of wine. That had to be what he was after. But who was the deep voice directing him?

She exited the bedroom and peeked into the *salle de bain* and saw a camera. A green light was on, which meant she was being filmed snooping around. Abdel would take care of that, she decided. She ran downstairs, feeling claustrophobic. Olivier and Abdel would be showing up any moment. Time to check on Vincent. She strode out to the car, key in hand, and was preparing to unlock the door when she felt an arm encircle her neck in a choke hold, almost pulling her down.

The pressure on her neck was blocking air, and she tried to use both hands to loosen his hold on her by kicking him hard on the shin, but he was prepared, and she missed. She was half-walked and half-dragged to a vehicle behind Vincent's car. Her arms were loose and she reached into her pocket and threw out her talisman, the little pen knife her brother had given her. The man was panting heavily. The door opened and she was thrust into the cab of a truck. Instead of running around the truck and risking her escaping, he got in behind her, and crawled over her to the driver's seat. When he turned on the ignition, they made eye contact. It was the foreman Yannick she had seen in the cellar. She spoke in French, her voice calm. "You made a mistake. I am Vincent's date."

"*Salaude*!" Yannick lit a Gauloise and said, "What did you do to Monsieur Barthes?"

"*Rien!* Nothing!"

He sped off. There was no seatbelt, and Max clung to the door handle as Yannick swerved, almost losing control. He made a series of turns. "Where are you taking me?"

"*La ferme*!" he shouted.

She shot back in French, "*You* shut up and listen! You better think about what you're doing. Kidnapping an American could land you in jail for years!" They were already at the bottom of the hill heading away from Bouliac and toward a highway sign. Olivier had told her a shipment of Vincent's wine was going to Antwerp and she wasn't going to end up there. "What did you do with Vincent?"

"I have him."

"He's back there?" she demanded, tilting her head in the direction of the back of the truck.

"He's asleep."

Yannick slowed down as they approached a roundabout that was bordered by large flowery bushes. She had a split-second in which to make a choice. The bass voice of the caller on the answering machine ricocheted around her brain. Tucking her head, she opened the door and rolled out, hitting her shoulder hard. She crawled a few feet, tucking herself under a bush. She was about to stand and make a run for it when she heard Yannick yell. She stayed put. She could hear him running, stopping, starting again, and swearing. He would find her in a minute, kill her, and claim she hurt herself leaping from the truck. Her shoulder throbbed.

Yannick wasn't giving up, but he had moved farther away in his search. She could hear him thrashing through a clump of bushes twenty yards away. She had noticed a taxi stand across the boulevard as they entered the roundabout, but what were the chances that a cab driver was working at this hour? I have to risk it, she thought. She got on all fours, then stood and made a wild dash across the street. She didn't have to turn around to know that Yannick had spotted her, but she was much faster. The taxi driver was dozing. She banged hard on his window, startling him, then leapt into the backseat, locking the door.

"*Dépêchez-vous!*" she yelled in French. "I'll pay you fifty euros!" The driver put the car into gear just as Yannick's hand grabbed the door handle.

"*Où*?" the man called back to her.

"To Bouliac. *Vite*!" She pulled Olivier's card from her pocket and gave Olivier's address. Soon they arrived at a two-story stone house. "I'll be back with your money," Max said. She knocked on Olivier's front door. Headlights went by and she waited for the car to pass, then ran to the back door and pounded harder. She heard a car door open and close. Yannick might be insane enough to pull right into the driveway and pursue her. A light was on. "Olivier!" she called. Someone tapped her shoulder hard. She screamed and swung at the same moment, her fist connecting with the taxi driver's cheekbone. He swore, and tried to grab her arm. They both froze when the door opened.

Zohra, her eyes wide, stepped out into the night. "She owes me fifty euros!" the taxi driver yelled. "*Ah, les prostituées*!"

"Mademoiselle," Zohra said softly. "Come in."

Chapter Twenty-two

April 5

Olivier explained to Abdel as he drove to Vincent's house that Vincent had put a drug in Max's wine, but she had managed to switch glasses.

"*Connard*!"

Olivier had never heard his assistant call anyone an asshole. "You hadn't mentioned his reputation for drugging young women to me."

Abdel hesitated. "I should have, but all that I have to go on are rumors. My fellow officers tell me that the calls come in, then Monsieur Yves Barthes gives a great sum of money to our department, and that's the end of it."

"What happens to those reports?"

"They are sent to the minister of the interior."

"I'll look into it when this case is over. There is no question now that Vincent is involved in some illegal activities."

Olivier hit the play button on the CD player and the music of the Trout Quintet resumed. The angler was now muddying the water in order to catch his prey. The theme couldn't be more apropos, Olivier thought. He explained the story in the music to Abdel.

"I wonder if Monsieur Barthes had some other goal in slipping a drug into Max's drink other than to have sex with her," Abdel said.

"Like what?"

"I'm not sure."

Vincent's house was dark but his Ferrari was parked in front. Olivier and Abdel exchanged puzzled glances. Olivier drummed his fingers on the steering wheel, wondering what to do while Abdel ran in to get Max. He got out and peered into the window of the car. No Vincent. His thoughts veered from the logical to the fantastic as he wondered what could have happened. Why was his gut telling him that something was terribly wrong?

Abdel ran to the car and said, "No one is here. The back door is unlocked."

They entered and turned on lights. Nothing overturned. Everything looked in order. Both stopped when they entered the foyer, looking up at the painting of a beautiful woman.

Olivier's mobile rang, and he almost dropped it pulling it from his pocket. It was from his house. "*Oui?*" He listened, then stuck the phone back in his pocket. "It was Zohra. Max is at my house, a little banged up, but fine. Let's go."

◇◇◇

Max was in the salon, sipping a cup of tea. Olivier went to her and pulled her up into his arms, all earlier tensions dissolved. She winced and grabbed her shoulder.

"You're hurt!"

"I put ice on it," Zohra said.

"I can't tell you what went through my mind when we arrived at Vincent's and the house was dark," Olivier said.

"Maybe close to what I felt when Yannick had me in a choke hold," Max said. She explained what had happened.

Olivier felt restless and angry, and craved a drink. "I want a nightcap. Will you go with me?" he asked Abdel and Max.

Abdel looked surprised. "To a bar? Now?"

"I'm not trying to corrupt you, but I need a driver."

"*D'accord.* I can do that. I'll change into street clothes so we can go to a local place."

"You carry clothes in the trunk?"

"Something Max taught me: Who knows what situation we'll be in next?"

Max smiled. "I'm game."

"But your shoulder," Zohra said.

"A drink will help. We'll get it X-rayed tomorrow."

"First thing."

Abdel drove to Restaurant Le Cochon Voloant, a small, classic bistro that had been around a long time, and stayed open until four. They were led to a table, passing a tiny bar on the way.

"If you're hungry the steak is good," Olivier said to Abdel. "I'm having a scotch."

"Sounds good."

"Max?"

"Scotch."

Abdel sat on the banquette facing the room, and Olivier and Max sat across from him. "A lot of artists come here," Olivier said.

"Don't look now, Monsieur, but behind you at a back table is Vincent Barthes."

"I thought he might be here."

"You did?"

"I've seen him here before. Vincent is a popular boy. I'm sure he's not alone."

"No. He's with Pascal Boulin."

"*Quoi?*" Olivier exclaimed in disbelief. He scowled at seeing the two men laughing like school chums. When he turned to Max she was watching him, and he thought her expression sympathetic, which didn't help. He said to her, "Vincent was knocked out by a drug? And now he's having a conversation and a drink in a bistro?"

Max explained that the effects of the drug had to do with the amount consumed. "I don't think he imbibed that much," she said. "Enough to be amnesiac, and a little out of it. But Yannick rescued him. He revived quicker than I thought he would, but don't forget, it's an antidepressant here. He may be taking a low dose."

"The evening continues to spin on its uneven axis," Olivier said, and Max laughed. Olivier spotted a table in a back corner that had just been vacated. "Let's take that table so they don't see us," he said. Abdel explained to the server and soon they had moved out of sight.

Olivier ordered, then turned to Max. "Do you think we'll hear more from the taxi driver? What I'm asking is, how hard did you hit him?"

"Repercussions guaranteed."

Olivier's scotch neat arrived, along with Max's scotch on the rocks. He sipped. "I'm not letting you out of our sight until you are on the plane to New York," he said to her. "Abdel might be right that Vincent pursued you to find out what happened to the missing magnum."

"That occurred to me," Max said. "Not half as flattering as having a guy fall in love with you on the spot, but I have to admit that Vincent is much smarter than I gave him credit for. He's a little too curious under all that charm."

Abdel offered Olivier some of his dinner. "I'm too worked up to eat," Olivier said. "I'd go and confront Vincent, but Pascal will jump in and create a scandal."

Max said, "Olivier, let it go."

Olivier looked across the table at Abdel, who nodded in agreement. "Tomorrow we'll comb through his business," Olivier said. "If nothing else, we will drive him crazy."

"Wait until he learns he was dealing with an NYPD detective," Abdel said, grinning.

"All I did was switch glasses," Max said. "I shudder to think what could have happened if I hadn't. Thanks for the tip, Abdel." She sipped her scotch. "It was Yannick who caught me off-guard. He knew I could beat him in a fight and he didn't give me a chance."

"Thank God Abdel had the strong hunch he was heading straight to Vincent's house." Olivier glanced behind him at Vincent's table. "He's enjoying himself, which I find infuriating." Olivier put up his finger to order another drink while Abdel bit into his steak.

"Monsieur, how did your role-playing go tonight?" Abdel asked. It was obvious that Abdel wanted to get Olivier's mind off Vincent.

"It was a challenge to stay in character, and at the same time curiously liberating. I admire the way Max does it with such ease."

"It's the way you problem-solve, I think," Abdel said to Max. "You take in a lot of information from the way people respond to your false persona."

Max said, "I worry that it requires a deceptive nature to be able to change roles the way I do."

"Not when there is intention," Abdel said. "You're speaking of human chameleons, who are constantly adopting new roles as a means of getting what they want."

"I have to admit I was at a loss with Vincent. I had the feeling at one point during the evening that he was interrogating me."

"The voice message confirmed that," said Olivier. "Vincent was trying to assess how much you knew." The scotch was producing a low buzz, Olivier realized. He stared across the room at the two men talking in animated fashion, and was surprised again at his negative reaction to Pascal fraternizing with the enemy. The booze had erased the knowledge that members of the wine world were like a club. Their late-night drink and conversation could be perfectly innocent, the wine broker and the wine producer meeting up in the wee hours of the morning to share notes.

Abdel, who had the best vantage point for watching the two men, said, "Pascal is leaving." He waited a beat. "Vincent has seen us." Abdel pretended to lean over to pick something up off the floor, then said, "Let's go."

Max agreed. "Come on, let's get out of here." She took Olivier's hand, and he walked out with her, barely able to maintain his balance. Abdel was in the car, and hopped out to open the passenger door for Olivier. Max climbed into the backseat.

"I'll be back here with your car in the morning," Abdel said as he pulled into Olivier's driveway.

The porch light was on. Olivier entered his house, tripping over a shoe. Holding onto the stair railing, he pulled himself up to the second floor. Max followed, having stopped in the kitchen to pour some sparkling water in a glass for him. He accepted it gratefully. She helped him undress, hanging up his suit, and then stripped down and climbed into bed. He lay down next to her and inhaled her wonderful fragrance. He kissed the back of her neck, her hair, and put his arm around her.

"I want to marry you," he heard himself mumbling in English, as though he were not the Olivier knew, but someone else entirely.

She laughed softly. "I'll answer when you ask in French."

Chapter Twenty-three

April 6

Max awoke to the aroma of coffee brewing. Her shoulder ached, and she cursed Yannick. She held up her dress to inspect it, and, seeing a tear, decided to borrow some clothes from Olivier. A casual shirt and pants would suit her nicely. She could hear him downstairs talking to Zohra.

Max entered the kitchen, and was greeted with a smile from Olivier. "*Comment ça va?*"

"*Bien. Et toi?*" She walked over and gave him a kiss.

Zohra rushed over to the table with a bowl of *café au lait* for her, followed by piping hot croissants. "*Merci beaucoup*," Max said, taking a seat beside Olivier who leaned over and kissed her. Zohra presented her with an ice pack, which she placed on her shoulder. "Abdel is just arriving with my car," Olivier said.

Abdel entered the back door and his grandmother brought him coffee. "Can we compare notes on last night, leaving out the altercation?" Olivier asked. "We'll start with the *Cheval Blanc* dinner and what I learned, and Max, if you can bear repeating your experience of last night that would be helpful. Abdel, step in with any new information you have."

The conversation continued for an hour, with Abdel taking notes, and stopping to clarify at times. At the end, he read from his list:

- Paula Goodwin: not a suspect. Was in NY night of murder. See if she can find the person at her company who sold the lot of *Mouton-Rothschild* to Bill Casey, and its provenance. Might lead us to clues as she knows everybody.
- Bill Casey: person of interest. Sent Ellen with second bottle, then demanded it back. Announced to friends what Jordan was doing with second bottle. In NYC at time of murder. Max will interview.
- Vincent Barthes: strong suspect. At hotel night of murder. Rented a room to host clients. Use of drugs (perhaps cover-up by father). Cameras in house. Voice on answering machine. Suspicious cases of wine found in NYC. Finances a mess. No strong alibi.
- Pascal Boulin: suspect. Why hanging out with Vincent Barthes middle of night? Finances a mess. With Ellen Jordan afternoon of her murder. Ended relationship. Lowered score. Alibi can't be verified.
- Laussac: suspect. At hotel hour of murder. No firm alibi. Publicly anti-Ellen Jordan. Has money to hire killer. Great loss of revenue from Jordan's bad rating, and from committee lowering score. Vindictive.
- Yannick Martin: strong suspect. Laussac foreman. Moonlights for Vincent Barthes. Fought Max in Jordan's hotel room. Kidnapped Max. What's in it for him? Wife offers alibi. Check.
- Cazaneuve: minor suspect. Bribed? Theft of bottle?

Olivier brought up the man with the heavy accent on Vincent's answering machine. "Are we assuming now that someone other than Vincent is directing this operation?"

Abdel and Max nodded. "What do you want the police to do with Monsieur Barthes?" Abdel asked Olivier.

"Have him followed."

Abdel nodded. "And Monsieur Martin?"

"I plan to pay him a personal visit."

"Neither of them is any good to us in jail," Max said. "Vincent might lead us to the people heading this counterfeit operation."

"We suddenly have a lot of suspects," Olivier said.

"And at least one presumably in New York," said Max.

"I was introduced to a man with a thick accent at the Laussac dinner," Olivier said. "I assumed he was drunk."

Max laughed. "There could have been twenty men from the New York area, or more. Here's the Brooklyn accent: Jeat?"

"No idea about this word."

"Did you eat?" Max translated. "Did the gentleman you met ask for a quafee?" Abdel and Olivier laughed. She next spoke with the nasal accent of a Queens native, then shifted to the Bronx, and quickly turned herself into a French diva. She was hilarious and Olivier and Abdel applauded.

"I hate to be the serious one," Olivier said, "but I have come up with an agenda."

"Serious and old-fashioned," Max teased. Abdel burst into laughter when Olivier looked puzzled.

"We'll drive to get your car, Abdel, and from there you can continue on to ransack Vincent's business. Call me if there's a problem. I'll take Max with me and we'll stop by the hospital to get her shoulder checked out." He turned to Max, "Plan to stay here tonight and Zohra and I will cook up something."

Zohra, who was back at the sink, said, "I have to know what that something is before I shop. And tonight, I do the cooking."

"Let's start with crab," Olivier said. He took a few minutes to discuss the menu with her before turning back to Max and Abdel. "I'm going to interrogate Pascal and Sylvie Boulin, and Abdel will accompany me there. After, Max, you and I will go and officially call on Yannick Martin in the Médoc region."

"Vincent is covered," Max said.

Olivier stood up. "*Bon*, I need forty-five minutes."

Zohra left with her shopping bag, and Abdel offered to drive her. "Back soon," he said.

Olivier appraised the outfit Max had put together. "My shirt suits you. Now let's go upstairs and find you a belt for those pants." He went straight to his closet and handed her a belt and a pair of suspenders just in case. "But you might like to look through my wardrobe and choose something else." Max removed her shirt and was about to try on another when he pulled her to him and kissed her. "I started to ask you something in English last night and you said to ask in French."

"You must have been dreaming," she said, hoping he didn't notice the panic rising in her. "We have to meet Abdel." Whoever labeled this guy old-fashioned she thought, as she wrapped her arms around him, couldn't have been more wrong.

Abdel pulled in just as they stepped out the door, and the trio took off. Olivier's mobile rang as they arrived at his car, and he held his hand up for silence. "It's my Dutch contact," he said. He reached for a piece of paper in his pocket and scribbled as he listened. "*Parfait. Merci beaucoup*," he said, slipping the phone into his pocket.

He turned to Max and Abdel. "French customs discovered questionable cases of wine going to an importer in New York two weeks ago, shipped from Barthes Négociants. They alerted New York customs, and it's just been collected by a trucker, who is being followed."

Abdel drove down the long, winding road. "I've been studying American importers on the Internet," he said. "It seems they make the most money in their hierarchy, just as the *négociants* are accused of doing here."

"What percentage do they get here?" Max asked.

"Fifteen. The *vignerons* and the *négociants* have a necessary but uneasy relationship."

"Who sets the prices?" Max asked.

"The vineyards, always comparing prices with their competitors. The 1997 is an example often used of how they overcharged on a poorly rated vintage, which put a lot of stock in the *négociants*' and importers' warehouses that they couldn't sell. This is predicted to happen with the 2012."

"Well put," Olivier said.

Max said, "My favorite motives are coming up: greed, opportunism, and disloyalty."

"All will most certainly come into play with this case."

"Got a name at the importer's?"

"Anson Richards."

"My first two appointments when I get to New York will be with the collector Bill Casey and Richards."

"I'll go to the wine tasting at Bill Casey's and follow up with Paula Goodwin. I'm fascinated by how the auction house works."

Max smiled. "I almost forgot. I learned just before going out with Vincent that I'll be in charge of our investigation in New York. This is a first."

"You deserve it," Olivier said, as they entered his car. At the Hôpital Pellegrin in the heart of the city Max was treated for a sprained shoulder. She moved quickly to her room when Olivier deposited her at the hotel. Now that she had convinced Olivier that she was okay, she began to quiver inside. The past twelve hours had become a reality.

Chapter Twenty-four

April 6

Sylvie and Pascal Boulin lived in a sixteenth-century stone house behind their shop in Saint-Émilion. The interior of the house was a mixture of old and new, with abstract paintings hung alongside ancient portraits. Olivier admired the old beams and wooden floors, burnished by sunlight shining through multi-paned windows. Sylvie led Olivier into the living room with a wall of books on either side of a stone fireplace, and comfortable sofas and chairs casually arranged around it.

Pascal, looking tired, shook hands with Olivier and Abdel. "I realize you were trying to help me when my shop was robbed, Commissaire," he said. "Sorry for being rude." Olivier and Abdel exchanged a hopeful glance. "Sylvie," Pascal said, "I need to meet with these men alone for a few minutes. Please excuse us."

Sylvie glanced at her husband before speaking. "No, I won't leave. I know, Pascal, that you're in trouble." Transferring her attention to Olivier, she said, "I'm not an idiot. Pascal and I argued about Ellen in the bistro, and it seems we've been arguing ever since. She held too many strings. I suspected the affair."

"Sylvie..." Pascal pleaded.

Olivier didn't have time for the couple to resolve a marital issue now. He said, "Witnesses tell us that you and Pascal met at the local bistro for a short time between 4:30 and 5:00. Where did you go after that?"

The silence in the room grew leaden. "To purchase some macaroons, and to the Hôtellerie Renaissance." She looked at Pascal, "The proprietor of the hotel, Madame Cassin...don't forget, Pascal, we are old friends... told me when I bumped into her on the street that you had spent much of the afternoon in Madame Jordan's room. I looked up at the clock in the hotel lobby and noticed it was 5:45." She looked to Olivier for encouragement, and seeing that she had his full attention, continued, "I knocked on Madame Jordan's door. I knew she was in there. When she refused to answer, I told her to go to hell and that if she gave us a lower score I would make her sorry."

Olivier interjected, "You said all this through the door? " When Sylvie nodded yes, he said, "Did she respond?"

"No. Not one word. I could feel her behind that door, guilty as accused." Would Sylvie have had the nerve to bring a poisoned cheese to her rival, Olivier wondered, as he considered Abdel's explanation about a woman choosing a specific target when poisoning someone.

"If you're thinking Sylvie might have killed Ellen," said Pascal, "think again. She is incapable."

Sylvie stared at Pascal. "I felt like killing her, Pascal," she said, and then began to sniffle. "At the moment I was knocking on her door I wanted Ellen Jordan dead." Pascal reached for her hand, but she withdrew it.

That accounts for the emotional turmoil that Max witnessed in the bistro, Olivier thought. "Did you go to the fromagerie that week?" he asked Sylvie.

"Of course. What woman doesn't go to the cheese shop daily?"

"Do you recall which cheeses you purchased?"

"Not all. There was brie... I buy it by the round...and there was a goat cheese that I can't remember the name of. I bought a *Beaufort* for making *raclette,* and a *Mont d'Or*, Pascal's favorite. Oh, yes, I purchased a blue. It was a *bleu des Causses*, my favorite."

Olivier hoped that his sigh of relief was only visible to Abdel. Pascal chose the brief lull to blurt out, "You know, I had told

Ellen that I couldn't continue our affair when I got back to my office at the vineyard."

"You did?" Sylvie asked her husband in a timorous voice. Pascal reached for her hand again and this time she didn't pull away.

Olivier said, "She lowered your score by quite a few points according to her assistant."

"Our wine has only gotten better," Sylvie said. "Proof of that is the Saint-Émilion appellation committee elevated our status this year."

Olivier wondered if the appellation committee wasn't too political a group to be fair about anything. On the other hand, it was possible that Pascal's score was a vindictive act on Ellen's part. "Madame Jordan's tasting book has gone missing. Someone about your size, Pascal, broke into Ellen Jordan's room wearing a mask, and happened to run into her assistant. They fought."

Olivier watched Pascal's face go from glumness to surprise. "Who won?" he asked. Olivier had already made note that Pascal was wearing a tee-shirt, and there was no sign of a bruise on his neck, or any other indication that he had been in a fight.

"The intruder escaped with the tasting book, but I wouldn't say he was the victor."

"Which means my score will be leaked to the press."

"It makes sense that you would want the scores suppressed forever."

"It's true that if I had known she was going to do that, I might have gone to her room to steal the tasting book, but as I didn't know, there was no point. Much more important than her book is the wine that was stolen from me."

Abdel said, opening his notebook. "The wine was insured for 100,000 euros. Your gambling debt is close to 80,000."

"You're really going to charge me with stealing my own wine?" Now Pascal was up and pacing.

Olivier interjected, "Pascal, I have reserved any judgment until now about you. But look at it from my perspective: You may have been the last person to see Ellen Jordan alive, she lowered your score after you left her room, and someone of approximately your stature broke into Jordan's room and stole her tasting book after she was taken to the hospital. Then you have your wine stolen, which almost equals the amount of your gambling debt."

Pascal glanced nervously over at his wife. "Sure, sure, my friends and I discussed stealing my wine at the local bar," Pascal said, brushing his hair out of his face. "But by the time I got home, the plan was forgotten."

"But your vintage wine was gone the next day?"

"Yes. Cases that were already paid for and being shipped to San Francisco."

Now fully back in her husband's court, Sylvie explained, "Pascal and his pals were partying in the local bar the night the wine was stolen. I heard them enter the shop and got up to see what was going on. Pascal and I fought and everybody left. The cases of wine were there. The next morning Pascal found them gone."

Olivier thought the story so absurd that the couple might be telling the truth. If that were the case, perhaps someone was trying to divert the police's attention to Pascal. Pascal asked Abdel to show him the bank figures, and Olivier got up to walk around. "Go have a look at my garden," Sylvie said, and he gave her a grateful smile. As he was leaving the room, he overheard Abdel asking Pascal if someone was attempting to collect a debt, and Pascal protesting.

The roses were starting to bud out in the garden. Olivier inhaled deeply and sat on a bench, trying to make sense of recent events. Max was right. Pascal had a strong motive to kill Ellen if she threatened to go to Sylvie or to lower his score. It would have been easy for him to find aconite growing in the fields, bring her a poisoned cheese, share a little wine with her and leave, knowing that she would be dead within the hour. The basic question then, was: Was Pascal capable of killing someone? Or, would he and Sylvie have planned Ellen's death together? He had been so sure of that answer before he arrived today, but not now. He went back to the salon, where Pascal had opened a second beer.

"What do I do about my wine?" Pascal asked him.

Olivier wanted to scream that what he should be caring about was his mistress' murder, not his wine. Convinced that Pascal's break-in had nothing to do with Opération Merlot, he said, "Abdel has filed a report, but if you lose your wine for good, it might teach you a lesson."

He couldn't resist bringing up seeing him in the bistro. "Vincent Barthes is in a great deal of trouble. I was surprised to see you with him at the bistro."

"What kind of trouble?"

"You'll know soon enough. I'd suggest you stay away from him."

"It seems as if everyone in Bordeaux is under suspicion for one thing or another," Pascal said.

Olivier was at the door. "Neither of you is to leave the area. Is that understood?" Looking contrite, the couple nodded.

"Pascal is at the top of Max's list of suspects," Olivier said to Abdel as they strolled up to his car.

"And why not?" Abdel asked. "We haven't ruled out a *crime passionnel*."

"True, but the murder, we must assume, was premeditated because the cheese had to be prepared."

Abdel said, "In which case, Monsieur Boulin knows how to do that. He's a farmer and a chemist by trade."

"I maintain for now that he doesn't have the character of a killer. I know him, Abdel."

"We were taught at school that knowing a suspect is often a deterrent when solving a case."

Olivier felt annoyed, but knew it was because Abdel could be right. He reminded himself that part of his reliance on Abdel had to do with his objective analyses. Maybe it was the moment to ask Abdel the question that had been haunting him. "Do you agree with Max that no one ever calls me on my shit?"

Abdel looked like he wanted to laugh, and Olivier wished he hadn't brought it up.

"Honest answer? Yes. On second thought, maybe my grandmother."

"Does anyone call you on yours?"

Abdel was all teeth when he laughed. "*Oui, Monsieur*. You!"

"Oh."

"We need to get back to Max," Abdel said. "She has probably solved Madame Jordan's murder while we've been interviewing the Boulins. She's like a pig digging for truffles. They never give up."

"Don't say that to her!" Olivier said. When he stopped in front of the hotel, Max walked with long strides toward them, wheeling her suitcase behind her, and carrying an oversized handbag. She was back in uniform—cowboy boots, white starched blouse, and skinny, black jeans. "Pop the trunk?" she said.

Olivier and Abdel exchanged amused glances before Abdel hopped out to give her a hand. Max chatted in French, "I'm glad to be out of there," she said. "The concierge is also happy to see me go." She lifted her suitcase into the trunk of Olivier's car just as Abdel was reaching for it. He closed the trunk and stood still, looking at Max. "What?" she asked.

"Nothing."

"Are you going to ask me not to break his heart?"

"If you do, you'll have to deal with my grandmother."

"Give him a word of warning while you're at it!"

"I'll tell him he'll have to deal with your father." They high-fived.

"What was that about?" Olivier asked when she climbed into the car.

"A secret pact."

"That sounds ominous." He drove off. "You feel prepared for New York?"

"I should have the case sewn up by the time you get there." Her statement was so close to Abdel's that it gave him pause. "You know I'm joking," she said when he didn't laugh.

Chapter Twenty-five

April 6

"How does an investigator get to drive an Audi-A7?" Max asked Olivier as they headed out to the Laussac's. "It's a snooty car where I come from."

"I drive it because it's fuel-efficient, has an excellent crash record, and is fast."

"Cars tend to match their owners, don't you think? You wear custom-made suits, carry a Hermès briefcase, listen to classical music, and drive a fancy car, all of which contribute to your prosperous bachelor status."

"What type are you, then?"

She laughed. "I drive a ten-year-old, beat-up Toyota named Lucy."

"That could be reverse snobbism, you know. As for your jeans-and-cowboy boots image, to me it says 'If you get too close, I'll kick.' Your tattoo says the same thing, but the vintage jacket says, I am also a woman who can be taken to the opera."

"Not bad. Once I overheard you telling Abdel that I'm the type of women who still needs her father's approval."

"I'm not accountable for anything said during the time you claimed not to know French. But we all seek our parents' approval," Olivier said. "It's important to come to a place of not needing it."

"For me it's about trying to fill my brother's shoes as well as my own. He would have made a star detective."

"He was twelve. If you had that impression by then, he was surely trying to please his father. What did he like to do?"

"He was a sports nut. And he loved music. He was taking guitar lessons when he died."

"That's what I mean. You don't know how he would have turned out."

"My mom might secretly agree with you."

"How's she doing with her friend's death?"

"I'm not sure. When I spoke with her she was deeply sad, but also a little upset with Ellen for her bullheadedness."

Olivier turned down a beautiful tree-lined road. "We're approaching the de Cheverny estate that was originally owned by Chantal's family. This is where they live. Though Laussac is part-owner of a vineyard in Saint-Émilion, it's a hobby for him."

"And why will you say you're calling on him?"

"I want to see if he's willing to discuss his foreman."

"I thought Yannick was just a thug until my ride with him last night. He has some power over Laussac. It's hard not to stereotype Laussac as the dapper Frenchman," said Max.

"He's rich, smart, and behind the charm is an aggressive bulldog," Olivier said turning into the driveway. "He also drives an Audi."

Max chuckled. She gazed at the castle they were pulling up to. "What do these people do all year? Have parties and invite each other?"

"Most of the famous vineyards are owned by large corporations. Insurance companies and the like. Chantal Cheverny Laussac is an anomaly. It's rare these these days to find a family owning and running a vineyard."

"If my parents and I decided to move here tomorrow, we might be able to afford the maid's cottage."

"You'd be happy there drinking *vin ordinaire*."

◇◇◇

A majestic fountain separated François Laussac's office—a small, beautifully designed outbuilding—from the *château*. He sat behind his desk, dressed like a gentleman farmer in a tweed jacket and corduroy trousers. On the wall was an original painting by Jean-François Millet. He said to Max, "I'm surprised you're still in Bordeaux."

Max answered in French. "I'm waiting to accompany Madame Jordan's body to New York. I decided while here to continue my education in wine, as Madame Jordan would have wished me to do."

"I assume you had an immersion class in French since I saw you," he said sarcastically. Laussac turned to Olivier, "Let's get on with your busines."

Olivier got to the point. "Someone attacked Mademoiselle Maguire in Madame Jordan's room and I suspect your foreman. I wanted you to know I'm going straight there when I leave here." A rapid blinking of the eyes was the only giveaway that Laussac was nervous.

"What would he have been doing in her hotel room?" Laussac asked.

"Planting a poisonous cheese? Taking Madame Jordan's wine tasting book? Stealing a magnum of 1945 *Mouton-Rothschild?*"

"I have my own, thank you. An authentic one. And I can't think that he has the intelligence to do all you're suggesting."

"About the magnum. A counterfeit ring is operating out of Bordeaux. I'm not naming names yet."

"Have you bothered to check in with your friend Pascal? I hear he's been reckless with cash." When Olivier refused to comment, he said, "Bordeaux is a billion-euro business, and our competition is much greater than previous years. We don't need a counterfeit scandal on top of a suspicious death."

"I'm afraid the two are interlinked."

The magnitude of the crimes seemed to register finally. "You have suspects?"

Olivier nodded. "Of course. I thought you'd be interested to know that Madame Jordan's tasting book went missing from her room."

François' eyebrows shot up. "And?"

"I've come up with two people who might want that book badly enough to steal it, or have someone steal if for them. You, and Pascal Boulin."

François spluttered, and he stared into Olivier's eyes, as much an indicator of lying as darting eyes. "Pascal stands to benefit the most. Did you know that he and Madame Jordan were having an affair?"

"What I find more interesting is your obsession with Pascal."

Chantal entered, looking regal, even in slacks and a crisp blouse. "*Chéri*," she said to her husband, "There is a crisis. I went to our private cellar to take out some wines for my mother's birthday and I noticed some cases in the corner that weren't there the last time I checked. Cases of Pascal Boulin's vintage wine, his Terre Brulée, are there."

"*Pas possible*!" François said, jumping up. "*Mon Dieu*! What next?"

"Let's have a look, shall we?" said Olivier.

The four of them tromped to the private cellar, which was like a tomb, Max thought. "Who was here last?" Olivier asked. "And who has a key?"

"Chantal and I do, of course," François said.

"And Yannick Martin?" Olivier asked.

François' glanced over at his wife who said, "I was told that he no longer has access."

"What do you mean?" François asked his wife.

"I don't know why, but you give in to him," Chantal said. "What did you do with his key?"

"It's upstairs in the kitchen."

"No, it isn't."

"Pascal Boulin could have brought his wine here, knowing it would be safe. He came a few months ago with a group of winemakers and Yannick gave them a tour of the cellar."

"*Arrête*!" Chantal cried. "François, you prattle on as though you know what you're talking about." She turned to Olivier and said, "I told him to fire Yannick six months ago. He could have stolen Monsieur Boulin's wine and been hiding it among my private collection when I caught him a few days ago. He may also have stolen my wine."

François had grown strangely meek. "I had nothing to do with this," he declared.

"If you know anything that will help us, François," Olivier said, "now is the time." They waited for a moment while François stood with a stubborn look on his face.

Chantal broke the silence. "I'll call Pascal and tell him it's here. In the meantime, you will all stay for lunch."

"Don't call Pascal," Olivier said to Chantal while following her into a small dining room that overlooked exquisite gardens. "I'll call my assistant to come for it. In the meantime, I will need records of every case of wine that has left this property over the past six months, whether legally or stolen."

"That could take months!" François sputtered.

The fragrance of the fresh lilacs bursting out of a vase in the corner was intoxicating. The round table was set with ancient earthenware and horn-handled cutlery. A maid arrived with a chilled bottle of Grand *Cru Classé Domaine de Chevalier*, and Max watched as Olivier took a moment to sniff the cork. "A wonderful combination of sauvignon blanc and semillon grapes," he said appreciatively.

A different server entered with pan-fried *chipirons*, or calamari. Talk had drifted away from the tense issue of stolen wines. Olivier and Chantal discussed the blooming season. The maid arrived again with plates of duck breast served with spring potatoes, accompanied by a 1989 *Laussac* red wine. A salad followed, and the foursome returned to the topic of collectors. Chantal lamented that collectors were driving the thefts.

"Do you have a keen interest in wine?" she asked Max.

"I'm no *amateur de vin*," she said, remembering that *amateur* in French meant professional. "But yes, I'm interested."

"When I saw you the other night, you seemed familiar," Chantal said, gazing at her guest.

Before Max had a chance to respond, Olivier interjected, "She's the granddaughter of Madame Isabelle de Laval. Max resembles her."

"Isabelle de Laval? *Vraiement*?"

François said, "Your grandmother is the mother-in-law of Ministre Philippe Douvier?"

Max nodded. François stared at her in disbelief. "And your mother?" Chantal asked. "Where is she?"

"Juliette? She was disowned by her family for marrying my father."

"Good for her!" Chantal said, tossing a smile her husband's way. The maid entered with a beautiful plate of cheeses, but Olivier said they had to move on. They shook hands with François and Chantal, and went quickly to Olivier's car.

"That was close," Olivier said. "You nearly lost your cover. She may have seen your photograph in the newspaper when you were lauded for your work in Champagne."

He didn't say it, but Max knew he would feel relieved when she was out of France. She had mixed feelings about leaving, for it felt as though they were making progress. "What do you think about Laussac pointing the finger at Pascal? Today at their house I had some serious doubts about his alibis."

"This is when my father would say that when one suspect becomes too obvious, and all fingers are pointing at him, then it's time to look elsewhere."

"Hmm. Just when I had arrived at the opposite opinion," Olivier said.

Chapter Twenty-six

April 6

Loud, argumentative voices came from within Yannick's small, wooden-framed cottage behind the Laussac château. Olivier and Max walked up to the front door and when the arguing didn't cease, peered in a window. A woman was angrily pointing at a television set. The sound was off, and the screen displayed a glamorous photograph of Ellen Jordan, taken at least a decade earlier.

"What'd I tell you!" the woman screamed. "You're going to get blamed for everything!"

"Go to hell!" Yannick said. "You're the one who wants, wants, wants! There's never going to be enough money for you!"

"I want out, that's what I want!" As the woman swore and started toward him, Olivier rapped loudly on the door.

"Answer that!" Yannick ordered his wife.

"What's my role here?" Max asked Olivier.

"Follow my lead. And please refrain from finishing your ongoing wrestling match with this man."

"My shoulder won't allow it."

A woman with dyed auburn hair opened the door and introduced herself as Corinne. Olivier had seen untidy houses, but never one in a shambles like this one. Clothes were piled up on the chairs, and beer cans were strewn everywhere. The salon reeked of cigarette smoke. Yannick remained in the same pugilistic stance in the middle of the room, eyes narrowed, switching his hostile gaze from Max to Olivier.

"This woman claims you kidnapped her last night and were planning to murder her," Olivier said.

Yannick fixed his gaze on her. "She was drunk. I had orders from Monsieur Barthes to take her to the hotel and that's what I was doing."

"All the same, if she decides to press charges, I'll have to take you in and let the court decide."

The woman had turned the television down and sat sipping a beer. Yannick lit a Gauloise and acrid smoke filled the room. "This better not be true," she said to Yannick.

Olivier had thought a lot about Yannick, noting that he worked for two men, both under suspicion. He was surely the intruder in Ellen Jordan's room, then he turned up the next night at Vincent's business to load up his truck, and only last night was hauling Max to god knew where.

"I understand you no longer have access to the Laussac's private cellar," Olivier said to Yannick.

He shrugged. "Some of their best wine was stolen. All the employees were told to stay out at first, but Monsieur Laussac gave my key back to me."

"Why?"

"I told him I'd quit if he didn't." It crossed Olivier's mind that what he was holding over Laussac was a certain wine tasting book, which he had been paid to steal from Ellen Jordan's room. And who knew what else?

"Cases of Monsieur Boulin's pilfered wine were just discovered in the private cellar," Olivier said.

"He could have stolen his own wine. I've heard of it."

"Oh, he did," Olivier lied. "We just don't know how he got it to the Laussac cellar. Did Pascal ask you to hide it?"

Yannick was thrown off his game. He shook his head, unsure. "Just so you know, Monsieur Laussac has a key to his wife's cellar. He has it in for Monsieur Boulin."

He was accusing his own boss? Olivier wondered. "Monsieur Laussac would hardly be stealing the Boulin wine."

"He would if he wanted to make him look like an idiot. If you ask me, he succeeded."

Olivier didn't buy it. By now, Max and Corinne were talking in the kitchen in French. He noticed that Max had accepted a beer. "I want to have a look around," he said.

"*Here?*" Corinne called from the kitchen. "What're you looking for?"

"Ellen Jordan's wine tasting notebook." Olivier moved at a painstakingly slow pace, peering into the small bedroom that contained only a double bed with a sagging mattress and a bureau, and then looking around the kitchen. Max sat at the kitchen table looking as though she belonged. He wandered back to the living room and scanned the bookcase. There was a romance series in paperback, an old dictionary, and a few of Georges Simenon's books.

"I see you are a fan of Commissaire Maigret. A favorite of mine," Olivier said.

"She's the reader," Yannick said, dipping his head in the direction of the kitchen.

Max and Corinne entered the living room, Max's face was flushed. Corrine whispered something in broken English which Olivier didn't understand and both women laughed.

Time to drop the bait, Olivier decided. "There's a big reward out for that notebook," Olivier said.

Corinne put her beer down. "How much?"

"One thousand." She shifted her eyes to Yannick.

"Who's offering that?"

"The police."

"We'll ask around," Corinne said.

"We're about to arrest Vincent Barthes in connection with a counterfeiting scheme, and maybe even to Madame Jordan's murder. He's agreed to tell us everything he knows."

Yannick stalked off to the kitchen and returned with a beer, and popped it open. Finally he's rattled, thought Olivier.

"I don't get it why Monsieur Barthes would do anything to go to jail for," Corinne said. "He has it all—looks, money..."

"It's like Simenon's mysteries that you and I like so much," Olivier said. "There's always a psychological component when people choose to commit a crime, and once that's uncovered, it becomes easier to find the criminal." He turned to Max, "Have you decided if you want to press charges?"

"Corinne talked me out of it," she replied in French. Corinne looked pleased.

"You still need to go into headquarters," he said to Yannick, "and allow my assistant to take fingerprints."

"Will Monsieur Barthes be there?" Yannick asked.

"We have him under guard at his house."

"He owes me money."

"We can make sure you get that. *Au revoir.*"

Max said good-bye to Corinne, who said she'd like to come to New York one day.

"How'd you get her to warm up?" Olivier asked Max in the car.

"You saw. Drinking beer. Talking about men and about life disappointments. She's a lonely, frustrated woman. And a little frightened, I think."

"Yannick feels things closing in."

"Saying that Vincent is ready to talk was a good move," Max said. "That got to Yannick."

"He knows who killed Ellen Jordan, I'm sure of that."

"Did you see the look I got when you told him I might press charges?"

"Vincent, Yannick, François...you've made some enemies here, some of them powerful."

As they passed the Laussac *château*, an SUV swerved dramatically onto the lawn and stopped. A large, muscular man emerged from the vehicle and made a dash to the front door. François Laussac suddenly appeared at the threshold and within seconds was poking a finger into the man's chest.

"It's Pascal!" Olivier said. He swung his car into the driveway and screeched to a halt. They both jumped out.

Pascal was pushing back at François and shouting, "You sent your foreman to steal my wine and I'm going to get it back! *Putain*!"

François, Olivier knew, would have to have the last word, and he was right. A few feet from the two men, he could see that the veins stood out in François' face as he bellowed, "I saw you enter Ellen Jordan's hotel room. *J'accuse!* You murdered your mistress!"

Pascal bellowed another obscenity, and drawing back his fist, swung and hit François hard, knocking him down. Olivier grabbed Pascal's arm. "*Arrête!* You're under arrest. Get the handcuffs," he said to Max, and she loped off to the car.

A drunken Pascal turned to Olivier, "I may as well admit the murder and be done with it. But not until I find who stole my wine!" He pushed past the magistrate, jumped in his SUV, and squealed off. Olivier pulled out his mobile and called Abdel who assured Olivier that he was a few kilometers away and would set up a roadblock.

François Laussac was nearly hysterical. He stared at Olivier out of his swollen eye. "I'm calling Philippe Douvier!"

Olivier decided that Douvier might have to hire another secretary to handle the complaints as he and Max ran to his car. Just as he pulled out onto the road, a truck passed him. Yannick! Olivier watched in horror as Yannick rammed his truck into Pascal's SUV, which spun out into a field.

"Yannick has pulled Pascal from his car!" Max cried. Olivier stopped, and saw the two men grappling on the ground. Max leapt out of the car and started running toward the fighters. Olivier called to her and when she turned, Yannick was upon her. She transformed into a whirling dervish, fists flying. Yannick had the upper hand because she was trying to protect her shoulder. He tripped her, and she fell to her knees. He picked up a handful of dirt and threw it at her face. Pascal jumped Yannick and knocked him to the ground. Olivier dove in, and attempted to pull Pascal off Yannick, but was pushed away. Abdel rushed up, gun in hand and issued an order for them to stop, firing a warning shot in the air. The brawl was over.

"Handcuff Yannick and take him with you," Olivier said. "Pascal, you are under arrest for assault-and-battery and drunk driving." Olivier went over to Max, who held her hands over her eyes. He reached into his pocket and brought out a handkerchief and handed it to her. While she dabbed at her eyes, he walked alongside Pascal to the car, and ordered him to get into the backseat. Abdel had Yannick contained, and was directing him to his car.

Pascal passed out before they had driven a kilometer. Olivier pulled into the parking lot of a café. "I'll get some water," he said to Max, and was back in a minute and dabbing her eyes with the cold water. "You simply can't resist a fight, can you? It wasn't necessary."

"Yannick had a knife."

"How do you know?"

She held up a small utility knife. "I saw it glint in the light when he took it from his pocket. When Pascal jumped him, he dropped it." She was, as usual, a step ahead.

"More scandal," Olivier said. "François Laussac will bring in Douvier when he presses charges against Pascal. I think you're leaving France just in time. I wonder if I should go or stay."

"To look on the bright side," Max said, "Pascal's wine has been found, and two suspects are about to be locked up."

"But nothing is solved," Olivier said. "The only reason anyone is arrested is because those two got in a fight. There's no proof of anything."

"My father would say the muddier the water the closer we are to the answer." Olivier wondered if her dad listened to classical music. "I'll wager another bet that the tasting book will show up now that you've offered money," Max said.

"How much?"

"Five euros."

"Forget it. I'll be so keen on winning the bet that I'll let the murder investigation go." She laughed. They drove along in silence for a few minutes, with Pascal snoring in the backseat. Olivier said, "I shouldn't have stopped you mid-motion. I'm sorry. But you must be more careful that the Jiu-Jitsu doesn't make you too confident."

"It was stupid of me to go near them with a bad shoulder. You know, though, I could teach you a few moves."

"I don't need to fight," he said. "I'm a magistrate, not a cop."

Pascal spoke from the backseat, "You should try it, Olivier. Do you know how good it felt to clobber Laussac?"

Olivier peered in the rearview mirror at Pascal's swollen face. "But not so good to be clobbered by Yannick, I take it?"

Chapter Twenty-seven

April 6

Photographers and reporters swarmed around the modern courthouse that resembled a *Star Wars* set as Yannick and Abdel entered. Max scanned the crowd as Olivier drove around to the rear of the building where they could enter unnoticed. She followed him into his office. Floor-to-ceiling bookshelves. A couple of antique Japanese framed prints. A set of brass justice scales resting on top of an antique desk. Several *paysanne* oil paintings hung along the wall behind it.

"These landscapes are wonderful," she said. "Who's the artist?"

He smiled. "*Merci.*"

"*You?*

"I almost went to art school instead of taking the justice route."

"What changed your mind?"

"Wanting to make a difference. Now I believe that art has a greater influence on the human psyche than bringing people to justice. I'm not including my feeble attempts at painting. I'm speaking of art that transports, the way music does."

"You sound like my mother. She dragged my brother and me to every museum in New York. Well, most of them."

He smiled. "Do you have a favorite painter?"

"I have an eclectic list. Basquiat, and an even more contemporary artist in New York, Wayne Ensrud. But I also love the ancient Caravaggios at the Frick Museum on Fifth Avenue. "

Abdel entered, notebook in hand. "Sounds like Martin won't be locked up long."

"Why?"

"His lawyer is Maître Georges Demarchelier!"

Olivier said, "Who's paying him?"

"I'd place a bet it's François Laussac."

Max said, "Is it possible that Laussac paid Yannick to murder Ellen Jordan? Maybe Vincent and the counterfeiting aren't connected to Ellen Jordan's murder."

"Motive for Laussac?" Olivier asked.

Max shrugged. "I once handled a case where a man murdered his wife for putting a knife in the wrong drawer. Laussac? Maybe he is connected to the counterfeiting operation. Think about it. His vineyard is going down. It's easy to take wine from his wife's cellar. He steals Pascal's wine, or has Yannick steal it and bring it to him. He could be sending cheap wine to America in vintage bottles."

"But no connection to Vincent, right?"

"No idea."

"I have no doubt that Laussac either has, or desperately wants, that wine tasting book," Olivier said. "Both to broadcast his higher score, and to try to ruin Pascal. He could be vindictive enough to have Yannick steal Pascal's wine and hide it."

Abdel said, "I have the names of everyone who was at the local bar the night Monsieur Boulin's warehouse was broken into." He handed a sheaf of paper to his boss. Olivier skimmed down the list of twenty names, and gave it to Max. She stopped reading when her eyes alighted on Yannick's name, and looked up at Abdel who nodded as if to confirm that Yannick must have overheard Pascal and friends planning their robbery.

Abdel continued, glancing down at his notebook, "We've had a report from the cheese shop. The young assistant there recalled Pascal Boulin coming to purchase cheeses the day he had the rendezvous with Madame Jordan, the same that were in her refrigerator."

"Was the blue that contained the poison among them?"

"No." He continued, "Madame Boulin was correct about the cheeses she purchased. The one she forgot was *Vacherin*."

"That's the camembert that's made in Switzerland and France," Olivier said. "It's best to eat it in the spring when the cows have better quality pasturage."

"So cheeses have *terroir,* too," Max said, a note of sarcasm in her voice.

"Absolutely. You can cut the rind off this cheese and eat it with a spoon."

Abdel exchanged a smile with Max over Olivier's food description, then read from his notes. "Chantal Laussac purchased cheese four times last week, and the concierge from Hôtellerie Renaissance, Monsieur Cazaneuve, stops daily for cheese at lunchtime. I've already mentioned Pascal Boulin. Someone bought *un livre de bleu* two days before the Laussac event, but the clerk doesn't recall which brand. A young woman purchased it, a secretary who had it delivered to a trader's business. She's looking for the receipt."

Olivier's eyebrows shot up, and Abdel said, "I had the same thought. I'll go straight to Monsieur Barthes' wine factory and interview the secretary."

Sylvie tapped on the door and stuck her head in. "Olivier, what are we to do?"

"Pascal was booked on assault-and-battery and drunken driving," Olivier said.

"May I take him home with me? The doctor said his nose is broken."

"Not yet."

"I don't think I can take much more," she said, looking limp as a wilted weed.

"You can see him. I'll take you there." Max and Abdel went along to the interrogation room, where Pascal sat, looking miserable. The left side of his face was badly swollen, and he wore a bandage over his nose.

Pascal jumped up, immediately on the defensive. "François was telling everyone that I killed Ellen. He may have sent his foreman to steal my wine. This man has tried to make my life hell from the time I started with my winemaking twenty years ago. He's doubly furious that my wine was given a higher rating by our appellation committee and his was knocked out of the competition."

"Why did you go to Laussac's? I told them I would call you."

"Laussac called me and told me to come for my wine and on the phone accused me of hiding it in his cellar."

Max wondered if all rural communities operated in this manner. She had started to see Pascal as a guileless farm boy who had made a big splash in the wine world, but was completely lacking in sophistication. He could have been a farmer in the Midwest, which made her understand why Ellen had been attracted to him.

"Everything is stacking up to make me look guilty of theft and murder," Pascal said.

Sylvie, who had remained quiet, said, "Pascal, I know you are innocent, but the theft happened because you were talking about it in public. You also decided to have an affair with a public personality and were with her on the day she died. I hope you will stop and take the time to mourn her, and the relationship, otherwise we will never have another happy day."

Pascal began to sob, and silence reigned for a few moments. Sylvie put her arm around him, and Pascal looked up at Olivier. "Continue."

"Did Madame Jordan ever talk about Vincent Barthes?"

"She was keen on matching Mademoiselle Maguire with someone, and I thought perhaps it was Vincent, but I'm not sure." Max didn't dare look at Olivier, but instead tried to look surprised.

"You'll be staying in jail for a couple of days, Pascal," Olivier said.

Sylvie protested, but Pascal put up his hand to stop her. "I deserve this," he said. He looked at Olivier, "I feel you growing unsure of me, Olivier. I feel like I'm losing a friend."

Olivier left the room.

"Any update on the missing magnum?" Max asked Abdel.

"Not really. Vincent Barthes could easily have bribed the concierge. Pascal says no, but he probably did know about the hidden bottle of wine. He would have had a hard time stealing it, though."

"What about the 100 euros we found in the maid Martine's possession?"

"We don't have that story yet," Abdel said.

"What a morass," Olivier said. "What about the concierge? He has access to everything at the hotel."

Max said, "I thought Madame Cassin was a little intimidated by him. And the maids are terrified of him." She looked over at Abdel. "Did you check to see if Paula Goodwin called Ellen?"

"A call was registered from her hotel room in Paris. It has also been confirmed that she was in Paris at a wine dinner on the eve of Madame Jordan's death."

The trio was stumped. Olivier said, "Search Monsieur Cazaneuve's apartment, Abdel. I'll issue a warrant."

"*Oui,* Monsieur."

Olivier remained pensive, "Pascal said Ellen was expecting someone after he left."

Max said, "I don't think she had a plan to invite anyone by when I left and she simply wouldn't have opened her door to most callers. That rules out Yannick, the concierge, and Laussac. If Pascal returned, she would have opened the door. She might have been receptive to Vincent if he called ahead."

"There is someone else," Olivier said. "But who?"

"I wish Ellen would send us a sign," Max said.

Olivier rolled his eyes.

A secretary ran up to Olivier and said, "A Monsieur Seurat called and is waiting for you in the tavern across the street from here. He said he must see you to give you something." Max couldn't keep from grinning.

◇◇◇

They rushed to the bar where the dead maid's husband was waiting. The television, perched high on a shelf in the dimly lit bar, was on mute. A couple of workers were at the end of the bar sipping Pernod. Alain Seurat, who was holding a glass of the *cuvée du patron*, motioned to them. Olivier ordered a glass of the same, then turned to Max and she nodded, while Abdel abstained as usual.

"What about my wife?" Alain asked, slurring his words. Max felt sorry for the farmworker who, until two days ago, eked out a living with no idea of the tragedy about to befall him.

"I'm terribly sorry to tell you that the blue cheese that she ate contained poison," Olivier said.

Alain swigged down the liquid in his glass. "I remembered something, Monsieur Chaumont. Martine said she overheard Monsieur François Laussac telling a hotel guest in the lobby that he planned to get even with Madame Jordan for refusing to appear at his dinner one way or the other." Olivier wondered if they had all run to the bar to hear what they already knew. "My wife was starting to tell me about the extra money she made when she became suddenly ill." Great, thought Olivier. Alain held something up. "My wife found this under Ellen Jordan's bed."

Alain handed Olivier a key ring with three keys attached to it, and four charms: a miniature bottle of Bordeaux in 24-carat gold, a martini glass, a wineglass, and a circular disc with the word *bientôt* on one side and "soon" on the other. Olivier took the set and fingered the charms. "Where did you find it?" Olivier asked.

"In my wife's jewelry case. I'm sure she was going to take it to the manager." It confirmed what Olivier had already concluded, that poor Martine was a kleptomaniac.

"Do you think this belonged to Ellen Jordan?" Olivier asked Max, handing the key ring to her.

"I never saw it."

The bartender turned up the volume on the television when François Laussac, dressed impeccably in a navy suit and tie, began speaking from a podium. "*We at the Syndicat des Grands Vins de Bordeaux deeply regret the death of a woman who was one of this century's greatest contributors to the international wine community, Ellen Jordan. Her sudden death is being investigated by the French police, as is the death of a hotel maid, Martine Seurat.*"

The questions from the press overlapped, but finally one could be heard over the din. "Did she taste and score any of the 2011 wines?"

How crass, Olivier thought. He waited with the others for the answer. Lausac paused, as if deciding how to answer. "She did."

"Any idea if she raised your score from the 2010?"

"I understand that is the case," he replied humbly. Olivier wished he could jump through the television screen and grab him by the neck.

"And the maid," someone asked. "Her name?"

Laussac looked down at his notes. "Martine Seurat."

"My wife is now famous," Alain whispered, obviously in awe that Martine's name was mentioned on television. Olivier shook hands with Alain, and marched out of the bar. Max and Abdel had to quick-step to catch up.

"Douvier must have given Laussac permission to make such an announcement," Olivier said.

"Speaking of which," Abdel said, "Monsieur Douvier called me." Olivier and Max turned to stare at him. "He said he knew you were going to be in New York for a few days, Monsieur, and told me to call him anytime I needed help,"

"He's trying to promote his good works around immigration."

"I don't know of anyone he's helped," Abdel said. "That must be why he said he'd like me to come into Paris when I have a break so that we can discuss the case."

"He'll use you as a role model," Olivier said. "Be careful."

"I will." Abdel explained that he needed to check in at headquarters, and was off.

Olivier reached over and took Max's hand, and told her about his and Abdel's meeting with Pascal and Sylvie."

"I don't know if I could be as forgiving as Sylvie."

"When my wife strayed, I was willing to forgive, but she didn't want to work anything out."

"Joe is a serial philanderer." The silence that followed was comfortable. "I'm ready to return to New York. I'll bet you a dinner at Restaurant Veritas in New York that the murderer is lurking somewhere in New York."

"We don't have enough suspects here?"

"No one who would literally hand Ellen the cheese that would kill her within an hour. I still have that mysterious voice ringing in my ear. The one on the answering machine."

"I see. And how do you know about this restaurant?"

"It's where the true winos go, and I'm not referring to street bums."

"It's a deal," he said. "But for tonight, *chérie,* Madame Zohra is preparing something very special for you."

Had Olivier just called her *chérie*? "I hope it's a repeat of last night."

"We're talking about food and wine, *n'est-ce pas?"* Olivier asked, his eyes twinkling.

The telephone rang as they entered the house and Olivier rushed to pick up. He spoke for a moment and handed the receiver to Max. "It's your grandmother." He went to the sink where Zohra was shelling the crabs and pulling the meat from the legs. It was tedious work that seemed to offer little return, but Olivier knew differently. He washed his hands and snitched a pinch of the fresh spider crabmeat to sample. Zohra gave him an exaggerated scowl, and he smiled at her.

"*Parfait,*" he said. "Only you can create a bouillon that allows the fennel to perfume the meat so subtly." While peeling the avocados and smashing them in a purée for the *verrine d'araignée de mer, vocet et gelée de fenouil,* he listened to Max explain her role in New York to her grandmother.

For the next two minutes Max nodded her head and said "*oui…d'accord, oui-oui,*" then "*merci,*" and finally, "*au revoir.*"

"That sounded like a one-sided conversation," he said, when she walked over and stood beside him while he decanted the wine.

"She wants me to join her in Burgundy this summer. My mother and Hank are also considering an invitation from her."

"And you'll go?" Olivier pressed garlic into the avocado purée and added pinches of various spices that were perfuming the kitchen—paprika, curry, five spices, Sichuan pepper.

"Depends."

Olivier laughed at her uncharacteristic coyness. He walked over to his music collection and put in a Gerry Mulligan CD, then took Max's hand. "Come on," he said, "let's decide on a bottle of wine." He opened a door off the kitchen and led the way to the cellar. The air was slightly musty, and cool. He flipped the light switch and moved across the room to the 200 bottles of wine, resting horizontally on their sides.

"You're more of a collector than I thought!" she said.

"All carefully selected. Here's my Burgundy section," he said, pointing, "and here is my Bordeaux. From the time I was ten, my parents have given me a special bottle on my birthday." He glanced over the Bordeaux section of his cellar and shook his head. He turned around to another wine rack that was behind and looked carefully at the aligned bottles. He lifted one, then another, and replaced them. His hand landed on a bottle on the lowest rack. "Aha, here is what I'm looking for," he exclaimed happily. "It's a bottle of *L'Insolite*, by a great winemaker, Thierry Germain, who is in the Loire region. It's a very nice white Saumur, to be precise."

"I'm surprised you're not selecting a Bordeaux."

"I don't know of one that would work with the crab. Besides, Bordeaux isn't the only part of France that has *terroir*. Let's have it rest in the fridge for half an hour."

She followed him back upstairs to the kitchen. Mulligan's baritone saxophone issued out the elegant and velvety sounds he was known for. Olivier placed the wine in the refrigerator, then took her in his arms and danced her upstairs.

New York
April 2012

Chapter Twenty-eight

April 7

Two fellow police officers recognized Max when she stepped into the customs area at JFK, and turned her arrival into a hero's homecoming. She was whisked through customs in minutes and one carried her bag as she headed out to the front of the building.

"Going my way?"

Max whirled around and threw her arms around Hank's neck. "Whoa," he said, obviously pleased. Her mother ran up to her, and bestowed kisses on her cheeks, as Max engulfed her in a hug. "*Chérie, ça va?*" she gasped.

"*Bien.*"

"Let's go," Hank said. "We have to go to American Airlines' cargo building. The funeral director is meeting us there."

"That's how they refer to a human body? Cargo?" Juliette asked in a disapproving voice, and Hank nodded. He parked and they headed to the terminal. The day was sunny and warm. Max walked alongside her dad, full of dread. They entered a vast building similar to a passenger terminal. A wide-shouldered man with a booming voice walked up to Hank and introduced himself, explaining that his employee was driving the hearse to the loading area. They followed him around the corner.

The casket was inside a container, or air tray, and covered in an exterior layer of canvas. Stamped at one end was the word 'head,' and Ellen's name written in large, green letters beneath it. Also stamped on the casket was HR-HANDLE WITH CARE. Max wished she had a placard with those words engraved on it to carry in front of her. This was her worst moment since discovering Ellen's body. Juliette reached for her hand, and they stood in silence as the hermetically sealed container was rolled into the hearse. The funeral director said he'd see them later, and was off.

On the drive into Manhattan they decided to drop Max off at her apartment in the East Village, then she would go to dinner at her parents' apartment. "You don't mind that I cleaned your apartment?" Juliette asked when Hank pulled up in front.

"I hope you wore a mask," Max said, and Juliette laughed.

"I want to hear the whole story when you can talk," Juliette said. "I've been asked to deliver the eulogy, you know."

"Really?" Somehow Max couldn't envision her mother speaking in front of a large audience. "That's brave."

"It's necessary." Max had always loved her mother, but now that she had been in the place where Juliette had grown up and met her mother's mother and sister, a new dimension had been added. Max thought that for the first time in her life she felt more French than American.

Hank put her suitcase down beside her. "Want me to carry it up?"

"Nah. I'm fine."

"Before you ask, Walt and I agreed there was conflict of interest and stayed out of the review process."

"Joe called and thought they were coming down hard on him."

"Your partner status is over."

"You're sure you stayed out of it?" Max asked.

Ignoring her retort, Hank said, "I was happy to hear you were put in charge of the counterfeiting operation you and Olivier..."

"Olivier."

"...are so riled up about. If it exists. And, by the way, you have to take a course in anger management."

"Was that your recommendation?"

"I didn't oppose the idea."

"I'm sure. Your retirement date is set in stone?"

He chuckled. "You got a couple of months left with me. See you tonight."

Max stopped by her neighbor Irene's to get Woof. The retired police dog, a German shepherd, went crazy when he saw her, and she rushed outside with him for a four-mile run, then took him with her to her parents' apartment. They talked over dinner about the events in France, and Max went into much more detail about Ellen's death. Juliette said, "It might help, Max, to realize that this was Ellen's *destin.* And maybe it's yours to find out who murdered her."

"That's the plan," Max said, tired of the destiny talk. She felt more guilt around Ellen's death talking to her mother than she had in France, and thought it had to do with every moment in France being filled with the search for the murderer. The adrenaline rush had dissipated, and now she was left with cold reality. Ellen returned home in a casket. She couldn't say that she knew Ellen, but there was a personal connection through Juliette, which made it tougher. Could I have saved her? Max wondered for the hundredth time.

◇◇◇

April 8

Max jumped up and put coffee on, then ran with Woof around the block. In an hour she was back checking emails. Olivier's flight wouldn't arrive until six in the evening. Bill Casey's driver was picking him up and taking him to Bill's New Jersey home for the professional tasting. Olivier, who would be presenting himself as French wine collector Pierre Guyot, was modest about his tasting talent, but Max thought he would know without a doubt if the second magnum of *'45 Mouton* was authentic or not. She had told Olivier that she wanted to confiscate the lot of four magnums, which she had the authority to do, and not waste time on Bill Casey's little party, but he had been more than mildly curious about the American collector, and the tasters who would be attending. She agreed to the event.

She picked up her ringing phone and agreed to meet with Walt at lunchtime at the precinct station. "I asked Joe to come," Walt said. "He's checking his schedule."

Max knew what that meant. Joe wanted to talk to her before he sat in a meeting. "I get the idea Hank thinks our international counterfeit operation is a crock," she said.

"What do you expect of a beer guy?"

Max laughed. She was back on her home turf, and officially a detective again, which felt like an injection of power. She called Bill Casey, who told her to come to his New York apartment mid-morning as he was waiting for a delivery. Within half an hour she was rushing for the subway. He lived in a four-story apartment building on East 79th and Fifth. The elevator opened to his apartment. They appraised each other as she stepped off the elevator.What she noticed was intelligent, blue eyes behind round glasses, a shaved head, and a sardonic smile.

He invited her in, cautioning her not to trip on the corner of the Oriental rug that needed to be fixed. The walls of the apartment were covered with art, most of it abstract. It seemed logical to Max that a man who collected wine would collect art as well.

"My wife is in Italy looking at paintings," he said. "She's as insatiable about art as I am about wine." A maid appeared and he asked her to bring coffee. "Unless you prefer tea."

"Coffee, please," Max said.

She was trying to buy enough time to decide whether or not to confide in Casey that she was a detective, again wondering how much Ellen had told him. He beat her to it. "In case you're wondering, I know who you are. Ellen told me that you were going as assistant-cum-bodyguard, and she was going to have an evening with *le juge* Chaumont."

"I wonder how many other people she told that to," Max said. "It seems that everybody I talked to in the wine world knew about the magnums you bought and that Ellen had declared one of them fake."

"I didn't see any reason to keep quiet about it," he said, sounding a little on the defensive. "I have a group of pros coming to my house to taste a second magnum in the lot this evening, as you know."

"Isn't this an expensive method of testing?"

He gave her a knowing smile. "If I don't do something, they'll be confiscated, right?"

"If Olivier hadn't agreed to come, they would have been."

"I figured."

"You still haven't found any record of who at Blakely's sold it to you?"

"Not yet, but my secretary is on it."

Max scribbled in her notebook for a minute. "Chaumont is coming to New York as a collector and not as a judge, or examining magistrate. These aliases enable us to mingle a bit more freely. The problem is if that information is leaked, our lives could be in danger."

"Give me the benefit of the doubt, Max. Believe it or not, I do have integrity, and no one wants the real culprit, if there is one, brought in more than I do."

Just in case, she decided to issue a threat. "I understand. You do know that OGA, obstructing a governmental administration, is considered a crime."

He hesitated a second to see if she was kidding and when he saw that she wasn't, said, "The commissioner is a personal friend. I didn't want to bring that card out, but I don't have much choice."

"Then you must know that Olivier and I are working to uncover a counterfeit ring?"

"Was it the magnum of '*45 Mouton-Rothschild* that Ellen took from here that started the ball rolling?"

Max hoped to avoid being the one to announce the fate of that bottle. "It started six months ago when an unusual number of rare wines were taken from some of the top *châteaux*. It's not uncommon for someone to break in and take a few cases, but the numbers made Olivier suspicious."

"It's uncanny in a way that this is coming on top of Rudy Kuriawan's arrest last month. Collectors are on edge. It's strange, but buyers wanted to believe him. They still do."

"Why? He made at least a million dollars off them."

"Do you know how stupid some of these people feel? You'd be surprised how many investors I know who'd rather suffer financial loss than be exposed for swooning over fraudulent wines. Besides, he was charming, and they liked him."

"Did you buy from him?"

"Not a lot. I bought some of his Burgundy wine through Blakely's Auction House."

"And that didn't make you mad?"

"They were screwed, too. They've sold a phenomenal amount of wine with their appeal to young investors. I applaud them."

"Paula Goodwin's the auctioneer?"

"And about to be CEO. She's the name there."

"Some people were dubious all along about the authenticity of some of those wines," Max said, "but they didn't think they'd be believed. Or they were overruled by the general consensus."

"That's true. A couple of my friends stayed away from that scene."

"Is it okay to assume that Paula's crown is slipping a little?"

"She's at the top of her game, and making more money than anybody else. As long as that remains true, I don't think so."

"Ellen didn't receive any support, I take it, when she voiced her intention of exposing someone who she thought might be counterfeiting?" Max asked.

"A lot of people thought she was being a little over the top. Her first plan was to take it to the Mouton-Rothschild Château and have them examine it. I wish she had stuck to it."

Max read from her notebook. "She had read about a physicist named Philippe Hubert who, by using low-frequency gamma rays to detect the presence of a radioactive isotope cesium 137, claimed to be able to test a wine without opening the bottle."

Bill suddenly grew annoyed. "Wine is like sex," he said. "Can be just as good, and just as short-lived. We must hold onto the romance. If we don't, we'll end up with test-tube wine the same way we have test-tube babies." Max thought Olivier and

Bill would get along. "The true test is taste, and that's why I'm having these people gather."

"What if the opinion isn't unanimous?"

He laughed. "Then I throw up my hands."

"Is it common knowledge that Ellen took a bodyguard to France?" Max asked.

"No. Everyone I talked to thought she had an assistant."

"I don't understand why she didn't tell anyone the name of the person she suspected."

"I'm not sure. I thought it had something to do with Pascal Boulin. She loved the guy."

Max disagreed, but it was based on feeling rather than fact, though Pascal was sitting in prison at this very moment.

"I assume the magnum I sent to France with Ellen will be returned, and that it's been treated well?"

"I have bad news. It was stolen from the hotel safe."

He jumped up, furious. "This is ridiculous! Why didn't you guys claim it right away?"

"We were all at the hospital and when we returned it was gone."

"Come on. Clues?"

"Nothing at the moment."

"Then what do *you* think? As the daughter of the famous detective, Hank Maguire, you must have an opinion."

She had to be careful. "Anything I say now would be speculation and it's against department rules to surmise."

"Well-spoken, detective. I don't have to follow your rules. Who needed cash fast? Someone who knew the bottle was there and going out that evening? Someone like Pascal, who had asked Ellen for a loan."

"He's being checked out."

"You know what? I'm going to call my friends in special places, Max. It's nothing personal. I have nothing else to tell you." She didn't blame him. "If you had gotten in touch with me while you were in France, I would have sent you to Vincent Barthes. I've been to dinners with him. He would know all the latest gossip."

"He's in some trouble that I'm not allowed to talk about right now."

"I'll find out. Probably to do with that business he started on his own to prove himself to his father. We all knew that would be a bust. It's too bad."

Max realized she needed to head to the station. "I hope something gets resolved at the tasting," she said.

Bill studied her. "We're playing roulette with my wine." His eyes narrowed. "So tell me, are you a gambler?"

She smiled. "Sometimes."

"If you were a counterfeiter would you mix up a lot like this, or make them all fake?"

"We thought of that. My pal Abdel, a policeman in Bordeaux, thought that once greed took over, the counterfeiters couldn't stand to put in an authentic one."

"He has a point. But what about you?"

"I'd mix them up. Keep everybody off-balance."

"So would I. I'm curious to know if you're into wine."

"Not on a detective's salary."

"So you've never consumed a rare vintage wine?" She shook her head.

"I must rectify that," he said. "That is, if you get the stolen bottle back." His eyes twinkled. She was glad to see the attitude change.

"I'll do my best."

"I'll be honest with you. I'm not at all convinced that there is a counterfeit operation, and even less convinced that's it's connected to Ellen's death. What does your dad think of all this?"

"You know him, too?"

"Only his reputation."

"He's not a part of the investigation. Look, I have to go. Paula Goodwin. Will you introduce me?"

"Of course." He walked her to the elevator.

"Would you say she and Ellen were friends?" Max asked.

"Friendly rivals, I would say. There's quite a lot of competition in the wine business, and both of them were striving to be at the top."

"But their roles were completely different."

"Ellen had entered the world of consulting, and that's where they overlapped."

Max realized that she was operating in a tiny, rarefied world of people who were at the top of the power chain, and who then had to hold onto all they had gained. Bill spoke slowly, searching for his words. "Paula is great as long as everything is going her way. She doesn't like to have her opinion trumped, nor does she like anyone on her turf. She can be a pitbull."

Max thought many women were labeled that way when they were extremely successful, which made her wary. "She isn't the person Ellen wanted to talk to in France, is she?"

"You mean about counterfeiting? Good god, no! What led you to even think that? She wasn't even there."

"I try to think outside the box."

"You're so far out now that I feel it's my job to rein you in."

"What's her background?

"Horrible childhood, I hear. Whose isn't? Paula got herself into the best schools and went into business. She married the CEO of an electronics company and has two sons, but is in the middle of a rancorous divorce now. One child is at Yale, and the other is in boarding school. She got into wine late, but became obsessed, like the rest of us."

"I know her job is prestigious, but does she make much money?"

"Not in real terms." Max would bet she earned ten times what she did. "Look, Paula is a good friend. I've lost one friend and I'm going to support the second through everything."

Max decided to switch back to Ellen. "Did Ellen advise you to buy the '45 magnums?"

Bill thought for a moment. "Actually, she was opposed. She never trusted auction houses. It was the first time Paula sold me wine, and I still think it had to do with that."

"So Paula Goodwin sold you the magnums." He hadn't wanted to reveal that information, Max knew, which was why he had said his secretary was looking. Judging from his expression, he knew he had slipped.

"So?"

"Do you think that's why Ellen chose the *Mouton* for her birthday out of your collection and declared it a fake? To prove that you made a mistake in buying from Paula?"

"It did cross my mind. Ellen could be a little vindictive."

Max knew that was true.

"She and your mother were great friends, I understand. You've got some interesting genes."

"I don't recommend them. They make me schizzy."

He smiled and walked her out to his private elevator, and pushed the down button.

"What about a boyfriend?" Max asked.

"Pardon?"

"Paula Goodwin."

"I don't go there. Rumor has it she has an on-again, off-again relationship with a distributor. No law against that."

"We have some marked cases that have shown up at Richards Importers. Know them?"

"Anson imports the best. A real straight arrow. Talk to him." She boarded the elevator. "I like your spunk," he said. "I want to offer a $250,000 reward to the person who brings Ellen Jordan's killer in."

"Talk to the commissioner."

He laughed, and the elevator door closed.

Chapter Twenty-nine

April 8

The news that the doyenne of the wine world had been murdered had created more commotion in the U.S. than in France, Olivier realized, as he walked through JFK Airport passing dozens of televisions, each of them displaying photos and videos of Ellen Jordan, with newscasters explaining the circumstances of her death. After exiting customs, he walked out to look for Bill Casey's driver. A man stood holding a placard that read "Pierre Guyot." Olivier almost passed by him, forgetting for a second that he had an alias. Within minutes they were in a black Mercedes SUV, on their way to New Jersey. Olivier double-checked to make sure he had Max's address, and then relaxed.

The driver introduced himself as Tim Shea, and told Olivier to "just call me Tim." Olivier said, "Okay, Tim." I'm in America, alright, he thought, with everyone on a first-name basis. He was amused when Tim offered to fix him a drink for the road, and was a little sorry that he had to decline.

He went over the lists that Abdel had put in his hand as he was leaving—the hotel guest list, the Laussac dinner guest list, cheese buyers at the local shop in Saint-Émilion, and a list of flights departing Bordeaux the day after Ellen Jordan's death. Once off the New Jersey Turnpike, they entered a small town, Tenafly, passing one impressive house after another. The driver rounded a bend and pulled up in front of a palatial home set back from the road which bore a resemblance to an Italian Renaissance villa. Olivier thought this was what people in America referred to as a trophy house. His gaze swept the grounds behind the house, where he saw horse stables below and what appeared to be kilometers of white fencing.

Tim hopped out and opened Olivier's door. A man whom he assumed to be Bill Casey waved from the front porch. He looked slight standing in front of his grand house. As any man would, Olivier thought.

"You're the first to arrive," Bill Casey said, "which was my intention. Come in." They entered a vast foyer with a gilt-framed mirror covering the wall on the right and a curved staircase that seemed to wind upward to eternity. Bill, smiling, led Olivier through a set of doors on the ground floor and on down a short staircase until they were in front of a medieval-type doorway. "I wanted you to see my wine cellar before the others arrive," he said proudly.

The cellar, as it turned out, was comprised of five cellars—one holding a concentration of Australian wines, another containing wines from the Bordeaux region, a third filled with Italian wines, and one full of oversized bottles. The fifth cellar was a complex consisting of a dining room, bathroom, and kitchen. All in all, Bill explained, the cellars comprised 9,000 square feet, and held 50,000 bottles.

"The Mouton has been decanted," he said.

"What, exactly, did Madame Jordan say about the one she tasted?"

"The taste was off. She speculated that someone had found the perfect old bottle and filled it with an inferior wine, which doesn't mean inexpensive."

"Did you agree with her?" Olivier asked.

"No. But it can be daunting to taste with a world-famous wine critic." Bill admitted to chronic ambivalence. "Sometimes I wonder if the whole business isn't a crock," he said.

"Crock?"

"Bullshit." He hesitated, "Forget I said that. What got me hooked a decade ago was the phenomenal experience of drinking a wine made by an artisan who had put his heart and soul into it. But I'm tired of the competition, and all the turmoil around the dark side of this business."

Olivier thought he might be tired of it today, but tomorrow he could be salivating again for that perfect bottle to show his friends. Bill led Olivier down another aisle of the cellar, which Olivier thought must be insured for millions.

"I heard through Paula Goodwin today that you were interested in one of the magnums from this lot," Casey said. "That true?"

"I wanted to see if you were trying to unload them through her."

Casey gave Olivier a shrewd look. "And?"

"She thought she could arrange it."

"I just learned that one magnum has gone missing, so there will only be one left after this evening. If anyone changes their mind about confiscating that one, I'll go through my attorneys, or drink it before they can get their hands on it. I could imagine it being stuck in a corner of a 70-degree office." They went back upstairs to the kitchen.

"You aren't trying to implicate Paula Goodwin in any of these thefts and counterfeiting shenanigans, are you?" Bill asked. "That's where Max was heading, for no good reason."

"My job is to ask questions," Olivier said. "And to observe. I try to do this without making assumptions." He looked around at the vast and well-equipped kitchen. "I assume you like to cook?"

"I'm a meat junkie. Grilling and roasting. My wife Ginny, who's in Italy for two weeks, prepares the gourmet fare. You cook?"

"I like to. I wouldn't know where to begin here, though." He picked up a bottle of Harlan Estate and examined it. "I've been meaning to experiment with California wines."

"I could set you up out there," Bill said. "I know everybody."

Olivier smiled at the typically American comment. "I think Max told you that I'm here as a collector by the name of Pierre Guyot," Olivier said. "I'm learning that people are much more reticent around authority."

"Max is a piece of work. She had the gall to threaten me if I told, and came up with a law to back up her threat."

Olivier laughed. "Who will be here tonight?"

"There are six of us," Bill said. The doorbell chimed a tune. "And here they are." Three men wearing casual clothes were at the door. Olivier was introduced to Winn Guthrie, owner of the most prestigious wine store in Manhattan on Madison Avenue, a sommelier from a restaurant whose name Olivier didn't catch, and Phil Ox, director of a cooking school.

Last to arrive was Paula Goodwin, who apologized for being late, but explained that she had a big auction taking place tomorrow after Ellen's memorial service. "I almost canceled," she said, "but then thought it could be a kind of paying homage to her."

She noticed Olivier and walked over and shook hands. "Pierre Guyot," she said. "What a surprise. I asked my friend Vincent Barthes if he was familiar with you after meeting you at the dinner at Cheval Blanc and he said he'd never heard of a Pierre Guyot. That surprised me, as I thought surely you must have at one time or another done business with the Bartheses."

"I only moved to Bordeaux last year, and remember, I've collected very few bottles compared to the investors you're dealing with." He was amazed that his luck was still holding as far as his alias was concerned. He and Max were moving in such small circles that it seemed inevitable that they would be found out. This had been his argument when they had discussed their roles in New York, but she had convinced him to at least start out undercover.

"Excuse me for a moment," Paula said. She walked over to Bill Casey, who greeted her, then seemed proud to introduce her around. Olivier watched them in discussion. He hadn't felt any warmth from Paula either time they had met, yet she was magnetic. Her face wasn't relaxed, but there was no denying that she was an attractive woman. He thought she must be around Ellen's age, close to fifty. Her blond hair was held back with a headband, and she was sartorially perfect.

The men gathered around Bill and her, and she held forth, telling stories about her travels in China, including meetings with heads of state, which he thought sounded exaggerated. A maid entered with a tray of champagne flutes, filled with *La Grande Dame* champagne. "Gentlemen," Bill said, "we salute one grand lady with another. Let's raise a glass to Ellen Jordan." Everyone solemnly lifted a glass and drank.

The table was ready. Bill motioned for them to sit. Out of seemingly nowhere, trays of delicious morsels had been placed on the table. "I want to introduce a friend—and fellow collector—who just flew in from France, Pierre Guyot," Bill continued, and they all nodded. He continued, "I have also brought into our fold this evening the head of the wine department at Blakely's Auction House. I don't have to introduce her." She stood, and looked from face to face.

"Speech!" one of the men said.

"Ellen and I were in the wine world together over a decade," Paula said. "She became *le palais* early in her career and I was a late bloomer when I entered the auction house circuit. Tonight she is our muse." She raised her glass again, and the small group followed.

Bill stood. "Gentlemen, you have a special assignment tonight. Ellen dined with Ginny and me the night before she left for France, and I opened a magnum of *1945 Mouton-Rothschild.* However, one glass into our dinner, Ellen was certain that what we were sipping was counterfeit." The room grew quiet. Bill continued, "Tonight I am going to risk opening another, and your opinion, as well as the expertise of Paula here, will hopefully determine once and for all if someone tampered with these bottles."

As if on cue, the maid arrived with a decanter of wine. "I'll take the empty bottle home with me," Winn joked to break the tension that had descended. "I read that old bottles are fetching large sums of cash on the Internet."

"May I see the cork and label from the bottle?" Olivier asked.

"Of course," Bill said, motioning the maid over.

Bill sipped first, rolling the wine around in his mouth, and swallowing. The others proceeded to do the same. "Ecstasy," Bill said. Olivier sniffed, then sipped, too astonished to say anything. He agreed with the famous American wine critic, Robert Parker who called it "truly one of the immortal wines of the century." The flavors entered his consciousness and as he swished the wine lightly he tasted first spicy black cherry, then coffee, tobacco, and mocha. Olivier couldn't believe the vitality of it. He heard the others in the room exclaiming in soft voices, but after another sip, he felt he had entered a realm beyond all imagination. What a smooth and polished finish, he thought. Eyes closed, he relished the lingering flavor.

"Monsieur Guyot?"

He was startled back into reality by Bill's voice asking him, sotto voce, if he had an opinion. "It's genuine," Olivier said. They all sat now in reverent silence, breathing in the perfume of the wine, after quietly sipping, and rolling a little more under the tongue.

Paula performed a perfect ritual of wine tasting. "Is there any question about the authenticity?" she asked. "There isn't a shadow of doubt in my mind." No one expressed a doubt. She looked smug, which annoyed Olivier. He also worried that he, Max, and Abdel had been foolish after all to focus so much attention on the stolen bottle in relation to Ellen's death. What if someone knew she had it, thought it authentic and simply stole it? Maybe the wine had nothing to do with her murder.

Winn smiled at Paula, "Who was this lot purchased from, Paula?"

"I don't reveal the names of people who sell to me," Paula said. She was smiling, in control.

Olivier made a mental note to see if Yves Barthes had responded to his email asking if he had any memory of the sale. He was ready to suggest to Max that they issue a subpoena to search Blakely's records if they didn't come up with the entire story behind the wine.

The maid brought the bottle and the cork to Olivier, who put on his glasses to study them. Everything looked perfect. Olivier excused himself, and went to the kitchen, hoping to sneak out for a breath of fresh air. To have had his mind set on a fake, and then to taste the authentic had jumbled his thoughts, and besides, he was tired. A little night air would bring him back to life. The maid was clearing a tray. "May I help you, sir?"

He noticed the back door. "I'd like to step out for a little air, that's all." She opened the door to the terrace. "The others will join you for cigars," she said. He stood quietly, looking at the horse stables. In the distance he saw a greenhouse, and beyond that a border of woods. He wandered along a path that appeared to lead back to the front of the house.

He heard a car door slam, and peered around the corner to see who was leaving. Paula was rushing across the driveway carrying a metal wine case designed for individual bottles. She unlocked her Jaguar and put the case in the back on the floorboard, and quickly went back inside, neglecting to lock the car behind her. Olivier walked over and looked into the car, and peering around to make sure no one was watching, opened the door and took out the case. Hands shaking, he opened the case. A magnum of *1945 Mouton-Rothschild.*

He hurried back to the kitchen, and noticed the door that led to the tasting room cum cellar. He dashed through it, with no one the wiser. He saw another aluminum portable wine carrier, and grabbed it, went into the dimly lit cellar and looked around. Rushing to the California section, he pulled out a magnum of a name he'd never heard of and put it in the case, and snapped it shut. He hadn't seen anyone. He pretended to be invisible as he scooted through the kitchen and back out to the parking lot. Quickly, he opened Paula's door and removed the metal case and substituted the one he had just found, then looked around for Tim. Recognizing the SUV, he went over and tapped on the window, waking him up.

"Whuttsup, man? You ready to go?"

"Soon. I wanted to leave this here. You never saw it, right?"

"Never did."

"Where the hell have you been?" Bill asked Olivier in a jovial voice when he joined him. He was obviously happy with the results of the tasting.

Heart pounding, Olivier said, "I'm sorry, but after the long trip my digestion is upset. I think I should leave."

"Okay, okay. I understand."

"Was Madame Goodwin here earlier today?" Olivier asked.

"Call her Paula. She actually decanted the wine. She had to see a friend in the neighborhood, and so came early. You met her, right?"

He nodded.

"Come join us for a minute!" Bill said.

"Sure."

The guests were on the terrace smoking Cuban cigars and chatting. Olivier took a few puffs and thought the aroma exquisite, but jet lag had set in. It was only 9:00, but by his clock it was 3:00 a.m. Paula was standing alone, and Olivier approached her, thinking of her fury when she opened the case he left her. She said, "Bill Casey's mother was an Irish maid in Boston, and look at this spread!"

"The American dream," Olivier said. "It's all quite Great Gatsby-ish."

"But this place is nothing compared to the *châteaux* in Bordeaux, huh?"

"There's a 500-year difference," he said, and was pleased to see her smile.

"I might have the fourth bottle of *'45 Mouton* for you," Paula said. "You said you were interested when we were at the Cheval Blanc dinner."

"My understanding from Monsieur Casey is that it's not for sale."

"I can convince him." She chuckled, "My wine investors are quite pliable. I call it the sandbox syndrome."

"What do you mean?"

"The kid happily playing stops and wants what the other kid

has. Collectors are like that. They also want to have *the* bottle, whatever that might be that moment. I'll find a burgundy that he can become obsessed with, and he'll be more willing to let this go."

"We can talk," Olivier said.

"You're different from the others," she said. "You do your homework, and you understand the subtleties involved in wine." Olivier thought his cover was blown, but she continued, "Maybe because you're French."

"How does that make me different?" Olivier asked.

"It's not about the money with American collectors," she said. "What's $25,000 to them? Some of them make that in an hour." She laughed, "In a minute."

"And where do you stand?" he asked.

She laughed but sounded bitter when she spoke. "Money's an illusion, and I know that's a cliché. There is never enough money in this city, and once a woman divorces, as I have recently, it feels like being on Skid Row."

He gave her an admiring look. "You don't look to be close to the edge."

She was pleased. "What'd you think of tonight's tasting?"

"Like everyone else, I found the wine transcendent."

"Spoken like a true Frenchman." She moved closer to him and put her hand on his arm. "I can give you a ride into the city. I have a vintage wine there, and I won't tell you which one. That would blow your mind. Where's your hotel?"

She was coming onto him! He hadn't anticipated that. "I'm staying with a friend."

"So? You can't have a drink before going home?"

"I'm sorry. She's been waiting for me for hours."

Paula gave him a hostile look and stalked off.

Chapter Thirty

April 8

Joe begged out of the meeting with Walt as predicted. Hank, on the other hand, was pacing around Walt's office when Max arrived. She updated them on events in Bordeaux. Hank broke into the conversation, furious that Vincent hadn't been locked up for attempting to drug Max. "I outwitted him," she said. "Plus we don't want him in jail for obvious reasons." Hank remained silent when the counterfeit ring came up, and Max knew this part didn't interest him.

"In a nutshell, what do you think happened?" Hank asked Max.

"I think Ellen accused her visitor to his face."

"But the murder was premeditated."

Max said, "The visitor entered her suite, probably nervous about being exposed, with a wait-and-see attitude. Ellen, unaware of danger, said everything that was on her mind. The sauterne was opened, and then the blue cheese was brought out as a special treat, just like in a fairy tale.

Walt said, "You and Chaumont have concocted a big counterfeit scheme, Max, but I don't see much proof. A magnum of wine was stolen from the hotel safe immediately after her death, but you haven't succeeded in linking it to Ellen's death." That damned bottle, she thought for the hundredth time. A third magnum from the lot Casey purchased would be opened this evening, she explained, which was predicted to be fake.

"It's going to be rigged, I bet, especially if Goodwin sold it to Casey. You've looked into that angle, right?" Hank asked.

"They were both reluctant to disclose that she sold it to him," Max said. "Now they can't recall the provenance."

"Ha! Subponea Casey's records, and hers, too!"

"I'm not having it," Walt said. "They can taste all they want, but I'm confiscating a bottle for the Fraud Squad. What kind of money are we talking here?"

"We're in the $30,000 plus per magnum category," said Max.

Walt gave a low whistle. "Have you ever tasted any of these special wines?"

Max shook her head. "I'm curious, though. There don't seem to be enough adjectives in either French or English to adequately describe the experience."

"How about delicious? What more do you need?" Walt said. He paused, "You think Casey might be involved in this ring of counterfeiters?"

Max said, "I don't think so. Casey's involved because he paid a bundle of cash for something that he's suddenly not getting a good return on. He's upset about Ellen's murder, and at the same time trying to protect himself from ridicule for buying a lot of fakes."

"Why would he be ridiculed? He's a victim, for god's sake."

Max was tired of explaining. She said, simply, "When saddled with fakes, collectors feel stupid."

"Stupid I understand," Walt said.

Hank said, "Casey's also protective of Paula. If he hadn't been such a loud-mouth, Ellen might still be alive today."

"I don't know if I'd agree with that," Walt said. "But I'm interested in meeting with Chaumont. This happened on French soil and I see it as a French problem to solve."

"That's what the list of suspects is about."

"None of them add up in my book," Hank said. "Except Barthes. Who do you have over here?"

"Nobody specific. We're going to be checking out a number of importers and distributors, starting with a small importer named Angus Richards. Some of the marked wine from Bordeaux showed up in Richards' office and customs let me know." Max knew she didn't sound very convincing.

Walt leaned back in his chair. "I'm going to send this report over to my buddy at the Fraud Squad."

Max knew what that meant. She got up to leave. "Go ahead."

"You look discouraged," Hank said.

"I am. We keep running into dead ends. Vincent's involved in shipping fake wines, but with his dad backing him, nothing much will happen."

"Let's go back to that message on his answering machine," Walt said "Had Vincent already listened to the message?"

"I don't think so. He would have saved it or deleted it. I deleted it, though."

"Good. One more question: Was the camera on?"

"I hope not, but honest answer: I don't know."

"Keep us informed," Walt said. He stood up and looked out the window. "I've got a new partner for you. Name's Carlos Vasquez. He'll start today."

"Who is he?"

"Just made grade three detective after being in narcotics. Kind of a runt, but I think he'll be okay."

"And Joe?"

"He's being transferred to the Bronx."

"What if I asked to go instead?"

"Why?" Walt asked, too surprised to remain detached.

"More autonomy."

Hank scoffed.

"Let's see how this case goes," Walt said.

"Whatever."

She left, and hopped on the subway, more determined than ever to break the case wide open.

◇◇◇

Time dragged by as Max waited for Olivier to arrive. At 9:00 she ordered Thai take-out, not sure whether he would have eaten or not. He hadn't called, but she also wasn't worried because she knew Bill Casey would take care of him. She had left the 20th Precinct office and gone to a Jiu-Jitsu lesson, arriving back at her apartment energized. Joe had texted her every twenty minutes for two hours, wanting to talk, but she hadn't answered. The buzzer went off in the kitchen, indicating that someone was in the small foyer asking to enter the building. She asked playfully who was there over the intercom.

"Joe."

"I'm busy."

"Max." It sounded like a command. She buzzed him in.

"I can only give you a few minutes. I thought you were sick."

"I had a quick recovery."

"Funny how that happens."

He got a beer out of the fridge and sat down. "My key didn't work downstairs."

"Hank changed the lock."

"He's given me hell since you left. I'm on probation now. So what happened at the meeting?"

"I knew it. You want the dirt from me before you sit down with Walt and Hank."

"What's wrong with that?" he said, wearing a hang-dog face.

"I requested a transfer, but they didn't take me up on it."

His eyes softened. "You'd do that for me?"

"I'm doing it for me. Let's face it, Joe, we suck as partners."

His gaze had shifted to the television that was on mute, and he reached up and turned up the volume. "Here's a report on Ellen Jordan," he said, interrupting her. After showing the coffin of Ellen Jordan being loaded onto the hearse at the airport, the commentator announced that two suspects had been arrested. Philippe Douvier's face flashed up on the screen. Standing beside him was Abdel! In two seconds they were off the air, and the commentator had moved on to a different topic.

Max wondered if her grandmother knew what was going on.

Joe got up. "I'm outta here. I'm heading up to Monaghan's Bar with some of the gang if you want to come along."

"Not tonight."

"Hey, Max," he said, looking into her eyes. "I'll say the words that will change everything. I'm sorry. Now will you put on your fucking cowboy boots and stop the game-playing?"

The door buzzer rang, and Max said, "I guess you'll meet Olivier."

"Who?"

"My French partner." She decided to run down to greet Olivier. "Wait here." She skipped quickly down the three flights of stairs. Olivier stood there, weekend bag in hand. She opened the door and threw her arms around him, and he laughed out loud. Hearing footsteps behind her, she turned. She looked up at Joe, who was trying to hide his shock, and introduced them. Joe nodded, then walked off into the night.

Olivier said, "I'm not interrupting something?"

"Thank God you are," Max said. She leaned over and gave him a kiss. Noticing the high-tech wine case like the one she had carried on the plane for Ellen, she said, "Don't tell me you've got another magnum of wine to protect!"

"You'll see." They walked up the stairs. "Joe's tall," Olivier said.

"I'll be glad when we're not dealing with each other's exes," she said.

Olivier sat quietly looking around the apartment while Max opened a bottle of white wine, and poured each of them a glass. "*Pas mal,*" he said.

"That's pushing it," she said. "How was the tasting?"

"The bottle Bill Casey opened was authentic."

"You're kidding!"

"I think Paula Goodwin switched bottles." He lifted the wine case. "I believe she took this one from Bill's collection, and had the opportunity to bring in an authentic one as she did the decanting."

"Which means she laid out a lot of dough to fix things. She probably had to buy that baby. How'd you figure all that out?"

"I saw her going to her car with a case, and watched her. I'm turning into you."

"How?"

"I stole her case and ran like a madman to Bill's cellar and stole a California and put it in a different metal case."

It was Max's turn to laugh. "What will we do with the stolen bottle?"

He picked it up and studied the label, then took out a loupe and analyzed it. "If it's counterfeit, they did a good job. This is the one that should go to the Fraud Squad."

"You got it. Bill Casey is going to be rip-shit." Olivier obviously didn't understand. "Furious," she explained. "You went behind his back."

"I had to move fast, and he would have objected." He picked up the bottle again. "I think you should subpoena Bill Casey's and Paula Goodwin's purchase and sale records. I want to go to the *château* directly when I return."

"That's what my dad just said."

"It's logical."

"I think she did something illegal five years ago when she sold this lot, and Bill knows it. It doesn't make her a counterfeiter because she sold wine illegally."

"We have reversed roles. You've become rational."

Max filled him in on the day, mentioning Walt's skepticism that the counterfeit operation would bring in the killer, then skipped to Douvier's press conference. Olivier said he would call Abdel. She went to her computer and brought up the justice minister on French television. She turned up the volume: *Minister of the Justice, Philippe Douvier, announced the arrest of two suspects in the Ellen Jordan criminal case, winemaker Pascal Boulin and vineyard foreman, Yannick Martin.* Abdel nodded grimly by his side.

"*Merde*! This could ruin their reputation if they're innocent. I should go back immediately," Olivier said.

He brushed the hair that had fallen onto his forehead back with his hand, a sign of frustration, and took another sip of the white wine. What a graceful man, she thought. What a fabulous, graceful man. She put down her plate and climbed into his lap and kissed him on the lips. "Not yet," she said.

The investigation was quickly forgotten as they made their way to her bedroom. They lay in bed after making love, her head on his shoulder. She had lit a candle on the bureau, which cast the room into shadows. Someone shouted down below on the street, and the retort was a barrage of vulgar epithets.

"It sounds as if the people on the street are in this room," Olivier said. "And they're not pleasant company."

"I never hear it anymore," she said. She was ready to drift off to sleep. "How did Paula Goodwin behave at the wine tasting?"

"Fine. She invited me home with her."

Max's eyes jerked open. "*Quelle* bitch!" Olivier laughed.

Max sat up. "That's a clue to her character. She goes after what she wants, but we know that already. Her abs means she has discipline. Appearance means a lot to her. She has the $400 hairstyle with extensions, she's had at least one facelift, and probably shops at stores like Barney's or Bergdorf-Goodman."

"What are you saying?"

"How does she do all that on her salary?"

"Didn't we learn she has a rich husband?"

"Ex-husband." She told him what Bill Casey had told her.

"Sounds like you're bored with our suspects in France?" Olivier asked. "Did you find out more about auction houses?"

"Sometimes they travel abroad and buy from the *châteaux*. Most lots come from private investors who are getting rid of cellars, or want to earn on their investments. They will purchase from a distributor if he's going out of business, or has so much stock that he needs to liquidate some bottles on the cheap." She turned over and looked at him. "Did you know instantly that you were drinking the real stuff this evening?

"Absolutely. I could write an essay about the nuances involved, so for the moment I will only say that it was incomparable."

"Maybe one day I'll be so lucky," Max said, yawning.

He put his arm around her, "*Chérie*, we must sleep." He

pulled the cover up. "Tell me a story while I fall asleep. How did your parents meet?"

"It's a short story," she said, "with a long ending." She told how her mother had been held up at gunpoint in New York when she was with a friend on the Upper West Side, and Hank had been the cop on duty.

"It's not such a sweet story," Olivier said. "She could have been killed."

"But she wasn't, and they married, and had me and my brother!"

He chuckled. "I'm not surprised that your mother's family disowned her. It was common back then, but the rules have relaxed in recent years."

"I wonder how much they've relaxed. Your parents wouldn't be thrilled to have you with an American cop."

"Who happens to have a stellar French background, but that has nothing to do with anything. They will love you for you." He took her hand, and she felt him relaxing. She thought he was asleep when he said, "I sometimes wonder if we have behaved like amateurs, Max. Vincent is making counterfeit wine, I don't question that, but it could be a small operation. Two people in Bordeaux are locked up, but for misdemeanors, not for Ellen's murder. And I don't think I see much enthusiasm from your father or Walt O'Shaughnessy."

"That's not their style. They've seen detectives spend twenty years on one murder case."

"We'll be old by then."

He drifted off to sleep and Max lay awake mulling over his last statement. Was she projecting, or did it sound like he was insinuating that they would still be together in twenty years?

Chapter Thirty-one

April 9

Mourners waiting to enter Saint Thomas Cathedral on Fifth Avenue stood in a single file line that went halfway around the block. Max had left the apartment early, and asked Olivier to take a taxi to the church. He showed his pass to the attendant at the front door, careful to avoid the cameras circling the front of the building. He had a double identity, and could be recognized by some viewers as the French judge, and by others as collector Pierre Guyot. Max was the assistant to Ellen Jordan in the minds of people in the wine world, and to others she was Detective Maguire.

The wine world was well represented in the great sanctuary. Olivier recognized critic Robert Parker, who was with friends. Mayor Michael Bloomberg and his entourage strolled down the aisle of the church, causing a mild stir. Max, looking chic in tailored pants and jacket, walked up the aisle with an avuncular-looking man in a well-tailored suit on one side of her, and a tall, angular man who seemed to take everything in without blinking on the other. They had to be the great investigative duo, Hank and Walt, Olivier thought. Max caught his eye and winked, then said something to Hank, who glanced in his direction and nodded. Walt and Hank sat down a few rows in front of Olivier, and Max joined Olivier, who squeezed her hand when she sat.

Olivier thought the funeral was like a state occasion, as people continued streaming into the church. He was admiring the Gothic architecture when Bill Casey leaned over to say "The Queen of Hearts is yelling 'Off with your head!'"

They were to discuss the missing wine now? Olivier wondered. Americans, he had decided, were never in the moment. "She's the furious queen in 'Alice in Wonderland,'" Bill whispered.

Whatever that was. Olivier sank into a state of relief when the organist started playing Bach's cantata, "God's Time is the Best of All." Glancing to his right, he saw Paula Goodwin, impeccable in a Thierry Mugler suit, hurry to take her seat. The church was almost filled to capacity when a petite, dark-haired, sparkly eyed woman walked to the chancel and sat in a chair resembling a throne. "That's my mom," Max whispered again to Olivier. The organist began Chopin's "Funeral March" after which Bloomberg walked up to the podium and gave high praise to the woman who had broken through so many barriers, and who had influenced millions of oenophiles.

The rector introduced Juliette de Laval Maguire. Juliette, elegant and displaying no trace of nervousness, began to talk about Ellen's earliest tasting days in France. She spoke of her friend's integrity, and how she had had little tolerance for those who didn't live up to her standards. With a voice laced with passion, Juliette said, "Ellen died because she was giving someone one more chance to come clean, to step forward and own a mistake, and rectify it. Poisoning someone is the ultimate act of cowardice. Ellen did not deserve that."

The silence that followed seemed eternal. Olivier had an urge to scan the crowd, wondering if the murderer was sitting among them. Juliette said softly, "*Adieu, mon amie. Adieu.* Farewell, my friend." She stepped down. Someone applauded, and in a moment everyone had joined in. It had been a simple statement of truth, Olivier thought.

"That French woman was amazing," a woman behind them said after the service as they stood in a small circle. "She has guts." Olivier watched Max's face flush with pride.

Feeling a tap on his back, he turned to see Max standing beside her mother, who addressed him in French, "Max is at last interested in the world of the French," Juliette said, smiling, "and I am pleased that she has you as an influence." Olivier admired her sagacity. He assured Juliette that there were many influences besides his, hopefully positive, and then they were interrupted by Hank, who came up and extended his hand. Olivier guessed he was at least three centimeters taller than himself.

Hank put his arm around his wife. "Maybe somebody will feel some remorse after hearing your declaration and confess."

"I hope so," Juliette said. A tender, little smile was Hank's only reaction to her earnest reply. Walt joined them, and shook hands with Olivier when introduced.

"What's the plan?" Hank asked.

"I'm going to interview an importer, and Olivier is off to Paula Goodwin's wine auction," Max answered.

They were heading to the exit door. "That takes care of the wine part of things," Hank said. "Who's going after the murderer?"

"I am, if you tell me who it is," Max said, matching his sarcasm.

"You can come with me if you'd like to see the auction house," Olivier said to Hank.

"I thought I'd tag along with Max," he said, smiling at her eye roll. "Actually, her new partner is going."

"Where? I'm taking him with me now?" The look on Hank's face was her answer. "He's blown his first day by being a no-show."

Hank put up his hand and Carlos Vasquez, wearing a baseball hat backwards, and slouchy jeans, ambled over. He looked like a boy, Olivier thought, reminding him of Abdel when he first tried to help him. Max glanced up at Hank, who was smiling. The new detective walked up to her, all five feet six inches of him, shook her hand, and said, "Carlos." Max introduced him to Olivier.

"Why don't you and Olivier come for dinner this evening?" Juliette said. "I'll ask Walt, too."

"Okay," Max said. Hank had gone off to get the car and Juliette told Max she needed to meet him out front. Olivier and Max followed her out. It was a cool, breezy April day, the sky cloudy. Max hugged her mother and said, "*Maman, très bien.* Where did you come up with your little scenario about Ellen giving someone a chance?"

"She told me."

"What?" Max exclaimed.

"She told me before she left. She was to meet with that person in Bordeaux. I have no idea who it was, Max."

Max and Olivier exchanged glances.

"I'm going to head to the importer's office," Max said. She turned to her mother, "I'm undercover, in case anybody asks who I am. Most of the wine people here think I was Ellen's assistant."

"Max, you have too many roles," Juliette said. She smiled up at Olivier, "Max has been play-acting almost constantly since she was two."

Max and Olivier agreed to meet up at her apartment no later than six. She kissed her mother and began walking south, her new partner practically skipping beside her. Olivier tried not to think about the red thong and lacy red bra she left the house in that morning as he watched her until she was out of sight. She fluttered her fingers behind her, and he knew she was aware of him watching her.

He turned to see Paula bearing down on him. "There you are," she said. "A metal case was taken from my car last night. Bill Casey said to ask you if you saw anyone as you were wandering the grounds after the tasting."

"True. I was admiring the architecture of the horse barn, and wondering who rode the horses."

"That's not what I'm asking. He could see that her patience was barely holding. "Did you see anyone suspicious out there? Anyone looking in cars?"

"No."

"Your driver? Did he mention anything? Bill is going to talk to him."

"No, he and I talked about how poetic a summer evening can be. It was after..."

"Jesus, Pierre!" She strode to a waiting limousine, an impressive sight in short skirt and stiletto boots. Hank pulled up to the curb and hopped out. He handed Olivier a cell phone and explained that he had recorded all of their phone numbers in it. "Tonight we'll create a game plan," he said. "We'll see you and Max at seven." He paused, "Max isn't up to any hijinks, is she?"

Olivier thought it was time to invest in a new American dictionary. He would guess what it meant. "This afternoon is about both of us introducing ourselves to people who might have some clues. No Wild West stuff."

"She complains that Ellen ignored warnings, but she does the same." Olivier had a hint of what Max had been complaining about when she called Hank and Juliette umbrella parents.

Bill joined Olivier as they watched Max's parents drive away, then the two walked a half block to Bill's waiting car. Tim jumped out and opened the back door, and said, "Hello, sir," to Olivier. Bill told him to drive to the restaurant Vin on Madison Avenue. "Paula claims some magnum she had for another customer went missing from the back of her car after the tasting. I told her to ask you," Bill said.

"Oh?"

"You were out getting air for a while. I thought maybe you saw something." His eyes were accusatory.

"I'd get her to tell you what precise bottle she had."

"Do you know?"

"I'd wager a bet on a *'45 Mouton-Rothschild.*"

"How much?"

"My career."

Casey looked shocked, but Olivier could tell that he didn't want to know any more about Olivier's snooping. Not now, anyhow. A quick eye exchange with Tim linked them in the little conspiracy.

"I thought the French were known for being rational," Bill said as his driver pulled up in front of the restaurant.

"We are. I am probably the most rational man you are acquainted with." Or was, he thought.

◇◇◇

Bill led the way into Vin, where they were greeted by a gentleman who whisked them to the auction room. Every attendee held a glass of wine. "Have a glass of the '81 *Billecart-Salmon Blanc de Blancs*," the restaurant host said, pouring a glass from the magnum in his hand, and giving it to Olivier. Paula, holding a glass of wine, motioned him over to the podium. She spoke over the crowd, "Did you ask your driver if he saw anything?" she demanded of Bill.

"Not yet. I had a funeral, remember?"

His tone stopped her from asking any more questions. Focusing now on the crowd that continued to grow, Olivier felt as though he was at a party that was about to veer out of control, which, oddly, felt like a metaphor for his investigation. There was no evidence of genteel tasting, but of reckless imbibing, followed by crass remarks. Olivier overheard one of the men say, "This wine has the bouquet of the pussy of a fifteen-year-old virgin," an assessment that was followed by raucous laughter. He had to be one of the group wine collectors referred to as the Dozen Dirty Dudes, who had scads of money to play with, and who turned auctions into drunken parties. He was disgusted.

Paula banged her gavel on the podium and the noise subsided. The consumption of wine, though, continued to pick up. The vintages poured were impressive. Paula began announcing cases of wine at hyper-speed, and paddles were raised all over the room. Bill Casey bid on twelve bottles of *Chave's 1995 Hermitage Cuvée Cathelin*, a Rhône wine, taking the lot for $8,000. She needs Casey, Olivier thought, far more than he needs her.

Paula announced a brief break. She and Casey walked over to Olivier. Paula didn't mention the wine again, but she asked Olivier if he had heard that Vincent Barthes was in trouble.

"I've been too busy to follow the news over there," he said. "What kind of trouble?"

"He hasn't been responding to any texts or phone calls. Someone told me this morning that his business is being investigated." Good, Olivier thought. Abdel has let Vincent know that his calls are being monitored.

He waited. Bill stepped away to speak to a friend, and Paula kept her focus on him, and he knew she was deciding if she should bring up the bottle again or not.

Bill turned back to them. "You have a bottle of 1990 *Romanée Conti*, I hear."

"The last one sold for $47,000," Paula replied.

"I'm interested," he said. Olivier thought Casey's addiction plain to see. He had to have the latest.

Olivier said, "I told Madame Goodwin when we were at a dinner in Saint-Émilion that I would like to add to my collection. After tasting the wine at your home last night, I knew that this was why I had come. I want the last magnum of this lot that has caused you so much trouble."

Bill's eyes bulged, as if he were asking, "What now?"

Paula said, "It's not for sale."

Olivier interrupted him before he went on another harangue about the money thrown into a hole. "I'll start at $50,000."

Bill stared at him, and a tiny gasp came from Paula. "You're going to put it out of range for Paula," Bill said, his face flushed, his brown eyes flashing.

"Isn't this the trend these days?" Olivier asked in a serene voice.

"The bottle that was stolen from my car was a *'45 Mouton*," Paula said. "If you can find it, it's yours." She went back to the podium.

"Can you let me in on what the hell you're doing now?" Bill asked Olivier.

"I'm muddying the water," Olivier said, and smiled at Bill Casey's expression of consternation. "Actually, I might be drowning."

They stopped to see what everyone was bidding on. Bill said, "Do you know that in 2002 a bottle of 1945 *Romanée-Conti* of Burgundy sold for $2,600, and last year a bottle went for $124,000. Blame Kurniawan."

"It's sad," Olivier said. "These rare bottles are only for the very rich."

"Which will lead to more counterfeiting," Bill said. "More retailers are buying directly from the *châteaux* because of it."

Olivier said, "The truth is that no one knows much about what happened with wine before World War II, no matter what they say. Even the *châteaux* don't have records of the amounts of stellar wines that were produced, or the format, or packaging. They sent vast barrels of wine to the traders who bottled it."

"It definitely makes it harder to catch these guys. In the case of Kurniawan, they went after him for being in the country illegally since 2003 and happened to find the counterfeiting operation. Suspicion was growing, but no one wanted to speak out."

Olivier glanced down at his phone and wondered why he hadn't heard from Max. "I must go," he said. "Thank you for your help."

"Olivier. Enough of the game-playing. Tell me if you took the case from Paula's car before I have to go fire my driver."

"Don't fire him before the end of the day tomorrow."

"You're picking on the wrong person. I'll pay whatever it takes to make you drop this ridiculous investigation. I'm the only one who has been robbed, and I'm willing to let it go."

"But this ridiculous investigation is about a lot more than you, Monsieur Casey. If Madame Goodwin has committed a theft, or gotten involved in something criminal, then Max's and my job is to make sure justice is served."

"Okay, then, end of the day tomorrow."

Olivier turned to see him hold up his paddle for yet another lot of wine.

◇◇◇

Olivier walked out into the drizzle and on an impulse walked up two doors and entered Blakely's Auction House, following the sign to the office area. A young secretary smiled as he introduced himself as Pierre, a friend of Paula's. There was a slight lull between phone calls. "I'm Anna, by the way," the young woman said. They were operating American-style, already on a first-name basis.

"I'm coming from the auction," he said.

"Oh, are you going back? I wonder if you'll drop off Paula's phone."

Gifts are raining down, thought Olivier. "Of course."

"Wait just a minute." She disappeared into an adjoining office. A smartphone was on her desk, vibrating against the wood, indicating there was a text message. Glancing around, and seeing no one, Olivier picked it up and saw the text was from Vincent: *Everything unraveling here. On friend's phone. Pierre Guyot not who he says. Name Olivier Chaumont. Investigating Ellen's death.* It was signed, *V.* Olivier deleted the text, and quickly put the phone down.

Anna returned, almost bumping into him at the door. She reached down and handed him the phone. "Paula needs her keys, too. The auction is ending and she has to be somewhere immediately."

She handed him a set of keys, and as he took them, he almost dropped them. His heart started pounding. Four charms dangled from the circle—a wine glass, a martini glass, a miniature bottle of wine Bordeaux, and a disc that had a word on each side. He turned it over and read the engraving: *Soon. Bientôt.* It was identical to the one Alain Seurat had handed him in Bordeaux. The rational side of his brain offered up that Paula wasn't in Bordeaux when Ellen died, but then, someone who had been in Ellen's room had a matching keychain.

Paula swept in through the door. "It was easier for me to rush over and get these," she said, picking up the cell phone and glancing at it to see if she had any messages before dumping it into her Hermès Birkin bag. "Pierre, I'll tell you what. You want a bottle of the '45 *Mouton* so much, I'll let you keep the one you stole for half of what you offered for Bill's. I'm sure you've opened the case."

"Why aren't you going to law enforcement?"

"Because it will drag on forever. I don't have the time or the inclination. Yes or no?"

Olivier couldn't believe he was negotiating with a killer about anything, for he knew without a doubt that Paula was responsible for Ellen's death. "I want the papers on it," he said. "The provenance. Where you purchased it."

"You have some nerve," she said. Her phone was buzzing and she looked down, "I have to go. Everything is off."

Her phone jangled and she reached into her bag, "I'm on my way!" she shouted. She rushed out the door. Olivier went out behind her, and watched her climb behind the wheel of an SUV. He tried Max's cell again, and then put up his hand to hail a taxi. He had to get in touch with Max and tell her that Paula should be arrested immediately.

Chapter Thirty-two

April 9

Max sat in the Manhattan office of Anson Richards, a slightly built man who sported a trim moustache, and black, horn-rimmed eyeglasses. He was a garruluous conversationalist, happy to explain the three-tier wine system set up after Prohibition. Carlos Vasquez sat listening intently in the chair beside her, a distraction she didn't need.

"Once the wine arrives on American shores," Richards said, "the importer notifies the wholesaler, or distributor, who in turn moves it to their customers, primarily wine stores and restaurants. That's the simplified version. On the European side, the freight forwarders, who are brokers, truck the wine to the steamship company."

"So if the papers are in order when the wine arrives at the port, then U.S. Customs generally doesn't interfere?" Vasquez asked. Max couldn't believe it. The least he could do was keep his mouth shut.

"Good question, Officer Vasquez," Richards said, and Vasquez smiled. It was the small, narrow patch of hair just below his bottom lip that turned Max off. When he glanced over at her, she kept her face immobile. She remembered now that this was his first assignment as a detective. Richards continued talking. "Customs will receive a document called an *acquis* from the

French exporter, and if that looks okay, the wine is picked up by the importers' licensed trucks. They might spot check, but we are talking millions of cases. American wine consumption has increased every year for the past fifteen. A few years ago, we became the biggest consumers of Bordeaux."

"A French judge initiated a sting operation months ago," Max explained when Richards finally drew a breath, "because two things were occurring simultaneously in that country: extraordinary wines were being lifted from *grand cru châteaux*, and as prices skyrocketed, counterfeiting was on the rise. A very recent example is the 1945 *Mouton-Rothschild...*"

Richards stopped her by putting up his hand. "Everyone knows the story now of Bill Casey opening a bottle for Ellen's birthday and her declaring it a fake. Max, this counterfeit conversation could go on all day. Let's discuss the pallet of wine that customs singled me out for."

With him being so dismissive of Ellen, Max thought maybe Ellen had broken an unspoken protocol by being so vocal about her suspicions. Either that, or people in the wine world were already bored by the case, and had moved on to some other heinous crime. "Cases of wine that were marked as suspicious at Barthes Négociants were sent to you. They have the initials *OM* on the bottom of the case," Max said.

"I saw that, and I'm incensed that they showed up here."

"What's the final destination?"

"Wexler's Importers is my distributor. I can't afford a warehouse, and I use them. Excellent company."

"What wines were in the cases?"

"I deal with high-end wines. Some old vintages of the *premieur cru* wines. *Haut-Brion* and *Cheval Blanc* are two. I'd have to check the others. I hope they don't get held up because they've already been sold and buyers are impatient." He removed his glasses and began rubbing them with a tissue. "Barthes is a traditional firm that wouldn't be involved in something this scandalous. Are you sure someone isn't planting the suspicious wines there and they are innocently shipping them out?"

"I suppose that's possible. The son is running things."

Richards made a face. "Oh, him. He doesn't have half the character of his father. He started making wine for the masses, certain that he would create a sensation. It hasn't taken off."

"Is Wexler's your only distributor?"

"I have a couple of others for lesser wines. I'll have my secretary bring their addresses. He put his glasses back on and looked at her. She thought him innocent. "So what are the fraud police doing in France?" he asked. "Is this under the Direction Centrale de la Police Judiciaire? If so, they are probably the best."

"They're involved."

Richards sighed, "Wine is on par with other high-end goods, and with the economic downturn we are attracting more counterfeiters. It's easier for them because there are more collectors out there, who think wine a stronger investment than the stock market." Angus' eyes narrowed behind his glasses. "You aren't accusing *me* of being in on this dirty little operation, are you?"

"We haven't tagged anyone yet. I'm doing the legwork and the French investigator will join me tomorrow."

"Sounds serious." His secretary entered and handed Anson a sheaf of papers. "Here it is, Wexler's. Port Elizabeth in New Jersey."

"Good. I'll start there."

Richards said, "He's a mover, Larry Wexler. Kind of an overnight success. The key, in the end, is being both importer and distributor."

"What's the difference?"

"Distributors have to own warehouses." He rubbed his thumb and finger together to indicate a lot of cash.

Max looked at her watch, and saw it was four. That was pushing it time-wise, as she and Olivier were going to her parents' for dinner. Still, though, she had accomplished nothing. "I need your help."

"Okay."

"I want to meet Wexler."

"Today?"

"I want to nose around, that's all. If I see something, I can go back tomorrow."

He picked up his desk phone. "Who shall I say is coming?"

"A woman named Bailey Blue who is opening a new specialty wine shop in Lower Manhattan." Damn, she thought, I have to include Vasquez. "And her…boyfriend." Richards' eyebrows sailed up to his hairline, as he glanced in the direction of the wiry, young detective. Vasquez stood up quickly, his head reaching Max's shoulder. "I'm a good boyfriend," he said. "Not the dude who gets drunk and beats the girl."

Richards spoke into his cell. "Larry? It's me, Anson. I have a woman I want to send over. She's opening a new wine shop, and I don't have some of the wines she wants." He listened, then implored, "Come on, do it for me. Say forty-five minutes?" He hung up. "He's terribly busy, but he said yes."

"What wines should I be asking for?" Max asked.

"Tell him you want some of Pascal Boulin's wine. The *Terre Brulée*. It's a popular boutique wine here. Wait here, and I'll get you a few labels that I don't carry." He left and soon returned with a couple of other names. "Wexler's is a huge complex, much of it off-limits to the public."

"Do you have a pass I can use?"

He reluctantly pulled out his drawer and handed her two special passes for entering the warehouse area. "Don't lose them," he said. Max thanked him, and he added, "I think you're wasting your time going out there."

Max and Carlos boarded the elevator to the lobby. Out on the street, she rushed over to a hot dog stand, and ordered two. Carlos said he wasn't hungy and she tossed his into a wastebasket. She wasn't sure she wanted to work with someone who didn't eat hot dogs. She checked her messages. Olivier's voice came on, "Max, call me. I have important information. See you at six." She looked down at her cell. The battery was low. She swore, and stood for a second, deciding. "Your cell okay?" she asked her new partner.

"Yeah." He handed it to her.

"Good. My battery's going." She took it and called Olivier's cell, and hung up when voice mail came on. She hailed a taxi and once they were on their way, she called Walt, and said she and Carlos were doing a quick check on a guy in New Jersey. She didn't mention his location. "A shot in the dark," she said. "See you at my folks' for dinner."

"You didn't give him the location," Carlos said.

Max gave him a hard stare. "Don't worry about it."

He turned his head and gazed out the window. I'm acting like Hank, Max thought. She said, "I just went to the funeral of the woman I was hired to protect. It hasn't been a good day."

He looked at her. "I saw the YouTube video."

"Did the damn thing go viral?"

"In the department it did. You hate men, huh?"

"I hate men who do bad things to women."

"So do I. Are we hoping to find Ellen Jordan's killer in Port Elizabeth?"

He doesn't know when to shut up, Max thought. "This is a short stop. A courtesy call on a guy who had some questionable wine arrive in his warehouse. I'll probably have you hang out in the parking lot."

"I like being your boyfriend better."

"I don't know why I said that. A high-end wine shop owner wouldn't be with you. No offense intended."

"You'd be surprised by the types of women who come on to me. I am."

"A lot of women like uniforms. Men not so much."

The cab driver maneuvered his car through the Lincoln Tunnel, and continued on to Interstate 80 through what was commonly referred to as the Jersey Meadows, a euphemism for the oil refineries that extended as far as the eye could see, billowing black fumes into the air. Dante's Hell couldn't equal this, Max thought. They continued west. She saw a sign for Port Elizabeth. Max felt the weight of her 19mm Glock tucked into her waist holder, then checked her pocket for the little knife her brother had given her, and dabbed on lip gloss. She couldn't believe the size of the parking lot. She texted Olivier: *C U @ 6.* She turned her phone off and dropped it back into the bag, then asked the cab driver to wait.

She and Carlos surveyed the vast network of buildings and vehicles. "I'm going in to meet this guy Wexler. The owner." She gave Carlos the once-over. "You look like a worker, so blend in. I'm not sure about the patch of hair…"

"It's called a soul patch."

"Whatever. Have you done any undercover work?"

"I'm just out of narcotics, so sure."

"Okay. You have your gun, right?"

"It's on my ankle."

"The main thing is to act like you belong. Move with purpose. And don't stray too far."

"I'm like a rat the way I can scurry in and out of places."

"Just don't scurry too far. My phone is almost dead and you need yours." Max was embarrassed to think that Olivier's arrival had turned her into silly putty. She couldn't recall ever forgetting to charge her phone. She waited while he keyed in her cell number, and she did same. "I've got enough juice for this," she said.

"I'll be around." He practically vanished before her eyes.

Taking a deep breath, and trying to imagine how a woman would behave who was opening a wine shop, Max entered Wexler's Wines Importers and Distributors. It felt like a sanctuary after all the chaos outside. She sat down to wait, looking around at the spare, attractive décor of the reception room. A woman got up from her desk and turned to Max. "May I help you?"

"Bailey Blue to see Mr. Wexler. I'm opening a new wine shop. He's expecting me."

The secretary returned. "Mr. Wexler is with another client. Do you mind waiting?"

"Not at all. May I look around?"

"Go ahead. There's a building across the walkway there that has a nice display area. Come back in ten minutes."

"Thanks." Max went outside and waved to the taxi driver.

"I don't have all day!" he shouted from the car.

It had stopped raining but was still overcast and chilly. She pulled her jacket tighter around her, and headed toward the taxi. He rolled down his window and stuck his head out. "I'm sorry," she said, handing him a twenty. He backed up and parked.

Max the building the secretary had pointed out to her. Approximately a hundred wine bottles were on display in a glass case. All the first-growth names from Bordeaux, along with what she assumed were impressive wines from many countries. She dug around in her bag and pulled out her phone charger, then found an outlet to plug it into. No one was around. She walked down the hallway to the right looking for a women's room. Doors to what she presumed were offices were closed. She tried one, and it was locked. The second one opened when she turned the handle, and she turned on the light. It was someone's private office, with photos of children propped up on the desk. She quickly scanned the room. At least a thousand labels were stacked on a shelf. She picked up a few and saw that they were from Bordeaux's first-growth *châteaux*.

She heard a light click and whirled around, reaching for her gun. "It's me," Carlos said.

"You nearly got shot on your first day. Whistle next time you're sneaking up on me."

In the corner were large UPS boxes. Max pulled the flap up on one that had been opened and pulled out two empty vintage bottles from the best *châteaux*. The address was Vin. The restaurant was sending Larry Wexler old bottles? "This is the biggest clue we've had," she said.

"Wanna make an arrest?"

"I want to make sure. I'll go meet the owner as planned and select wine for the store. As soon as we're out of Wexler's office, see if you can get in there and check out his computer."

"You don't want me to go with you?"

She pointed to the main building. "I'll be there. Meet me outside Wexler's office in half an hour."

"Got it."

Max grabbed her phone and charger, and rushed back to the main office. A man she assumed to be Wexler appeared, and she went forward to shake hands. He was fit, that was for sure. Muscles bulged beneath his jacket. They shook hands. His was damp. "Anson Richards said you were the man to see," she said in a loud, cheerful voice. "What an operation you have here! I was just looking in the other building at your display." She realized she was feeling nervous after her discovery in the display building, and reminded herself to speak more naturally.

"What specialty wines are you looking for?"

It was the creepy voice on the answering machine. He asked her again, with impatience in his voice, what she was looking for. She noticed that her hand was shaking. She reminded herself that Wexler didn't know who she was. Play it cool, she said to herself.

"I was thinking about Pascal Boulin's wines."

"You're going for the boutique stuff. That's what it's called here. Garage wines in France."

"I think they will have appeal for my customers. I'm really interested in the artisanal wines, too. The organic."

He removed a handkerchief from his pocket and mopped his brow, though the air was frigid. "Come with me," he said, leading the way. They entered the huge warehouse, where she studied the rack and tier system that took up space the size of a parking lot. Everything was on pallets, each made up of a block and tier configuration four blocks across and eight high. Cases of wine were identified by numbers and letters. Workers were running all over the place, men were driving carts filled with cases, and phones were ringing. Wexler received a call, and glancing down at his phone, excused himself. He stepped away a few feet. Max went outside hoping to find Carlos. She decided to try Walt, but her battery had not charged enough.

A black Volvo SUV pulled up beside her, and Paula Goodwin stepped out. Max slipped her cell back into her bag. Paula stared at her. "You're Ellen's assistant," Paula said. "Sorry, what's your name?"'

"Bailey Blue."

"Right. What on earth are you doing here?" Max almost gasped with relief. Women like Paula rarely remembered names of people who didn't matter to them. "Buying wine for a big event," Max said.

"Which one?"

"It's up in Connecticut. My wedding, actually," she lied. "My fiance's inside." She was about to ask Paula why she had come here when she looked up and saw Wexler walking toward them. Then she remembered. Bill said Paula was in a relationship with a distributor. Shit and *merde alors*, she whispered to herself.

"Paula."

"I hope it's important that you dragged me out here, Larry," Paula said.

Max noticed the tension between them. "Excuse me a second," Wexler said to Max, taking Paula's arm and guiding her a few feet away. Max studied them, growing more worried by the second. Paula turned abruptly and strutted to the main building. Wexler smiled at Max, "Let's finish placing your order," he said, leading the way to his office.

Max spoke rapidly to Wexler, "I didn't realize it was so late. I'll take a quick look, but can come back tomorrow." They walked down a long aisle until they came to an exit door.

"The wines you are interested in are in my new warehouse," Wexler said. "I'm doubling the size of my operation." With your new millions, Max thought.

"Impressive," she said, thinking she should have told Carlos to trail her. They exited a door and went directly through another. Against the right wall were shelves filled with bottles. The rest of the building was empty, except for a giant sea-tainer in the middle, evidently waiting to be loaded or unloaded.

"These are my boutique wines," Wexler said.

Paula entered, and Max was glad to see her, though she was terrified that she would remember her real name. "When's your wedding?" Max could barely hear over the sounds of the trucks and construction work outside.

"Next week."

"You're getting married and opening a wine store in the same week?" Wexler asked. Max tried to feign a laugh. "It's crazy, I know."

Paula wasn't amused. Her face grew hard. "Ellen Jordan's assistant who knows nothing about wine is opening a wine store?"

"Assistant?" Wexler asked. "What's going on?"

Max's gun was out. "You're under arrest for counterfeiting, Mister Wexler."

He blinked hard. "You bitch!" he yelled.

"A gun's on you, and don't think I don't know how to use it." Max saw out of the corner of her eye the .22 Paula was holding on her. Only one choice. She ran in a zig-zag pattern toward Paula, who fired the pistol but missed. Max lunged at her and Paula dropped her gun. Max grabbed her arm, but too late. Wexler was upon her, using her as a punching bag. Max used her arms to ward off the blows, but her shoulder was still weak. She slumped to the floor.

Max awoke in a cold and dark place, shivering, hurting all over. She felt around, but couldn't find an object to help center her. She thought she couldn't have been out too long because Paula and Larry were still arguing about what to do with her. "How'd you know she was a cop?" Paula asked Wexler.

"She used Vincent's phone to call her precinct from a bar." Max moaned over her stupidity. "He called the number and got a NYPD detective, then texted me. He also caught her on camera listening to me on the answering machine."

I'm dead meat, Max thought.

"What do we do now? Wexler asked.

"We follow the plan, only we leave tonight. Vincent shipped money to the Australian account."

"What about her?"

"We get rid of her."

"Max heard Paula's voice moving closer. "Open it," she ordered Larry. The side of the container went up like a garage door. Max pretended to be unconscious. Wexler moved in closer with a flashlight. "Shine it on her face," Paula commanded. Max didn't move. The door slammed and the container went dark.

"She's in a sea container that goes out late tonight, correct?" Paula asked.

"We haven't finished emptying it," Larry complained. "There's one more pallet of fine wine still in there."

"Leave it. Make sure she's out and cover her with the tarp."

"She'll die in that thing."

"Duh."

"I think you get the death penalty for killing a cop."

"It will take eight to ten days for her body to reach France. Anybody could have killed her and thrown her in there."

"I need a drink," said Larry.

"Verify while I'm here that she'll be picked up." Max heard him make a call to ensure that the sea-tainer would be picked up within two hours and the ship would pull out at eleven, heading to France. The irony, Max thought. She rolled on her side, against the cold, hard metal side. The idea of dying of hypothermia and thirst in a sea crate was horrifying. Her hands crawled up the side of the container and she found that she could stand, and even limp around. She placed her head against the side of the container in order to hear well.

A door opened, and the noise from outside the building roared in. Paula said, "I'm not here, no matter what, and if you give me away, Larry Wexler, I'll shoot you dead before I go down."

A man's voice echoed across the warehouse space. "My passenger told me to wait. Tall blond woman. I gotta' get paid."

Max felt a surge of hope. It was Carlos pretending to be the cab driver. Brilliant!

Wexler yelled, "She left. This space is off-limits. Construction site." His voice faded as he moved toward the door, then she heard voices raised.

"NYPD!" Max heard next, followed by a gun report, then a man yelling in pain. But who had been shot? Carlos or Wexler?

My only chance, Max thought. She yelled help, but the noise of a machine outside the building drowned out all other sounds. She crawled around on the floor of the container until she bumped into the pallet of wine, the whole lot encased in shrink-wrapped plastic. Reaching in her pocket she pulled out her brother's knife that she carried around like a talisman and began jabbing it into the plastic. It took tremendous effort, but Max finally managed to extract a bottle. It shattered when she threw it against the wall. She screamed at the top of her lungs. The ear-splitting sound of metal banging against metal next to her ear caused her to cry out in alarm. Paula was screaming epithets and hitting the siding of the container with great force. The noise reverberated throughout Max's body. She rolled into a fetal position, covering her ears. The interior of the container reeked of wine now.

The machinery outside droned on and on. Max lay on the floor thinking about her kidnappers. Neither of them would have any qualms about her dying a slow death crossing the Atlantic in a portable morgue. Walt knew by now that she was in trouble. Olivier would be sitting in her apartment, worrying. He said he had something important to tell her.

Max summed up the story she had figured out: The French exporter, Vincent, met up with Larry Wexler on the international wine circuit. Though it was illegal, Wexler surely provided wines to Paula, which she sold at auction, claiming to have gotten them from other people. Larry and Paula were romantically involved. And maybe Vincent and Paula. Ellen had stuck her nose into their business, and paid with her life. And for all she knew, Carolos had just paid with his.

The machines stopped abruptly. The workers were probably changing shifts, as it seemed this was a twenty-four-hour operation. Max heard a tap-tapping across the wooden floor. She heard a door open and slam. Paula Goodwin was free.

Just then, Max felt something pressed against her thigh. It was the pocketknife that she had stuck back in her pocket. "Hey kid," she whispered, "Hank and Juliette can't survive another loss. Help me out here." She gripped the knife tightly as her mind drifted off into darkness.

Chapter Thirty-three

April 9

Olivier sat in Max's kitchen checking emails, waiting for her to show up. Abdel had news: François Laussac was pressing charges against Pascal Boulin for assaulting him. Yannick Martin was out on bail, the 10,000 euros paid by Laussac, presumably. Abdel and his team had found new corks and a large number of old vintage bottles in the cellar of Vincent's office, but no equipment for making labels. Vincent had been trailed to a bank in Switzerland, where he had removed a large sum of cash, and wired another large sum to a bank in Australia, which they intercepted. Since his return he hadn't left his house, but his father came by to say good-bye, and Yannick had stopped in twice. Abdel assured Olivier that Vincent was under guard. Pascal remained in jail, and Olivier typed a response to Abdel that he could be released. The concierge, Monsieur Cazaneuve, had resigned from the hotel, and Abdel asked Olivier if he should interrogate him at his apartment. Olivier was about to sign off when Abdel wrote, "You were right about Douvier exploiting me. I wish I had listened to you."

"D'accord." Olivier tried Max again, then called Anson Richards, whose secretary explained that Mr. Richards was indisposed. Olivier asked her if a woman named Max Maguire had met with him. "You mean a tall, blond, girl, all in black?" That was the one.

She said Max had been gone for a while now. He stayed on hold while the secretary tried to find her boss to see if he knew where Max was headed. She said she'd have to call him back. At least he knew Max had been there. He took a moment to look up the word 'indisposed' on his laptop. *Ill, or disinclined or unwilling* was the definition. He wondered which definition applied to Monsieur Richards.

His phone rang and he picked up quickly. "It's Walt. I've got some bad news. Max has disappeared from a wine warehouse in New Jersey. I'm on my way to get you."

"Disappeared?" He felt panic growing.

"I'll call her folks," Walt said before ending the call.

Olivier was ready when the unmarked car pulled up. Walt stuck his big hand out the window, and shook Olivier's. "Hop in," he said. "Her new partner Carlos called me and told me he was bringing in Wexler, but that Max was nowhere to be found and no amount of threats would get any answer out of Wexler."

"You must have ways of making this man talk."

"For sure." Walt continued with the story. "She and Carlos met with a guy named Anson Richards, who sent them to Wexler's Wines in Port Elizabeth."

"They didn't stay together?"

"Max was posing as a new wine store owner, and so had Carlos get into Wexler's office and break into his computer. They were to meet in half an hour. What about you?"

Olivier told Walt about exchanging bottles with Goodwin, then about the keychain. It was obvious from Walt's expression that he was now taking every aspect of this case seriously.

"We'll bring her in on that basis," he said. He radioed in for someone to pick up Goodwin, adding that he needed search warrants for Wexler's warehouse and apartment. With nothing else to do, he said, "Don't worry about the kid, she's tough." Olivier thought Walt was trying to reassure himself. Walt next barked an order on his cell to someone to find the taxi driver who had taken Max to the warehouse.

Olivier was impressed with the detective he knew to be approaching retirement. He had already observed that Walt had the kind of demeanor that made people, whether colleague or criminal, unload their secrets. He wore a Smith & Wesson Model 10 on his hip. What Olivier found interesting was that it wasn't an automatic, and that it had a four-inch barrel and a wood grip. He had noticed earlier a more compact five-shot revolver strapped to Walt's ankle.

"Max said you're one of the most senior detectives in the precinct," Olivier said, as Walt drove through the Lincoln Tunnel.

"Forty years," Walt said. "I'll soon be sixty-one. When I started back in 1973 there were no female officers on patrol, no counterterrorism division, and few minorities. Now the minorities make up the majority of police officers. It's a different world, with way too much paperwork, but I still love it. What about you?"

"You could compare me to your state prosecutor. My position is constantly in jeopardy, especially with some of our ministers trying to abolish courts and the *juges d'instruction*."

"I never wanted to get into the political aspect of police work," Walt said. "My father and my grandfather before him were cops, and that's all I ever wanted."

"We thought uncovering the counterfeit operation could take weeks," Olivier said. "And suddenly we have two strong American suspects.

"I've found that when cases start to unravel it goes fast," Walt said. "It takes diligence, and a stroke of luck. You being handed the key ring in France by the maid's husband and then seeing it on Goodwin's desk is what I mean by luck."

"The Champagne murders and now my Opération Merlot have taken me into a world of greed that has shocked me," Olivier said. "Except for German officers resorting to violence during World War II, I don't know of a case when wine has been associated with murder."

"The world's gone crazy," Walt said. He slowed the car down. "Here we are." They entered a vast parking lot and followed signs to Wexler's Importer and Distributor. Hank pulled up behind them, and got out of his car and walked briskly over, leaving Carlos behind on his phone.

"You must have taken a helicopter here," Walt said. Olivier thought the two detectives an incongruous twosome, Walt sartorially elegant in a suit and Hank in cowboy boots and leather jacket. Olivier stood back when Hank went into a diatribe about how he should have gone with Max, how headstrong she was, and what the hell was the point of being a cop if he couldn't save his own kid. Olivier thought he was displaying a rare vulnerability.

"You're irrational about her," he overheard Walt say. "Where she is right now has nothing to do with Frédéric."

"That's enough." Hank's voice was steely.

"If I don't say something, nobody ever will. You can't keep her safe, Hank. None of us can control fate."

"I can sure as hell try."

"If you don't let her go, she'll have to take off. She told me once that the only time she feels really free is when she's in France, or in a Jiu-Jitsu fight."

"Let's deal with the psychology stuff later," Hank said.

A car from the Port Authority police pulled up. Walt walked over and shook hands with the driver and talked with him for a few minutes. He came back to Hank and Olivier, and said they had to wait a couple of minutes. He explained to Olivier, "The Port Authority police are in charge of crimes connected to regional airports, train stations, and shipping. They handle thousands of ships carrying more than 32.8 million metric tons of cargo every year, including the wine you're looking for. They have over 100 detectives trained for crimes occurring at transportation facilities. I could go on, but I think you get my point."

"Let's stop the lesson and go in," Hank said. "Show us where you saw her go in, Carlos."

Olivier felt like he was part of what he imagined an old-fashioned Western posse to be like as they entered the warehouse and followed signs to the office. A receptionist said that Mr. Wexler had left for the day. Walt pulled out his shield and said they were looking for a young woman who had met with Mr.

Wexler around 4:30 this afternoon. She shook her head and said she had just come on for the night shift.

"I guess we'll have to conduct a search," Walt said. Hank had already disappeared.

"I'll need to contact Mr. Wexler," the secretary said.

"You do that," Walt said.

Chapter Thirty-four

April 9

The solitude and darkness of the container, along with the fear that Max was trying to keep at bay, reminded her of a time when her parents took her brother and her to a country fair where they rode in a small car through a tunnel of horrors. Max was ten and her brother four, and while he had laughed, she had been frozen with terror as monsters with ghastly faces lunged out from the walls. She had experienced a much greater fear years later when her brother's life had hung in the balance, and when his death was announced, she entered a world that was like the tunnel, where images of him crushed by a car tormented her for years.

She had taken the cue from her parents to hide the grief that threatened to topple them over on a daily basis. Juliette had tried to get pregnant again, to no avail, and Hank had worked obsessively and become a hero. Max rebelled and started hanging out with the wrong crowd, but eventually got a degree from NYU in French literature and soon after applied to the police academy. It had been twelve years since Frédéric's death, and she realized that she and her parents had never discussed it. Note to therapist, she said out loud: deal with brother's death. Note #2: Tell Olivier you love him and don't worry about his response.

She had no idea how long she had lain in this box. She had heard a shot ring out, and a cry of pain. Several scenarios passed through her mind. The one she clung to was that Carlos shot Wexler, and by now Walt, Olivier, and Hank were on their way to her. What she feared, though, was that Wexler had a hidden gun and had shot Carlos, and he was lying on the floor nearby, dead. Paula and Wexler could be on a plane to Australia by now.

Pain brought her back into her body. Her head hurt with a vengeance, and she couldn't get warm. She lay there, and then remembered the wine that was her only company. She got up and found her way to the pallet, then dug out her penknife, and began to cut through more plastic. It took half an hour, but she pulled out a bottle, and stuck her knife down the side of the cork until it released. She turned the bottle up and took a sip. It was delicious. Ellen's wine tasting instructions came to mind. "It's a scintillating wine," she said out loud, "with a hint of blueberries and yes, tobacco." She had another sip, and another, imagining a headline in the *New York Post* announcing her death: *Detective Dies with $5,000 Bottle of Wine Clutched in Hand*. She eased back into the void.

◊◊◊

The Wexler warehouse was a beehive of activity at eight at night. Small trucks wove in and around the pallets of wine, and in and out of the vast warehouse. Olivier observed the rack-and-tier system, eights pallets high. Bottles were identified by numbers and letters. He could see Hank and Carlos far ahead, and he and Walt hurried to keep up.

Through the exit was a shell of a building that appeared to be a new warehouse under construction. Hank peered in through the window but it was dark inside. The door was locked. Carlos explained how Wexler raced at him when he entered this space, and when he raised his arm, Carlos had no choice but to shoot.

Walt said, "He hasn't said anything?"

"All's he's said is that a woman named Bailey Blue was in there buying for her new store, and by the time I showed up she had left."

"He didn't have a gun, but went aggressive when you yelled NYPD," Hank said. "Something had gone down."

Carlos said, "I kept my eye on Max until she told me to check out the office. She met up with a lady in the parking lot and talked to her."

"Describe her," Walt said.

He did. Olivier said, "Paula Goodwin. She drove out here?"

"She's in with Wexler," Hank said. "The picture is clearer. Did you see Max leave?" he asked Carlos.

"No. I waited for her, then looked all over, and when I didn't see any sign of her I called Captain O'Shaughnessy."

"Max walked into a trap," Hank said.

"I'm calling the office," Walt said. "Joe's still there. He'll get Wexler to talk." He walked away from them to make his call.

"Open this door," Hank ordered Carlos, who took out a wire and began working it through the door handle. Olivier walked to the far corner of the building and peered around the corner. A wide door was raised and a flatbed truck was parked in the cavity of the building. Olivier beckoned to Walt and Hank, who followed him to the truck that was blaring hip-hop music. The driver was looking over a worker's shoulder; the worker was busy readying the mechanism that would lower the container onto the flatbed.

Hank and Walt approached the driver, holding up their shields. Olivier watched as the driver stared at the shield, then hopped up into the cab and turned down the music a half notch.

"How come you're the only truck in here?" Walt asked.

The driver, his dark hair pulled back in a ponytail and sporting a scraggly beard, looked around and shrugged. "This building ain't officially open yet. I have an order to pick up a container. That's all I know."

It occurred to Olivier that all truckers shared the same responses, as though their ignorance of what they were delivering was part of their DNA.

"Let me see your license," Hank said. The driver dug it out of a beat-up wallet that he kept in his back pocket and glanced around at the men who were walking around the building as if they were searching for something.

Displaying no nervousness, he said, "All's I'm doing is taking an empty container back to the dock to be returned to Europe." He paused, "What's going on? Drugs or something?"

"Something," Walt said. The night manager, a short, nervous man, ran out from the office at the other end of the warehouse and demanded to know what was going on.

"What time did you come on?" Walt asked.

"Four."

"Did you see a tall young woman anywhere on the premises? Tall woman with short blonde hair?"

"Only woman I saw was Ms. Goodwin."

"What time?"

"Five-thirty, maybe. She was moving quickly down aisle three."

Walt turned back to the driver. "Give me your *acquis* papers."

The driver handed him a sheaf. "I'm taking it to the *Mary Honeycut.*"

"I take it that's a boat?"

The driver nodded. He stood on one foot and then the other waiting for Walt to finish looking at the papers. "I gotta get movin, chief. This is a rush job."

Walt waved him on. The driver turned back to his truck and continued his preparations for loading the large container that was suspended four feet off the cement floor with ropes and cables. A worker held a control box. Swearing, the driver moved his truck beneath it. A song of loss and abandonment issued from the cab of the truck.

Another sound cut through the lyrics, and Olivier looked around to see if there was nearby construction. "Stop!" he shouted to the driver, running up to the side of the container. The driver cupped his hand behind his ear as if to say he didn't understand.

Hank was taking impatient strides toward the truck now. "Turn the damn radio off!" Hank yelled.

"What's going on?" Walt asked Olivier.

"I heard something like glass breaking," Olivier said.

They all froze in place in order to listen. "C'mon guys!" the driver complained. "You're making me late."

Hank turned to the driver, "Open this thing up."

The driver started to protest, but seeing Hank's face, obeyed. "I need to lower it first," the driver said, and the worker hit buttons that brought it to ground level. "Now don't go accusing me of nothing," the driver said, sounding defensive.

The manager pulled the rope that lifted the door. Hank stepped inside, Walt behind him holding a flashlight. "See anything?" Walt hollered.

"I got her!" Hank said.

Olivier entered, and saw Max lying on a tarp with broken glass all around her. She appeared to be covered with blood. As Hank ripped off his jacket and placed it under her head, she said, "I think I drank too much."

Walt went into action, issuing loud, barking orders to police officers, some who showed up the minute they heard Max was missing on their radios. Walt called for an ambulance.

Hank stood up, and Olivier heard him speaking in a soft voice into his cell phone. "She's here. She'll be okay. Now stop your crying, Juliette." He quickly left the container and found a quieter place to finish his conversation.

Olivier knelt down beside Max. Seeing her bruised cheek, and half-closed eye, he felt coldly vengeful toward Wexler. "You almost had a fermented body show up on your shore," she said. "Glad you didn't have to deal with that."

He picked up the broken wine bottle. "You chose a really fine wine to throw against the wall! You also won our bet that the killers were on American soil," he said, switching to French, "We'll dine at Veritas tomorrow night."

"I have a day to pull myself together then." She sounded winded, and her eyes were closed.

When the ambulance arrived, Olivier heard Hank say, "Mom will meet us at the hospital."

Walt marched to the unmarked police car, with Olivier behind him. "This would have been another murder on their hands if they'd been successful," he said. "If you hadn't heard that glass breaking, who knows what the outcome would have been."

Olivier didn't want to think about it. "What will you do about Paula Goodwin?"

"The night is young," Walt replied. He maneuvered the car around a city bus. "I assume you'll want to stop by the hospital so we'll head there first."

They both seemed lost in their own thoughts when Olivier said, "I have a ring for Max."

"Here a ring says a lot, if you know what I mean."

"She doesn't wear rings, I notice," Olivier said.

"She'll wear yours." He glanced over at Olivier, "Max reminds me of my wife who was a detective for twenty years. She didn't make it."

"I'm sorry."

Walt sighed. "What can you do?"

Olivier didn't know.

Chapter Thirty-five

April 9

When Max was released from the hospital two hours after her arrival, she insisted on going back to her apartment. Olivier had stopped by the emergency room and offered to take care of her if they released her. He sat reading a book with Woof at his feet, sipping a glass of scotch, when she and her parents arrived at the apartment. He stood and walked over to Max. "You're okay?" he asked, kissing her on each cheek, and leading her to the sofa. "Do you want a glass of something?"

Woof jumped up and barked excitedly until Max calmed him down. "She's on pain pills," Juliette said.

"I didn't swallow them," Max said, leaning down to pet her dog, who was jumping around in excitement. "I'll have a sip of scotch." She and Olivier exchanged un-selfconscious smiles. Juliette bustled around, and Hank, looking uneasy, accepted the glass of scotch Olivier offered him. Juliette declined. "Don't forget your promise to me," she said to Max.

Hank announced that he would stay out of the search for Paula Goodwin. "I don't need to kill somebody on the eve of my retirement."

"I *will*," Olivier said. It was hard for Max not to laugh at the out-of-character remark.

Juliette said, "They killed my best friend, and were trying to kill my daughter. I wish I knew this Jiu-Jitsu."

Hank grinned. "You French are sounding awfully violent." Growing more serious, he said, "I figured Max was going to run into one of the hard-hitters in this group. I just didn't figure it would be today. Who would have thought a woman like Paula, at the top of her game, would be involved?"

That's what people will say about Vincent Barthes, Olivier thought. He knew the general belief in France was that the elite were incapable of committing crimes. He wanted to remind them to look back at the history of the kings and queens of France to see real crime at work.

"All I could think in that box was that my partner of half a day was dead. And I hadn't been friendly."

"He thinks he's failed, and should be fired for losing you. I'm afraid from now on he'll be your shadow."

"We'll work it out."

"What about the collection that started all this mess?" Hank asked. "How do you know Bill Casey isn't part of this ring of counterfeiters?"

Max said, "It sounds weird but he wouldn't stoop to that, and besides, he doesn't have to. He's not an avaricious guy. His problem is that he has a soft spot for Paula, and thinks we've made her into a scapegoat. He takes care of the underdog."

"He was good to Ellen, too," Juliette said.

Hank said, "A lot of this is about his ego. All the bottles taken care of?"

Max spoke up. "Ellen and Bill and friends killed one magnum. The one stolen from the hotel safe in Bordeaux is still unaccounted for. Olivier has the one that Paula switched on Bill, which is surely counterfeit. And Bill has one left."

"She was willing to pay $30,000 to fool him?"

Max nodded. "And she offered Olivier $25,000 to buy back the fake bottle that she knew he had taken."

"She covers all the bases. So all you're missing is Paula Goodwin," Hank said.

"Australian officials are on high alert," Olivier said.

Walt buzzed from downstairs and Olivier grabbed his jacket. "Now you see why I love my job," Max said.

"I may change careers," Olivier said, and was off.

After the door closed, Hank said, "He doesn't have the chutzpah to be in this line of work."

"You're saying that after he went undercover and caught Paula switching bottles, then stole the bottle and noticed the key chain, plus…"

"You're stuck on the guy, huh?"

"Yep."

"Your ma and I were married within a month after meeting each other. This thing with Olivier has been dragging on almost a year."

"Olivier doesn't rush anything, and that's fine with me." Max sipped her scotch. "Let's go back to Paula Goodwin. I was fooled by the suit and friendliness."

"She's a sociopath," Hank said. "Brutally cold inside, but on the surface they can make themselves charming to get what they want. What a crime is to us is expediency to them. Ellen had to die because she was about to expose Paula. People like her who have social status are acquitted more than any others because of their charm and smarts. It drives me crazy." He drained his glass of scotch.

Juliette began arranging books on the shelf. Max recalled her promise to herself to have the "talk" with her parents. Her mother made it easy when she said, "I don't want to leave you here alone."

"Olivier could be out all night," Hank said.

Max watched her mother for a moment, then took a deep breath, knowing that she was keeping herself busy in order not to face the trauma of her daughter being injured.

"*Maman*," she said.

"*Oui, chérie*?"

"I've had some time to think. While I have you both here, I have a couple of questions. If I don't ask now, I never will."

Hank leaned against the doorjamb. "Fire away," he said.

"Did you two have to get married?" They looked at each other, and back at Max.

"We would have married anyhow," Juliette said softly.

Hank said, "I disagree. She would have gone back to France and lived happily ever after in some castle..."

"Not true, Hank," Juliette said. "I was in love. I still am." He stared at his feet.

"Dad," she said, "I was stuck in that coffin long enough to think about us. How much you mean to me, and how grateful I am to you."

"You're going to get sappy on me?"

"I am. And *Maman*...the day Frédéric was hit by the car..." Juliette's eyes instantly welled with tears, and Max knew why she had avoided for years bringing the topic up. "Do you think the accident wouldn't have happened if I'd been with him?"

"Max," Hank said, a hint of warning in his voice, "it happened a long time ago. This is hard on your mother..."

"Think how hard it's been on me!" Max said. "It was my fault!"

Juliette sat still for a few moments before she spoke. "For a long time, *chérie*, I wanted to believe there was some reason for the accident, that we could have prevented it, that I should have gone for him, that you should have been with him and not doing what all eighteen-year-olds do, which is to be with their friends...I even believed at one time that our son had to pay with his life for the people his father had killed in the line of duty."

"Juliette." Hank looked shocked.

"But it was none of those things," Juliette said. "It was fate. Or destiny. Or whatever you want to call it. We don't have to know everything." Her voice trembled, "I know I can't go through losing another child, though."

Max moved into her mother's arms, crying. When they looked up, Hank had disappeared. "He worries about you, too, Max. I think he wishes he hadn't pushed you to follow in his footsteps."

"But I did and I'm glad. I love my job. Maybe eventually I'll be following in yours and spending more time in France. Mamie has invited me to Burgundy in the summer."

"*Vraiment?* You would see where I grew up. Is my mother the only one luring you back to Burgundy?" Her eyes twinkled.

"It seems that Olivier has family there, too."

"Hank will be retired. *Maman* wants me to come."

"She told me. I hope you'll go."

"Really? Hank has been telling me that you are ready to be on your own, that we need to release you. I don't understand this. The French never do all this releasing. We don't have the term 'empty nest.' For the rest of their lives the children come for dinner on Sunday and bring their children."

"Good thing we're French then, huh?" Max said.

Juliette walked into the kitchen to prepare a few "neebles," but paused to add, "I'll make a deal. When you stop leaping into dangerous situations, we will stop being helicopter parents."

"How can I stop when I don't know they're dangerous?" She hesitated, "I wonder what Frédéric would be doing were he alive?"

"I thought he would go into music."

"Really?"

"All this talk about him becoming a detective. He wasn't interested at all. He was quite gifted with the guitar."

"I wish he were still with us."

"He is," Juliette said simply. Max closed her eyes, feeling that some great load had been lifted.

Chapter Thirty-six

April 9

Olivier watched, fascinated, as Walt set up a command post at the 20th Precinct station on West 82nd Street. All airports under Port Authority supervision were covered, and train and bus stations had been put on watch, too. It was the vastness of their operation that floored Olivier. The Port Authority police had been called in and Interpol was on alert. Carlos had come in to report on their search for Paula, and said that her eight-room Fifth Avenue apartment was under tight security. Hank had sent a detective to Yale University to make sure her son wouldn't disappear. Her younger son in boarding school was also being watched.

Paula would have a hard time leaving the country, Walt said, though he was concerned that she had too much of a head start. Olivier learned that Wexler's offices and warehouses were flooded with police combing through everything looking for counterfeiting equipment. They had found labels to be affixed to old bottles, and the boxes of bottles sent from the restaurant, Vin, which Wexler was filling with lesser wines and selling for a fortune. Olivier predicted that much of the lesser wine was sent from Barthes' business, along with hundreds of old bottles. It was a perfect set-up. As far as Olivier could tell, nothing was left undone in the pursuit of Goodwin. Walt checked in twice with Hank, and was told that Max was resting.

"What's going on in France?" Walt asked Olivier.

"Vincent Barthes is under surveillance," he said. "I want to interrogate Wexler about anyone in France who is involved."

Walt said, "He's all yours after we're done. Your buddy Douvier called an hour ago. I don't think the guy ever sleeps. He needs to talk to you."

"Okay to use your phone?" Olivier wondered why Douvier hadn't called him directly.

Walt handed over his cell phone.

Douvier picked up immediately. "Captain O'Shaughnessy?"

"*C'est Chaumont,*" Olivier corrected.

"*Ah. Bon.* How is New York? I was there last year and had a remarkable time of it."

This is a social call? Olivier wondered. "We're making progress. I'm leaving late tomorrow night, and can fly into Paris if you want to confer the following afternoon."

"Abdel is keeping me informed."

"Yes, I know."

"He's an upstanding young officer, proof that these guys can make something of themselves." Olivier knew that "these guys" meant Arabs. How, Olivier wondered, can our social problems be altered when our leaders talk this way? Douvier, it was easy to see, was making a smart political move by using Abdel. By placing his sudden support of immigration in the forefront, Douvier might stand a chance of being appointed minister again, or at the very least, leave on an impressive note.

"By the way," Douvier said, "I've talked to the *procureur* and we want to remove the twenty-four-hour guard from Vincent's. We could arrest him, you know."

"Philippe, if this woman makes it to France I have a feeling she'll go right to Vincent." He explained in as simple terms as possible about the night before.

"You have no idea which direction she went in?"

"We've lost her."

"Like you lost the magnum of wine. What next? We've already had two arrests, Olivier, with a lot of publicity, and both suspects have been released." Now that he had gotten his point across, he said, "I'll keep a policeman on until you get back, but then… *Olivier, êtes-vous là*?"

Hearing activity in the other room, Olivier touched END and handed the phone back to Walt. How could he possibly explain in a few sentences the scene at the precinct, Max's experience with the counterfeiters, the arrest of Larry Wexler, and the disappearance of Paula Goodwin? He had to call Abdel as soon as it was daylight in France, and try to put a stop to Douvier's interference in the New York investigation. For now, though, he was upstairs in the 20th Precinct station with Walt beckoning to him. He wore no jacket, offering a full display of his gun.

Walt had removed his jacket, offering a full display of his gun. Hank came in and paced around the room while Carlos sat in front of one of the large, gray desks that seemed to fill the room, typing notes into a computer.

Olivier had been surprised to see a cell in the officers' room when he entered, and was told it was a temporary holding cell. Wexler sat inside the cell, his head in his hands.

Walt spoke to the group, "Here's what went down after those two shits left Max in the container." After explaining what happened in New Jersey, he added, "I'm sure that Goodwin thought when Max's body was hauled off the container in France in eight to ten days that no one could ever prove she was involved. Carlos, let's unlock the cell door and invite our guest to join the conversation."

"It's not locked," Carlos said.

Larry Wexler walked out, a defiant look on his face. "Look," he said before anyone had addressed him, "I want my lawyer here."

"I'm Captain Walt O'Shaughnessy," Walt said. "We're booking you now, that's all. You were read the Miranda Act." He turned to a young detective, "Turn on the recorder."

"Your cop last night tortured me."

"Is that a formal complaint? If so, we'll deal with it later."

"What am I being arrested for?"

"You mean you don't know which crime? How about counterfeiting? Illegal importation of wine? Assault? Murder?"

Olivier could see that Wexler was panicked. "What murder?"

"What about the attempted murder of NYPD detective, Max Maguire, to start?"

Wexler's voice was firm. "It was self-defense."

Walt leaned over him, not taking his eyes off him. "You knocked out Detective Max Maguire and left her to die in a sea-tainer. We have the facts from your victim." Sweat dripped off Wexler's face. Olivier knew from meeting him in Bordeaux that his hands were clammy. "Which reminds me," Walt said. "Where's Paula?"

"I don't know," Wexler said. "Australia, maybe."

"What happened?"

The room was silent except for a fax machine starting up.

"We have enough proof already to lock you up for a long time," Walt said. "Detective Maguire has told us everything. It'll go a lot easier for you if you tell us where she went."

"Okay, I'll cooperate."

"Do you need water?" When he nodded, Carlos went to the water cooler and filled a cup with water and handed it to Wexler. "My question is simple," Walt said. "Did you kill Ellen Jordan?"

"No."

"Who did, then?"

He paused. "Vincent Barthes."

"How?

Wexler said, "He has a lab and knows how to make poison. He put it into a blue cheese, and took it to her…"

Vincent's alibi isn't foolproof, Olivier thought. He had taken the room at the hotel to talk business with clients, which meant he had access to the upstairs at the hotel.

"That's interesting," said Olivier. "I thought it might have been Vincent, but it was your key chain that was found on Madame's floor. It has your DNA on it."

Wexler's face grew alarmed, and he thought a couple of seconds before he said, "Vincent had a set, too. Paula had them made for us at Cartier."

"But only one set has your fingerprints."

Wexler's jaw tightened, and he took out a handkerchief and wiped his brow. Olivier was sure now. Wexler had paid Ellen Jordan a visit, after Paula called and asked Ellen to meet with him. He brought in the cheese and the sauterne.

Walt said, "We know Ellen Jordan was aware that Paula Goodwin sold the *'45 Mouton-Rothschild* wine to Bill Casey. Jordan suspected her of counterfeiting and had decided to have a talk with her before going to the police. We know from her phone records that she was to meet with Paula Goodwin at the *en primeur*, but Paula canceled. You went instead."

"I didn't know Ellen Jordan."

"But Paula knew her quite well. You were her emissary."

"Ellen Jordan was also acquainted with Vincent Barthes."

"She knew his father. She wouldn't have opened her door to Vincent. "What did you do after you left Madame Jordan's room?"

"I didn't say I was there."

"I said it." Walt asked for a cup of coffee for the prisoner and the officer brought it to him. "You know Paula Goodwin's going to throw you to the dogs. While you're rotting in prison, she will be out in the world, making tons of money, living the good life."

Wexler's head dipped, and his body slumped. He explained how he and Paula Goodwin had started sleeping together two years ago. "We figured we could make a fortune selling counterfeit wine to investors who didn't know what they were talking about. When we attended a wine event in Bordeaux six months later and met Vincent Barthes—who, by the way, Paula also had a fling with— Paula told Vincent about a scheme for earning millions through the use of his facilities. He signed on finally because his business was failing."

They had started simply: they paid Yannick to steal a few cases here and there, then sold them in Japan and China. Vincent, Olivier knew, was aware that the families wouldn't report the thefts. It worked for a while, Wexler said, but then stories of the thefts began appearing in newspapers. That was when they decided to fill a few fine bottles they found in the basement of

Vincent's father's building with a lesser wine that was made at Vincent's new processing plant and pass those off to investors. It was a success from the start, mainly because they all had excellent connections to people who were clamoring to invest in wine.

Olivier interjected, "The *Mouton-Rothschild* magnums were from Yves Barthes' business?"

Wexler nodded "Vincent's grandfather was the *négociant* for the vineyard back in the 40's and 50's. The bottles and the labels were authentic."

"But not the wine that went to Bill Casey," Olivier said.

"One of the four bottles was authentic," Wexler explained. "I think that's the way we did it. Ellen tasted a fake. The authentic one was a birthday present to Vincent from his father when he turned twenty-one."

Olivier thought how different the outcome would have been had Ellen opened that one. It was this kind of randomness that made him believe in fate.

Walt started to pace. "Finish your story." A detective sitting quietly in the room started the tape recorder again.

"We were making millions. If people got suspicious we agreed we would quit, but for Paula it became an obsession. We stashed a lot of the money in Switzerland."

"And spent."

"That, too. Finally, Paula thought things were getting out of hand and wanted to give it a rest. She had the apartment and the car she wanted. Vincent could show his father a big profit, and sell his supermarket operation. I was fully established. It was perfect."

"Then Ellen stepped into the picture and told Bill Casey that the *Mouton* was a fake," said Walt.

"How'd you know that?"

Walt, irritated, said, "It's not rocket science. You take over, Olivier."

Olivier said, "Bill Casey told Paula that Ellen was taking the wine to France to have it tested, correct?"

Wexler nodded. "Vincent was in New York when Paula decided that Ellen was going to bring us all down. She decided to kill her. Vincent sent Ellen a warning note, because he didn't want to be a part of it. But Ellen ignored it."

"So who killed her?" Walt asked in a loud voice.

"I told you. Vincent." Wexler held his stomach and said he had to be excused, and an officer took him out.

"What do you think?" Walt asked Hank.

"A man who would beat up a woman, the way he did Max, would easily kill."

Olivier said, "It makes sense that Vincent put the poison into the cheese."

"And where did the aconite come from?" Walt asked.

Olivier answered quickly. "The foreman, Yannick Martin."

"Paula Goodwin was in New York feigning illness, clever woman," said Walt.

Hank spoke at last. "What's Paula Goodwin's status?"

"MIA. We've checked out everything."

"Put it out there that the killer has been found," Hank said. "It might slow her down if she knows Wexler's been caught."

"I'll put it on the news tonight," Walt said. "She'll want the cash that Vincent retrieved from Switzerland. I wonder if he was to meet them in Australia?"

"That was my thought," Olivier said. They had started to go around in circles.

"I'm going to pick up Juliette and take her home," Hank said to Olivier. He looked at Olivier. "Need a lift?"

For the first time, Olivier allowed exhaustion to wash over him. It was midnight. "I accept," he said, and they went out to the street and got into Hank's unmarked car.

"You did some fine detective work," Hank said.

"I wish events had coincided better," Olivier said.

"Meaning you would have gotten to Max in time to warn her? You tried." He wove in and out of traffic as he made his way down Second Avenue. "I've never come across a murder occurring over wine."

"It could have been art, but happened to be wine," Olivier said.

"Do you invest in wine?" Hank asked.

"I have around 200 bottles. I'm not competing, though, for rare wines. I purchase mine in a good year and wait patiently for them to come into their own."

"How long you talking?"

"A decade for many of them. Some will be perfect in twenty years."

"You're that patient?"

"Sometimes not."

"Max mentioned that her grandmother wanted her to come to Burgundy for the summer. I hope she'll go and stay a month. She has a lot of vacation time built up. Maybe she'll get out of police work altogether."

"I think she'd be surprised to hear you think that. It's her passion."

"You really mean that? Everybody assumed after Frédéric died that I wanted my daughter to replace him. That may have been true at first. But now…" When Olivier didn't respond, he continued, "All parents really want is for their kid to be happy, right?"

Olivier nodded, but thought his parents wanted much more than their child's happiness. "Patience is a good quality," Hank was saying, "but maybe overrated. I didn't think I stood a chance with Juliette, but I went for it. Everything happened fast after that."

They were in front of Max's apartment building. "Goodnight," Olivier said, not giving Hank the opportunity to ask any questions about Max and him.

Chapter Thirty-seven

April 10

Olivier was asleep on the sofa and opened his eyes when Max entered the living room. "*Bonjour*," he said. "You were sleeping soundly when I came in and I didn't want to wake you."

She yawned. "I ended up taking a pain pill. I was thinking about the bottles of wine I broke when I woke up."

He sat up. "A couple of bottles of *Margaux '82* were broken, and the bottle you opened for your last communion was a lovely wine from Burgundy, a *Nuits-Saint-Georges*. Good choices, by the way." He watched her take a package of coffee beans from the freezer, then waited while she pressed the button on the coffee grinder.

"I wish I had a better memory of the taste."

"Too bad you didn't have the experience of drinking the genuine *'45 Mouton* at Bill Casey's gathering, a rare experience for anyone."

"Something I have in common with several billion other people. I'll manage the way they do." She sat down beside him on the sofa while the coffee was brewing. "Now tell me about last night."

He filled her in, ending with, "but no sign of Paula Goodwin."

"She must have friends all over the world willing to jump in to help her."

"They'd aid a suspect?" Olivier asked.

"There's no reason for them to know, but even if they did, their disbelief that their 'wine guru' would cheat them would take over."

"I'm surprised she left Wexler alive," Olivier said.

"She left Wexler to be picked up, which makes me think he murdered Ellen. All the better for her if he confesses."

"You seem to understand her well."

"Hank's been giving me a few lessons."

She jumped up. "I have to get ready to meet my mother in a couple of hours, and I have police files to write up before I do."

The apartment phone rang and she switched to French. "Ah, *bonjour, Mamie!* She glanced over at Olivier and smiled. Olivier got up to pour some coffee. "*Oui, oui. D'accord. Bon. Vraiement? Okay, merci, Mamie, au revoir,*" she said into the phone, nodding her head the entire time. She hung up. "Mamie told me Douvier was excited to learn of the capture of Larry Wexler last night," she said to Olivier. "He's about to present to the French public that Ellen Jordan's killer was found in New York, and that the case is closed."

Olivier said, "Captain O'Shaughnessy is focusing on the Wexler arrest which will make Goodwin think she got away with setting up her partner as the guilty party. It seems to be working with Douvier, too, though that wasn't my intention. I want to know how Paula and Wexler both knew your identity."

"I called Joe from the bar at the Hôtellerie Renaissance bar the night Ellen was murdered to get the code to break into her computer. Vincent lent me his mobile to make the call, and we figured that later he called that number and Detective Joe Laino answered. I also might have been filmed listening to the answering machine in the bedroom."

"Any idea when Vincent let Wexler in on your identity?"

"Probably seeing me in the bistro with you and Abdel made him suspicious, and he began investigating." She went to her little desk and pulled out files. "Hey, did my shoulder bag come with me from the hospital?"

"Your father would know. I need to verify that I'm leaving on the 11:30 flight tonight. I should arrive in Bordeaux around five tomorrow afternoon."

"Don't tell me. A group decision has been made to leave me here. Thus the dinner."

"What do you mean? My plan is to check on things in France, then meet you in Australia in a few days. By then your injuries…"

"I'm fine. Paula Goodwin is on her way there to find Vincent. You want to use your power of persuasion to get Walt to let me go?"

"I'll see what I can do. You think Goodwin slipped through before airports were put on high alert?"

"I do. And if she has my bag, she has my passport, gun, detective shield, and credit card. Walt can find out if Max Maguire has entered France."

"There's no way she could be mistaken for you."

"We're both blond. And with my credentials she's carrying, do you think security officers will study the photo?"

"The French may be more skeptical. My gut is telling me she's on her way to Australia, if that counts for anything. Check to see if someone has charged anything to your credit card."

Max decided to ignore the sarcasm, as she felt a fight brewing. Hank was emphatic that a detective mustn't second-guess that first intuition, but she felt herself weakening slightly. "She wouldn't get far with a $3,000 limit," Max said lightly. She stood up and glanced in the mirror, feeling disgruntled about giving up work for a few hours of pampering with her mother, but a promise was a promise, even though she had promised while almost unconscious.

"I'll go to the precinct while you're with your mother."

"Are you sure you want to do dinner tonight?" she asked. "I'm fine with take-out here again."

"Max, do you know how many times you've asked me if I'm sure?"

"It seems weird to be going to a fabulous restaurant when we have a crime to solve."

"You just came up with a theory about your shoulder bag while having coffee and talking to your grandmother. You were relaxed."

"Okay. Point taken." He disappeared into the bathroom and she heard the shower start. She got up to check the bedroom closet once more, in case her mother had put her bag there. Olivier was humming a tune. On impulse, she opened the sliding door to the shower and stepped in.

◇◇◇

Max entered the front door of Veritas, on East 20th Street, a restaurant that a food critic for *The New York Times* had called "an elegant little jewel box." She walked through a hip crowd at the bar, carrying her weekend bag, which the maitre'd offered to store for her. He then led her into a cozy room humming with the conversation of a small group of diners. Pendant lights cast a warm glow onto the bare, dark wood tables, contributing to the intimate atmosphere.

She smiled as she sat on the banquette that ran the length of the wall. Walt had said yes to her returning to France, and Hank hadn't interfered, which surprised and pleased her. She and her mother had spent the afternoon being pampered with a manicure, a new hairstyle, and even a new dress. They had finally settled on a short, red, soft stretch jersey number, which was as far from Max's norm as she ever cared to go, and now she sat second-guessing their selection.

The sommelier came to greet her and Max readily accepted the glass of champagne he offered. She didn't see Olivier until he was upon her. She smiled up at him, where he stood calmly behind his chair, looking at her. "What's wrong?" she asked, feeling self-conscious. "Lipstick on my teeth?"

"*Au contraire, tu sembles...parfaite.*"

"I'm far from perfect," she laughed. "My mother went a little crazy, don't you think?"

He sat down across from her and picked up her glass of champagne, and sipped. "*Louis Roederer*," he said. The sommelier appeared with the wine list that was thick as a Bible, and Olivier decided on a white burgundy to start, a 2008 *Domaine Leflaive Les Combettes,* a *Puligny-Montrachet Premier Cru.*

"Are you okay with the tasting menu?" he asked. She nodded, knowing that it was just that: a way to sample multiple tiny portions that the chef thought best represented his talent.

The server arrived with an *amuse-guile.* "It's a roasted wild mushroom shooter with hen-of-the-wood, oyster, and shitake mushroom crostini," she said.

Olivier sipped. His eyes sparkled. "Do you taste how the light and airy Porcini foam betrays the woodsy, earthy note of a mushroom that's been distilled down to its essence?"

"Uh…no."

Olivier laughed. "I love how the earthiness of the mushrooms brings out the brioche in the champagne."

"You took the words right out of my mouth."

"You're making fun of me," he said.

"I can't help it. I thought brioche was bread."

"It's special bread, very yeasty and sweeter than usual toast."

"How depressing that I will probably never develop that *je ne sais quoi…*perhaps the extra olfactory sense that some French people seem born with."

"It's not an extra sense, but the way all our senses work together, perhaps?"

The sommelier returned with the wine, and waited for Olivier to give his approval, which he did with a subtle nod. The server brought small, white plates upon which rested Montauk Pearl oysters with tequila lime mignonette. The sauce enhanced the acidity of the *Puligny-Montrachet* perfectly. Max savored the sensation of cold stone that the oysters had clung to before being picked, and the vibrant tang of the wine, making her think for a second she was sipping a sparkling wine. Maybe this was the extra-sensory something that happened when a perfect marriage occurred between certain foods and wine. Or perhaps it was the way Olivier kept looking at her, as though *she* were an *amuse-gueule.*

He was behaving true to form when dining. Nothing else existed. While sipping wine, he told her about the first time he tasted wine at his grandmother's birthday, and how French parents often put champagne on the lips of infants, a ritual intended to make them a *Champenois* for life.

He looked at her. "You're not in pain."

"I've felt worse after a Jiu-Jitsu tournament, so yes, I'm fine. I turned my body to ward off the worst blows."

The server came to the table and announced: "Smoked salmon served with a crispy poached egg over a mimosa of egg and crème fraiche."

"Sounds poetic," Max said.

"The salmon has a terrific hue and delicate texture," Olivier said. Max took a bite. It melted on her tongue with just a hint of smoke in the sweet finish.

"The poached egg is deep fried," Olivier said in French. "Notice how the wine shines through the egg and complements the smokiness of the salmon." She looked at him to ascertain whether or not he was showing off, but he was focused, tasting the food the same way he tasted wine. "Let's go back to talking about our nemesis, if it isn't too much like pouring vinegar over our dinner," Olivier said.

"Paula? She could disappear for years."

"So far she's looking pretty innocent as far as evidence goes. She was in New York when Ellen was murdered by either Vincent or Wexler. Wexler beat you up, not her. She may get pegged for selling fake wine, but there isn't proof that she was involved in the counterfeiting."

Max nodded. "She blew it when she held a gun on me, but she's thinking now that I'm going to be dead before I become a problem for her."

"Perhaps you will get to surprise her," Olivier said.

"I hope I'm armed."

Olivier said, "That's why I'm keeping a guard at Vincent's, until we decide to arrest him. My thought is she needs him, and will try to persuade him to go wherever it is that she has planned out."

The sommelier arrived to announce the red wine to be served with the house-brined wooly pig, a half-bottle of a 2005 *Bordeaux, Pichon-Longueville Baron.* "It's bold, but with refinement," Olivier said. "It will hold up well with the rest of the dinner."

Just then, Chef Sam Hazen, a handsome bear of a man, ambled over and shook hands with Olivier and Max. Olivier asked about the name 'wooly pig," the course that was to arrive next, and Hazen said it was their version of the American BLT. "The pork is served over flash-sautéed lettuce with charred grape tomatoes and a crispy pork croquette."

Max was intrigued that a man resembling a lumberjack had created the delicacies that had been placed before her. He moved on to another table.

"I feel like I'm on a movie set," Max said. "And everyone has rehearsed but me." She glanced around the room. "I wonder how many people in this room are wine connoisseurs."

Olivier, resting between courses, said, "Connoisseurs used to be a rare breed; they questioned and investigated, and over time developed a sixth sense called taste. But the act has been democratized."

"Meaning anyone today can call themselves a connoisseur of anything?"

"Well put. People who are vastly wealthy want the best, but they're often not sure what that is. From what I observed at the auction, they are buying something that makes them feel important. I think most of the true connoisseurs of wine don't have enough money to purchase $500 bottles of wine."

"So people like Ellen Jordan and Paula Goodwin come along to tell them what to buy, right?" He nodded. "Paula is surely a connoisseur."

Olivier said, "She has a Master of Wine certificate, but taste is a different matter. There is an old expression my father taught me: to taste wine, one must have soul. I rest my case."

The filet arrived next. The center had concentric circles of pink that provided contrast to the crisp, seared deep brown of the edges. It was topped with willowy spears of vivid green asparagus, a wonderful play against the soft, buttery decadence of the meat. Next to arrive were large ravioli as soft as pillows filled with rich, braised short ribs. The pasta was translucent with lacy, crisp edges that floated on top of the mushroom infused broth. The short rib flavor was enhanced by the umami of the mushroom broth. The wine, from the Left Bank, was cabernet driven, fabulous with the mushroom broth, the mushrooms bringing out the earthy qualities with a subtle spicing, black pepper and nutmeg.

"Now that I've consumed this wine with you, I don't think I'll ever taste it and not think of you in this moment," Olivier said. "That's another charm of wine. The taste is often associated with a particular person in a particular setting."

"As I will probably never have the chance to taste this particular wine again, I'll have to come up with something else to remind me of you."

She liked seeing him laugh. She wanted to add that she carried a vivid memory of every second she had spent with him, from walking along a path with him in Champagne, to dancing on the terrace the night before she left, to the moments they had spent in the shower earlier today. She glanced at her watch.

"My intention is to never drink it without you," he said, and she felt herself blush. He reached for her hand, and she thought it could never be better than this.

Dessert and glasses of champagne arrived. The server said, "You have a *framboise pate des fruits*, a salted caramel tart, and an Earl Grey-infused chocolate truffle."

Max bit into the chocolate and Olivier asked her what she thought. She remained quiet, focusing, then said, "I love the interplay of deep bittersweet chocolate flavor with the herbal intensity of bergamot.."

Olivier gave a boisterous laugh. "How did you come up with the bergamot?" he asked. "It's perfect!"

"No one ever asks me," she said. "And I don't go around volunteering information. I think my mother introduced me to bergamot."

"Max," Olivier said, gazing into her eyes, "I have something for you." Max watched as his hand reached into his suit jacket pocket, but was distracted by a noise behind him.

She turned and saw Walt gingerly weaving his way over to them, not at all gracefully. "We have news that can't wait," Walt said. "Vincent Barthes has been found dead in his home. An accident, they say. Slipped in the bathtub. I'll drive you to the airport." With both of them speechless, he said, "I'll be out front while you decide where to go. The flight to Bordeaux is at 10:30."

"Paula *is* in France, then," Max said, "and predictably, has taken out Vincent. We've got a hell of a job ahead."

Walt was waiting for them in the bar, observing a world he didn't know or care anything about. He handed her the necessary official papers that would replace her passport and shield, and took off to bring the car around. Max took her bag into the ladies room and emerged wearing jeans and boots, and her usual t-shirt and jacket.

Once on the sidewalk, Olivier yelled, "Predictably! What are you, some psychic? Do you ever let a case just rest for a minute without proclaiming your certain knowledge of what is going on?"

"We're wasting time if we go in any other direction."

"Walt said it was an accident!" he said, glaring at her. "If it was, then Paula Goodwin is here, or on her way to Australia! Which is where we should be headed!"

Max knew when Walt said "flight to France" that he and Hank also thought France. She remained calm. "I'm still betting on France."

Walt had pulled up and now stuck his head out the window, "Make up your minds."

Olivier got into the front seat with Walt, and Max climbed into the back. "France," Olivier said in a resigned voice.

They rode in silence for a few miles before Walt said to Olivier, "Sounds like she rejected the ring."

Ring? Max wondered. That was what he was digging around for! She rode the rest of the way to the airport with a smile in her heart.

Chapter Thirty-eight

April 11

Olivier sat mesmerized by the blinking light at the end of the airplane's wing, glad to have a brief respite. Max had dropped off to sleep immediately. He hated fighting with her, but logically, it made much more sense for Paula to go to Australia, where she had contacts and probably a nest egg. She was on the lam, but he had no doubt that so far her actions would not lead to extended jail time. Her hands were clean. That was why, in his mind, she wouldn't blow it by killing anybody.

He was unaware that he had drifted off to sleep until the captain came on the intercom announcing their pending arrival in Bordeaux. Max sat up, groggy. "Paula is running around France as me, with all it takes to pull off another murder." Olivier wondered if he was only in love with Max when she was sleeping. He had been just about to apologize for snapping at her earlier, but now remained silent.

Abdel called before the plane came to a complete halt. "Monsieur, I have really bad news." Olivier tried to remember when he had called with good news. "We found the body of the policeman who was keeping an eye on Monsieur Barthes' place. A single shot through the head."

Olivier barely spoke above a whisper. "I'm sorry, Abdel."

"D'accord."

"Is someone waiting to meet me here?"

"Oui, Monsieur."

Olivier put away his phone. "What's going on?" Max asked.

"The guard is dead. Clean shot through the head."

She brought her hand up to her mouth. "Check to see if it was a Glock 19mm." Her voice had become whispery like Abdel's. Olivier thought if she started to cry he'd lose it. Two more deaths!

"Olivier." It felt like a command. He looked at her, and saw a female Hank, the fiery eyes, the set jaw, the determined mouth. "We three can beat her in this lethal game. Paula has to have a sidekick. Somebody doing her dirty work."

He snapped to attention. "Somebody who speaks French." They were in the police car on their way to Vincent's, where Abdel waited. Olivier called him. "Did you check airports?"

"No one named Max Maguire arrived at any of our international airports," Abdel said.

"She must have a different alias," Max said. "I'm calculating she left JFK at the approximate time we were picking up Larry Wexler at Veritas, and arrived in Bordeaux twelve hours later. Somebody was with her."

Abdel ran out to greet them, and escorted them through reporters and paparazzi up to the *salle de bain* where Vincent still lay in the tub, his head lobbed over to the side. The medical examiner looked up. "He has a depressed skull fracture from a blunt force wound. It could have come from the fall, which means he would have slipped backwards. His position doesn't correlate to the type of injury he has."

"Could the body have been moved from somewhere else?"

"Yes."

"I'm calling for a forensic autopsy."

Max and Abdel followed him downstairs. "What about the policeman?" Olivier asked Abdel.

Abdel's face was grim. "Cold-blooded murder."

"You knew him?"

Abdel nodded, then said, "Monsieur, let's get on with it." Max touched his arm, and he put his hand over hers for an instant.

He straightened his shoulders. "Some videos are missing. The ones from the bedroom and the *salle de bain*."

"Monsieur Douvier has them all under lock and key at Bordeaux headquarters so he can review them later. It turns out that a number of calls had come in over the past months from young women who claimed they were drugged by Monsieur Barthes."

"Who were the reports sent to?" Olivier asked.

"The *procureur* had sent them to Monsieur Douvier's office. He was about to launch an investigation."

"After months?" Olivier was disgusted. "Is Douvier coming here?"

Abdel nodded. "He's about to announce to the public that that Monsieur Barthes drowned accidentally."

"What about the policeman?"

"The ministers have convinced themselves it's a separate incident. The policeman was an Arab like me, and they're giving it a racist slant."Abdel hit the refrigerator with his fist. "I feel like I've done everything wrong. I should have been hanging around here instead of checking airports. Two more murders and where is that woman? She could easily be in Spain!"

"I'm going to look for the missing magnum," Max said. "Vincent also had a cache of money here, which I'm sure is gone, but we can check."

Abdel brightened for a moment. "The missing magnum was in Cazaneuve's apartment. He was bribed by Monsieur Barthes to steal it, and then held out for more money. We have him locked up. The bottle is tucked away in your office, Monsieur."

Olivier said, "Is there anything else, Abdel? Any reports of anyone showing up here?"

"Nothing of consequence. Yannick stopped by, and the policeman allowed him to go in to see Monsieur Barthes. He was picking up a check."

Olivier said, "I want you to drop Max at my house, and then drive out to see what Yannick is up to."

"Now?" Olivier nodded, not missing the look of skepticism on Abdel's face. He thought each of them needed a short time to be alone to think. He knew he did.

"Bring Yannick in, but don't let the press get word of it. He might know something."

"But there is so much to do here."

"We have all night."

"Okay."

"I have to talk to the minister of the interior and convince her to involve every unit in the country in this investigation," Olivier said. "Paula Goodwin could be sipping wine in Paris. She could be anywhere."

"She could also be watching from across the street," Max said. Olivier told Max he wanted her to go home, and that he would join her soon. "Zohra is preparing a meal," he said, giving her a tired smile, and reached over and squeezed her hand.

After agreeing to meet up later at his house, Abdel and Max left out the back door, and Olivier stepped out the front into glaring lights. He told reporters that Vincent Barthes had fallen in the tub and drowned. Someone shouted a question about the policeman and he said it was a separate incident. He had decided when he opened the door that Paula Goodwin was watching the news, and agreed with Walt's theory that if she relaxed her guard, she might make a mistake.

Chapter Thirty-nine

April 11

Abdel sounded frustrated. "Did Monsieur Chaumont have some hunch about Yannick? It feels stupid, going out to Médoc."

"He wanted to get rid of us so he could think," Max said.

"I hope he doesn't go off the deep end like he did last year."

"It was pretty bad, huh?"

Abdel nodded.

"You know this case is going to rest on those missing videos," she said.

"I'm certain Goodwin has them," Abdel said. "And if she's as smart as we presume her to be, she destroyed them."

They drove along in silence. Max said, "I think Olivier's hunch might be right on. We're thinking she's in train stations or airports disguised as somebody else. What if a farmer agreed to drive her over a border to another country? The Netherlands, for example."

"Yannick?"

"Why not? You can interrogate his wife, Corinne. She might be ready to turn him in."

"That gives me something to work with," Abdel said.

"On the other hand, he and Vincent had a friendship of sorts."

"The class difference is much too great. Neither would think of the other as a friend. They had deals."

Abdel pulled into Olivier's driveway, and Max hopped out. "I'll bet Zohra has something delicious in the oven."

"No doubt."

They high-fived, and Abdel backed up and was gone. Max walked up onto the porch and put her bag down to knock on the door. "Zohra!" she called out.

A figure stepped out of the shadow and she felt a gun pressed against her side. "Detective. I thought you were on a cruise."

Max had never felt such dread as she followed Paula Goodwin into Olivier's salon. Paula went to stand in front of the fireplace, where she sipped a glass of water. Max sat on the sofa, with Mouchette leaning into her, purring loudly.

"Where's the commissaire off to?" Paula asked.

"Home."

Yannick entered from the kitchen, holding a beer, and grinning at her. She had never noticed before how bad his teeth were. Maybe because she had never seen him grin before.

Paula said, "The Neanderthal only drinks beer, and bad beer at that."

"Where's Zohra?" Max asked.

"Dead." This is some psychological ploy to get me to react, Max thought. She had to stay calm in order to think. Her biggest worry was that Olivier would be coming soon, and she saw no solution.

"Where's the body?"

"Garden shed." Certain that they were engaging in psychological warfare, Max decided to join in. "One more out of the way, huh?" she said.

"I'm not joking, you know. I think she had a heart attack."

"May I go check on her?"

"No."

Corinne came rushing in the door, coming to a halt when she saw Max. "What are you doing here?"

"I came for dinner."

"You know everybody," Paula said to Max. "How'd you leave Wexler?"

"Guilty as charged."

"I saw the news. Poor Vincent. What's this about French men and you? He really liked you."

"I didn't get that impression." Max's only hope was Corrine, but how could she get to her?

Paula turned to Corinne. "How's the maid?" Paula asked Corrine.

"Not good. I put a blanket on her."

"Leave her. We should be ready to go when the judge gets here. Ask your husband if the truck is gassed up."

Corinne went into the kitchen and said upon her return, "Everything's set."

"Tell your husband to take Max out to the shed and shoot her."

"Shoot? Are you crazy, Madame? He won't kill."

"If you don't do as I say, I'll shoot you. Go!"

Corinne scooted out of the room again and was back in a minute, Yannick trailing behind her with another beer. Corinne took a seat and lit a cigarette. Max caught her eye, and Corinne looked away.

"I have to use the toilet," Corinne said.

"Hurry up!" Paula said. Corinne scurried away.

"Tell him to stop drinking," Paula said to Max. "And know that I understand more French than you think."

Max decided to test her. She said to Yannick in French, "You are being accused of killing Monsieur Barthes and a policeman. I know you didn't do it. I want you to help me overtake her."

He stared at her hard, slurping his beer, and she realized she was shaking.

Paula yelled for Corinne, who ran in. "*Oui, Madame*?"

"Tell him to stop drinking. And ask him what Max said to him?"

Corinne translated for Yannick, who replied to her in French, "The broad wants me to help her overtake the other broad. No way."

Corinne glanced over at Max and then fixed her attention on Paula. "He said that the detective asked him to spare the judge's life."

Max's emotions veered from panic that Yannick wasn't going to be persuaded to help, and deep gratitude to Corinne for not giving her away.

"How touching," Paula said sarcastically.

If only they leave before Olivier arrives, Max thought. The antique clock bonged nine. Paula's cell rang. "Okay, we're ready. We'll meet you in two hours." She ordered Corinne to tell Yannick to take Max to the shed.

"Okay." Corinne hesitated, then said in a soft voice to Yannick, "She wants you to shoot the detective. Nod your head." He did as told. Corinne said, "If you shoot her, I'll turn you in."

Max thought the beer she shared with Corinne in her kitchen was turning out to be one of the most rewarding moves of her career.

"I'll drive to Spain like we agreed, and ditch the broad," Yannick said. "There's a lot of money. I saw it."

"What's taking so long?" Paula demanded. "Move!"

Paula's losing control, Max thought. She's paranoid, and desperate. Yannick marched over to Max and grabbed her arm and hoisted her up. She winced from the pain in her shoulder.

Rectangular lights streaking through the room made them all stop. Olivier had turned into the driveway. "Everybody freeze!" Paula said. Corinne explained to Yannick, who dropped his grip on Max. Paula commanded Max to open the door, and warned her that she was holding her gun on her.

Chapter Forty

April 11

Olivier said good-night to the officer who brought him home. He was ready to sit down and have a scotch. He made his way to the porch and saw through the glass in the back door Max coming to greet him. Noticing the stricken look on her face as he entered, he was about to ask what was wrong when Paula Goodwin stepped out from behind the door, pointing a gun at Max. "Welcome home, Judge," she said to Olivier.

He assessed the situation in a flash. His hunch about Yannick had been correct. It was apparent that the foreman had been drinking, which made him unpredictable. Corinne was acting as translator, and was in way over her head. Paula needed him, but she didn't need Max, which was dangerous. Zohra was nowhere in sight.

"Where is my femme de ménage?" Olivier asked, looking from Paula to Yannick.

"She's resting," Paula said. A quick glance at Max told him that the truth was grim.

"What do you want, Madame Goodwin?" he asked.

"I need to get to Spain, where I have someone meeting me. You will accompany Yannick and his wife and me in his truck in case we run into problems."

"Is your passport in order?"

"I'm traveling as your girlfriend. Up until now I've been Jennifer Casey, but after we enter Spain I will take Corinne Boudreau's ID with me. We'll leave her at the border."

It all became instantly clear. Bill Casey had helped her to escape by flying her to Bordeaux and giving her his wife's passport. Casey's arrogance, the need to be right, had put his and Max's life in danger. He looked at Paula, "I won't be much good to you once we're in Spain."

"You'll be a hostage, then. It's time to get moving."

"What about Max?"

"We're leaving her behind." She motioned to Yannick, who moved toward Max.

Olivier began speaking in rapid-fire French to Yannick, saying that if he killed the detective he would spend his life in jail. "So far you haven't killed anybody," he said. "I know that." Paula screamed at him to shut up, but Olivier continued, "Help us and you'll get off easy..."

The report of the Glock was earsplitting, and only a second later did he realize that the bullet had grazed his arm. Corinne yelped, and Paula turned the gun on her. "Go get antibiotic ointment," Paula said. "It's nothing." She pointed the gun at Olivier again. "Consider that a warning. The next time your brains will be on the floor. Sit down."

His arm felt like someone had touched his skin with a hot poker, though he could see the wound was minor. He shifted position and was made aware of the tiny box in his pocket containing the ring for Max. He had always pooh-poohed the power of talismans, and teased Max about carrying her brother's knife on her for good luck, yet he felt strangely comforted by the ring. He wished he could convey some of this to Max. He felt her attention on him and raised his eyes to meet hers. In a flash he knew that she had understood his thoughts. Corinne returned with the ointment and fabric, which she began to wrap around his arm.

"We'll all go out together," Paula said.

Olivier was surprised at how easily the decision came to him. He would rush Paula the minute they were on the porch, and if he died, so be it. If something happened to Paula or him, Yannick would not kill Max. The foreman pushed Max out the door, and onto the porch and down the steps. Corinne followed, then Olivier, and Paula brought up the rear, gun in hand. Olivier took a deep breath, and was just about to whirl to confront Paula, when he heard a gun report. Paula swore. Before she could issue a command, Corinne rushed into the yard, calling her husband's name. A bloodcurdling scream pierced the air, and Paula shot into the dark.

Max had disappeared. Paula yelled out, "Max, you have two seconds to appear or I will shoot the judge!" She dug the gun into his back, and Olivier uttered a prayer he had learned as a child. He heard Paula make a gagging sound then a thud as she dropped her gun. He jumped back. Abdel had come from behind and jabbed his left hand across her throat, cutting off her oxygen. Dropping his left hand into the crook of his right elbow, he squeezed her neck in his forearms, until Paula went limp, and fell to the ground. Two beats of shock followed, as Abdel panted hard, and Olivier stared at the lifeless form. Max ran up to the porch, and leaned down to check Paula's pulse. She looked up at Olivier and Abdel. "Her windpipe's busted," Max said.

Olivier and Abdel exchanged glances. "She's dead?" Abdel whispered.

"You can see how easy it is to use too much force with Jiu-Jitsu," Max said. "Zohra's in the shed, Abdel. We'll deal with this."

"But..."

"Go!" Olivier ordered.

Abdel ran off, and Olivier called for ambulances. He and Max walked briskly to where Corinne sobbed over her husband. "He won't wake up," she said.

Olivier knelt down to examine him, and saw that the bullet had gone through his heart. "I'm sorry," he said. His words were genuine. He was deeply sorry that Ellen, Vincent, Yannick, and the police officer were dead. He didn't feel the same regret about Paula. It had been a trade-off: Abdel eliminated Paula and Yannick in order to save Max, Olivier, and his grandmother.

Olivier knew that Max and Abdel had worried that he might sink into depression again, but as horrible as the losses were, he had never felt stronger.

Abdel carried Zohra inside and gently lowered her to the sofa. Zohra's eyes fluttered open. Olivier sat next to her, holding her hand. Max sat quietly in a chair. "What happened when you and Yannick went outside?" Olivier asked Max.

"Yannick and I had just walked down the two steps to the lawn," she said, "when Abdel stepped into the light and pushed me hard. Yannick turned his gun on him and Abdel shot him at close range. He had to. He told me to hide behind a car, and he took off around the house and entered the front door in order to come up behind Paula. Brilliant maneuver.

"Monsieur, I shot someone at close range and killed a woman with my bare hands," Abdel said. "I've never harmed anyone." Olivier saw that he was shaking, and knew the flashbacks that would occur before he could accept how necessary the violence was. All Olivier could do now was to reassure him. "You saved three lives, there is no question about that."

Blaring sirens filled the air. In moments Zohra was on her way to the hospital. Olivier and Max walked outside, where ambulance attendants were trying to revive Yannick, to no avail. Olivier turned to Max, "Help Abdel. I need to do something."

He went to Corinne who stood alone near the porch, watching. Olivier said in an apologetic voice that he needed to get some details from her.

"I told Yannick to stay away from that woman from the start," she said. "I want it clear right now that he didn't kill anybody."

"I hope you're right, but we have no proof. I know some justices who would be happy for the story to end with him as a serial murderer. He was carrying the .22 that killed the police officer." He invited her into the house, and she agreed. Once inside, he went to the refrigerator and removed a beer and handed it to her and she thanked him. He poured a shot of scotch into a glass and sat with her.

"Yannick told me that Madame Goodwin killed Monsieur Barthes and the police officer," Corinne said. "He swore on his mother's photograph."

"The only way we'll ever know is if we can put our hands on the most recent videos that have gone missing from Monsieur Barthes' house. The ones in the bedroom and the *salle de bain*. Did he mention the videos?"

"Madame Goodwin gave him a thousand euros to destroy them."

"And?" Olivier waited, barely breathing, for she held the key to the entire investigation.

Her eyes narrowed. "What if I told you he burned them?"

"I wouldn't believe you."

She sniffled, and sipped her beer. "Why not?"

"Because you want to see them in order to prove to yourself that Yannick didn't commit murder. You're not sure, are you?" She began to cry.

"What if I say I believe you?" Olivier said. "I'm so sure that he's innocent that I'll offer you another thousand for them." Her head jerked up, and he knew that the offer had made her much less ambivalent.

"What about me?"

"Explain."

"What will happen to me?"

"If you tell me where the videos are, I'll keep you out of it. As it is now, you are an accomplice to a kidnapping, which will put you in jail."

She sat slumped in the chair. "I gave them to the pub owner where Yannick and I hang out. I told him to hold onto them until I got back and paid him a hundred euros."

"The money will be in your hands by tomorrow, and you will know the truth. One of my officers will drive you home."

"*Merci, Monsieur.*"

"Oh, one more question. The wine tasting book. Who paid Yannick to steal it?"

"Monsieur Laussac paid him to steal it, but then Yannick offered it to Pascal Boulin for a sum."

"How much?"

"Five-hundred euros."

"And?"

"Pascal said no. It should be in Monsieur Laussac's library." Olivier couldn't believe how the knowledge that Pascal had said no boosted his faith in humankind. "I trust that the offer you made a few days ago is still good," she said.

"It is, but you will be much happier, Madame, if you accept a simple life."

An officer entered and he asked him to drive Corinne home. He followed them out and saw Max sitting alone in a lawn chair. He joined her, taking her hand as he sat. "What was going on in there?" she asked.

"I have work to do in town."

"Do you want me to come?"

"No. It's something I need to do alone. I have all night. There is dinner if you're hungry."

"I think I'll call my parents."

"You're okay, Max?"

"I am."

"Do me a favor."

"Sure."

"Tell your father that I understand what he was telling me about patience."

"You're going to let me in on this conversation?"

"I will once the case is officially closed."

She looked concerned. "Are you okay, Olivier? I know how in Champagne..."

"I've never been better." He squeezed her hand.

Chapter Forty-one

April 12

Philippe Douvier joined Max, Abdel, and Olivier in Olivier's office. He refused a chair, but stood before them, close to the door, as though he was due somewhere else. They were to meet with other justices in fifteen minutes for a preliminary review. Max diverted her attention from her uncle to Olivier. He hadn't returned until five a.m, and now sat at his desk, looking serene. She wondered if he had gone back to the bistro that stayed open until four, sipping scotch. Nothing had been mentioned about the case over their morning coffee.

"There are more questions than there are answers in this case," Douvier said. He glanced at his watch. "You won't be surprised to know that I've opened a separate investigation into the brutal death of Paula Goodwin and close-range shooting of Yannick Martin. There's no proof of her being a murderer from the reports that I have, nor do I see any wrongdoing in her being flown to France by a friend. As for insisting that Monsieur Casey…"

A light knock on the door interrupted him. He opened the door and when Bill Casey entered, Douvier shook his hand, introducing himself. "Monsieur Casey, I apologize for making you come from Paris," he said, obsequious as ever.

Max, shocked, looked at Olivier, who raised an eyebrow in response. "Thank you for coming," Olivier said, politely. "It was I who insisted that you be here for the wrap-up of this case."

"I've only learned this morning of the carnage that went down last night," Bill said. "My god, killing a woman."

"Not just any woman," Olivier said. "Which will be made clear shortly. She entered France on your jet, using your wife's passport, when there was an all-out alert for her."

Bill looked confused. "There was nothing on the news about the alert," he said. It's true, Max thought, that he had no way of knowing that a mad chase was on for Paula, as the NYPD had kept that information secret in order to lure her in. "I had a meeting in Paris and Paula knew about it," Bill continued. "She told me she had to get her hands on a special wine, and I said sure."

Max wondered which rare wine she had bribed him with to get him to say yes. "And the passport?"

"She must have stolen it. We met at my apartment and she may have seen my wife's passport on the hall table."

"You didn't know Paula had it?"

"No, she got off in Bordeaux, and I continued on to Paris. I was unaware of anything that happened at customs."

Olivier glanced at his watch. "We need to address Monsieur Barthes' and the policeman's deaths before we meet with judiciary members."

Douvier's eyes grew wary. "Without absolute proof, we're going to keep the cause of Monsieur Barthes' death accidental drowning. At least for now." Max thought she could see the direction he was headed in, where politics would supersede truth. "The policeman's death could have racial implications."

Max started to object, but Olivier motioned her to remain quiet. Douvier turned his gaze to Abdel. "There might be some questions from the minister of the interior about your shooting a man at close range and choking a woman to death."

Olivier's voice was firm. "Abdel, please prepare my presentation." He waited as Abdel left the room, and turned back to Douvier. "Max Maguire and I were witnesses," he said. "Commissaire Zeroual saved our lives. The session today, however, is about Vincent Barthes. I have proof that he was murdered, and will now lead the way to the courtroom where you and Monsieur Casey can see for yourselves. As a footnote to all this, my housemaid's life teeters on the edge as a result of the invasion of my house."

"What happened to her?"

"She was bullied."

Bill Casey said, "I still don't know why I'm here. I sure didn't kill anybody."

"Monsieur Casey, I wanted you to have a full understanding of the carnage as you call it, and what led to it," Olivier said. "You didn't pull the trigger, it's true, but you shall not go blameless."

Abdel stood by the computer as they entered the courtroom. The dozen ministers and justices, including the local procureur, sat talking among themselves, waiting for the routine wrap-up before they went off for lunch. Douvier went before the group, explaining that there had been a new development that he had not been informed about until a few moments ago. He emphasized that it had been a complicated case, and veered off topic to wonder if perhaps the case was in the end about a deep rivalry between two American women that had little to do with France.

Max wanted to scream.

"Two Americans have been arrested," Douvier continued, and there now seems to be some evidence that one of them, the auctioneer Paula Goodwin, was involved in the death of Vincent Barthes." No one stirred as they allowed the information to sink in. Douvier turned the proceedings over to Olivier, who clarified that in fact the case had nothing to do with rivalry between two women. He explained in great detail how it had unfolded. Everyone sat mesmerized. He talked about Barthes' video system that had obviously become an obsession, and how it had led to the proof that they were about to witness.

Olivier then instructed Abdel to run through some of the office scenes at Vincent's business. There were frames of Vincent in his office speaking to a group of reporters about his wine, and workers moving bottles down a conveyor belt. Next, they were in the cellar of Vincent's father's company and the video flashed images of hundreds of old vintage wine bottles lined up against a wall. In a moment, the video tour took them into Vincent's townhouse. The front of the building was displayed, and various people were videoed entering and leaving the house. There on screen were the women arriving with Vincent, most of them appearing to be drunk. Some of them were beautiful. Some were underage. The viewers shifted in their seats. Olivier, moving up the side aisle in the darkened room, slipped into the chair beside her, and took Max's hand.

On screen, Vincent bustled around in the kitchen, removing a roast chicken from the oven. Someone knocked on the kitchen door, and Vincent walked across the room and opened it. Paula stepped in. He seemed shocked to see her. She told him she had come back for him, just as she said. He smiled as she explained that Yannick was out back with his truck. Max could see that Vincent felt vivified by her presence. Yannick entered and opened the fridge and took out a bottle of beer.

"Vincent," Paula said, "you need to get ready. I'm a fugitive right now because of that bitch detective who can't be stopped."

"Max? Is she okay?" Vincent asked.

"She's on a cruise."

Max felt the hair on her arms go up.

"And Larry?"

She smiled at him. "He's confessed. He'll get life."

"That's horrible," Vincent said, taking a bottle of white wine out of the refrigerator. "You forced him into it."

"Everyone has free choice," Paula said. "Go upstairs. I'll bring a glass up to you." After he left the room, Paula turned to Yannick. "Kill him," she said, handing him the .22." She pretended to pull the trigger.

He shook his head and said, "No. You."

Paula turned the gun on him, and he laughed. Corinne was right, Max thought, Yannick would not kill. Looking annoyed, Paula opened the bottle of wine and took a bag of powder from her pocket and dropped it into the drink. Max wondered if she'd ever draw a full breath again. Paula went upstairs and Yannick followed. The screen went blank for a few seconds. Abdel fidgeted with the computer.

In the next frame Vincent, shirtless, was in his bedroom, sipping from the glass. He had obviously taken a shower because his hair was wet, and the towel was on the bed. Paula entered the room, a jade horse in her hand, which Vincent paid no attention to. She was wearing a raincoat, and gloves. Vincent said he would only be ten minutes. "Where's the cash?" she asked.

"In my closet."

He opened the closet door and pulled out the suitcase, and opened it. "Great," Paula said. He walked around to the other side of the bed to find his shoes. He said, stumbling slightly. "My head is fuzzy. I feel disoriented."

"Are you sick?" Paula asked.

"Nervous," he said. "I hope we make it to Australia."

"We will."

He looked at her. "You look amazing in that trench coat," he said. "You're an amazing woman." He stumbled and fell onto the mattress. He tried to get up. Paula said, "Let me help you."

He laughed. "You're so beautiful," he said, slipping off the bed onto his knees. Paula, Max thought, had given him a big dose of the GPA. Paula smiled grimly, and walked over and stood behind him. She lifted her arm and struck him on the head with the jade horse, and he collapsed onto his stomach.

"Yannick!" Paula called. The foreman wandered in, his eyes wide. Paula demonstrated lifting the body. Vincent moaned. "The *salle de bain*," Paula said. The last frame was of the two struggling to lift Vincent into the tub with the water running. The screen went blank.

Olivier got up and walked to the front of the room. "What about the other suspects?" someone asked from the audience.

Olivier explained that Larry Wexler delivered poisoned cheese to Madame Jordan and probably watched her become ill, but that it was Vincent who had put the poison into the cheese, and Yannick who had collected the aconite in the field. Madame

Goodwin was the leader throughout. The authorities slowly filed out, Douvier leading the pack.

Bill Casey remained in his seat. "I'm in a nightmare," he said. "I can't believe I was delivering a woman intent on murdering. What happened to her?"

Max and Olivier joined him. "Greed," Max said.

"And you?" Olivier asked. "What happened to you, Monsieur Casey?"

"I trusted this woman," Bill said.

Max said, "It's not about a woman. Or women. It's about your arrogance and pride. When you return to the states you will be arrested, and your story will be on the news. I will see to it."

Casey said, "Spare the lecture, Max. It's over. I'm the one who has lost two friends."

"You forget that Ellen was my mother's closest friend," Max said.

Casey got up to leave. "Do what you have to do, Max. I'm not the type to hold grudges, but if you put me in a corner I will fight. I'll come up with a different spin. I'll go on talk shows and explain about Paula's history of growing up with an abusive father after her mother died when she was two. How she was abandoned by her husband, who went off with another woman. Over time the American public will develop sympathy for the woman who had to claw her way to the top of her profession."

Max grew silent. Her father had told her in the beginning of her career that there was no hard justice for people like Bill Casey. Her mother would remind him that there was karmic justice. Hank hadn't bought any of that.

Casey looked at Olivier, "I brought the fourth magnum with me to deliver to you personally," he said. "My chauffeur has it downstairs."

"That's very gracious of you," Olivier said. "I accept."

Max gave him a hard look, which he ignored. He and Casey shook hands and Casey left the courtroom.

"How can you accept his wine?" Max asked.

"Captain O'Shaughnessy had a little talk with him. The deal was that he had to either turn it over to me for testing or the Fraud Squad would pick it up. Your dad and the captain are not done with him, by the way. Aiding and abetting is a crime. At a minimum, he will spend many hours in court testifying."

"I have this desperate need to make him pay," she said.

"Now you see why I spend my few extra hours going after people who stand little chance of being made culpable." He closed the door to the courtroom after they exited. "Abdel is waiting in my office."

They joined him. Abdel said after they entered, "You're quite the detective, Monsieur." Olivier smiled.

"We want to hear how you found the videos," Max said.

"Later," he said. She turned to Abdel, "Where did you learn the Jiu-Jitsu move?"

"From you."

"The video in Central Park?"

He nodded. "I think I need more lessons."

"And Zohra?" Olivier asked.

"She will be out of the hospital in two days."

"We'll stop by," Olivier said. "Take the day off, Abdel, and we'll do the same."

Max jumped up and gave Abdel a big hug. "Jiu-Jitsu and hugging. See what you've taught me," he said.

"Not a bad combo," she said, laughing. "I'll see you before I leave France."

He waved and was gone. Olivier looked at Max. "I'm making dinner this evening, and will try to make sure there aren't any interruptions. I'll build a fire and open a special bottle."

"The one from Bill Casey?"

"It's a gamble. One is authentic and the other fake. I must choose between the one Bill Casey just delivered, or the one retrieved from Cazaneuve's apartment."

"I'll bet on the one Casey brought with him. Dinner in Paris at a modest restaurant?"

"Done."

"That means it's all up to you. You could cheat. What the hell do I know about how it's supposed to taste?"

"Trust me, you will know if it's authentic. The taste will be subtle at first, but after a moment it will explode. The experience then becomes ethereal, some might even say…" He couldn't find the word in English. "*Jouissif*," he said.

"Are you saying orgasmic?"

"*Exact*."

"Are we still talking about wine?"

Olivier's laughter reverberated around the interior of her skull.

To receive a free catalog of Poisoned Pen Press titles, please contact us in one of the following ways:

Phone: 1-800-421-3976
Facsimile: 1-480-949-1707
Email: info@poisonedpenpress.com
Website: www.poisonedpenpress.com

Poisoned Pen Press
6962 E. First Ave. Ste 103
Scottsdale, AZ 85251